A HUNDRED KISSES

JEAN M. GRANT

A Hundred Kisses

Copyright © 2017 by Jean M. Grant

All rights reserved. Printed in the United States of America.

No part of this publication may be reproduced, distributed, or transmitted in any form or by any means, including photocopying, recording, or other electronic or mechanical methods, without the prior written permission of the publisher, except in the case of brief quotations embodied in critical reviews and certain other noncommercial uses permitted by U.S. copyright law. For permission requests, write to the author using the contact form on jeanmgrant.com.

This is a work of fiction. Names, characters, places, and incidents are either the product of the author's imagination or are used fictitiously, and any resemblance to actual persons living or dead, business establishments, events, or locales is entirely coincidental.

Book cover and scene break art by AK Westerman, AK Organic Abstracts | OA Graphic Design.

Map by David Lindroth Inc.

First edition, 2017

Print ISBN 978-1-5092-1441-9

Digital ISBN 978-1-5092-1442-6

Second edition, 2024

Print ISBN 979-8-9898854-5-9

Digital ISBN 979-8-9898854-4-2

www.jeanmgrant.com

To my mother, Mary,
whose love of poetry and art inspired me
to follow my own dream.
Lapich Knewel.
I will see you again.

SCOTLAND

Glen Shiel, Scottish Highlands, 1296

Strife abounds. King Edward of England has invaded the southern strongholds of Scotland and is pressuring King John of Scotland to abdicate. Several Scottish nobles, called Claimants, vie for his throne. The Cause divides the country, as each clan must choose and support a Claimant. Many contenders seek fortune and power, but a few seek Scotland's independence. Only by a great force can this be achieved. However, the road to independence is fraught with those that wish to see the Cause crushed, at any cost.

PROLOGUE

Only one word describes a woman widowed for the second time on her wedding night—cursed. Deirdre had never believed in such a thing until the moment she awoke on the morning after her nuptials to Cortland, her second husband.

One breath.

One breath?

She shot upright in the bed. She listened to her lone, rhythmic breathing as her body was jarred from its deep sleep by a bolt of energy—or rather, by the lack of energy—she felt beside her. With her eyes still clamped closed, she roused her other senses.

Everything she heard and felt was heightened. The spring wind whistled through the crack in the window shutters. The scent of baking bread stirred her stomach as servants below prepared for the day. Peddlers prepared for the market in the courtyard. Footsteps sloshed through puddles; wagons creaked. The world buzzed with activity...louder, harder. She pushed aside the scratchy and suffocating bedclothes.

Then inhaled and tuned out the chaos. One breath.

Last night returned to her in a flood of images as she opened her eyes. Her gaze darted across the ceiling and around the room. Even without dawn's light, hidden behind the closed shutters, she knew something was amiss in her wedding chamber. But she couldn't bring herself to look beside her.

One breath. One heartbeat. It was hers.

A dark weight crushed her chest. She drew on her ability and detached herself from the hum of humanity, closing her eyes once again. She didn't feel his color anymore. A weak, blue lifeblood emanated from his body. It encircled her, wet and frigid. The sole heartbeat in the room was hers. The truth sank to the pit of her stomach before she rolled over to confirm what she already knew to be true. His body was lifeless. Her new husband, her groom from last night, lay dead beside her, and it was all her fault.

Again.

CHAPTER ONE

Glen Shiel Wilderness, One Month Later

H eavy breaths.

Deep, erratic, in and out.

Alasdair scanned his surroundings as he settled his racing heart. *Focus. Focus.* Through extended breaths, he allowed the air to flow in and out of his nose. He had run hard and fast, slipped, and now found himself tangled in a thicket of gorse.

He couldn't make out the sounds anymore, as they were drowned by his own labored breathing. He chided himself. *Recover. Breathe in.* Drawing in another deep breath, the cool air rushed down his throat. It took a moment, but his body cooperated.

He closed his eyes. The disadvantage of no sight was foolish, but it allowed him to home in on the sounds of the forest. His hearing told him more than his eyes ever could in the shadows of late afternoon.

He heard no hooves, no feet, and no swish of movement against the brush.

Waiting awhile before moving, he was well aware of the pain rising up his arm from his fall. Nearly every muscle in his body ached. He removed his torn jacket and inspected the wound—a large gash traced his forearm. The bleeding wasn't profuse, but it would need stitching. After wrapping his kerchief around it, he rose and scanned the area for a sheltered place to sleep.

An hour of searching yielded no appealing spots, so he kept on. Distracted by the baron's men, he had veered off the path and was now far from his original route. Unfamiliar with this area of the Highlands, he cursed himself for being ill-prepared. Then again, his hasty departure hadn't been his fault.

His stomach growled. It'd been two days since his last proper meal.

Alasdair slumped down. He wrestled with the sleepiness that lured him. If he surrendered to his exhaustion, he would dream, and dreaming was the last thing he wanted. Hours passed as he sat in silence, listening to his own pulse, the birds chirping, the wind rustling leaves. No blades, hooves, or soldiers.

He ignored the throbbing in his arm and thought upon his mission. Thomas's message had seemed urgent and troubling. Robert Bruce's workforce had run into problems with readying the ships, and they questioned his authority over the navy. If Alasdair didn't get there soon enough, this entire plan would crumble. Bruce was the lone legitimate Claimant who could prevail against King Edward. He needed this navy.

Alasdair pulled the parchment sheets from his satchel. He ran a finger over the thick red wax seal of Bruce. The sheets contained a coded dispatch that only he, Thomas, and the foreman in charge of the fleet's construction could decipher. He had to get to the isles. Thomas's message arrived nearly a month ago. God knew how many workers had abandoned the project already.

He grew lightheaded and could fight it no longer. He closed his eyes. The baron was gone. Only the sounds of dusk kept him company.

As soon as he fell into the fitful stage of sleep, the nightmare imprisoned him again.

The scene unfolded before him as though he were a ghost.

His mother stood on the raised stump, her body tied to the tall stake behind her. A pile of wood encircled her feet. Only a small crowd had gathered in the courtyard, despite his father's commands that all should attend. Alasdair sobbed at her feet, calling out to her. A cloud overtook her normally serene eyes. "Step back, Ali. Step back. It will be all right. Hush. Go. Go to the keep, love," she whispered. Alasdair remembered how her voice faltered.

The young Alasdair climbed on the pile and clutched her flowing gown. She had been dressed in her finest, not stripped down to her undergarments like the handmaid who stood tied to a post beside her. His father had always liked a display. Alasdair's hands reached and passed over his mother's large pregnant belly. With that, she sobbed, too. "Oh Ali, be good for Mama. I'll see you in the pearly white heaven that God has promised us. Be steadfast, son. Trust your heart."

"Light it," his father ordered. The men hesitated, but his father barked the order again. They ignored the child that stood upon the wood pile, his hands tight around his mama's legs. Wee Alasdair cried louder. He remembered the soft feel of her silk gown against his wet cheek.

"Get down, love. Get down. Go, close your eyes!" his mother cried. The fire began to lick the wood logs.

"Light the other one!" his father said, and the soldiers moved over to the handmaid. The movement drew the attention of the gathering away from his mother. Alasdair felt a hand upon his back, pinning him to the wood pile. Realization had awoken in the five-year-old, and he struggled to get down.

"Let him go, you bastard!" his mother screeched.

"I'm not the bastard, Cassandra!" he countered, pushing Alasdair with emphasis.

"You know that's not true! Release him, or I will unleash my wrath upon you from the grave!"

This attracted the crowd, and they returned to the first stake. Alasdair's father grabbed his son and pulled him down, but not before the boy's shirt sleeve caught on fire. Alasdair screamed and rolled on the ground. The sound of his mother's cries penetrated his soul.

The aching awoke him, as it always did. He rubbed his arm from shoulder down to fingers, feeling the rippled scars under his shirt. He forced that memory away.

Dusk had turned into dark, and he rose. Sweating and thirsty, he followed his intuition through the trees to a clearing that hopefully opened to a loch or burn.

Deirdre's weekly visits to the loch were her refuge from the energy of the village. The water's iciness was a thousand fingers prickling her skin, but she submerged farther as she entered in from the shore. The world's humming and warm colors faded as the water consumed her. She let out a loud sigh, then inhaled and dunked her full body in.

For that brief moment, as air expanded her chest and the world of the dark, shallow water swathed her, she felt free from her powers.

The water's nip at dusk was a welcome from the heat that radiated off all the living during the day. It was as though the life force of every living being ceased during the hours when the sun set. Most importantly, she could no longer see *him*, and her vision of him—the man from the wood. The trees didn't appear ablaze before her while the man cried out for help, his dark blue eyes wide, his black hair catching aflame, and his vibrant red lifeblood draining.

She massaged her scalp, hoping to erase the image. The visions would never cease. They never did. The more she fought them, the more her powers gripped her. *Oh, Mother, why couldn't you be here to teach me how to control it?* She trembled as the chill sank into her bones. Her lungs grew empty, and she struggled to remain under. She didn't want to face the world. Her ears rang, and with open eyes, a welcome blackness crept over her vision. Maybe she could stay under and let it take her.

Her only escape from obligations as laird's daughter danced around her with a chilling caress. Although she had left the village unnoticed, she knew by morning that somebody, most likely Crystoll, sent by her father, would be knocking on her door. Or Moreen would need her to taste a new recipe in the kitchen. Or Caite would want to whine about something. Nay, but not now. Now, she was alone. Her father had been too distracted with the news the sentry brought about Dunbar. This wet, numbing escape was not accompanied by one of her father's escorts.

So, by God, she succumbed to it.

She sensed no colors in the murky, lifeless water, and it was freeing! The last tendrils of breath escaped her now. Muted visions passed before her eyes—her mother, her father, Gordon, and Cortland. Just a moment longer, she thought...

Suddenly, a burst of warm light invaded her thoughts as air filled her lungs. Red-hot hands burned her shoulders and ripped her from her icy grave. She breathed life into her body with a gasping inhalation. Then she coughed, gagging on the change.

Muffled words yelled at her. Somebody had pulled her from the water.

Oh, God, so hot. His fingers were like hot pokers. Her head pounded as she slowly returned to the present. Heat radiated from her rescuer.

"Wh—?"

"Hush, lass. You nearly drowned."

His voice was as soothing as a warm cup of goat's milk on a winter's day and a red-hot glow emanated from him. Never before had she felt such a strong lifeblood, and it nearly burned her. She struggled to disentangle herself from his arms. She blinked, only seeing a blurry form before her. "Release me!"

She splashed and wriggled, and he did as told. Clambering to the shoreline, numb and shaken, she began to dress. It wasn't easy as she fumbled with slick fingers to put on dry clothes over wet skin. She instantly regretted her naked swim. She pulled on her long-sleeved white chemise first.

She faced the forest, away from her rescuer. He quietly splashed to shore as his lifeblood burned into her back. He wasn't far behind, but he stopped. She refused to look at him until she was fully clothed, not out of embarrassment of her nudity, but for what had just happened. He released a groan and mumbled under his breath about wet boots. His voice did not belong to one of her father's soldiers.

When she put the last garment on, her brown wool work kirtle, she squeezed out her sopping hair and swept her hands through the knotty mess. She fastened her belt and tied the lacings up the front of the kirtle. Blood returned to her fingertips, and she regained her composure. Belated awareness struck her, and she leaned down and searched through her bag for her dagger. Then spun around.

She gasped as she saw the man sitting on the stone-covered shoreline, his wet boots off. It was not the hint of a scowl filling his strong-featured face that sent her pulse soaring like a hawk. She staggered back, caught her heel on a stone, and fell, dropping the dagger. Dirt and pebbles stuck to her wet hands and feet, and she instinctively scrambled away from him.

His glower, iridescent dark blue eyes, and disheveled black hair were not unfamiliar. Staring at her was the man she had seen in her dream—it was the man from the wood.

Alasdair rushed toward the woman as she fainted. He knelt and caught her limp body by the shoulders. What in blazes? First, she was in the water drowning, and now she had passed out right before him, but not before he saw her face drain of color. Without thinking, he cupped her cheek and rubbed his palm on her cold skin. He wrapped his arm around her and sat her in his lap. He needed to get her somewhere warm for only a sliver of daylight remained. "Wake!" he pleaded. Soaking ringlets of long dark hair enveloped her ashen face.

He pushed aside a few tendrils and softened his tone. He didn't want to startle her with his roughness. "Wake, lass. Wake. 'Tis safe."

She moaned, and her eyelids fluttered as though she were caught in a horrible dream.

Well, she wasn't dead. Not yet at least.

She began to mumble and not in the Gaelic.

"*Hvítr andlát...*" she slurred.

She needed body heat and a fire for she was talking pure madness.

She spoke finally in English. "Who?" Shockingly blue eyes with mossy green circles around the pupils stared at him.

"You're safe. Is your home near?" Although she was awake now, he felt the urge to hold her until she was no longer shivering.

"H-Home?" Her lips were tinged gray.

Alasdair noticed the blood on her kirtle. "Are you hurt?"

She shook her head slowly, settling deeper into his lap, and leaning her head against his shoulder.

His arm stung. Damn, it was his blood. The wound had opened.

That sat in silence for a long moment.

"I-I am well. You may let me go." She motioned to rise but stumbled.

"You're not well. Sit and I'll make a fire."

"You're injured." She reached for his arm.

He shifted, causing her finger to brush against his wrist. A light pink began to fill her cheeks as warmth breathed into her, but he could tell she was fighting the chill. "'Tis fine. Stay. I'll gather wood." He hesitated. Any woman in her right senses would run from him once he left her alone. He probably looked like a madman, dirty from days of traveling, bleeding, and soaked after pulling her from the water. But, they needed a fire.

He was quick in his search for wood and kindling, and to his surprise, she was still sitting on the loch shore when he returned. He reached into his bag to find his flint and winced with the movement.

"I can help you with that." She pointed to his forearm.

She had nearly drowned, and she took pity on him? He held a hand upon it and found some torn fabric in his satchel. "I'll be well." He wrapped the cloth around his arm, knowing that it wouldn't be well until it was stitched.

As the flames lit the wood, he sat across from her, unsure what to say. At least the color had returned to her face.

Ah, the water. He pushed aside the thoughts that were stirring an unwanted response in him—her naked as she bathed, the wavy hair that flowed down her pearly back… It was as though she were a selkie come ashore for her mate. Oh God, it had been too long, and he felt ashamed for having watched her from the trees. He had meant to travel on once she was gone.

But then she had submerged herself for what seemed like forever. Her head hadn't broken the water for air, nor had she appeared to struggle. He had no bloody idea what she had been doing, but he couldn't let her drown. He had never seen a person hold their breath that long.

He shook his head, his damp hair chilling his neck. Perhaps this entire meeting was naught more than a figment of his exhausted mind. He was about to ask her why she had disappeared beneath the water when she spoke.

"I was well."

"Well?"

"In the water. I didn't need your assistance, sir."

"Oh?" He felt a strange sense of wanting to throttle her. Didn't need help? She had been under for many breaths! The water wasn't deep, but perhaps she had lost awareness. "So you had wished to die?"

She hugged her arms around herself, obviously trying to work heat into her body. "I can hold my breath."

Alasdair muffled a groan. This was the last thing he needed. He had to get to the isles, and soon. The baron was close.

"I should return home," she said, rising with difficulty.

"It's dark. And there could be—" He grabbed her wrist to stop her. She ripped her arm from his clutch and sat back down as if struck by a sudden pain. He wanted to warn her that there could be unscrupulous men about, for he knew the baron and his men had been near, but then again, who was he? To her, he was a stranger. Possibly a dangerous one.

"I-I—" She tightened her hand into a fist and rested it against her forehead.

"Does your head hurt you?"

"Nay. 'Tis just the chill." Abruptly, her demeanor changed. The hint of a smile tipped her lips, which grew pinker by the moment. She held his gaze. "My name is Deirdre."

On each of his encounters with strangers, Alasdair had grown more confident in his guise. He didn't blink at his lie. "Aleck Stirrat. Do you reside nearby? You shouldn't be alone, my lady. Where has your escort gone?" The question was very belated, but needed to be asked. Why would she be alone?

"I'm well on my own." She released an exasperated sigh. "From where do *you* hail? You speak with a southern accent. Edinburgh?" Her eyes glowed, too aware, too...something.

"Lennox. My work takes me to the isles." *God's teeth, why had he said that?* The isles were not part of his ruse.

She chewed her lip and scanned his attire. "What takes you there?"

"Trade."

Her expression grew suspicious. "Lennox? Who is your overlord?"

"The king, my lady."

"And God bless him, sir."

Oh, she was a tart lass.

He rubbed his chin. "Specifically, Laird Cunningham is my liege."

"Cunningham," she repeated, as if mulling it over.

"And you, my lady?" he said. A woman of nobility shouldn't be out alone in the woods, far from her home with brigands and English about. Where was her handmaid? Her entourage? She might be dressed in a work kirtle, and not a fine gown, but she did appear to be a crofter.

She waved a hand. "It's only Deirdre. No lady," she said, avoiding both his gaze and his question. "And I'm well," she said again.

He didn't believe her but asked no more.

For being well-prepared with his story, he had forgotten to appear the part of a trader seeking work in northern Argyll. Highlanders were rudimentary and almost barbaric in their ways. He wore his leather-lined trews, long belted shirt, and quilted jacket, although he looked as if he had rolled in the mud for a week. At least he remembered to remove all his rings and fur pouch, which were tucked in his satchel for bartering. Highland and Lowland traditions were different, especially with England's influence and hold on the south. He had to keep reminding himself of such. He poked at the fire and cleared his throat. "You're shivering. Sit closer to the fire. I can find us food."

"Nay bother. I've my bag, over there." She pointed toward it but made no move to rise.

He gave her a permission-seeking glance before picking it up.

She nodded. "I don't have much in there."

Her bag held a light wool plaid, a flask, bannocks, cheese wrapped in cloth, and herbs, among other trivial items. "Here." He brought the plaid over and wrapped it around her shoulders, pausing a moment to rub his hands on her forearms in a warming gesture. She was like ice.

He picked up her wayward dagger and placed it beside her along with the cheese and a bannock.

She didn't touch the food, but she did slide the dagger into a sheath and then tucked it into a pocket in her gown.

Hunger rolled in his stomach, but he didn't eat either. "You should rest." *So I can slip away during the night.*

"I can't." She pulled the plaid tighter, as if trying to quiet a voice from within. She rose again, a bit unsteady.

He could almost see thoughts churning in her mind. Her face said it all—distrust, worry, fear. This woman of few words and bold expressions baffled him. "Please stay or at least let me escort you home. I'll not imperil your virtue. I promise."

She made a soft, throaty sound.

"Your home can't be far. Oblige me, my lady."

She gave him a sideways glance with a lift of an eyebrow.

"Deirdre," he corrected, her name a song on his tongue. "You can trust me. No harm shall befall you, by my own hand or another's."

She sat slowly, clutching her temple as if pain overcame her. "Aye, just for a moment, then I go. By myself."

It was the best he could get from her. He didn't like the idea of this woman, lady or not, stumbling off in the dark. As much as exhaustion crushed him, he vowed to stay awake and watch over her.

A radiant energy swirled around Deirdre. She embraced the fire and warmth that took hold of her body. A sweet whirring played in her ears and her heart sang along as the melody danced down her spine and through the depth of her belly. She had not felt this appeased in years. Was she dreaming?

The pleasant sounds changed from the tiny, ever-present tune to a deep, vibrant rhythm.

In and out. In and out.

It grew louder, harder. She rolled over toward the glowing red sensation, delighting in the joy of it.

She opened her eyes. A man's face rested no more than a hand's distance from her head. She studied his features in the dawn light. An old scar traced a large, dark eyebrow. Thick black eyelashes fringed his lids, and a long nose led down to wide lips with days of stubble around them. Wavy hair fell against his forehead and brushed his neck. Dirt and blood smudged his round chin.

Heavens, not only had she fallen asleep in the presence of this stranger, but she lay right beside him, his breath hot on her face as he snored. Something prevented her from shooting upright in that moment. She brushed her palm against his cheek. The hot sensation penetrated her hand. Instead of fleeing the heat, she accepted it. The warmth slid down her wrist, to her elbow, and in toward her chest. He was unlike anything she had ever felt or sensed before. His lifeblood, embodied by heat, was contradictory: powerful and invigorating, yet soothing. The low hum quieted her incessant thoughts. It was strange...

Although she could feel his lifeblood, she could not sense his emotions like all the others.

He stirred. She froze. The red life within him grew hotter. He would wake soon.

She removed her hand and rose. Clenching her hand, she could still *feel* his lifeblood, as if it stayed with her. It had burrowed itself into her bones. Heavens, how she longed to question him more. Taken aback yesterday by the circumstance, she had lost all sense.

She knew better. She had to get far from him. Oh, by the graces, there was something about him, about her visions of him...

Perhaps it was Cortland's death that upset her so much. *Her second husband.* Dead in her matrimonial bed. She shivered, not from cold.

If her father found out about this, there would be hell to pay. She grabbed her bag, hurried from the river bank, and rushed into the trees without another moment's pondering, praying she'd never see the stranger from the woods—from her dreams—again.

Alasdair waited until Deirdre was out of earshot before he stood. He muffled a curse. He had slept on the injured arm, and it hurt something fierce. In fact, he was upset with himself for falling asleep at all.

He hadn't been the only one exhausted; Deirdre had fallen asleep quickly. He shook his head as if to dislodge the remnants of the dream. Nay, he couldn't remember any of it, but it had been warm, almost heavenly. Then he awoke and felt her soft hand upon his cheek. He'd feigned sleep, but he sensed her awareness of his wakefulness. Regardless, he relished the touch. Her smooth palm had been welcoming after a long time without the touch of a woman.

He stretched his arms and legs from another night on the stiff ground. The sound of his groan rebounded off the nearby trees and water. He would press on. The baron followed closely—too damn close yesterday. The man would not relent.

Fatigue and indecision plagued Alasdair, and he lacked the energy to ponder his options. His good sense told him to continue west. He was getting closer to the isles. Another day or two and he would be in a seaside town where he could gain passage and be freed of his burdens, at least for a while. Thomas awaited him, and it was imperative he get there soon. King Edward pushed farther and farther north by the day, and the fleet had been delayed enough.

But...

He needed a new horse, and his food was depleted, as well as his coin. He grabbed his satchel, swiped the dirt off his trews and shirt, and re-entered the woods. A unexplainable pull drew him north instead of west as he began to walk. If that lass Deirdre lived close, that meant there was a town or village nearby. It was risky, but he needed to get provisions. He prayed he could slip in, steal what he needed, and get out unnoticed.

CHAPTER TWO

Deirdre slammed the door behind her and fell into the chair beside the hearth. Hamm jumped into her lap and purred. His calmness transferred to her as she stroked his marbled fur. He shoved his head into her chin, and the purring pulsated into her bones as she scratched his ears.

If only she had been born a cat. All they did was sleep, pounce, and eat, with the occasional frolic over a butterfly. Human life wasn't that simple. She frowned for she was too old to be thinking about the simplicities of life anymore.

Perhaps what she loved most about Hamm was that she couldn't feel his energy. He radiated no color; his warmth was purely from body heat. She was thankful her ability didn't extend beyond people. In animals, she found a natural serenity. Besides, animals didn't judge, crucify, and burn people out of fear.

Her fingers tingled. She wasn't deaf to the talk that circulated about her within the village.

As if he could read her mind, Hamm nuzzled harder into her chin, begging attention. "Aye, you wee furry beast. Hush, hush," she cooed and continued with her petting, working her fingers through his matted and dirty fur. "Where have you been playing?" She plucked a few brambles. "In my blackberry bush?"

Her father disliked Hamm. He thought all cats were filthy, mewing nuisances that served one purpose—to catch pestilence-ridden rodents that raided the grain and food stores. In fact, Cortland hadn't liked Hamm either. Her heart felt heavy as she thought of her late husband, and the cold blue color that emanated from him on the morning after their wedding.

Hamm jumped off her lap as she rose.

Nervous energy spurred Deirdre to clean the cottage, which was her hideaway from the keep. Her father didn't approve of it, but she found solace here. It was quaint, quiet, and away from the noise of the town. Of course the laird's daughter couldn't live in such a place, so she slept at the keep in her bedchamber with the plush linens, fine garments, and always-tended fire. She dined in the hall with her family, entertained visitors, and maintained the castle's gardens, all keeping with her daughterly duties. *And the façade of being content.*

When she wasn't needed to oversee the lady's chambers of the keep and the servants, she escaped. There was something tranquil about working her small garden of herbs and vegetables, sewing by the hearth, drafty though it might be, and meditating on life's grander topics of life, death, and purpose.

Death. *Oh, Death, why do you haunt me?*

If only her mother were alive to explain it all. Had she been gifted, too? Why had death followed Deirdre into her matrimonial bed, not once, but twice? And Auld Kenneth MacDougall, who died before they could wed, would make three dead grooms. She was ever grateful for at least *that* death. He had been a boar of a man in both stature and disposition. If he had died in her bed, the MacDougalls, who already hated her family, would have been even more sore. She needn't further strife between their clans.

She opened the chest at the foot of her cot and searched through the items within it. She held a tiny nightgown and rubbed her fingers along the soft wool. It had been her infant gown. She laid a hand on her still flat belly. Death haunted her, but it seemed as though life did as well. One night of bedding was all it took. Her mood soured in a similar fashion to her stomach.

If only...

Many *if onlys* cluttered her thoughts lately. If only she had never married Gordon or Cortland. If only she had been born second. If only she had not been bestowed this unnatural gift of sensing lifebloods and emotions. If only she could journey to Uist, to see the people of her mother's culture. She had known for a long time about her mother's history there, but her father never allowed her to join any of his political forays. A venture to the isles was a foolish idea that would never reach fruition. Unless? That stranger from the woods, Aleck, had mentioned the isles. Perhaps...? No, she shook her head. He was far away by now. Besides, she'd rather not see him again.

Unable to escape her thoughts today, she placed the infant gown in the chest and found herself in front of the table beside the hearth. She ran a thumb over the dozen books on the table, her fingertips gliding over the embellished fabric-bound prayer books, and then pausing on the goatskin-bound book. She picked it up and traced the simple metal fish on the front. It had been her mother's.

She drew it open with care, the parchment pages thinned from her years of perusing. It lacked a title.

Nearly fifty pages were filled with drawings, symbols, and words she couldn't read. Her only guess was that it was written in Norse, for that was the language of the isles. Or rather, it was the former language. Only a few pages had Latin words.

She flipped to the page that always intrigued her. *Eir* was written at the top, and below it was an ornate drawing of a noblewoman, she presumed, by her dress. She sat surrounded by several maidens, all of them atop a wide hill. An etched dark red sun shone down upon the burn of vibrant blue water that encircled the hill. Deirdre traced over the intricate lines of the illustration, imagining the effort it must have taken to create.

She had once asked Moreen, her father's cook, what *Eir* meant. Moreen, after all, had been from Uist, the land of the Norse before their expulsion by her grandfather's generation of Scots. Moreen had said that Eir was the Norse goddess of healing and mercy. A Healer. Moreen had insisted she couldn't read Norse and had shrugged away Deirdre's inquiries. More than once, Deirdre contemplated asking Gilford to help her translate it, for he was one of the few servants that could read. Asking their castle steward meant her father would know, so she refrained from doing so. Once again today, she found herself wondering.

Perhaps one day she would journey to Uist, meet with her kin, and learn more about her godforsaken gift. "Mm-phmm." She shut the book.

A gift was the farthest description from it. Her power killed her lovers. It was no gift. Before another unlucky soul shared her bed, she needed to learn the truth of it. How could her touch, loving a man in that intimate way a wife could, kill her husbands? It was impossible. Yet...

The door flung open and interrupted her fretting. Deirdre's sister burst into the cottage. "There you are! Da's been looking for you all day!"

"Why? So he could scold me again?" She tucked the book into a sack to take with her to the keep tonight. Certainly her father would insist upon her sleeping there again.

Caite scowled.

"Could you not attend to his needs in my stead? I've tasks to tend to."

Caite scoffed, hands on her hips. "Where were you yesterday? I looked and couldn't find you! You're fortunate Da was distracted after supper."

Deirdre sighed. "It doesn't matter."

Caite pressed with her diatribe. "I know where you go."

When Deirdre didn't respond, Caite tried a different tactic. "Your place is in the keep. Da allows you to spend your days here at the cottage because you're mourning and need your time away from the keep and reminders of..." She paused, the heat in her tone cooling. She closed the door. "Oh, Dee. It's been a month. You never loved Cortland anyway."

Deirdre adored her sister and never grew tired of her sunny lifeblood, but today she didn't wish to be bothered by anyone, even Caite. She gave her a sidelong glance. "I still do not wish death upon anyone."

"Aye," Caite said with a shrug, not needing to say more. She flopped into the seat Deirdre had occupied a moment earlier. She twirled a lock of her wavy brown hair. "There's time to find another husband. You're young."

Deirdre pinched her forehead with her thumb and forefinger, soothing a dull headache. She was in no mood to be discussing her marriage difficulty. Her father had already been imploring her to find another suitor.

Who would marry her now? Cortland's bairn grew within her, and God alone shared her secret. She could not bring herself to tell her father. She couldn't even tell Caite. Not yet. Maybe another suitor would rectify things... She banished that thought. What man would marry her with another's seed growing in her womb? "Sweet Caite, I grow tired of this. Time is no longer my ally." She lifted her gaze from the floor and smirked. "But... Crystoll finds you fetching. He's told me himself," she said, taking the conversation's focus off herself. She was already a disgrace to the clan.

Caite's cheeks colored fiercely. "Oh, Dee! Do not speak of such things!" She tossed a look over her shoulder to the door, though Deirdre caught the light that shone in her sister's youthful face. She was besotted.

"You've come to marrying age, as well," Deirdre said, suspecting her father's soldier was waiting outside to escort Caite to the keep. She felt his earthy brown lifeblood, a perfect complement for her sister's glow. "Men should stay far away from me." The words hadn't come out as playful as she intended. Two men had not lived past the day after their marriage to her.

Caite stood, patted down her skirts, and brushed her hair behind her ears like a fussy hen. "Love will find you again, Dee. Now, you need to return to the keep at once. Da ordered it!"

Deirdre stopped her pestering. "What could possibly be so pressing? 'Tis midday. We have no guests. Perhaps I'll stay here tonight." She covered a yawn.

"Och, but there is a visiting noble at the keep. He arrived this morning. Da needs you to speak with Moreen about supper. I can't handle such things!" Caite shuffled her feet. Pleading blue eyes stared at her. That pretty face charmed the men in the village when her sister wanted something, but it did not work on Deirdre.

Deirdre decided against arguing with her sister. Instead, she brushed past her and opened the cottage door. Aye, it was as she had expected. She motioned Crystoll Murchison over.

"My lady?" he said. He bowed and beheld Caite as she appeared beside Deirdre in the doorway. "Are you ready to return, Lady Caite?" His cheeks were tinged pink from either the day's unusual warmth or his obvious infatuation with her.

Deirdre grinned brazenly at her sister. Caite gave her a look of daggers.

Deirdre couldn't fight obligation any longer. "Please take Caite home, Crystoll. Inform my father that I'll be there soon."

"Aye, my lady." He offered Caite his elbow.

Deirdre watched with a near maternal pride as her sister strolled to the keep with him. She gloried in that brief happy moment. Hopefully her father would approve of the relationship because it was a good match.

As the two faded from view, Deirdre was assailed by a heaviness in her belly. That sort of love would never happen for her and not for lack of wanting or trying.

She pulled herself from her melancholy by keeping busy. She cleaned the cottage, and placed a bowl of goat's milk down for Hamm, who lapped it hungrily. Moreen would be delighted to have fresh herbs from her garden to make the evening meal. Picking up a basket, she hurried outside. In no time, she found herself up to her elbows in the patch of overrun herbs and vegetables, plucking out weeds and brambles that had run wild. She abandoned all thoughts and enjoyed the simplicity of hard work and soft soil. Like the cold loch water or the stroke of an animal, digging through the earth appeased all the colors constantly battering her.

When finished, she leaned back, rested her dirt-covered hands behind her, and lifted her chin toward the sky with a sense of renewed energy. The later afternoon sun sank toward the horizon.

"Graces!" How had the time passed so quickly? Disheveled, she rose, wiping dirt from her soiled and splotched skirt. She then grabbed her basket and sack and hurried to the keep.

She had been unlike herself the past few days, ever since her dreams started again. She shut the idea away. This had *nothing* to do with the man in the wood or her dreams or the life now growing in her womb. "Mmphmm!" She picked up her pace.

Brilliant hues of pink speckled the cloudy sky as the sun set but she she had hardly a moment to enjoy it for she was terribly late.

A HUNDRED KISSES

She felt Moreen's discontent before she rounded the rear of the keep. Although she had been able to tune out the lifebloods of the villagers in her haste, the slap of frenzy and tension hit her as she approached the kitchen. She faltered a moment. Heaving a sigh, she rubbed her temple as the anxiety of others took a beating on her. "I'm sorry! I'm sorry!" she said in a breathless gasp, rushing through the side entrance. She dropped her basket on a table next to Moreen.

Moreen shook her chubby face and cast a fraction of a glance up from her preparation. She sliced through a slab of venison, clouting the meat as if it fought her. "Tsk tsk. Milady, bless the heavens that I can handle this myself! What hiv ye for me?" She poked a large nose into the basket and took a deep whiff. "Ah blessings, garlic and rosemary! I'm afraid my garden hasn't been as bountiful as yers this moon."

Deirdre's stomach growled at the scent wafting from a boiling pot. Cooked cabbage with spring onions and fresh-baked bread were all too enticing after a day of forgetfulness and fasting. Servants hurried past her, the kitchen alive with readying the supper. A servant bumped into her, apologized, and continued around her with a platter of meat.

Moreen blew a wisp of unruly hair out of her eyes. "Lass, ye look a muddle."

Deirdre reached for a piece of bread. "How many guests will be attending?"

"One noble, milady, but ye ken how yer father is." Moreen lobbed a glance at Deirdre's dirty kirtle. The crease in her aging forehead thickened. She pulled herbs from the basket and scuttled over to a few servants.

"Chop this and add it to the stew." She returned to Deirdre and shooed her. "Go ready yerself. The laird's guest is already here. I am well here, milady."

"Aye, ma'am," she said, kissing Moreen on the cheek and grabbing another slice of bread.

Deirdre hurried through the narrow passageway behind the kitchen toward the second tower, hoping that her father wouldn't be angry with her delay. As lady of the household, it was her duty to greet all guests and nobles. She almost collided with Gilford as she turned up the spiral staircase. She quieted a yelp.

"By the—" He grimaced. "Oh, it's you, milady." He gave a quick bow.

"Sorry, Gilford!"

A guttural groan escaped in irritation from her father's steward, but he urged her on without a word and continued with a servant following closely.

She climbed the staircase to the tower to find Maddie pacing in her room.

"Milady!"

Deirdre waved dismissively. "Och, I know."

"I've laid out yer gown."

"Thank you, kindly." She didn't care what she wore to yet another boring nobleman's visit. "Do you know who our visitor is?"

"No, milady. Perhaps a suitor?" Her rosy complexion glowed as she untied the laces on Deirdre's brown work kirtle.

Dear God, she hoped not. "Perhaps."

Maddie helped Deirdre step out of the kirtle and assisted her into a new one of cream wool to match the long-sleeved chemise beneath. She tied up the front laces and then pulled the dark green gown over Deirdre's head. The fabric fell in a heavy whoosh to the floor. A chained belt completed the ensemble. Maddie then brushed Deirdre's tangled locks, which hung halfway down her back. "Milady, shall I plait yer hair?"

"No need. Thank you, Maddie." She took the comb from her maid.

"Aye, milady." Maddie curtsied and departed.

Deirdre hurried through her grooming, sweeping part of her hair back with a small golden comb, but refusing to put it up. Her father always liked her to wear it up plaited or in a coif to impress, but she was in no mood for it tonight. When her hair hung free, her soul felt unburdened. She grimaced at the dirt beneath her nails and did a cursory clean of them in the water basin. She then hurried downstairs as soon as she was ready.

Thankfully, the grand hall was not filled with the usual weekly attendees. She counted table place settings: herself, her father, Caite, her brother Edmund and his wife Fiora, and two other seats—she presumed one for Crystoll and the other for the guest. Uncle Kendrick was away in Edinburgh this month.

Why were there no additional seats for the visiting noble's soldiers? Most nobles were like roosters, coming in with their flock of vassals, servants, or ladies.

An empty seat remained for Laird MacCoinneach's commander, but alas, she thought, that is—or rather, was—Cortland. Her father had yet to replace his most faithful and highest ranked soldier. Perhaps Crystoll would be appointed to the position. He was kind and able, and Deirdre always enjoyed his presence.

She paused in the entranceway and inhaled, preparing herself for another dull evening of talk on the court in Edinburgh or England, the latest in the market trade down the coast, or more political banter. News of King Edward's attacks in the south moved fast. Their guest tonight was likely another nobleman who was north seeking support for a Claimant in the Cause for the Scottish crown. From what she had overheard, her father had not yet declared allegiance to anyone. *Dear Heavens, please don't be another suitor.* War raged in the south and Scots bickered among themselves over the throne, and all she could think about was her own needs.

A booming cough from the opposite entrance announced her father's presence. Edmund walked at his side, taller than their father by at least a head's length, with the full, rounded shoulders of youth. They were thick in conversation, and their voices echoed across the hall.

"Auld Hugh Cunningham is his chief?" asked Edmund. "Why would he send a nobleman north on such a task? What about his vassals or soldiers? He came alone. We should be wary, Father. Certainly he's here seeking supporters for the Cause...or perhaps he's an emissary with other intentions, to bring word back or to—"

"There is no need to be troubled yet." Her father patted a hand on Edmund's back.

"Father, we can't get involved in this Cause! Please reconsider. Joining in this madness is—is...'tis treason to King John and to Scotland and—"

Laird Simon MacCoinneach shot a look of warning to Edmund. Deirdre's brother clamped his mouth shut and scowled like a five-year-old boy.

Her father approached his oldest child with a scrutinizing gaze. She curtsied and patted down her skirt, her hand pausing on her belly. She felt his displeasure, and it afflicted her further.

"You've been in the gardens?"

It wasn't a question. The air of disapproval was all too apparent. She stuck her chin out but remained quiet. His hawk-eyes were penetrating.

"Tomorrow you'll stay here, at the keep. No more idleness. You've mourned enough."

Deirdre winced. He was riled, and she felt it, a pang through her middle.

"See to our guest. He's in the first tower. Please escort him down." There was no room for question in his tone.

"What? Shouldn't—"

His look silenced her question.

She saw no rescue in Edmund's equally glowering face. Her brother was a sour man and even more so lately. While their father continued to arrange marriages for Deirdre, Edmund's wife Fiora suffered another loss of the bairn she'd carried within her. Each time, Deirdre had known before the news came to her. Deaths caused pinches of pain in her chest, like little dagger slices, and would result in a painful headache as their cold, deathly blue washed over her.

She curtsied. "Aye, Father." She left the room and made her way to the tower, where the guest bedchamber was located. It was usually a responsibility of Cortland's or Gilford's to escort a noble guest. Of course her father had put *her* on the errand... This visitor was indeed another suitor.

She bit her lip, thinking. Cunningham? Why did that name sound familiar? Certainly a noble from there had come to meet with her father before. Numerous had frequented their mighty keep of Eilean Donan in the past two years, thirsty for her father's sword and allegiance.

She fussed with her hair, tucking in loose tendrils behind her ears. She patted her skirt and exhaled. This unlucky soul could be the next to share her cursed bed. She'd been foolish to think that she could do it all on her own. Her father would not relent. He would double his efforts once he learned of the bairn. She pinched her cheeks, wishing Maddie had finished her grooming ritual after all. Her fingertips still smelled of the earth, despite the hasty cleaning of nails and fingers. She hoped that this suitor would at least be kind. She cringed, remembering Auld Kenneth MacDougall, a man far from kind.

Heavy footsteps sounded above her. Her own unease ran rampant, and it caused her to be distracted, unable to discern his lifeblood and emotional energy. She could sense an insincere scoundrel from afar, and even though her father never spoke of or acknowledged her gift, he had relied upon it many times to help him weed out the miscreants who came calling. Nearly at the top of the spiral stairs, she looked up to greet the man, feeling winded from her haste. The stairwell was steep and dark with a low overhang, and all she saw were his finely-made trews and leather boots. She bowed her head and dipped into a curtsy the best she could on the narrow steps. "Sir..." She paused. Her father had not mentioned his name. "May I please escort you down to the hall?"

"I admire a laird who sends a lady to retrieve his noble guests. A beautiful face is always an enjoyable sight." His voice was deep and amused.

"His Lairdship is in the hall. Shall I take you there?"

He stepped down to her level. She lifted her gaze to meet his as she rose, and a warm and familiar face greeted her. "Dear me." His smoldering lifeblood crushed her with its heat, and she lost her footing a bit.

The man from the wood took her hand to steady her, and he kissed her knuckles.

Dizziness struck her. He caught her by the elbow and held her upright. "Are you all right, *Lady* Deirdre?"

Was he laughing at her with that disparaging tone? By the heavens, he was!

He smirked. She grimaced.

Thankful for his hold, she recovered her poise. His life energy didn't cause her to cringe or turn away; in fact, she felt quite the opposite. She found she wanted to be near it, near him, even though it appeared to steal her footing. "I-I...please excuse me," she replied. Her stomach was in an uproar, a queasy mix of nausea and hunger. She silently reprimanded herself, both for her lack of grace and her ignorance. How had she not sensed that it was *him*? His heat prickled her soul!

His dark blue eyes smiled at her. "I surprised you."

She swallowed. Her breath quickened, and heat warmed her cheeks at remembrance of their last encounter—asleep, together, on a bed of dirt and leaves. "I didn't expect to see you again, Sir Stirrat." She paused, carefully processing her thoughts before she spoke. She added, "So soon. Shouldn't you be on your way to the isles?" She blinked, forcing herself to control her senses.

"Dornie is en route to the isles."

A thought dawned on her. "Did you follow me?"

He chuckled lightly, leaning in closer, loose locks of wavy black hair falling into his face. "You mean after you left me at dawn? I should be the one questioning you. You are indeed a lady."

She stepped back and glanced down the stairs. Nobody was near. "Please, sir, I-I hadn't meant to lie, but you see…"

He saved her from her discomfort. "No. I didn't follow you. Luck brought me here, my lady, and your father is a most convincing man. He insisted I stay."

She muffled a grunt. Indeed, Sir Stirrat was yet another noble after her father's pocket or an alliance. It was odd that she didn't sense that. This man's lifeblood radiated strength, faith, and something else she couldn't put a word to. Yet…she couldn't read his emotions, the man beneath his fiery shield. Aye she felt his blazing red lifeblood and his character, but not the emotions beneath them. Very perplexing! Was he friend or foe?

"Believe me, my lady," he said, with an almost sly grin, "I'm weary from my journey and could use a night's rest that is not on a bed of leaves. That's my single reason for visiting."

"As you say, Sir Stirrat." God's graces, was he the same man she had seen in the woods last night? There, he seemed raw, unrefined. Now, he bore the air of a nobleman and was dressed to match, with clean dark trews, white linen shirt, scrubbed boots, and fingers adorned with bright jeweled rings that he had not worn in the woods. His hair was pulled back in a low coif, although the unruly dark waves that circled his high forehead fell loose to his ears. The stubble that had peppered his chin was now gone. Had he lied?

"May I escort you down, sir?" she repeated. She pondered more about his presence. He had no liege, servants, or horse with him when they had met. She had truly thought him to be a lone trader journeying by foot.

By the heavens, though, his energy was overpowering, and it seemed to drown her other senses when she was near him. Her head ached when she tried to discern the true motives for his appearance at Eilean Donan.

"It's Aleck. No 'sir' needed, my lady." He looped his arm into hers and guided her down the stairwell.

They descended in silence, but Deirdre swore he could hear her pounding heart. She stopped short of the hall. The words caught as she contemplated how to say them. "Sir—"

"Aleck," he corrected.

She licked her lips. "Aleck. When we met, er, in the woods, I—"

He turned toward her and took her free arm by the elbow, causing her to spin and face him. His fingers trailed down her forearm, and he lifted her hand. He brushed his lips against her knuckles as he had only moments before. The ruby in his gold ring sparkled, almost winking at her. *My, he was cunning in his play.*

It was then she noticed the scars that traced all of his fingers on his right hand. A rush of chills ran up her arm. He stood upright and whispered, his breath hot in her ear, "I'll not speak a word of our meeting."

"Thank you kindly," she said, too taken aback to say more.

"I ask one thing in return, though."

"Oh?"

"Don't leave me again?"

"Pardon me?"

A playful smirk spread his mouth wide. "During supper. I find all this political conversation disagreeable. I would be grateful for an ally."

She mustered a chuckle. "Of course. So would I."

Her head spun. God, who was this man, and why was he here?

Alasdair had never tasted such a delicious supper, and so he told the laird. Granted, he had not eaten much in the past month that he would consider a quality meal.

"Aye, Moreen is the finest cook in all of Glen Shiel," Laird Simon MacCoinneach said in between gulps of stew.

"Without a doubt, Laird," Alasdair agreed. He emptied his goblet of ale, and a serving lass came to refill it. "Shiel is a beautiful glen, Laird. What are those mountains north of you?"

"The five sisters of Kintail. Magnificent, aren't they? You've not been through here before, Sir Stirrat?"

"No, Laird. This is my first charge." He rubbed his chin in interest. "I'm afraid I am not as familiar with this route as I had thought. How far are you from the isles?" Supper had gone on long enough, and Alasdair needed to be on his way as soon as possible. In a last moment decision, once he had realized his location—Eilean Donan, the castle that served as gateway to the isles—he opted for meeting the laird instead of stealing horses and provisions. It was a perilous move, seeing as the baron wasn't too far behind him, but Laird MacCoinneach's allegiance would prove valuable when the navy was ready. Perhaps on his return trip, he could forge an alliance with him.

Edmund, Deirdre's brother, exhaled loudly. He had been quiet during the meal, sneaking in glares at Alasdair when he could. The laird's son looked plenty able to run him through if he wanted. There was a striking similarity between him and Deirdre. They shared the same eyes, those of a blue-green seaweed come washed ashore. Except, with Edmund, a thick scowl hovered over his while Deirdre's glowed with a depth Alasdair wouldn't mind exploring more.

Finding her here *and* to be the laird's daughter had been a surprise. And admittedly, not a bad one either.

"'Tis a few days' ride to reach the nearest port. Glen Shiel has seen many battles in the past because of our proximity to the isles. Are you familiar with our history?" Simon asked.

"I'm afraid not." Alasdair spooned a mouthful of stew onto a crusty piece of bread.

Most lairds loved to boast of their glories or pursuits, and Simon appeared to be no exception. "My father and I fought against King Haakon of the Nord Land and those *Lochlanach*, and we were granted the glen for our service and loyalty. The king, Alexander himself, came to our castle and bestowed it upon us," he finished, beaming with pride. He stroked his auburn beard, whilst deep in memory. He reached across the table with a beefy forearm and broke a loaf of bread in half, dipped it in a sauce on his plate, and devoured it as if he were eating the sweet rewards of a good pillage.

"Eilean Donan is a beautiful keep and well deserved, Laird MacCoinneach. I've heard the tales of the Norse of the isles." And of the bloodthirsty *berserkir* and *úlfheðnar*, the selkies, and the mystical peoples... Many were just that: embroidered stories of pretend.

"They are more than tales told to wee bairns. They are our truths." Simon's grin deepened, and his eyes held a faint glimmer, one of a deeper appreciation or fond memory. There was another story hidden in that look, a story that went beyond one of swords. One of the heart, perchance?

The laird was a stocky man, well past his prime, but still robust for his age and lacking gray hair in his bushy red-brown mane. He didn't look much like his children, so Alasdair assumed that they acquired their good looks from their mother, who wasn't present. Ill or deceased, he wondered. A lady of the keep did not typically leave her husband and laird to go visit the countryside.

Laird MacCoinneach's boasting substantiated Alasdair's knowledge about the Norse raids on the isles and mainland. Both the loch that surrounded the castle and the town of Dornie and its proximity to the ports made this area integral in a sea war. Now...for him to discern who the laird supported in the Cause. From what he had learned, the Highlanders were hard to persuade and were passionately loyal to their clans over siding with a Claimant. The lowland lairds had already openly declared their allegiances.

Alasdair eyed Deirdre. A different woman from his earlier encounter sat across from him. She appeared bored with the conversation. Instead of drenched dark hair cascading down her back, it was now pulled half back, tendrils fighting to come free. In place of a homespun wool kirtle, a green gown bedecked with small jewels on the low-cut bodice hung from her womanly frame. It complemented the jade flecks in her eyes and her high cheekbones. Apparently the laird showed off more than just his stronghold and fruitful gardens and woods, for the lady was a sight to behold.

Crystoll, the silent soldier on the other side of Simon, listened as though he had never heard the stories before, but Alasdair suspected otherwise. Many lairds did not grow tired of vainglory.

"How do the clans fare in the south?" Edmund asked.

"With King Edward's recent attacks, the court is unsettled."

"The clans, family, and duty rule the north. We do not allow the court to sway us," Edmund said, his gaze locked with Alasdair's. He took a slow sip from his goblet. "We are bound by blood."

"Certainly Sir Stirrat is well aware of the clans' precarious situation, as well as the whole of Scotland," Simon said.

Alasdair didn't hesitate. "Aye, Laird. As long as I live, I shall not bow to King Edward of England."

Simon's expression remained guarded. He rubbed his bearded chin in reflection. Brown piercing eyes searched Alasdair. "What have you heard about the Claimants, Sir Stirrat?"

"Many honorable men contend for the throne. They've all made their declarations clear in court."

"The Scottish contenders are fools. This entire Cause is a farce," Edmund said, clenching a fist on the table. "Pride leads them to think they can defeat a king of England who has such wealth and force."

The laird cleared his throat with a guttural warning.

Hmm. So father and son disagreed on this matter?

"I'm sorry Fiora couldn't join us this evening," Deirdre said, directing her soft-spoken voice toward her brother.

All eyes turned to her, for she had remained silent for most of the meal. Alasdair was grateful for her interjection. She smiled at her brother but not before sharing a brief bat of her lashes at Alasdair. He winked in thanks. Perhaps he did have an ally at this table.

Edmund was terse. "She's doing better. Perhaps on the morrow she'll join us for supper."

"I shall visit her."

A sad, dark shadow settled on Edmund's features. "No need."

Alasdair wondered what this was about but dared not ask.

Simon cleared his throat. "Sir Stirrat, do you hunt?"

"Laird?"

"Stags?"

"Aye. I killed a hart of ten last autumn."

Simon's eyes lit like a child who had just stolen a sweetbread from the kitchen. "Och! Then you must stay for a few days and join me on my next hunt tomorrow. No reds right now, but we might be able to take a roe."

"Laird, you've been most gracious, but my work takes me west."

"Your affairs can wait a few days." Simon measured Alasdair with a scrutinizing gaze. "Do you prefer bow or spear, or perhaps blade?"

Alasdair relented. He needed to stay in his host's good graces if anything may come of the relationship. "Short bow."

Simon grinned. "Able choice."

"Do you require dogs as well?" Crystoll asked. He had been a quiet attentive observer, speaking and agreeing where needed throughout the conversation, but silence didn't equate to submission or ignorance in Alasdair's opinion, so he remained wary of this man's scrutiny as well.

"Whatever the laird wishes."

Crystoll nodded and returned to eating his meal.

Edmund's glower deepened. "Sir Stirrat, what sort of trade do you oversee in the isles?"

Deirdre surprised Alasdair with speaking again. "Edmund, why do you persist with this inquest? Sir Stirrat must be tired from his journey."

Edmund scowled at Deirdre, and she returned the look.

The inquisition continues, Alasdair thought, reminded that he had already been through this dance with the laird. Though he had passed the preliminary inquiry, it seemed he faced a second round. "My laird oversees export of fish and salt as I have informed your laird upon my arrival. Since the departure of the Norse, we have seen opportunity flourish with France and trade with the isles." Through the corner of his eye, Alasdair watched the laird. His face said nothing. Edmund's, however, hid nothing. Alasdair inhaled faintly, hoping he played his hand well. "If there is war, then our soldiers will need to be fed."

Edmund was undeterred. "A nobleman sends his vassal on such errands."

"My laird entrusted me."

"How is Auld Hugh?" Edmund asked.

A shrewd test, Alasdair thought. He hid a smile. The benefits to having been dragged to court all these years meant knowledge he could use. "He died this winter. His son, James, is chief."

Father and son appeared to have opposite methods for testing his lies. His trial with the laird would be tomorrow, during the stag hunt. Right now, it was Edmund's opportunity to interrogate him. Simon was a lenient laird, allowing his son to be so brash.

Edmund leaned in, both hands tight on the edge of the table. "You have spent many days on the road, yet you arrive with no horse?"

"The animal grew lame a few days ago." Alasdair sensed Deirdre's eyes upon him.

"You didn't purchase another mount or hire more servants?"

Deirdre coughed and tossed Alasdair a fleeting glance of apology. He locked eyes with Edmund, not allowing his resolve to falter. "No. Some kind people advised me to come here. They had mentioned your laird's most agreeable hospitality. Indeed, I was going to purchase a mount here in Dornie."

"Edmund, enough. Let him finish his meal. He needs his rest before a day of hunting tomorrow." Simon plunked his goblet down, ending the conversation.

As Laird MacCoinneach, Edmund, and Crystoll continued their talk on other matters of the estate, Alasdair stole another look at Deirdre. A smile softened her lips. He couldn't help but return the gesture. It was a shame that he was going to need to slip away during the stag hunt on the morrow. He was just starting to like the lass.

CHAPTER THREE

Deirdre found herself in the pantry, among the preparation at dawn, unable to sleep and oddly famished. She poked through the large jars on the table. Then picked up a hot bannock from beside the hearth and slathered honey atop it. Suddenly, nausea quenched her appetite with the first bite. She put the bannock down and rubbed a hand over her middle. She sat at the table and rested her head on her forearms.

"Ye should eat it."

Unable to raise her head, Deirdre swallowed the chunk of bannock caught in her throat. Her stomach lurched, but it was a quick spasm and she felt a smidgen better. "I'm weary. Crystoll was telling me about the rat pestilence and those furry devils have been raiding the stores again. I may need to bring Hamm to the keep. Or perhaps I have the same sickness as Fiora."

"Fiora's fever isn't catching, but her other condition is," Moreen said. She added in a gentle voice, "Or was."

"What do you mean?" Deirdre lifted her head with a start, regretting it.

Moreen hurried over, cross in her manner. "Milady, yer lies may fool yer father and brother, but ye'll not fool me."

Deirdre felt her face grow warm, unsure if it was from Moreen's statement or her own fatigue. "You're fortunate I love you, Moreen," she said in light jest. Other ladies would not allow such insolence. But Deirdre adored her mother's friend.

"Och, dearie. Does yer father know yet?" Moreen sat beside her and rubbed a circle on her back.

Genuine love radiated from Moreen's yellow lifeblood, and her emotions were always reeled in even when vexed. Joy seeped into her soul around Moreen. Deirdre shook her head.

"Caite?"

Again, she shook her head.

"It is Cortland's?"

"Aye!"

Moreen was silent. Deirdre could feel Moreen's mind spinning with ideas.

"We need to get ye wed again," she said crisply, and rose. She maneuvered around the table, deft despite her plump and short stature. She stepped up onto a stool to reach higher shelves.

Deirdre lamented, "Not you, too. Why does everyone think I need a husband? Edmund can rule in my husband's stead. He'd be more than delighted to do so."

Moreen cast her an earnest sidelong glance. "Aye, lass, he could, but poor Fiora keeps losing the bairns. He will have no heir. Besides, ye're the oldest child."

"By a few breaths! That shouldn't matter. I don't want to hold this power." *I have powers enough beyond my control.*

"Ye won't, milady. Yer husband will." Moreen looked over her shoulder at Deirdre. The corner of her mouth curved up into a smile of pity and wrinkles creased the sides of her eyes.

"I don't see why Edmund can't be laird, and he can pass the duty on to my child."

"It doesn't work that way."

"You sound like Da."

Moreen stepped down and busied herself with slicing a loaf of bread. "He's a keen man with a kind heart."

Deirdre had never heard Moreen praise her father before. She lifted her head and evaluated the woman, her closest friend besides Caite. Moreen was her father's age, but still possessed a youthful glow in her face, with round pink cheeks, always smiling lips, wide brown eyes, and a head full of curly brown hair. She had been a blessing in Deirdre's life ever since her mother's death.

Moreen looked up from her work at Deirdre's silence. "What is it, dearie? Is it the bairn? Dinna get het up over that matter. Yer father will think of something—but ye need to tell him."

Deirdre grinned. "'Tis not that."

Moreen's eyes narrowed. "Did you lose your tongue? The sun is heading up, dearie. What is it?"

"You're besotted! Why didn't I realize it sooner?" Deirdre's smile deepened and she crossed her arms.

Moreen stopped her work, crimson flushing her cheeks. Very seldom did Moreen have few words to say.

Deirdre rose from her seat and hugged her from behind, resting her chin on Moreen's shoulder. "Oh, does he return the token? It would please me to see him happy again."

Moreen shrugged out of the embrace. "Hiv ye gone daft, lass? That bairn pulling the lifeblood from ye? Yer father's my laird, and I his servant. Besides, nobody can replace yer mother, especially me."

Deirdre's stomach wrenched, and not from the nausea that plagued her this morning. She slumped onto her seat. "What did you say?"

"I'm sorry. I didn't mean—"

"No, it's not that. Although I do wish my mother were here to explain things to me."

"Aye, lass. I miss her, too."

Deirdre lowered her voice. "You said my *lifeblood*. What did you mean?" The term had been something Deirdre thought of on her own to describe the energies she felt from people. Never before had she heard another person utter the word.

"Och." Moreen waved a hand. "Nothing."

Deirdre's strength dimmed. Moreen was not normally this evasive.

"Here." Moreen pushed the loaf of bread at her. "This will pass. The bairn takes much from ye in these early weeks. Eating small meals throughout the day will help."

Deirdre began to sniffle. She had never allowed the truth of it all sink in. Tears hovered on her eyelids. She couldn't escape the dull ache in her soul—her obligations, the bairn, missing her mother... It was all too much. "Moreen," she croaked, determined to find out more from her longtime friend.

"Hush, dearie. Women tend to cry more, too."

"I will not be silenced." She held Moreen's gaze. "Where have you heard of lifebloods before?"

Moreen's lips formed an O. Heaving a sigh, she said, "The isles. A long time ago." Her words were a whisper.

"What do you think about the Ancients and their *powers*?"

"Ye're special, Deirdre, and don't ever think otherwise."

"That's not what I asked." This conversation had been avoided for many years. She would not let Moreen escape it this time.

Moreen tapped her lips in contemplation. "The Ancients? They're simply folks people of the isles have imagined to explain the unexplainable. Tales told to children."

"I don't believe you."

Moreen held her ground. By the heavens, she was being stubborn today.

"I wish my father would take me to Uist, though he insists there isn't much left of Mother's kin."

"Perhaps one day ye will go." Moreen placed a calloused hand on hers. "Most of the Norse hiv gone, but the king's men remained, clearing out their followers and rebuilding settlements these past thirty years. Och, it's a lonely, dreich place, lass. Not much to see except..." She drifted off as though recalling a fond memory. "Hiv ye heard of the circles?"

"No." Deirdre leaned in closer.

A small glimmer lit Moreen's eyes, and she lowered her voice. "There are grand circles, built of slabs of stone. The Ancients and my kinfolk used to worship at these places. The people of the land hiv learned to harness the powers of the stones. They hiv special gifts—of sight, healing..." she said, pausing. Telling eyes stared at Deirdre.

Moreen's words vibrated within Deirdre. "Gifts?"

"Aye." Moreen beamed as if she'd come to some internal decision.

Finally.

"So you *do* believe in these abilities?"

Witches. The devil's work. That is what others proclaimed.

Moreen shrugged neither a yes nor a no.

"Did my mother possess a power?"

Moreen frowned, her face looking suddenly aged. Deirdre felt her hesitation. "Tell me."

"She was a Healer and her sister, yer aunt, a Seer."

Deirdre tried to swallow the lump that lingered in her throat.

Moreen's whole face broke into a smile. "Ye're a *Feeler*." She laid a hand on Deirdre's cheek. Heat pulsated from Moreen's hand, making Deirdre shudder.

"A Feeler?" There was a name for this ability?

"I've always kent of it."

"Do ye think Da—"

"Ne'er ye mind him. He was married to a Healer. He's stubborn and wants what's best for ye." She made a low throaty sound. "He doesna admit it, but aye, he kens of yer gift. He uses it for his own purposes, doesn't he?"

Deirdre nodded. She had always suspected he had known about it, but why protect her from such a gift? "I know no aunt."

"I'm sorry, lass. It wasn't my place to tell ye. I had wanted to, a lang time ago, but yer da—" She paused and straightened her back, apparently done with secrets. "Her name is Venora, and she still resides in the small settlement of Port nan Long, on the northern coast of Uist." She added, "That was years ago. She may be dead."

"Oh, Moreen!" A lightness filled her chest. She had kin alive in the isles? She had always wanted to journey there, but now she had a reason. "I must go then! Before the bairn arrives. Perhaps..." She didn't finish her sentence. Sir Stirrat was going to the isles. Mayhap he would...oh, she cringed with that thought. The idea of journeying there alone with him was a foolish one. Yet, that was twice now that the idea had entered her mind.

"How long have you known about my—oh heavens—whatever it's called?" Deirdre said, feeling a squeezing hurt. All these years and Moreen hadn't told her?

"A gift, lass. A gift. A woman of the isles knows. I ken ye weren't ready yet, and your da asked me not to, but now I see that yer powers hiv grown. It was time to tell ye," Moreen whispered. "Yer da—och, please don't say anything to him!"

Footsteps sounded in the hallway. Deirdre stood and hurried around the table to Moreen. She grabbed her hands and whispered, "Tell me more!"

Gilford entered the room. "Good morning, milady."

Deirdre recovered her composure. "Good day, Gilford."

"Your father requests your presence on the stag hunt. I'm to send you with the afternoon meal." He evaluated Moreen with suspicious eyes. Their castle steward always wore a wrinkled expression as if deep in thought. He was a phantom on the wind, whisking in and out of chambers, barking orders.

Moreen pulled out a basket and satchel and began to ready the meal's components.

"He requests that you be at the inner stable in an hour, milady." Not expecting a protest, he turned on his heels and was out the door.

Deirdre grabbed her middle, unsettled. "Och, will this ever cease?"

Moreen reached into a jar. "Here," she said, shoving a brown root and a bag of herbs into her hand. "It will ease the aches. Use a knife to shave off a few pieces and put them in yer water, or when ye can, steep with hot water to drink at night."

Deirdre eyed the root—ginger. "Why hadn't I thought of that? Thank you, Moreen." Piles of her mother's herbal books resided in her cottage, collecting dust and waiting to be read. Lately, Deirdre lacked the motivation. They were simple books, unlike the book of Eir. A *Healer*. Her mother had been gifted, too. Maybe it was time to read the books with more intention.

Her predicament was a heavy stone in her belly. A voyage to Uist was just a dream. It would never happen, not with Cortland's bairn growing in her womb to be born come year's end. She was trapped here.

Although...

She couldn't shake the idea away. Perhaps there was a way to get there sooner. Crystoll was too loyal to her father; there was no persuading him to take her there and secretly, at that.

"Promise we'll talk more later!" Deirdre said, rushing from the kitchen.

Moreen's words floated after her. "Aye. I promise."

Deirdre's worries dissipated—or at least she was able to stifle them—as the day drew on. The spring sun broke through the clouds, blessing them with a pleasant midday. As she sat on a blanket below a tree beginning to burgeon with leaves, a cool breeze sent ripples of gooseflesh down her exposed arms. She closed her eyes. Like with animals, she couldn't feel the life of trees. Instead, a quiet vibration emanated from them that drowned the hum she always felt around people. She supposed that was the reason why she enjoyed her isolation in her cottage or garden. It was restful and unstimulating to be surrounded by plants or animals.

Commotion interrupted her respite. Shouts and movement came from the trees across the meadow. Instead of seeing a boisterous group of men emerging with a stag in tow, two soldiers ran out. They reached her and began rifling through satchels. She rose and joined them. "Is something amiss?"

Peter, a young man of maybe sixteen, didn't look up. He pulled out a cloth and a flask of what she presumed was whisky. "Aye, milady. Sir Stirrat's been hurt."

"Hurt? However so?" They weren't boar hunting. Stag hunting was safer. Albeit, the men still tended to overindulge in whisky prior to taking up their bows resulting in misaims and errant arrows.

"S-Sorry, milady, we must tend to him," Peter said, running back to the trees.

She turned her interrogation to the other man. "Sham, do we need to send for Gilford?"

"I'm no' certain, milady. Milaird didna say. Edmund's arrow only grazed 'im, I believe." Sham left her gawking and he returned to the trees empty-handed, leaving behind ransacked satchels.

She huffed, lifted her skirts for better mobility, and entered the tree line. Just as she did, Edmund bumped into her. He was filthy, as though he had just spent the morning mucking the pigpen. With no apology, he stomped toward the clearing.

"Edmund, what happened?" She followed him to his horse. He removed his flask and downed the contents. The heat stemming from his red-orange lifeblood intensified as the tang of a spiced whisky fell off his breath. He radiated his usual obstinate energy, and his emotions reflected an even stronger defiance today than usual. Being twins, she had always wondered if they shared the same lifeblood, for she could not sense her own.

He grunted.

"You hit Sir Stirrat with an arrow? Whatever for?"

"I didn't do it on purpose. He got in the way of the stag."

"In the way?" she said, her voice rising.

He turned toward her and gave her an icy glare. He ruffled his hair with a fidgety hand. "Aye. I had my sights on a beautiful stag, six points. Six, Deirdre! He released first though I had already taken aim."

"I doubt he did that deliberately. Certainly, he didn't see you." She wasn't clear on the etiquette involved in a stag hunt. Thankfully, her father had never dragged her on one. She served as dutiful lady, providing refreshments and pleasant company for the visiting nobles while they boasted about their glories in taking down a stag. She crinkled her nose.

"So you say," Edmund mumbled.

She straightened her back and neck, attempting to meet him at eye level. It was to no avail; he was at least a head taller than her. She hardened her tone. "I would not like to think that you purposely did it, Edmund. Killing nobles that may or may not wish to court me is cavalier, even for you."

He closed the distance between them and growled the words through clenched teeth, looking down his nose at her. "Just because I don't like him doesn't mean I want to kill him. Shame on you for implying such a thing, dear sister."

She didn't flinch and gave him an equally hard stare. She clamped her mouth shut, feeling abashed but not remorseful. Ever since Fiora's latest loss Edmund had been more angry than normal. She finally said, in a whisper, "You know how much I wish for it to have been you born first, Edmund. I don't want to marry a noble who will be our laird, but Da..."

Edmund turned back to the tree line as others began to emerge. "Aye, I know how Father is," he said, his voice breaking.

Several other men were in jovial spirits as they strode out from the thick trees. The men conversed with broad hand gestures as the grooms took the stag's carcass to prepare it for the ride home. The dogs barked and paced, their tails wagging in excitement after a job well done. Though dirty and sweaty, the men were nonetheless upbeat and boisterous.

Finally, Crystoll entered the meadow. Aleck hobbled next to him, leaning on Crystoll's shoulder. Her father was on the other side providing support. He then patted Aleck on the back and released a throaty laugh as if they already had established a kinship. Aleck's face held a mixture of pain and exhilaration.

She turned to her brother. Edmund had already left to assist the men with the stag. Was she the only one concerned about Aleck taking an arrow to his leg? She rushed toward Crystoll, Aleck, and her father. "Please let me tend to your wound."

Aleck was dressed in the hunting clothes of her clan with a dark green shirt and brown hose. She glanced at his leg. His hose were torn clear across his thigh, and the cut was still bleeding due to it being improperly wrapped.

"Please do not fret over me. Just a graze," Aleck said.

"Then why are you limping? And it is still bleeding. It is more than a graze."

"Deirdre..." her father began in his commanding tone.

She ignored him, her gaze rapt on the injury, while considering the best options for treatment.

"My laird, let us sit him over there," Crystoll said with a head nod to the meal Deirdre had laid out.

They maneuvered him to the blanket. Aleck grimaced as he was eased down. Deirdre pushed her basket aside and looked within it for a cloth. She had clove ale and water, no whisky, which was both better for pain and cleansing.

"Can you ride?" her father asked Aleck, clearly not concerned about the injury.

Deirdre pulled at the torn hose and inspected his wound with a closer look. It hadn't been cleaned well. She took the cloth, dipped it in water, and pressed it firmly to the wound. She had to at least stop the bleeding, which was minimal. The wound was located on the outer side of his thigh. It didn't appear deep, but it was far more than just a graze. He was fortunate it wasn't lower or more toward the inside of his thigh, for she had seen men die from wounds there.

"I'm afraid not, Laird MacCoinneach." Aleck inhaled sharply. "Easy, lass!" He winced with her touch.

She didn't apologize, her attention fixed on the injury. "We must apply pressure to stave the bleeding. It will need mending."

Her father gestured to Crystoll, who immediately made for his horse. He then rode at a gallop from the meadow. Of all the days for Deirdre to insist on riding her mare instead of the horse-drawn cart for the hunt!

"Can you manage until Gilford arrives, Deirdre?" her father asked, no hint of worry in his tone. He knew she could.

"Aye." She pressed harder.

Aleck muffled a groan. Through gritted teeth, he said, "Mind you please let up a wee bit, lass?"

"Mmphmm." She blew a wisp of hair from her face and pressed harder. "You will not die on my charge, Sir Stirrat."

He inhaled sharply but shared a brief smile with her.

She had observed Gilford, who served as their village surgeon in addition to being the laird's steward, work on the injuries of the men through the years. In fact, he quite often requested some of the herbs from her garden to assist in ailments. However, that was the extent of her learning. The wound's bleeding had to be stopped and then the cut sewn and perhaps a poultice with herbs added to prevent sickness. Gilford would know if more needed to be done beyond that. She was no Healer. She wondered how her mother healed others. With herbs, or laying of hands, or spells?

"I suppose you found a way to keep me here longer," Aleck teased.

"Certainly that was my intention when I asked Edmund to loose his arrow upon you instead of the stag."

Her father had already left them and stood by the grooms and Edmund, admiring the stag.

"Edmund said you took the kill from him," she added.

"I never saw your brother. I was on the other side of the animal. Our arrows released at the same time. Mine hit the stag in the neck, and your brother's whizzed past its hind leg and glanced off my thigh."

"I daresay this is more than a glance?"

"I've had worse."

She glared at her father from afar. How could he be laughing with the men while Aleck sat here injured?

Aleck must have followed her line of sight.

"Your father is an admirable man."

"Oh, and did you two talk much on the hunt?"

He shifted his weight, moving to lean more on one elbow. "The usual formalities." He licked his lips. "I hate to be a burden, but could you pour me some of whatever you have to drink?"

"I do not have whisky. Does it hurt you?"

"Nay, just parched."

"Here." She took his hand closest to hers and placed it over the cloth and wound. "Put pressure on it. No, harder like this."

He did as told but kept her hand between both of his. His dark blue eyes shimmered with flecks of lighter blue and amber as he shared a lengthy look with her. By the heavens, was he trying to woo her? Heat poured from his hand into hers, and he squeezed softly. She pursed her lips and wrestled her hand free. "I do need both of my hands to pour."

"Of course."

"My assistance goes as far as wound-caring, Sir Stirrat." She handed him a small goblet of clove ale to drink with his other hand.

Her father returned, a smile splitting his bearded face. His cheeks were ruddy with scheming and delight, nearly matching the deep auburn of his hair. Deirdre had seen that look before. "How are you faring?"

Aleck didn't lift his hand. "I am well, Laird MacCoinneach."

"I'll ride back with the rest of the men, get this stag readied for supper. It appears you'll be staying with us a few more days, Sir Stirrat." Simon's voice carried a breezy, albeit sly, lilt.

"Aye, Laird, for at least a day or two to let this mend. Truly, my laird, I must be on my way soon thereafter."

"Of course, of course," Simon said, swatting that comment away as if it were a fly. "Deirdre, lass, please stay with Sir Stirrat. Gilford and Crystoll will return with the cart and dressings."

"But, Da—"

Her father cut her off with a whistle to the men. They emptied the meadow before she could even protest further. She watched in disbelief. At least he thought her able enough to be left alone with Aleck without an escort.

She fumed with how her father had manipulated the moment. First Moreen's enlightenment, now her father's contrivance—the day was not even half over, and she was already wishing to be in her cottage, asleep. She fought a yawn.

Her father wouldn't concede until he saw his daughter wed again, and it seemed he had grown more brazen than ever, reducing himself to consorting with southern nobles. If a man had gallant blood, he was suitable for his daughter. He had no regard whether the suitor was Lowland or Highland Scot. Gordon had been a political move, an arrangement with the MacRaes, while Cortland was from within the clan, their own commander. Auld Kenneth had been a failed arrangement that still left a grudge with the MacDougalls. Sir Aleck Stirrat was affiliated with the Cunninghams, and by the discourse at supper, it appeared he supported the Cause. That was good enough for Simon MacCoinneach.

Sir Stirrat was a reasonable choice given the circumstances, for she was a ruin upon her clan and family and her father was desperate. She was not ignorant of the rumors spreading through the village.

She sipped the root water Moreen had suggested. It settled her queasiness a bit. She pulled a wool plaid around her shoulders and over the cap-sleeved blue gown with the fitted long sleeves. Her father hated her wearing just her brown work kirtle, so today she had relented.

Her observations fell upon Aleck again. She couldn't suppress the sensation she felt from him. She pinched her forehead as a headache began to return. Closing her eyes, she tried to remember her dream. Aleck was most certainly the man she had seen. She had *felt* it in the dream...and she felt it now. His color was strong, like the sun itself. It was intoxicating—and perplexing.

"My father is fond of you," she said, allowing her anger to subside. "He doesn't befriend clans from the south—or anywhere—easily." She turned away from Aleck. A soft mist began to fall as the clouds covered the sun. She shivered.

"Shall we eat? Crystoll may be a while," Aleck said, tapping the spot next to him.

She remained seated where she was, thankful for the basket that separated them on the blanket. "How much has my father offered you?"

"Offered me, my lady?"

She turned toward him, arms crossed. "For my hand in marriage. You've not come to court me?"

"Should I have?" He reached for a loaf of bread, but his puzzled look passed between the hand clamped on his thigh and the food.

Deirdre took the loaf, broke a piece off, and scooped meat upon it. She prepared a small meal and handed it to him. "Then why are you here?"

He didn't answer.

Curses, if it weren't for his injury, she'd ride back to the keep alone. She blew a breath out to calm herself and sipped more of the root water. The mist grew into a drizzle as the clouds darkened, warning them that their meal would soon be cut short, but she had to wait for Gilford.

"Moreen is quite the cook," Aleck said, deftly scooping another serving of leftover supper's lamb and sauce onto a slice of bread with one hand.

Deirdre was happy for a change in conversation. "That she is."

"Your father did nothing but praise her cooking last night."

She gladly obliged him with idle talk. There was nothing else to do while they waited.

"Aye. She's been with us for twenty years. I was a young lass when she came here. She's like a mother to me ever since..." She stopped herself, surprised at the tears pricking her eyes.

"I'm sorry. I didn't mean to upset you."

She waved a hand in nonchalance, but inside she couldn't help but feel a distant hurt well up whenever she thought of her mother. She stiffened upright and drew in a breath. "My mother died when I was young. Moreen has been, well, she's a servant, but she's been kind to me all these years."

He smiled again, successfully disarming her. Between that, the dark stubble that peppered his jawline, the soiled hunting clothes, loose dark hair, and the beads of sweat on his forehead, he looked ruggedly handsome. She pulled her scrutiny from him. Where was Crystoll? The keep wasn't that far away, and he was an excellent rider.

Deirdre struggled to find something to talk about. "How is your arm?"

He stretched the limb in emphasis. "Och, good. Gilford stitched it for me upon my arrival yesterday. I'm afraid I'll be employing his services twice now."

Out of nowhere, the pressure of responsibility weighed on her spirit. Aleck appeared to be a nice man, and he was trying to be approachable. She, on the other hand, was not being gracious. Her father had worked hard during the past years to find the right suitor, and he *had* found two men who had been fond of her. Providing an heir rested on her shoulders. Deirdre was the oldest child, if just by a few moments. And though her father could choose Edmund, his first and only son and Deirdre's twin, to be laird, Edmund seemed cursed to remain childless, and father did not seem confident in Edmund's discernment with political matters. So, like Moreen said, Deirdre's husband would be their clan's next chief.

She bit her lip. And now, Aleck had already entranced her father! She searched her mind for a plausible explanation as to why Aleck was actually here. She didn't believe his tale. Her dreams and fate had not brought him by a magical spell, either. A gifted power is one thing, spells were another. "Why are you here?" again she asked.

"I already told you—trade."

"So you've said. The isles are…not fruitful."

"There's plenty of fish and salt. And there is a war. Men need to be fed."

She peeled her eyes from him. "Mmphmm. So you are to exploit the war then?"

His left eyebrow raised a fraction, causing the other one to crinkle.

She probed further, pretending that his stare did not arouse unwanted feelings within her. "May I ask where in the isles you journey?"

"Uist."

Both her breath and voice left her, a bite of cheese catching in her throat. "Uist is small, hardly inhabited," she managed to say as she swallowed the last bit. "There's naught there."

"Have you been there?"

"No." Deirdre focused on her senses. Once again, his lifeblood was a thick hot shroud masking his feelings. She couldn't read him. Why couldn't she read him?

"Well, the better reason for trade. It is quiet, unsullied now with the Norse long gone."

She fought to control her racing thoughts, but she pressed him. "What did you and my father speak about on the hunt?"

"You," he said, "...among other things."

She fought a blush. Why did this man unsettle her so? "Of course. Well, I am in no need of a husband. If that's what you truly came here for, then you may take your leave."

He laughed. "I've not come for your hand in marriage, my lady. Shall I instead beg you *not* to marry me to convince you of such? I've enough troubles without taking a wife."

"Troubles? What would a trader be troubled with?"

He was silent. Again.

Oh, she hit a mark! Like the men and their practice with the bow, her arrow felt impact.

She wasn't as weak-minded as most men thought. In fact, men tended to forget when a woman was present, even the laird's daughter. To their mistake. She had learned much while sitting in the hall, as suitors doted, noblemen boasted, and neighboring clansmen conspired with her father about the fate of Scotland. Each time, her father requested her "account" afterward. All this time she had thought he appreciated her keen ear, but instead he was relying upon her ability.

Despite her ire at her father's deception, there was something not quite right with everything Aleck said.

Unfortunately, she couldn't use her abilities to read his emotions. 'Twas like he had a fiery shield around him!

No more subtleties. Time to test her knowledge. "This war will not sit in the Lowlands alone, Sir Stirrat. Berwick was sacked, as was Dunbar. A storm besieges all of Scotland."

"I'm aware, but a man must still make his coin."

Did all men think her dim? She persisted. "We don't have long before Edward presses north. When King Alexander cleared out the Norse settlements in the isles, he left behind a fleet of ships and able-bodied sailors scattered among the isles and Highlands. King John or his successor will need them. I dare not think trade alone takes you there, Sir Stirrat."

"You are knowing, Deirdre."

A compliment? It wasn't exactly an answer. She pursed her lips, steeling her temper. "I'm wary of the Claimants vying for the crown. My father thinks King John will abdicate soon...that the bloodshed at Berwick and now Dunbar will send John fleeing into hiding."

"He's Edward's..." He scratched his head, trying to come up with a word. "He is disposable to Edward."

"So I've been told. Rumor tells that King John is already imprisoned. The true power lies in the twelve guardians of the council. Edward has marched too far north. We are losing this war."

"Unless the right Claimant arises," Aleck added.

"Indeed. My father favors the Cause. As you saw, my brother is against it. Where does *your* allegiance rest?" She nibbled on her lip before saying any more. Her father would have her hide should he learn that she discussed such matters with Aleck. She had already taken the conversation too far.

He popped a dried plum into his mouth. "With the right man."

"So you believe in the Cause?"

He gave a casual shrug.

"I presume the baron in Lennox has sent you here on orders to..." She contemplated and gauged his response. "...relay word to the lairds of the isles and rally a fleet for his supporters."

"That has nothing to do with fish and salt, does it?" Levity danced in his eyes.

"Are you laughing at me? I thought women were supposed to be the demure ones, Sir Stirrat."

Her questions were unsettling him. Good. She focused on his energy—it glowed a brighter red, but she couldn't feel the emotions masked by it, as hard as she attempted. Tension, perhaps? Unease? Her power could be a curse most days, but it was also an asset. What did his posture say? Confidence...and something else. "The question remains—which Claimant do you support, Sir Stirrat?"

He captured her eyes with his. "Who does your father support, my lady?"

"Only my father can oblige you with that answer." She grew exhausted by his circumvention and closed her eyes to shut out his energy. Mmphmm. Futile!

"Do you always talk to men you've just met in such a manner?"

"No, but you are...different."

"Do I vex you?"

She felt him lean in closer.

"Why would you ask that?" she said through gritted teeth, not opening her eyes.

"There are other things?"

He lingered near her face. She inhaled deeply instead of answering. Musky sweat and Moreen's earthy clove ale fell off him. "You smell."

"Aye."

She opened her eyes. His eyes stared back, both searching and inviting. She licked her lips, refraining from doing what her body wanted. She subtly repositioned herself farther from him. Aleck's vague confirmation of war and his involvement was disquieting. Glen Shiel and the keep of Eilean Donan were a gateway to Skye, serving as a stepping stone to the larger isles—both as protection and doorway. War was a horse galloping toward them.

"How's your leg?"

He lifted his hand. The bleeding had stopped. "Thank the heavens," she said, surveying it.

"A question, Deirdre..."

"Aye?" She wiggled back from him more. Although she had been the one questioning him, he excelled at turning it back to her.

"Why were you in that loch, in the woods?"

Her emotions surged, then welded together as she turned away from him. Words could not convey what she felt that eve. "I enjoy the cool water to bathe—to block out the world. I get headaches." It was a half-truth, and saying that was too much for her to admit.

"You were under for a while."

"I can hold my breath and swim well, Sir Stirrat. I thought we ceased with this discussion." She wanted to ask how long he had been watching her, but the thought that he had seen her naked quieted that question. Her father never approved of her ventures to the loch and if he had known about the rest of what happened that day? Och, nay, no good would come from it. He would insist upon a marriage this very eve!

"That's an interesting skill for a lady. You like to swim? And please, I prefer Aleck."

The sound of the cart and horse hooves freed her from responding. A moment later, Crystoll and Gilford arrived. She rose and busied herself with gathering the rest of picnic items while Gilford tended to Aleck's injury.

Gilford muttered a few words under his breath here and there, but overall, his grumblings sounded nothing out of the ordinary. "You will see more suns, Sir Stirrat. You'll be riding again soon enough. Stay off your feet for a week at least," she heard him say while she loaded baskets into the carriage with Crystoll.

A week? Deirdre caught Aleck's expression. He didn't seem too fond of that idea either.

In no time at all, they were on their way. A steady rain had joined them by the time they reached the village of Dornie. Deirdre slid off the back of the cart. Crystoll came around from the front and offered Aleck his shoulder to lean upon.

"Wait here, Sir Stirrat, while we take the cart to the other stable. I'll return momentarily to assist you inside. You can stay dry here," Crystoll said, ushering him under the awning of the inner stable.

Aleck reached for Deirdre. "You're shivering."

"I'm f-fine," she said, regretting not bringing her cloak today.

"Please have my plaid," he offered, pulling the larger blanket off his shoulders. "Your gown is sodden."

"If you insist, but please, Aleck, you need it. You don't want to catch a chill or fever."

"I'll be well."

Crystoll drove the cart with Gilford to the other stable outside the courtyard. A horse from within the stable nickered at Deirdre.

"Ah, who is this beautiful mare?" Aleck said, stroking the horse's nose.

"Delilah. Be heedful of her. She's feisty in this weather." A loud clap of thunder rolled. Delilah jerked away from them as if she heard Deirdre's warning. She danced in her stall, letting out a frightened neigh.

A painful headache suddenly took hold of Deirdre as a shudder rolled down her spine and nausea twisted her stomach. *Oh God, not again. And not here in front of him.*

The vision returned to her in a sudden flash of colors.

Brilliant crimson embers sprang from the forest. His red-hot lifeblood had transformed to a cold blue death as the blood drained from his body. He reached out to her, and she felt his heat dissipating from his body, but her legs and arms would not move. They were confined, as if tied to something. She tried to cry out, but the words remained lodged in her throat. She tugged and her arms would not budge. His lifeblood dimmed quickly. The fire consumed him and everything around them. His glimmering eyes and crooked smile became blurry as he began to die. The flames licked at her fingers and a heart-wrenching horror gripped her. Her soul cried. Her heart broke.

She rubbed the side of her head as she succumbed to the dizziness. A loud droning pounded in her ears, and then all was quiet as she slipped into deep black oblivion.

"My lady! Deirdre!"

She opened her eyes but didn't speak. The same crooked smile and piercing eyes from her vision stared back at her. Unlike the dream, his lifeblood was strong. His heartbeat drummed.

"Wake, lass. Are you all right?"

She blinked. Velvety warmth encircled her as she lay cradled in his lap—again.

There was no point in her asking what had happened, for she already knew.

"We need to stop this habit of you fainting."

"Mmphmm."

His smile deepened. Blood traced the bridge of his nose. He sat her upright. "Although I don't mind the afterward." He slowly released her.

"I'm fine." She heaved a sigh and stood, shaky.

"Are you certain?" His voice was direct, yet pacifying.

"Aye, 'tis just a headache. What happened to your nose?" she said, tracing a hand down the lightly bleeding cut.

"You hit me."

"Och, I'm sorry."

Delilah snorted behind them, either alarmed by Deirdre's fainting or the rolling thunder. Deirdre stood and attempted to get her wild horse under control. "Hush, hush, sweet thing. 'Tis just some wind." The mare's large head knocked her, and Deirdre fell in a splatter of mud.

"Whoa!" Aleck tried to pat the mare's snout. Just as he reached for her, more thunder clapped.

"Aleck, I wouldn't do that," Deirdre said, looking up at the skittish beast.

No sooner did she say that, then the horse reared up, neighed, and broke down the wooden door to her stall.

Deirdre was in no mood for this. The stable master had just repaired that door. She wiped the mud from her face.

A young stable lad came running toward them. The horse was frightened and kicked again, rearing up. The lad, Ewan, was new to helping their stable master and unfamiliar with her temperamental mare. He approached the horse.

"Whoa! Whoa!" the young boy cooed.

"Ewan!" Deirdre shouted. "No! Back away!" The commotion drowned her voice. The poor boy would be trampled by her horse if he got any closer. Deirdre belatedly stumbled farther back, out of the horse's range. She still spun from her moment of darkness.

Despite his injury, Aleck shoved the boy aside and placed himself between the horse and Ewan. He held out his hands and stood his ground as if daring her to come to him. In a surprising move, Delilah settled into a dance, then began to nicker again, still waving her head to and fro. Aleck kept talking to her, in a soft, indistinguishable soothing voice. Finally, with gentle coaxing from him, the mare retreated into a nearby stall.

Crystoll reappeared. He stopped in the doorway when he saw what was happening.

Deirdre rose and swiped the wet mud from her brow onto her skirt. Young Ewan came to her side, his face flushed and excited. "Milady!" He appeared unbothered from his near trampling.

Aleck returned and offered her a hand, and she accepted it. He smiled at her, his sopping dark hair a stringy mess down to his jaw. She wanted to scold him for such reckless behavior. Her horse could have killed him.

Realizing she could deny her predicament no longer, she reciprocated the smile. Moreen and her father were right and after word of this event reached her father, there would be no stopping him from requesting the marriage arrangement. She needed a husband, and perhaps this unlucky soul had arrived to provide her with one. She prayed that he would not die in her bed, too.

CHAPTER FOUR

Thunder awoke Deirdre, and she was grateful, for her dream had disturbed her more than any clamorous storm outside her bedchamber could. She pressed her palms against her eyes and sat upright. It was the third night in a row she had dreamed of *him*. It mattered not that a thick stone wall divided their bedchambers; she felt his lifeblood as though he lay beside her. *That* thought was what had stirred her from the dream.

A searing heat throbbed within her core. The bairn pulsed with a vibrant life. She couldn't pinpoint its hue yet, but her own belief and sense told her it was there. The heat was not the bairn though. It was something sensual. She may have lain with men only twice before, but she understood desire.

She inhaled, recovering her breath. Her nipples grew taut at the thought of his hands upon her skin. In this dream, she had met him in the woods, but it was not a death-filled vision. Instead, he held her, his fingers scalding hot upon her.

She opened her eyes and touched her lips, as though he had just kissed them. She could taste him.

Something compelled her to rise and push the bedclothes aside. A bolt of lightning brightened the room, followed by thunder's growl. Her skin prickled with the clouds' energy.

In the pitch dark, she allowed his sensation to guide her to the door.

Alasdair tossed to his side. He moaned and rolled to the other side. "By the saints!" He threw the bedclothes from himself and sat up, stretching his toes to the floor. The winter rushes had been removed, and his bare feet welcomed the cold stone. What he needed was to soak his entire body in the icy loch water outside. His thigh throbbed with movement, though he wasn't concerned by it. Gilford had seemed adept with the needle. What Alasdair had told Deirdre was true—he had been injured worse than this. Blazes though, he couldn't ride, not yet. His muscles hurt just from walking.

He had to leave Dornie though. The baron had been close. He could come at any time, and Alasdair needed to meet with Thomas on Uist. Why in God's name had he agreed to the stag hunt? God's teeth, he knew why. Well, part of the reason why. He wanted to earn the laird's trust if the opportunity arose where he would need to forge an alliance with him. And, well, the other part of his reason was sleeping in the chamber next door. But now look at him. He was a bloody mess.

He rose and took slow and deliberate steps. If he was going to sneak off and ride away tomorrow then he needed to move, get his muscles working. He prayed the laird would understand his hasty departure. He squinted out the loophole window but couldn't see the loch water as it pounded the island. The night was as ferocious as his thoughts.

The thunder could not compete with the hammering of his heart or the hard longing beneath his loose undergarments. He paced, the pain wrapping around his thigh like a clamped claw. He clenched and unclenched his fists. He had awoken…yearning to be with her. The dream had been vivid, as though she were with him, her soft fingertips stroking his chest and her small, sweet lips kissing his neck. She had invited him with her touch.

He groaned in remembrance of the fine body he had seen at the loch on their first encounter.

Blowing deep breaths in and out, he sat. As he massaged his sore upper thighs, being careful of his wound, he guided his thoughts to more mundane ones. She slept in the chamber beside him, and he fought with the provocation that lured him there.

Bloody hell. Sitting didn't help. He rose and made his way to the door. He had to get out of the room and pace.

The night wind blew through the narrow window at the end of the corridor, howling an eerie tune as Deirdre stepped into the hallway. Dimly lit sconces flickered upon the walls, casting strange shadows. She moved, compelled by some unknown force. Her long-sleeved chemise fluttered in the breeze, sending shivers down her spine once more.

She quelled a scream when she saw Aleck in the hallway already. They met without speaking, and Deirdre saw the desire in Aleck's face as the light defined the chiseled edge of his chin and his long nose. His eyes appeared black, hidden beneath a wavy mess of equally dark hair. He blended in with the shadows, save for the white loose tunic he wore over his undergarments which stood out like moonstone.

He approached her with small, unsteady strides and before she knew it, she was close enough to smell clove ale on his breath mingled with the scent of his nighttime sweat. She swallowed, trying to find an explanation. "I-I...how is your wound? I thought somebody should, er, check on it." Now *that* sounded ridiculous. Why in heavens would somebody need to tend to him in the middle of the night? "Or see if you have a fever?"

"I am well," he said, his voice husky.

"You shouldn't be moving about," she managed to say, moving back a half step.

"I need to stretch it. You shouldn't be wandering the hallways at night, my lady."

"Eilean Donan is quite safe, I assure you. Do you need anything?" She pulled her shawl tighter. She wore naught but her chemise beneath it. *But he has seen more.* Instead of feeling modest and abashed, she felt even more drawn to him with that thought.

"Let me return you to your room." He gestured toward her with his hand.

She stepped back, fighting the urge to take it. "No need, Sir Stirrat. Please, rest."

"Aye." He hesitated, staring at her for a long moment as though entranced. Deirdre shivered, and a tingle danced along the fine hairs on her neck.

Then, he finally nodded and turned, snapping out of his daze.

His foot caught on a loose stone on the floor, he fumbled in his stride, and released a groan. Deirdre rushed in and put her arm around his waist, preventing his fall.

"Y-You mustn't strain yourself," she stammered. "Here, let me assist you."

Warmth began to well within her at their shared touch as she guided him to his chamber. She realized how heavy and tall he was when he leaned on her. She tucked her head against his shoulder and wrapped her arm low on his waist. His muscles tightened with the movement. She brought him to his bed, although he seemed quite able to do it on his own. Sitting, he kept a hand interlaced with hers. Once he was seated, he made no move to unlock their hands. Nor did she.

Pulling her closer, she stood between his spread thighs, their bare lower legs touching. Her other hand fell upon his forehead, feeling for fever, although she took her time taking her hand away. Without thinking, she ran her hand through his hair. She brushed it aside, then retracted her hand. Somehow, she found her voice. "You're warm, please rest. If you have a fever, I can send for Gilford."

The glow of the hearth cast soft shadows across the room. The expression on his face matched the one from her dream—the kind of look that begged her to stay with him.

He said, "Your father wishes us to wed. Is that what you wish as well?"

So he *had* discussed an arrangement with her father. She tore her gaze from his and stared at the hearth. The fire almost flickered in response to her unrest. *I don't know what I want*, she wanted to scream. "I hardly know you."

"But you *do*," he responded.

His words struck her. She ripped herself from his embrace. "Please rest, Sir Stirrat. You're not well." She hurried from the room. Her heart pounded so loudly that she could no longer hear the thunder and rain. She shut her door with a thud and bolted it. She slid to the floor, chest heaving. Abruptly, the warmth of his lifeblood left, and a cold darkness consumed her.

A part of her wanted to say yes. She had married a stranger before. How was this any different? However, the same fate lay ahead for him as it had for Cortland and Gordon if she welcomed him into her bed. She was reluctant to admit *that* was the real reason for her hesitation. Their deaths had been her fault. Yet if she didn't marry Aleck, an uncertain fate remained for her unborn child and her father's land. She muffled a curse under her breath. She was damned either way. Maybe Father could be swayed to reconsider letting Edmund rule until her child became of age.

Despite her swirling thoughts, she forced herself into bed, burrowed beneath the bedclothes, and allowed the sound of the fierce storm and the remembrance of his touch lull her to a colorless sleep.

By the time Deirdre reached the kitchen to break her fast, it was late. She grabbed a handful of dried fruit and a bannock and left to oversee the courtyard's garden workers. The usual servants greeted her with nods and g'days as they toiled, pulling weeds and tending to delicate roots and seedlings. She crouched down to assist them.

"The rain turned the roots inside out, milady," Galina said as she hunched over a row of newly planted onions.

"It appears that the night's heavy rain was not kind to many of Moreen's seedlings."

"Och, she'll be crabbit!" Galina said, half in jest, half in fear.

Deirdre nodded at the fair-haired servant and set to work, which was a welcome distraction after the night encounter with Aleck. She dug into the dirt, enjoying the feel of the soil between her fingertips and the sweat down her back as she labored.

She had just finished settling the plants when Gilford beckoned her. "Milady, the laird wishes your presence at once." He was flushed and winded.

"Is something amiss?"

If he knew, he wouldn't divulge it. Loyal to her, more loyal to her father. He raised an authoritative gray brow to the quizzical looks around him. The servants returned their eyes, but not their ears, to their planting. He stiffened. "Nay, milady. The laird awaits you in his chamber."

She rose and wiped her hands upon her apron. They stepped aside. Once out of hearing range of the garden workers, she spoke. "Did you check on Sir Stirrat this morn?"

"Aye, milady. He is in good spirits and recovering well."

Deirdre's nerves were unsettled as she entered the hall and parted ways with Gilford. As she entered her father's chamber, he didn't look up from his papers on his desk. "Close the door."

She did as told and remained standing.

"Sit."

Thoughts of what she did wrong *this* time raced through her mind. She had been attentive yesterday at the hunt and tended to Sir Stirrat's wound, hosted the evening supper, and seen to her duties around the keep—what was it now?

He turned a serious eye to her. "I've arranged your marriage." Her father had never been one to waste words.

Even though another arrangement was inevitable, she was beset by a painful lump in her throat. She opened her mouth to protest, but he waved a hand, ordering silence.

"You need a husband, Deirdre."

She clenched her jaw and leaned forward in the chair. "Who is the man I shall call husband?"

"Sir Stirrat, of course."

She stifled a cry. "I don't need a husband! Let Edmund and his children rule. Perhaps Fiora and he will have another?" she said with little hope. *I don't need another dead husband.*

Her father snapped, "Edmund has no children. And your brother is brash, not fit to be laird. Your husband will be laird."

She tried another approach. "I don't know Sir Stirrat."

"You'll have ample time to become acquainted with him."

"I don't care for him!" Well, that was a partial truth, she thought.

"Who said marriage had anything to do with liking your mate?"

She stood, stung by his callousness. "What about my mother?"

He pursed his lips, obviously annoyed. "That was different."

She pulled out her last shred of courage. "Why *him*?"

"Do not question me. You think me a fool?" He vibrated with anger. "He will be your husband. This is not up for negotiation, Deirdre."

She crumpled into her chair. "Has he agreed?"

"You shall wed him as soon as my emissary to Lennox returns."

"An emissary?" She blinked back the combination of pregnancy nausea and the sickening anger that welled within her. Her father's lifeblood caused a throbbing ache in her bones.

He looked at her with derision. "You've more to learn, lass. Aye, I've sent a messenger to Cunningham's keep to confirm Sir Stirrat's story. You will wed him upon the emissary's return. In the meantime, we are to keep him here, delay him."

It was all political. It always had been. This was more than an alliance with a lowland clan; it was about the

Cause. She was about to say something that she would have regretted, but he subdued her with an implacable expression. She clamped her lips shut. Instead, she returned the look.

He shot upright. Heat filled his round cheeks, and he had the look of the devil, the auburn flecks in his brown beard glowing in the sunlight to match his face.

She never flinched, even when his hot ire burned her. Her father would never strike her, even when she was being the most obstinate.

He drew out the words like a snake's hiss. "Do you think that I am fooled by your lies?"

Her hands quivered. Fury bubbled in him and she recoiled from the discomfort his emotions pounded into her body.

"What man will want to raise another's seed?"

Her knees weakened. *Moreen.*

"You *will* marry him."

The laird softened his tone and came around the desk. He clasped her hand in his. "'Tis the only way, lass. You must wed. Sir Stirrat seems keen on you and a good match. Meanwhile, until we can assure this match, I need you to become *acquainted* with him. Your bairn will need a father, a father who does not question the paternity," he said, with subtle emphasis.

"What do you mean?"

Her father appeared unabashed. "Beguile him. Persuade him of your worth."

Dear heavens, was he saying what she thought he was? Her own father was telling her to ensnare Sir Stirrat, to be his lover! Well, she was no chaste maiden anymore. She was nothing more than a widow who killed her husbands and now carried the seed of her last lover. And talk of witchery circulated in the village after Cortland's death... Had Father heard, too?

He must have seen the shock on her face.

"My child is legitimate. Edmund can—"

"—Edmund cannot, and will not. Your child needs a father. Your child will be the heir. Your husband needs to think the child is *his*. All the more reason for the union. Do you understand?" He lifted his bushy eyebrows in earnest.

His words were ice sliding down her back. She nodded, mute. Despite the legitimacy of her child, she needed a husband to rule before the child was of age. Her father was not young. He needed a capable replacement now. Besides, if she had a daughter... Her stomach swirled and she wished for a basin, should her breakfast decide to reappear. Her father was right, though. No man would want to raise her child as his own. She needed a husband, and needed him fast.

She wanted to scream at him. Her father seemed too confident in his resolution. There was only so much a daughter could say to her father and laird, though. Her bold defiance withered to a deep, wallowing fear. She almost asked if Edmund could marry another. But what about poor Fiora? She was ashamed to even contemplate such thoughts. Instead, she mumbled, "I'd rather marry a MacDougall."

"Dinna jest. The MacDougalls are none too pleased with you either. They believe you to be a wi—" He stopped himself and returned to his chair and began sorting through papers. Apparently, the discussion was over.

A witch. A spellcaster. That's what they all thought she was. Had her mother been looked upon in the same way? She fought the sobs. "I do not jest! I feel the weight of this every moment I breathe. This is my life!"

"No, it's not just your life. It is the life of the clan and the future of Scotland."

"So it *is* all about the Cause?"

His face was stoic, unaffected by her outcries. "I'm well aware of your familiarity with my doings. I've not allowed you to Hall for your bonnie face alone. Lass, you'll make a fine laird's wife."

Never mind that all this time he had manipulated her ability to his benefit. She ventured another counter argument, choosing to fight her battle with reason, since her own needs meant nothing to him. "You don't know which Claimant he supports!"

"I will soon enough." His mood shifted. He almost pleaded to her, very unlike him. "War has already begun, Deirdre. We need to support the right Claimant to safeguard our home and our future. I am confident that Sir Stirrat is linked to the courts and a Claimant, and if it happens to be the wrong one, then you can persuade him otherwise. Women can turn even the most vengeful man into a peace-seeker."

He spoke in such a tender way that it confused her. Had mother done the same with him? Uncle Kendrick had once mentioned her father's thirst for vengeance against the Norse so long ago. She'd only seen her father fight with words, not sword. She asked, "What if Edmund is correct? Supporting a Claimant may lead to retaliation from King Edward."

"Edmund is wrong. He doesn't understand the ways of laird."

Her head spun. Aleck was connected to a powerful southern clan. What more did they know about him? Not only was her father asking her to wed a stranger, but she was to deceive him, too. And before they were married. It wasn't unheard of for a woman to lay with a man before they were wed. "So, we are to be allies with the southern clans? The Cunninghams?"

"We shall see." His attention returned to the papers on his desk. "You are excused."

She left the room, numb. There would be no more negotiations.

Deirdre abandoned all responsibilities for the day and sought the seclusion of her cottage. Her senses were always heightened when she was upset, and she had to just get away from the castle.

Contemplating the matter further would not bring her comfort, so instead she threw her efforts into her garden. She hated being a pawn in her father's deceptions and political schemes, but she needed to accept her position for what it was. She was powerless.

By mid-afternoon, exhausted, she sat at her hearth, drinking warmed milk. A knock on the door interrupted her dour musings. Expecting to see Crystoll, she was taken aback when Aleck smiled at her.

"Why do you pester me so, Sir Stirrat? Pleased with yourself, are you? And why are you walking all the way down here? You need to rest," she snapped, wishing she could take the words back immediately.

"Good day to you, too, my lady." A steady rain had overtaken the afternoon sun, and Aleck stood outside, sheets of water rolling from the roof of the cottage, soaking him. His hair was a dark wet mess of loose curls. "May I come in?"

She wanted nothing more than to slam the door in his face but refrained from doing so and gestured toward the glowing fire. She allowed him to limp over without assistance. He could manage the few steps to the hearth.

He drew his hands through his hair, slicking it back, but didn't sit. Rather, he turned to face Deirdre as he wiped wet palms on his trews. His lifeblood calmed her as though a knot within her had been slowly loosened. Damn him. How did he do that? And damn her for allowing it!

She fumbled with the pot on the fire. "Goat's milk with ginger and honey?" she offered. "I'm sorry your trip will be delayed further, Sir Stirrat." She poured a cup and handed it to him, the fragrance of ginger wafting to her nostrils in a pleasant aroma that helped to settle her nerves.

He accepted the cup, his fingers pausing on her hand. Her eyes darted from his face to his hands. She stared at the shiny white scars that traced the length of the back of his hand and along his fingers. The scars appeared old, not well healed. A negative energy associated with them caused her to shiver.

"Och, because of my leg? It'll be fine," he said.

She forced her look away from the scars and found her face close to his. "No. That is not why."

His eyes were gentle. "What then?"

She stepped back. "You've secured an alliance with my father and future lairdship of Glen Shiel. That's the real reason you came here anyway. You can cease your pretending."

"I have done what?" he asked again, his thick dark eyebrows drawn together.

She relied on reading his face rather than his emotions. Eyes, voice, movements...they were another way to read a person's intention. "You can cease your circumvention, Sir Stirrat. I grow tired of it. I know why you're here. I hope you find yourself content with marriage to me."

"I didn't make any covenants with your father," he said, his face staunch, revealing nothing. "Last night, when I asked you, it was of my own volition."

She huffed a breath, blowing wisps of hairs from her face. "Sir—"

"It's Aleck."

"I'm afraid, *Aleck*, that you'll be Laird of Glen Shiel soon enough. Well played, sir." She rose and turned to the fire, poked at it, and hid the tears that begged to be released.

"I didn't ask to be laird."

"That is what you will be. Or did my father neglect to tell you that when he negotiated his contract with you? Edmund has no children and his wife has lost another bairn. And my father does not seem him fit to rule. We may be twins, but I was *blessed* with being born first. It will be my husband that rules. I hope you're content with your prize of Eilean Donan."

And pregnant, cursed wife..

"You're twins?"

She rubbed the side of her head, the heat from his lifeblood overwhelming her. That's all he had to say? Had her father gotten him in his cups during their bargaining? Och, well that would explain his behavior last night. "Aye." Her voice faded, losing its edge the longer she was with him. "Good day, Aleck. Unless there was something else you wished to tell me."

He hesitated. "I came for another reason."

"Oh?" she said in feigned interest. Boasting about his new acquisition—land and wife—wasn't enough?

"I wanted to—"

She threw him her best attempt at a poisonous look. He was silent, but a muscle twitched in his jaw.

Finally, he exhaled and ran another hand through his hair. "Last night. It wasn't proper of me to... Please forgive me."

She said nothing.

"Until supper, my lady," he said, with a bow. He rose and was out the door in a swift motion, leaving his untouched milk on the hearthside table and a rainwater puddle on the floor.

Deirdre stared at the closed door. Aleck wasn't the only one feeling regretful.

Alasdair plodded in a dense fog—one of both mind and in the world around him—to the keep, the rain pelting him. Each step hurt, but he had to force the thigh muscles to regain their strength if he was to leave tonight. He prayed the stitches would not open. He knew he had to rest, but he lacked the time.

What in heaven had Deirdre been speaking about? Had the cunning Simon MacCoinneach played him, like a fool to a king—in this case, a fool to a Scottish laird? He had gone to Deirdre's cottage to apologize for his behavior last night in the hallway. Instead he was left staring like a dolt.

His mind raced with thoughts. He and the laird had circled the topic of a marriage alliance, but no agreement had been forged—not even close! God's teeth, *he* would be laird? Certainly he had impressed Simon, but why was the laird eager to marry his daughter off in such haste? It smelled foul, even if she was a delightful benefit to such a union, for her touch ignited a fire within him.

Alasdair's escape from Glen Shiel had to be tonight. He couldn't allow himself to get seized by this right now. As enticing as Deirdre was, he had a mission to see through.

He should have gone directly to the laird's chamber to speak with Simon, but he found himself near the kitchen entrance of the keep, seeking answers of another kind. He didn't want to admit he cared for Deirdre, and as daft as it sounded, he had also gone to her cottage to ask her if she wanted to come with him to Uist. It was pure madness, but there was a spirit about her from which he couldn't pull himself and she seemed interested in the isles, as if she longed to go, too. Perhaps he was just lonely from his month of running.

Blazes, he liked her sharp wit and tongue, too.

A plump older woman greeted him with a toothy smile. "G'day, Sir Stirrat. Could I fetch ye bread and cheese and a warm drink?" She looked him over. "And a dry cloth?" She carried a basket weighed down with spring vegetables.

He reached forward to help her, and she shooed him away. Her round cheeks were rosy from exertion. She stuck her lip out and blew loose, damp gray strands from her forehead with an exasperated puff. "No need, sir. I am able. I see that Gilford has done ye well. Moving about already, sir?"

"Might you be Moreen?"

"Aye, sir. What can I do for ye?"

Once in the pantry, the nutty scent of baking bread lured him to take a seat. Yet, he couldn't help but sense that something else had led him here.

As Moreen sliced a loaf of bread and laid out the butter and honey, he got to the thick of it. "You've been at Eilean Donan many years?"

"Aye, twenty." She smiled.

"Are you well acquainted with Lady Deirdre?" He needed to be cautious, but damn it, he wanted answers.

Moreen didn't appear startled as she bustled around the pantry, putting a few items in crocks and crates. "Aye, Sir Stirrat," she said, winded.

"And her mother?"

A trace of question danced across her face, but she answered with indifference. "I'm afraid not, sir. My obligations were bestowed upon me after Lady Mac-Coinneach's death."

He did not believe her. Against his better judgment, he leaned across the table and grabbed her hand, squeezing it softly, as though pleading for help. "Moreen, what troubles her?"

Moreen pulled it back and staggered, as if she had been touched by hot coals. She stared at his hand, then her own, and cradled her hand into her bosom. Fear clouded her eyes. He turned his hand over. There was nothing wrong with it, albeit it was chilled from the rainy afternoon.

He rose, and she cowered. "S-Sir, I can send a servant to assist ye with readying for supper."

Alasdair stepped closer, ducking with the lower ceiling. He hated to resort to intimidation, but she knew something. "What is it?"

"I-I'm sorry, sir. I don't ken what ye mean. Please, I shall send somebody straight away to tend to ye." She stepped back farther.

"Do I need to take this concern to the laird?" He cringed internally to even issue such a threat. This was unlike him.

She inhaled sharply.

Alasdair stood his ground, waiting for her resolve to break while using his size to his advantage. He towered above her.

She shook her head like her mind was somewhere else. "The curse," she mumbled, her voice quivering in a whisper. "By cravens, why didn't I see it? A dark stranger with eyes of a deep blue loch..."

"Curse?"

A frown tipped the corners of her lips and she stared across the room as if through him. Her expression was tight with strain. "Th-The curse," she stammered in a panting whisper. "Of course! It has to be..."

Moreen awoke from her trance and grabbed Alasdair's hands within her own strong grip. "Oh, sir! Please don't tell the laird or Deirdre that I told ye! Oh, please...they would think me an evil caster or worse!"

"I have nothing to tell them. My patience grows thin, woman. What curse?"

"A man from the wood. A stranger from afar. He will break the curse by a hundred kisses..." She began to mumble under her breath, stuttering and incoherent. Then as suddenly as her rant had begun, it was over. Moreen heaved a loud sigh, clasped her hands together, and her expression grew serious. "It requires a hundred kisses with the lass before ye bed her. Or else..." She stopped.

Well, this was madness. "A curse?" He was not foolish enough to consider what she said to be true. He put no faith in curses—or any of the old tales of the Ancients involving faeries, the wee folk, or magical stones. He stifled a snort. They were all implausible, crazy notions created by bored old women and superstitious men. He had no tolerance for it.

Moreen nodded. "Aye, sir."

"I think you've had too much of your own brew, Moreen. Curses exist in a fool's imagination," he scoffed. The pungent scent of yeast in the kitchen overtook his senses, and he coughed. Turning on his heel to leave the deranged cook, her final words halted him in his tracks. They floated over to him as a whisper, perhaps not meant to be heard, but he heard them well enough.

"Tell that to Deirdre's two dead husbands who didn't heed my warning."

He turned and locked eyes with her. She said no more, but her face said enough. Injured or not, he had to leave Eilean Donan—tonight.

Crystoll was Alasdair's steadfast companion for the remainder of the day, assigned to "show him Eilean Donan and the village." The laird had yet to speak to him about solidifying a marriage agreement, which made him question the truth behind Deirdre's accusation… But on the hunt, Simon had been very keen to talk about finding a husband for Deirdre… After his visits with Deirdre and Moreen, Alasdair did his best to avoid private conversations with anyone. He just needed to make it to nightfall. Alas, it appeared that Crystoll was going to be his watchman now.

The young warrior was obliging and obedient. It was either a ploy, and a good one at that, he mused, or he was being genuine. He favored the latter observation as Crystoll took him around the castle grounds unaware that Alasdair was using the time to assess his chances for a nighttime exodus. He considered leaving a note of explanation to the laird, but he knew better.

"The movement helps, aye?" Crystoll said.

"Aye, it does."

"I'm not one to sit idle, either," Crystoll said with a chuckle. "Many men, soldiers even, would stay bedridden with an injury like that, allowing themselves to be tended to like children. To heal, we must move it, build up our strength. But, Sir Stirrat, please don't push yourself or your stitches will open. Gilford's not the most tolerant when it comes to tending to his patients more than once."

Alasdair laughed. "Aye." He eyed the guards going in and out of the two flanking corner towers in the curtain wall. In the evening shadows, it was hard to see any movement behind the thin archer slits. "Have you seen disturbance here? You're quite north."

"Our laird is well aware of the impending dangers and has doubled his guard."

"That is prudent. Eilean Donan is a desirable keep, but I assure you, King Edward busies himself in the south."

"Our laird is not convinced of that. Eilean Donan is the way to the isles after all, and she's seen her share of strife." His high forehead furrowed as he pointed to a part of the castle where something had taken a big piece out of the stone wall. "If needed, I'm confident our laird will protect her. If we can expel the Norse, we can defend against the English. We've allies north and south as well."

Alasdair inclined his head in respect. If the situation had been different, he might have stayed. Laird Mac-Coinneach would have been a good ally, but after his secret escape tonight, he doubted the laird would want to join forces. Alasdair had already pressed his good fortune enough. He needed to leave yesterday.

They walked down the long bridge connecting the isle and the mainland. A bustling village surrounded them as men and women prepared for the evening. They passed a second large stable tucked within a cluster of crofts beside the blacksmith and separated from the stable within the bailey. Alasdair turned and marveled at the castle behind them. It jutted from within an ornate stone wall and sat on a small isle. An equally impressive stone bridge connected the isle to the mainland town of Dornie. Now that the storms had passed, he took it all in. The waters of Loch Duich lapped against the moss-covered rocks and grassy shores. Majestic mountains, late winter snow blanketing their peaks, towered over the open glen. It was indeed a jewel tucked away in the Highlands. 'Twas a shame.

He had been delayed long enough. He clenched his fist. Thank the heavens the baron had not located him here yet. Perhaps he had also detoured elsewhere to replenish supplies.

"Are you well, Sir Stirrat? Do require a rest?" Crystoll asked, all too attentive.

"Och, I am well. What day is it?"

"Sunday, sir."

"I'm afraid I missed Mass. Might we have a moment to stop by the chapel on our way to supper?"

"Indeed. This way." Crystoll led him to the chapel that bordered the northern tower.

"Could I have a moment alone?"

Crystoll nodded.

Small, round windows of colored glass were welcoming eyes on the front of the chapel. Creamy yellow Caen stone formed the building, clean and white-washed as though heaven had planted it there yesterday. It reminded Alasdair of his trip to London with his father years ago, when they'd visited the White Tower, which was also adorned with Caen stone. Of course, at that time they'd been honored guests. Now, he'd be more likely to visit the deep bowels of the prison rather than ever be entertained in the grand hall again.

His intent had been to scout the chapel and its potential use for tonight, but when Alasdair entered, a strange desire to meditate fell upon him. He approached the altar and knelt. He had always been a person of faith, something his mother had instilled in him. The irony of her death was almost too much to comprehend. Despite anything people might have said, his mother had loved and feared God. She had been wrongfully accused of witchcraft by an evil man.

The chapel was cold, drafty, and lit by a few candles, but he found solace within. It quieted his soul and brought peace to his heart.

He was doing the right thing. He had been entrusted by Robert Bruce to see the mission through.

He said a brief prayer and rose. Tonight he would make his escape.

Although she couldn't hear him, Deirdre felt Aleck rise in the late hours. She concentrated on her senses. Closing her eyes, she laid a hand on the wall that separated their chambers, and listened. A subtle hum emanated from the stones and vibrated into her hand.

Moments passed. He stirred and then his energy dissipated. He had left.

She sat on her bed for what seemed forever, contemplating. Her heart pounded in her temple, and her fingers tingled. Was she really considering it? Moreen's revelation had roused a new curiosity within her. She was a Feeler. Her mother had been a Healer. Her aunt was a Seer. She needed answers. It was better than staying here, seducing Aleck, and waiting for her father's emissary to return with good news.

Oh my God, but she didn't know him.

Yes, you do. The man from the wood, a voice in her head said, making her rise.

By the heavens, it was foolish, but his lifeblood drove her. Fully dressed in gown and cloak, she stood, her decision made. She picked up her satchel, weighed down by her mother's book, and departed.

She passed the stable within the bailey. It was empty. She presumed that he wouldn't steal a horse from there. There was no way for him to get past the tower guards and across the bridge unseen. She hid among shadows, relying on her senses to guide her as she concentrated on the guards' energies. She made it to the village unseen. Even though she could feel him already, her breath caught when she entered the stable.

Aleck stood by Samson, Edmund's horse. "No, not him," she said.

He swung around, his dagger drawn. A beam of moonlight spilled into the stable through the door and cast a shaft of light on his face. Her breath caught. He looked the same as he had in her dreams—hair dancing about, eyes narrowed, and scowl deepening his forehead.

"Why not?" He lowered his dagger and turned back to the horse.

"You won't get there fast enough. Samson's my brother's and an unruly beast. Besides, I would hate for Edmund to dislike you further."

"I don't think that's possible."

She muffled a small chuckle.

"Samson and Delilah, och?"

"They were foaled from the same mare and share an equal disposition."

He approached her. "Why are you here?"

She didn't answer.

"You wish to come with me," he said, lifting a dark eyebrow. "Are you unhappy here, my lady?"

She inhaled his nearness and ruddy warmth. "I..." She hugged her arms to herself, fortitude escaping her by the moment. "It is not for a marriage arrangement for surely if that were so, we would go to my father's chambers and sign the covenant this very eve and he would hold the grandest of halls."

Disappointment danced across his face and her chest quivered in response. Perhaps this was a mistake. She bit her lip, turning the questions away from her. "What are you running from, Sir Stirrat? Certainly my father has not frightened you so," she asked, ruefully.

He stepped even closer. Dark eyes commanded her attention, his breath hot on her cheek. "Why do you wish to leave?"

She did not respond.

Not waiting for her answer—which would not come—he said, "Come with me." He took her hand in his.

"If I come, then my father will hunt us down, and any alliance you had hoped for would be ruined."

"I can fend for myself."

"As can I."

Heat seared into their clasped hands, followed by a wave of calm. "How far is Port nan Long from your destination?" she asked.

"Why?"

"That is where I need to go. There is someone I must see."

He paused, and she was grateful it was hard to see his face as he moved into the shadows. "It's not far."

"Can you take me there?"

"You come for this one reason?" His voice faded to a near whisper.

Beguile him, her father's words echoed. "Yes."

He was silent for a moment. He hovered close to her face. "I ride hard."

"I can keep pace."

He turned to the horses. "Make haste."

CHAPTER FIVE

Agmus stared at his reflection in the shallow stream. He knelt and swirled a hand in the water, rippling his image. The small waterfall cascading over a protruding section of moss-covered granite caught his eye. The clear water spit and frothed over the edge, but it slowly became tinged with a coppery red that eddied into the whirlpool he made with his hand, churning streaks of red and brown. He looked again at his appearance in the moving water. His black hair danced about wildly as though a lion's mane, and his nose was exaggerated in the waves, seeming like that of a devil. Instead of abhorring his distorted reflection, he laughed. It was the face men saw when they cowered before him.

He stroked his beard and rose from the water's edge, knees cracking as he muffled a grunt. With his whistle, Ronat and Carney emerged from the forest. They were silent, their brows furrowed and eyes averted.

"Did you find the trail?"

Neither spoke. He stepped forward in a quick motion, regretting the move on his sore joints but doing it nonetheless.

Ronat cast a momentary glance over Agmus's shoulder to the stream behind him. "We think the trail leads north, Baron Montgomerie."

"You *think*? Can you follow it?"

Ronat shifted his weight from foot to foot, and Carney, an overweight and foul man in both girth and odor, blinked rapidly. "Aye, Baron, but it'll be hard on our mounts."

Then they would get new mounts if need be. He cleared his throat. "Ronat, you take the lead. Do *not* disappoint me, or it'll be your blood staining my boots next." He brushed past them toward his steed, sloshing through soaked ground. Agmus hoisted himself into the saddle, feeling the pain slide from his knuckles to his wrists. The horse neighed in agitation at his less than gentle movements. He gritted his teeth. They had spent two days collecting provisions and combing the area, and he was eager to press on.

Ronat and Carney rode ahead, and the two other soldiers who had been waiting by the horses took their place behind him. Agmus trotted his horse alongside the stream, their entourage quiet except for the hooves crunching on the wet pebbles and rocks.

He paused a moment, pretending to take in the stretch of Glen Shiel crags ahead of him, the Kintails' spring peaks still dusted with winter snow. This glen was a wild refuge for many in hiding. The lairds here were willful and loyal and kinships were strong between clans. Integrating here would've proven difficult for Alasdair, he imagined, but Alasdair was a cunning bastard, likely using his clever wit on the lairds and his handsome lure on the ladies. Agmus clenched his right hand and rubbed it on his thigh, massaging the ache in his knuckles and grimacing. He had himself to blame for Alasdair's training.

The soldiers gasped as they reached the body of Stewart—yet another disappointment. Agmus grinned, delighted by their response. They knew he made no idle threats. He continued on, guiding his horse around the dead and incompetent commander, and straight toward the keep of Eilean Donan.

Deirdre had not expected the first leg of their journey, the ride to Caol Loch Aillse, to be as detrimental on her body and spirit as it was. She had left Eilean Donan in a good state of mind, given the situation, but as her reliable and mild mare rode along the uneven path, whinnying and faltering here and there, her mood deteriorated along with her body. The clouds had rolled in, and a light rain accompanied them. The jolting ride didn't help her nausea at all, and she fought the bile.

They had ridden all night, and she was already weary. How was she to make it the rest of the way?

"You've said you've never been to the isles, Deirdre?" Aleck asked.

"No. The farthest I have been is Caol Loch Aillse."

"This is the farthest north I have been as well."

"How will you know where to go? You've not been to Uist before on your trades?" She held onto the reins with white knuckles as they maneuvered around a bend. How come she thought he had journeyed there before?

"Indeed it is my first trip."

Tingles rose up her back. This knowledge did not help the doubt running amuck in her mind. She passed another look over her shoulder. It was midmorning, and certainly by now her father had discovered their absence. She cringed knowing full well how fiery—and responsive—her father would be. She looked over her shoulder once more.

"Dinna fash, Deirdre. You'll be safe with me."

"I'm not worried about myself."

His smile was too smug for her. "You came of your own accord."

"That was before I knew you had no idea where we're going!"

"We'll make our way. The sun sets in the west, and that is where we ride."

Her mood shifted with her words. "My father doesn't forgive a person who backs out of agreements."

He slowed his horse to ride beside her. "I never agreed to anything."

"What do you mean? The marriage arrangement." She eyed him dubiously.

"My lady, he may have made his intentions clear to you, but we never forged such an agreement, although certainly he tried."

"I suppose the thought of marrying me is enough to make anyone flee." She slumped in her saddle.

He halted his horse and took her hand in his. "Any man that flees you is a dolt."

"But you—"

"As I've told you, my issues are pressing. I was not fleeing *you*."

Was that a glimmer of jest in his eyes? He leaned down and kissed her knuckles. "Will you please stop that?"

"Stop what?" He rubbed a thumb over each of her knuckles.

"That."

"As you command, my lady." He clicked his tongue and urged his horse forward.

If his thigh was hurting him, he masked it well. She shook her head. Men could be so stubborn.

As they drew on, the rocky terrain of Ardelve with the occasional ocean inlet was their quiet companion.

"Would you mind greatly to tell me more about the clans in this area?" Aleck asked.

Deirdre searched her memory. Laird Mathieson was a young, amiable chief. Her father had attempted a marriage arrangement with him. However, young William Mathieson had eyes on a Clan Donald daughter. "Aye, William, *err*, Laird Mathieson married Laird Donald's daughter a few years ago. So, the Mathiesons and Donalds have a strong alliance."

"Do we need to be concerned about this kinship?" Aleck asked, slowing his horse to keep her pace.

"Nay. Laird Donald is a capable chieftain who follows the old ways of his father. After the Battle of Largs, and the retaking of the isles from the Norse, he acquired this stretch of land. We also have a blood kinship with the Donalds." Deirdre eyed the satchel on Aleck's horse's saddle. She was both famished and nauseated, which was an odd feeling.

Aleck rubbed his chin. "Och?"

"My uncle, Kendrick, was married to Laird Donald's sister many years ago, but she died in childbirth..." She wondered if Kendrick's bad fortune, Edmund's lack of bairns, and her dead husbands were all a punishment from God or some divine fate. Why else would they all suffer so?

"So the Mathiesons and Donalds are your allies?"

"Aye."

"What about other clans in this area?"

"The MacDougalls have a feud with the Donalds tracing back many years, and despite his best efforts, my father has been unable to hold an alliance with both clans." She shivered, leaving out the part about her failed marriage alliance with Auld Kenneth MacDougall. "We maintain loyalty with Laird Donald and, in turn, Laird Mathieson. The MacDougalls reside east of here. We ride away from their keep." Or she hoped. Her head spun from lack of sleep. She shivered.

"Chilly?" Aleck asked.

"Nay. Thirsty."

He handed her the flask.

When they decided to camp for the evening, Deirdre let out a less than ladylike groan as she slid off her horse. She pressed her knuckles into her lower back. Then looked around. They had advanced a short distance inland from the road and settled on a clearing beside a copse. It was shielded by large granite boulders on one side, with a slope leading to a gurgling stream about fifty paces below.

"I'll make a soft bed for you," Aleck said, busying himself with collecting meadow grasses and ferns.

"Thank you, but I can do it. You should rest your leg."

"I'll see if I can catch us supper." He turned effortlessly toward the stream but then stopped halfway. "Will you be all right?"

"Aye, but your leg—" Her stomach growled at the thought of a cooked meal. At least she was too tired to feel the queasiness right now.

He laughed. "I'll do my best, my lady."

As a flush crept across her cheeks, she walked to her horse. She had packed a thick wool plaid, but other than that luxury and her heavy cloak, the ground would be enjoying her company tonight. She distracted herself with stroking her mare, and it nuzzled its head into her, seeking a scratch. Afterward, she stretched, laid her cloak on the ground for her bed, and collected firewood. Then, she picked her way toward the small rocky cliff that overlooked the stream.

Aleck was below, at the stream's edge. Watching him work the line and hook with dexterous fingers gave her a moment to reflect. She couldn't fight the notion that his mission to the isles was for something beyond feeding hungry soldiers or to build his wealth, and she would bet a hundred pieces of silver that it was related to the Cause. His evasion of her questions only reinforced her suspicions. She would be damned if he was going to the isles for salt and fish.

Her father never divulged which of the Claimants he backed, but she understood the weight of such a decision. King Edward was making his way north through Scotland, sacking towns, and weeding out contenders for King John's throne. It was only a matter of time before he reached Glen Shiel. Then what? If they backed no Claimant they would be left to fight alone. Clans would come to their aid if the cry should be released, but would it be enough?

She shuddered. She shifted her thoughts to Aleck, an equally vexing, but albeit, less dire thought. She wouldn't care if Aleck offered to lie near her tonight. Heaven knew that she had already shared a heather bed with him once, and that encounter in the hallway was hmmm...

She trembled again, but for a different reason. She rubbed her belly. *Beguile him.* Did she have the audacity to do that? To take him to her bed and deceive him into thinking the child was his?

She banished that thought. No, she wouldn't. She couldn't. She would have to suffer the consequences when she returned home. Aleck served a single purpose: to get her to Uist. There, she would find some of her answers.

After all these years, she would meet her kin—her aunt. That was, if she was alive. Although her father had gone to Uist several times to barter and forge alliances, he'd never taken her. He'd known all along that her kin were there, yet he never took her and she wondered why. What was he hiding?

Suddenly, Aleck reacted, jumped into the water, and pulled the line. A fish wriggled on the end of it.

Deirdre released a squeal of delight and clapped. "Well done!"

He turned up to her. "You will not want for more tonight, my lady!" he said, beaming. He staggered, the fish flailed, and the hook came out. Their meal dropped into the burn and swam away.

She covered her laugh.

He said playfully, "I doubt you could do better!"

She smiled and made her way down the rocky gradient with care. At the bottom, she pulled off her boots and unrolled her knee-high stockings. She felt his stare, but heard no protest, as she stepped into the burn. Cold water licked her calves. He handed her a prepared hook on a line that he had attached and wrapped around a stick. "No bait?" she asked.

"The fish ate the only worm I found."

"Hmm, how about digging for grubs? They hide in stumps, under logs, or wet areas, like over there." She pointed to a rotting fallen tree next to tall wet grass.

After some digging, they pulled out a handful of creepy-crawling larvae.

Aleck's grin widened. "You're quite the surprise, my lady."

She wiped her hands on her skirt. "You never dug for grubs when you were a lad?"

"I'm afraid not. My father sent me abroad to learn and study. He didn't neglect to teach me the blade though." He kicked at the sheath on the ground that held his sword.

His statement held a subtle pain. Since she couldn't read his emotions, she had to rely on ears and eyes to understand Aleck. She put a hand on her hip and held out her palm, filled with squirming creatures. "Well, I've the grubs. You have the line."

He set to work. After a moment, he handed her the prepared line. "Here."

"I am to fish for you, too?" She flashed him a smile.

"I won't lie. I don't mind watching you pull that skirt to your knees and hop upon the rocks like a selkie out of the water."

She paused, released her skirts, and allowed the water to soak the bottom hem.

He feigned exasperation, clutching a hand to his heart. "Och..."

She chuckled, giddy with sleep deprivation and fatigue. She prepared to cast the line. Failing a few times, she kept getting it tangled within itself, and twice she lost the grub. "Oh, curses!"

"Are you having trouble, my lady? A woman as keen on gardening and grubs as yourself I would think could catch a fish."

"'Tis a faulty line," she retorted. She had lost her mirth due to hunger and impatience. The seriousness of their journey floated into her mind, too, as much as she tried to bat it away! She was about to give up, toss the bloody stick, line, and hook into the burn, when warm arms enveloped her from behind.

"Here," he said. "Let me help."

Instead of taking it from her, he laid his hands over her forearms. He embraced her and guided her arms in the motion of casting. She shifted her feet on the slippery rock beneath her. "I am well on my own," she assured him, eager to be free of his hold.

"Are you certain?" His breath on her neck teased the fine hairs.

She moved again and lost her footing. The line and stick slipped. He caught her in one arm and the stick in the other. Just then, the line went rigid, and he pulled, whipping the line, with a fish dangling from the hook, from the water. Against her better judgment, she tried to right herself. Instead, she found herself tumbling and Aleck with her.

They landed in a heap of wet grass beside the burn.

She was in his lap—again. *Oh, curses.* Was this thrice now? All she could muster was, "Do you have the fish?"

He held up the line. "Aye." His narrow eyes shone in the late afternoon sun.

They were lovely loch blue eyes.

She wriggled to stand, but he kept a firm hand on her waist. "May I kiss you?" he asked.

Humiliated, she felt her face heat again. Why was she so frustrated around him? "I don't think you should." Even as she said the words, she found herself tilting her head closer to his.

His dark stubbly chin brushed her face and his breath was heavy from exertion. Their faces were close enough that she could feel the sweat on his cheeks against her own. "...but I shall not say no. *Should* and *could* mean vastly different things..." She allowed it.

He kissed her softly. His hand on her lower back held her firmly against his chest and she reveled in the intimacy of sitting in his lap, feeling the whole of him wrapped around her. She threaded her hand through his tangled hair and reciprocated the kiss with a heat she had never felt before. Oh, he was heavenly. He smelled like hard labor, tasted like ale, and felt like the warm earth his lifeblood radiated.

Then, her stomach growled again.

He stopped and laughed, their mouths still close. "I've kept my lady hungry for far too long." He eased her to standing and then stood beside her. "Come, I've a fish to prepare."

His smile was catching. It was like the comforting heat of his lifeblood transferred into her with his kiss. Gone was her embarrassment and unease like whispers on the wind.

They climbed to their camp, and Aleck sat beside the unlit fire. He dangled their small catch. "Your bountiful supper, my lady."

"Well, we are fortunate that I stole some of Moreen's bannocks and cheeses." She held up her satchel and cast a sideways look at him.

His mouth curved with humor...and something more. Something that stirred her insides.

She hastily turned her gaze to her food. His face was too inviting, and she licked her lip with hunger of a different kind.

They enjoyed a meager supper and remained quiet, the crackle of the fire the only sound. As the joy of the moment dissipated, a chill crept over Deirdre's skin. Even though Aleck's lifeblood was vibrant and warm, it was his body heat that charmed her senses more. She positioned herself closer to him and pulled her cloak tighter as daylight dimmed.

"Are you cold?"

"A wee."

He wrapped his plaid around her. "You can lie next to me tonight. I promise that your virtue will remain as before."

His arm fell upon her shoulder, and he was too enticing to deny. She bit her tongue. She was hardly worried about her virtue.

"You're shivering," Alasdair said, pulling Deirdre closer to him.

"Hmmm," she murmured, hinging on that delicate precipice of sleep and alertness.

He slipped an arm beneath her neck, and she curled in toward him, releasing a cat-like purr. Her skin was cold, and he rubbed her arms.

Alasdair could see his breath in the early light of day. Somehow, Deirdre had kicked off her thick plaid, and with the fire dampened, their camp was chilly. He pulled the plaid back over her.

Without thinking, he leaned down and brushed a kiss against her forehead. She was still, asleep. He pulled back, memory flooding his mind. *A hundred kisses.* Moreen's warning brought him to full awareness. Did he actually believe in this curse? A curse! He snorted. Deirdre stirred.

Impossible. Curses were for witches, spell casters, and the weak-minded.

Two dead husbands.

He ordered his inner thoughts to silence themselves. A curse was inconceivable. Their deaths must be coincidence. Sad, yes. But fated? A curse? Nay. That was blasphemy. At least he saw now why she was agitated about the idea of another marriage. The poor lass.

Though he denied her situation to be nothing but ill fortune, Deirdre also wished to go to Port nan Long. How could that *not* be fate?

Port nan Long was a quiet village on the isle of Uist. Of all the places for her to want to go! There was no hiding from her while there. Not that he wanted to.

Fate and coincidence aside, he couldn't just leave here there alone, for that was not proper or safe. Instead, Thomas and Annella would provide Deirdre with their usual hospitality, and she would stay at the keep. There would be no argument...and the lass loved to disagree with him.

Alasdair cursed the saints. Of all the clans to have run into, why had fate landed him at Eilean Donan? *Well, that wasn't fate*, his mind chastised him. *You had made that decision, you dolt.*

Everything could be explained.

He groaned, shifting his position. His guise was quickly falling apart and he fought with the idea of telling Deirdre more. Would she tell her father once she knew? Would knowing put her in danger?

He stroked her hair. Obviously she had a reason to go to the isles. Secretly, he had hoped she had come along to be with him. She had been none too pleased about an arrangement with him, though. Was she fleeing marriage all together? Or just her father? Did she have a lover that escaped to the isles and with whom she wished to be reunited? Was this the person she mentioned? Or, family perhaps? Gentle persuasiveness might get it out of her. What harm would it do? He had outrun the English. Even if this curse was true—which it wasn't—he could manage a hundred kisses...and defy this "curse."

It would take another week to reach Thomas on Uist. A week was a long time. Alone. With a desirable woman. He felt himself grow hard with yearning. There could many kisses...

He moaned, and Deirdre's eyes opened. She looked like an enchantress who might cripple him with the slightest touch. It was too much. Reminded of their earlier moment with her in his lap, Alasdair kissed her again.

She returned the gesture to his surprise and arousal. She curved her body into his. His mouth moved over hers, devouring its softness. She was like a refreshing drink on the parched palate. By God, he wanted to do more than just kiss her. They kissed far longer than was proper, as he got lost in the dreamy haze of early morning, half asleep, half awake. Gasping for a breath, her body heaving against his, she rested her head into the crook of his arm and shoulder. He inhaled the scent of her.

They rested for what seemed like forever as sleep began to wash over Alasdair again.

Endurance and patience produce character, and character produces hope. His father's biblically invoked words invaded his mind, though he tried to push them out. The father of Alasdair's youth would be proud of his son's patience and endurance at the moment. Too bad his father was a despicable bastard, with no morsel of decency or character left in him. Alasdair's father had slowly descended into darkness after King Alexander had taken most of his estate after the Battle of Largs. The former king of Scotland may have been kind to the Highlanders after the Norse invasion, but the clans in the southern uplands didn't fare as well. His father had lost nearly everything.

Alasdair tightened his hold on Deirdre and rested with half an eye open. Curse or not, he would enjoy the remainder of his journey with her so long as neither the baron or Laird MacCoinneach's men found them.

"By the heavens," he mumbled.

What the hell had he gotten himself into?

A quiet drizzle on her face awoke Deirdre. Her sleeping partner was so close she could feel the heat of his breath tickle her eyes. Aleck slept hard. She also had slept better than she had in months. A warm hearth of a man beside her probably helped. Or perhaps it was something else.

By her observation of the low cloud-obscured sun, it was at least an hour or so after dawn, far later than she expected them to rise. Her poor bottom ached, having felt the brunt of their hard ride yesterday. She rose, rubbed the soreness in her back with an exaggerated sigh, and stepped behind a larger boulder to relieve herself.

Letting Aleck rest, she decided to refresh herself by the stream.

She removed her shoes and pushed up her skirt hem. Modesty prevented her from undressing and submerging the rest of her body, for now she *knew* there was a man about. The thought that Aleck had seen her naked didn't bother her though. She wondered what he may look like beneath his traveling shirt and trews...

Inhaling chastity of the mind, she sat upon a large, flat rock, allowing the current to massage her ankles. She lifted her skirts higher and eyed her legs. She poked at her chafed and pink thighs. She couldn't imagine what her backside looked like. The chapped legs were the unfortunate result of riding without the leather trews her father allowed her to wear at home—of course beneath her gown, because what lady wears breeches? Regardless, she hated the sidesaddle, and it would have been impossible to ride through rocky terrain with it. So riding lacking trews and a sidesaddle was the only way.

A slice of sunlight through the clouds warmed her eyelids, and she enjoyed a long, peaceful moment.

A loud neigh from her mare disrupted the stillness. As opposed to Delilah, this mare had a mild temperament, but when something frightened her, she had vocals like a siren. Something was amiss. Deirdre pulled her boots on and climbed to their camp. The mare was dancing about, shaking its head to and fro.

She reached the empty clearing and strode over to where the mare was tethered to a nearby tree beside Aleck's horse. "Hush, hush." She patted her side. Aleck's horse whinnied and tossed its head high. Aleck was nowhere in sight. Graces, where was he?

Suddenly, the lifeblood of a nearby stranger struck her. Despite being a tepid amber hue, the lifeblood felt disingenuous and cold. For the briefest of moments, she inhaled and concentrated on the emotions of the person.

Fear, malice, and death nearly slapped her. She stumbled. The negative emotions always took a heavier toll on her.

Her pulse quickened, and she scanned the clearing.

Where in blazes was Aleck?

The glow of the stranger's lifeblood grew closer as did his sound, a rushing wind in her ears, not like the soft humming she felt from others with more passive lifebloods. This man was a few steps behind her. She pretended to be absorbed with stroking the horse, and she panicked for a split moment—she had forgotten her dagger. She knew exactly where it was—tucked away in the ornate box her father had given her, safely resting on her dressing table. Oh, she was a fool!

The droning sound that released from the person's lifeblood tore into her. Her head throbbed.

She turned to see a man only a horse's distance away, his dagger drawn.

She stepped back, her body pressed against the agitated mare. Finding her voice, she said, "Move another pace and my man will strike you down." Pain screamed in her bones.

He stopped, but his malevolent stare held hers. "I see no soldier, milady."

The man wore a thinned shirt and simple trews soiled by days on the road. His face was pitted with high cheekbones and the saggy skin of an underfed man. She didn't recognize him as one of Laird Donald's clan, and she had a good memory of the lifebloods she felt. Especially one as foul as this man's. Her gaze jumped, searching for companions.

They shared a battle of looks. She leaned back into the large belly of her horse, the touch irrationally soothing her. He stepped no closer, but he didn't lower his dagger as he looked her over in anything but a friendly way.

His ill thoughts twisted her stomach.

"Ye're far from home, milady. Laird Donald has become too bold."

He was a MacDougall. She gulped. She prayed that he didn't recognize who she was. "We're only passing through. We're heading to Caol Loch Aillse. We're of no bother to you. Please, just let us go on our way."

"Is that so?" He waved his dagger with threat and stepped closer as a sick grin spread across his face. He eyed the satchel over her horse and licked his lips.

She fought against the pain his unbridled evil emotions elicited. The roar in her ears magnified to a forceful gale. She began to shake. *I will not faint. I will not faint.* "I've no coin or jewels, sir."

A sudden realization replaced the lethal calmness in his eyes. "By the de'il, ye—ye're that witch Auld Kenneth was going to marry, aren't ye?"

Her lip trembled. "I'm afraid you're mistaken."

His grin turned dangerous, and he shook his head side to side. "Aye, ye are! Luckily for 'im he died before he could share his bed wi' ye. Aye, that's right, lassie, I've heard about yer men. Why, my laird would be quite pleased with me bringin' ye back...not to say he was sore about his father dying, leaving the seat for 'im."

"I didn't kill Auld Kenneth." Cursed or not, she had never shared her bed with him. They never even made it to the chapel before the old boar died in the midst of their betrothal supper.

"Ye poisoned him."

"I did not!"

"Leave that to my laird to determine, milady. Ye're coming with me—bringing ye is far better than coin!"

She wanted to scream, but who would hear her? Where was Aleck? Instead, she gritted her teeth and stood steadfast. Flee or fight? Lacking a dagger meant she would not win in a battle of body.

Shifting her feet, she readied them for action. He lunged toward her, and she stepped aside right before he barreled into her mare. She ran into the woods, hoping to find a hiding place if she could somehow outrun him. He swore, and the sound of snapping tree limbs followed behind her. The whirring grew louder as he closed their distance. Her head throbbed from his sick thoughts.

He caught her gown, his fingers digging into her skin. She fought blindly with elbows and feet as well as a high-pitched scream. His emotions tore through her with more intensity than his grip. She tumbled through thick shrubs and trees, fighting back with all she had.

Then, suddenly, the whirring stopped as she fell from his clutches and into a large prickly gorse bush. She smacked her elbow on a rock and cried out as the bush swallowed her. Tears burned her eyes, and pain raced through her arm. Her head vibrated, and darkness lured her. The small yellow flowers of the gorse blurred with their thick green leaves.

I will not faint. I will not faint.

Taking two deep breaths, she centered her energy. His brown-yellow lifeblood was gone, replaced by the white of death.

She tried to stand, but her skirts and hair were tangled in a thorny mess. Then, a familiar blinding heat overtook her. A large hand thrust through the nest of branches, and she clutched it, a smoldering wave rushing down her arm and searing her core as though it had been pierced by a hot arrow. She could taste the sweat and his intoxicated rush from the kill.

Aleck said, "Are you all right?"

She cradled her elbow and nodded, the burning from his presence more overwhelming than the pain from her injury. The fight had brought his own lifeblood to a pinnacle of heat, and it disturbed her how it radiated from him. Never before had she felt a lifeblood of such strength. Perhaps his lifeblood masked his emotions by its powerful dominance. Regardless, it debilitated her.

"Where were you?" she said, dizzy.

"With the other one." A scowl carved a ridge in his forehead. He steadied Deirdre as she stood and attempted to walk with him.

A crumpled and bloodied body blocked her path. Her stomach clenched, and she was sick, turning from Aleck's grasp. She retched in the grass.

She had seen plenty of dead men, but something about today's encounter was different. Unable to control the spasms, a knot formed in her throat and sweat fell into her eyes. She wiped her mouth on her sleeve and stood.

"Can I get you water?"

She heaved again, coughing and gagging. An unwelcome wave of discomfort raged within her. Death hurt her more than life.

Aleck held her, and she shrugged him away. She took purposeful breaths. It took her a long moment before she began to rein in the sensations. Slowly, his simmering lifeblood cooled to a warm and relaxing manifestation. "I'm w-well."

"By cravens you are. Did you hit your head?" He looked her up and down, turned her arms over, and ran fingers through her hair.

"No," she said, taking the water flask from her satchel on the horse and forcing herself to sip it. She wanted to yell at Aleck and tell him that his fiery glow was the issue. The water didn't help. She leaned over and was sick again in the bushes.

Aleck held her and cradled her hurt elbow. The engulfing heat from his touch had dissipated, perhaps as his own pulse slowed and the thrill of the kill had dampened.

He pulled out his satchel and tenderly felt her arm. "It's not broken."

She blew a wisp of hair from her face.

He dabbed and cleaned in silence. When finished, he looked upon her. She self-consciously ran fingers through her hair and felt somewhat comforted by the fact that Aleck's appearance didn't fare any better than her own. His eyes were glassy and dark and a new gash had joined the one on his nose, and she wondered if it was broken by the amount of blood.

"There was a second man?" she asked, her throat scratchy. She took another sip of water, sloshed it in her mouth and spit it out. 'Twas unladylike, but she didn't care.

"Dinna fret, lass." He straightened his shoulders.

A large red welt covered Aleck's cheekbone. She laid a light hand upon it. The distance in his eyes disappeared, and that familiar awakening she had come to appreciate returned. She cleared her throat and removed her hand.

He sat back. "Do you know who those men were?"

"MacDougall's men." Deirdre shuddered with her own words.

"I thought we were in Donald land, and we have no foes?"

"We are."

Aleck's temper flared. "Bleedin' Christ, Deirdre! You could've been killed! We're not safe here at all." He rose from his spot and paced. He blew out a breath.

She suppressed a whimper. God, if he knew. She'd thought that the MacDougalls' anger against her family had lessened over the years.

"I'm sorry. I didn't mean to raise my voice, but I do need you to be honest with me."

"I did tell you! You're the one who is journeying for trade. Shouldn't you be familiar with where we are and the dangers of the countryside?" she countered, her head throbbing.

"I think those were sentinels. One rode off. He'll return."

"I thought you killed him?"

Aleck rubbed his face. "He's injured, but he got away."

"Should we bury the other man?"

Aleck gave her a narrow glare.

They packed with lightning speed, and Aleck hoisted Deirdre onto her mare without a word. Within moments, they were off. She prayed they would make Caol Loch Aillse by nightfall.

Alasdair's nerves unwound when they reached the small settlement of Caol Loch Aillse on the western coast unscathed. The sun was already dropping in the sky. Could they secure a boat at this late hour?

Deirdre let out an audible sigh and dismounted. As her legs buckled, she grabbed the saddle. Alasdair swooped down and held her elbow. With a swipe of dirt from her face with shaky hands, she said with a breath of resilience, "I am well." A dullness clouded the usual glow of her vibrant blue eyes, and her face was ashen. She tucked her wind-blown hair behind her ear with an exaggerated "Mmphmm."

"Letting me help you will not hurt your pride."

She nodded with tight lips.

Though they had distanced themselves from those men, Alasdair looked again to the horizon. The heat flushing his chest would not abate. He didn't need petty arguments between clans to interfere with his plan, and apparently, the blood war between the Donalds and MacDougalls was formidable. The sooner he left the warring mainland, the better. Deirdre had been silent all the way to the port, equally aware of their predicament.

"Will you be all right on a boat?"

"Aye," Deirdre said.

As she gained her footing and they tied their horses to a pole outside a tavern, Deirdre tensed suddenly under Alasdair's grip. Her gaze was rapt by something over his shoulder. He turned to see an indistinguishable lone rider quite a distance out. The man rode at a full gallop, heading directly toward them. Another MacDougall?

"Quick, Deirdre. Into the tavern." Alasdair pushed her.

She held fast to her spot, rooted like a tree. "It's Crystoll," she murmured.

"Do you have the eyes of a hawk? We can't see who it is. Get inside!"

"No. It's him. I feel his—" she said, stopping herself. Her eyes pleaded with him. "It's him! I-I recognize the horse."

Deirdre moved with the will of a headstrong mare.

"Take this," he said, slipping his dagger into her hand.

She looked at it like it was foreign. "Why? I don't need it."

"Take it," he pressed. "Stand behind me."

She huffed but did as told. "I told you. 'Tis Crystoll. We are quite safe."

Safe? Not here. Not anywhere! He pulled his sword out of its sheath and slid it under the plaid on his horse's back. He rested a hand there. He calmed his pulse with deep breaths and waited.

The rider drew close enough that Alasdair confirmed Deirdre's perceptive guess. It was Crystoll Murchison, Laird MacCoinneach's dutiful soldier. Alasdair didn't move his hand from the sword's hilt though. How had she known it was him? Nobody could see that far.

The young, ruddy-cheeked soldier appeared weary, but relieved. "My lady! Thank God!" He dismounted and approached them. The crossbow slung over his shoulder shook with the man's quick movement. "Our laird was worried. He thought—he thought—" he started, but then turned toward Alasdair. A glower hooded his features. "Sir Stirrat, our laird is not pleased, but he is willing to reconcile upon your return." He beheld Deirdre. "Our laird believes you were taken under duress?"

Alasdair was about to speak, but Deirdre did so first. She clasped her hand in his. "We're not returning yet. And my father knows me well enough, Crystoll—I came of my own accord."

Crystoll observed their joined hands with a deeper frown. "What do you mean? Didn't Sir Stirrat take you by force?"

Alasdair's fingers danced on the hilt of his sword, still in its sheath.

"No," she said firmly. "I came by my own choice."

"I've been ordered to protect you and bring you home, my lady. If Sir Stirrat has compromised your virtue—"

"I most certainly have not!" Alasdair interjected.

"Come with us if you want to protect me, but I'm not returning home yet," Deirdre said, crossing her arms.

His gaze passed between Alasdair and Deirdre again. "Sir Stirrat has business there. You don't. He didn't—"

She cut him off. "No! I am of sound mind and body, Crystoll."

"I don't understand."

Deirdre looked at Alasdair when she explained, "I wish to see my mother's people. In Port nan Long on Uist. Moreen told me about kin I have there."

Now it made sense. He had suspected that. Why hadn't she just told him?

"My lady, you've no kin left there," Crystoll assured.

"How do you know?" she accused.

"Your father, Cortland, and I went to Uist a few winters ago to see Laird MacRuaidhri when he was ill. Yer father mentioned no kin."

"My father is a man who shares little. Moreen said I have an aunt," Deirdre countered, bitterness in her tone betraying her.

Alasdair's heart softened and he wanted to take her into his lap again.

Crystoll appeared to be contemplating that and said with quiet admission, "Your father suspected you'd try to journey there."

Although Crystoll's expression was a mask of stone, Alasdair saw the shift in his stance, the clenching of his fists. "Sir Stirrat, where does your trade bring you?"

It was futile to lie at this point. "Port nan Long. To the keep of MacRuaidhri. It appears we have shared acquaintances." He sighed internally. Bringing Deirdre was all well, but now Crystoll would soon enough learn the truth about him. The soldier would surely not return to Eilean Donan alone now that he had located Deirdre.

Crystoll's eyebrows lifted. "Plainly we do. How fortunate," he said, sourly. "I'll negotiate with a merchant, yonder," he said, pointing toward the small docks. He paused and directed his statement toward Deirdre. "My lady, I am ordered to send word to our laird of our whereabouts and your safety. You do understand?"

"Of course." She placed a hand on his arm. "Thank you."

Alasdair removed his hand from his hidden sword. He counted his blessings that Crystoll had conceded to Deirdre. Retaliation ran thick in Scots' blood. Alasdair didn't need another adversary. Laird MacCoinneach had been amiable, but all men had their point of tolerance. Alasdair had been daft to allow Deirdre to come along with him. And now the soldier was sending word of their whereabouts. If the message fell into the wrong hands... "Are there emissaries you can trust here, Crystoll?" he asked.

"Aye." Crystoll strode into the tavern.

When the soldier was out of earshot, Alasdair whispered, "Can we trust him?"

"Crystoll has never faltered with his charge. Why would you ask such a thing?"

The encounter with the MacDougall men was fresh in his mind. "I will not let harm befall you, Deirdre."

Her eyes locked with his. "I know."

A wave of guilt coursed through him. She trusted him. He hoped that when the moment came, he would be able to part ways with her. She didn't deserve his lies.

A short while later, Crystoll returned, cheerful. "Good news. A merchant knows Finn Kinnach," he said, pausing to explain for Alasdair's sake. "He's our stable master in Dornie. Do you remember him?"

"Och, aye."

"Captain Tuach's daughter is married to Finn's cousin." The youthfulness shone in Crystoll's smooth, suntanned skin. He ruffled his brown hair and massaged his neck, letting out a sigh. He drew his pleas to Deirdre one more time. "My lady, I cannot convince you to return home?"

"No," she said firmly.

Alasdair gave Crystoll a thorough appraisal. He was taller, built like a soldier, and Alasdair would bet his horse that Crystoll could wield a sword and his crossbow with accuracy. He had been quite agile on their stag hunt and now caught up to them quickly after their secretive departure from Dornie. Having Crystoll along was not an entirely bad thing. "Can we gain passage tonight?"

Crystoll shook his head. "A storm is brewin' on the outer sea. 'Tis too dangerous to depart tonight on a small ship, even for the short sail. He leaves at daybreak if the sea has settled."

"How much did he ask for?" The only barter Alasdair possessed was horses or his rings. His coin was gone.

"No need to concern yourself with it."

Alasdair tightened a muscle in his jaw. He suspected that the laird had sent Crystoll along with more than a strong fighting hand to retrieve his daughter. He squelched his pride. "My gratitude is yours." He pulled

Crystoll aside. "We may need the coin later to get to Uist. Please accept my promise that I will repay your laird."

"You'll need to discuss that with my laird upon our return. He wishes a truce."

His words stung deeper than Alasdair thought they should. There was no going back to Glen Shiel. "Of course."

"There's an inn," Crystoll said, pointing to the handful of buildings—a tavern, cobbler, cooper, smokehouse, a small kirk, boathouse, and cottages—not too far from the docks. "I will locate a messenger." As they walked to the inn, Crystoll pulled Alasdair aside. "Sir Stirrat, there are men in the region that are less than gallant. We should keep watch."

"Och. Of course," Alasdair said, rubbing his injured nose.

Deirdre settled in one of the three bedchambers upstairs after a light meal. Crystoll took the floor outside the door. Alasdair went downstairs to take first watch. He maneuvered through the smoky main room, thick with the scent of salted fish, body odor, and whisky. A lively group of men enjoyed their drinks with local lassies at the center table, while a few others laughed by the hearth regaling each other with tales of the sea. Alasdair sat outside on a stool, breathing in the fresh seaside air while gulls squawked in the evening sky. The last glimpse of orange light began to sink behind the low-lying clouds. He could taste the briny wind and feel the energy of the impending storm.

The first leg of their journey was complete, and the week's ride across Skye lay ahead, followed by a larger stretch of deep, cold sea taking them to Uist. He hoped he would arrive in time. He couldn't afford any more delays. The past few days had proven to be more eventful than he would have liked, and he prayed that no more unexpected encounters or companions awaited them.

Agmus came upon the town of Dornie to find the folk of the western Highlands deep in their daily drudgery. It appeared to be market day. He rode past two men in a heated conversation over mispriced goods, their arms gesturing whilst they tossed curses at each other beside a cart brimming with wool. He maneuvered through the ruckus, his soldiers closely following. A child chasing a loose pig cut across his horse's path. The horse reared up, and Agmus pulled on the reins to prevent the child from being crushed. A large wagon transporting barrels drove past him, and the driver gave him a subtle nod. Well, at least one person among these heathens recognized a noble.

He shook his head in disgust. These northern villages with their small stone—and some wood!—castles were nothing compared to the great fortresses in the south. With his army of well-trained and better educated soldiers at his command, he could storm through and wipe out the bowels of Scotland in one fell swoop. He didn't doubt that the clansmen were braw and able-bodied fighters, yielding their claymores with accuracy and conviction, but the clans and their blood-loyalty did not rule the south. Money, land, and king governed the lowlands. That was where the true Scots could be found. Soon enough, Edward's rule would extend north, and Agmus would be rewarded for his efforts after all the disloyal Scots were weeded out.

He took in the castle ahead of him. It was impressive in its simple beauty, as Highland castles were—abutted by a loch or coast as a means of fortification. It reminded him of his first home, long ago, when he was a modest laird in Eaglesham, under the Earl of Shrewsbury's rule. That mundane life of landowner and tax collector was a distant memory now. His true glory awaited him.

A handful of guards marched down the stone bridge that connected the keep's island to the mainland. Two men stepped forward, spears pointed up in respect, for Agmus wore his full noble dress. "G'day, sir. What business hiv ye here?" one asked.

"I'm here to see the laird."

The soldier eyed Agmus and his entourage. "Who might I say calls upon him?"

Agmus spoke coolly, but decided to be kind to these impudent fools. He might need the laird's cooperation, after all. "Baron Montgomerie of Eaglesham."

The soldier lowered his spear slightly and inclined his head in deep gesture. "Welcome, Baron."

Agmus smiled. These northern heathens at least understood nobility when they saw it.

"Please send word," the soldier ordered another man behind him who then marched toward the keep. "We can settle yer mounts, Baron." Two men approached Agmus's horses.

His two soldiers accompanied the horses, and he gestured to Ronat and Carney to remain with him, but not before giving Ronat a stern look of warning.

Agmus grimaced as he dismounted. Each day his discomfort was becoming harder to hide. He walked off the burning in his knees and followed the MacCoinneach soldiers to the inner courtyard.

In contrast to the energy of the village, within the curtain wall all was quiet. The soldiers took their place, flanking the entrance to the grand hall, spears in hand. A man approached Agmus upon his entry. Agmus presumed that he, although exuding an air of confidence, was not the laird. He was dressed in the traditional Highland clothes of "nobility," if he could call it that. An older man stood behind him, a quill and parchment in hand.

"Good day, Baron Montgomerie. We're honored by your presence."

"Where's your laird?"

The man's face puckered with an unwelcome frankness. "I'm Edmund MacCoinneach. My father, our laird, is hunting, but he will return soon. How may I serve you, Baron Montgomerie?"

"I shall wait." He flicked his hand to Ronat and Carney, who proceeded back out the entrance to the inner courtyard to take their posts.

Edmund turned to the man behind him. "Prepare refreshments for the baron in our laird's reading chamber." The man nodded and scurried from the room along with two servants who had been silently standing at the wall beside the hearth.

Another servant met them in the chamber with a basin of water and clean towel. Agmus dipped his hands in and washed the dirt away. He then sat in a plush chair, his knees creaking with the motion as the servant departed the room.

Edmund stood, not dare taking the seat of his laird. His expression was taut with a forced congeniality. "I hope your journey was uneventful."

"It was most agreeable."

"To what do we owe your most gracious visit, Baron? Dornie is far from Eaglesham."

Agmus hated pointless conversation. "I seek someone."

A glimmer of interest passed across Edmund's face. "Och?"

Ah, not pointless after all, Agmus thought. This impetuous young man didn't hide his emotions well at all. He wondered how his father's disposition fared. "Eilean Donan is a fine keep, Edmund," Agmus said with a subtle wave to the walls around him. The laird's personal library was simple, but well kept. In fact, the entire stone keep and its inner bailey walls were as pristine as the outer curtain. It was a new fortress hardly touched by war—yet. Delight slithered into his mind. Perhaps King Edward would bestow this keep upon him for his efforts. The location—on the brink of Skye—was advantageous.

"Aye, Baron."

Agmus rose and strolled over to the farthest wall, which held a shelf of leather-bound books. Laird MacCoinneach appeared an educated man. Books required a labored process of drying and stretching skin, binding the parchment, and not to mention finding a scribe. Glen Shiel held no monasteries that he knew of. The closest abbey was at least a week's ride away, south, from his recollection. He skimmed over the bindings. Most of the books on the shelf were in Latin or Gaelic. At least this Highland laird was learned.

Edmund closed the door. "May I inquire about the person you seek?"

Agmus appreciated the man's boldness, and he loved a game of cat and rat—the latter burdened with pestilence, and the former willing to rid the world of it. He gave Edmund a shrewd smile. This man made an ideal rat. "He's nobody of substance to you."

A shadow passed over Edmund's eyes, but he said no more. Wise man, Agmus thought, grinning. The castle's steward returned with a platter of bread, cheese, and dried fruits. He poured a goblet of ale and handed it to Agmus. Edmund motioned for the steward to leave. Then paced the room.

Agmus enjoyed his discomfort. "Tell me more about the area, Edmund."

"Have you passed through here before, Baron?"

Playing the cat, was he? He waved a hand. "When I was a young laird. Voyages to and from the isles for trade with my father," he said, lying. He watched Edmund's face.

"It appears that many men journey there now that trade has arisen since the Norsemen were expelled," Edmund countered.

Agmus stroked his beard. "Many indeed. Have you encountered any?"

Edmund chewed his lip. "Not recently."

This could be amusing, Agmus thought.

Edmund resolved himself to pacing. The awkward conversation lingered, a few servants came and went, and finally, the laird appeared.

A HUNDRED KISSES

Pink tinged the heavyset laird's cheeks, and he stopped in the doorway, slightly winded. "I'm sorry to have kept you waiting, Baron Montgomerie. It's a pleasure to meet you. I'm Simon MacCoinneach. I daresay you've been well taken care of?" He darted a look to his son.

"Aye, most certainly."

Simon said, "Edmund, please see to it that Gilford has our supper ready and a bedchamber for the baron."

Edmund shifted on his feet, hesitating for a brief moment before leaving. Oh, the lad did not like being excluded. Agmus tittered to himself. What a weak foal.

Simon sat in the chair at his desk. "To what do I owe the pleasure of your company? Glen Shiel is far from Eaglesham." He sipped from the goblet poured out for him. He waved the last servant out.

"No need for formalities, Laird MacCoinneach. A traitor is among us."

Simon coughed, spewing drink. "Pardon me?" He pounded his chest with his fist.

"You're familiar with the rumors of the Claimants who seek the throne even as King John sits upon it?"

Simon nodded as the red faded from his cheeks. "That is well known."

"I am a Guardian. You've heard of us?"

"Baron, Glen Shiel may be remote, but we are abreast of the happenings in court. It is an honor to have one of the Guardians visit our keep." He raised an eyebrow. "I was introduced to the Laird of Badenoch by the bishop at court last year."

It appeared Simon MacCoinneach was indeed an educated man. Badenoch was one of the Guardians Agmus didn't despise. He had been easier to manipulate than the rest.

Simon continued, "The Guardians rule by joint council, correct?" He paused and took a long sip from his goblet.

"Indeed."

The laird said, "However, I've been told that not all of you stand unified. Several Claimants have emerged from within the council to contend for John's throne."

Agmus grinned and flitted a hand as if in dismay. "Truly. The council is in upheaval. Our overlord and sovereign, King Edward of England, to whom we pay homage..." He paused, waiting for Simon's agreement.

Simon responded with a nod.

"...has been more than lenient with us. King John is compromised." King John, was in fact, a fool. A pawn in King Edward's game. He would be gone soon enough. Agmus continued, "Instead of remaining united, as was conferred to us, our council has become fragmented. War is on the front."

"So it seems. Do you come seeking my support, Baron?" Simon's brown eyes narrowed.

"I seek no rights to the throne. On the contrary. I seek a miscreant who poses a threat to King John, King Edward, and the council."

"I see."

"My trackers place his path here, through Glen Shiel."

Simon rubbed his beard in earnest and said nothing, apparently undeterred by Agmus's threats.

Agmus pushed. "He's relayed sensitive information to one of the contenders. He, along with all who've assisted him, has committed treason against King Edward."

"And against King John," Simon added.

"And against the council of Guardians," Agmus said, his tone deepening. The aching in his knees hurt something fierce, and he needed to stand and move. This had to be his last venture north. King Edward would have to find another man to complete his task of vanquishing all the Claimants.

Laird MacCoinneach gave him nothing of worth, but Agmus's observations and Edmund's response to his queries told him that Alasdair had been through here.

"Well, I hope you find him. In the meantime, Eilean Donan welcomes you."

"Have you had any recent visitors, Laird MacCoinneach?" Agmus sipped the ale, wishing there was willow bark in it for his swollen joints.

"None other than you." Simon's eyes were thin and unrevealing.

He lied well. Agmus pondered for a brief moment. Many of these Highland lairds supported the Cause, what with several Highland Claimants vying for the throne. Agmus was most concerned with Bruce, Comyn, and Moray. He was ordered to determine who each clan supported. Of course, Alasdair backed Robert Bruce of Annandale. The Earl of Ross's dominating presence in the Highlands meant that supporters of John Comyn dwelled in the area. These contenders were such a bloody headache. If they only knew the force Edward would soon unleash upon them. The clans would meet their end soon enough. In turn, the contenders would be found, hung, and the council would be united again under their rightful ruler—King Edward—and Agmus duly rewarded for his loyalty. The king had already taken towns in the south, and King John was unhinging. Abdication was inevitable. It was just a matter of time.

Simon rose from his desk. "Please join us in the hall for supper. Our kitchen cook is the best in all of Glen Shiel. You'll not leave the table pining for a better meal."

Agmus followed the laird from the chamber, annoyed but enlightened nonetheless. He had gotten the information he wanted, even if the laird had not outright told him. Now he just needed to determine which way Alasdair had gone. He had a feeling that the laird's son Edmund may be a good means to an end.

CHAPTER SIX

Deirdre's stomach sloshed back and forth as the cog ship floated across the sound toward Skye. The night's storm had left a dead calm in its wake. The sailors kept adjusting the single large sail, but it was no use. It just couldn't hold the wind, making their trip nauseatingly slow. If the short day sail to Sligachan, the busiest port on Skye, was this ghastly, she didn't wish to contemplate what setting sail across the sea for Uist would be like—they would be at sea for a long overnight trip. She focused on the horizon ahead, as Captain Tuach suggested. At least her bottom could get a rest.

They sailed on a vessel that transported barrels and bags of goods, which she presumed were ale, whisky, and grains. However, the ship lacked animal stalls, so she had been forced to leave her mare behind. Crystoll had paid good coin to a local stableman to care for her horse. The other two were sold. As hopeful as she wanted to remain, she suspected that the mare would not be there when they returned. 'Twas a shame she hadn't taken Delilah, that unpleasant mare, she thought with a smirk.

The morning's drizzle began to subside, and the sun struggled to brighten the day through heavy clouds. She found the day matched her mood.

"Lass looks the color of me wife's porridge, Sir Stirrat," the weathered captain, with a beard clear down to his belly, said with a chuckle. He approached Deirdre near the bow, the scent of unwashed male and salty fish infiltrating her nostrils. She discreetly covered her face as if wiping a wind-induced runny nose, focusing on anything else. She need not lose her breakfast over the edge of the vessel.

She ignored his comment and stared at the reddish hills on the shore. Aleck approached from behind and wrapped her in his plaid, standing beside her. She was ever grateful for the heat he radiated both in spirit and in body just by being near.

"We'll be there soon enough."

"Aye," she mustered, allowing her shoulder to touch his. Inappropriate or not, after their shared kisses, she felt a stronger pull to him and allowed his affections. She knew nothing would come from it. Her father may have given her orders to beguile Sir Stirrat into her bed, but she could do no such thing. She would just suffer the consequences upon her return home. It didn't mean she couldn't appreciate her time with him.

"Ye'll find good fish pies and warm baked sweets at Jemma's tavern," Captain Tuach said.

Aleck flattened a loose lock of Deirdre's hair, his fingertips lingering on her earlobe and then her neck. A shiver slid down her back, a pleasant distraction from the seasickness.

"What are those red hills called?" he asked.

"The Red Cuillin." Captain Tuach leaned over the edge of the bow, pointing. "And in the distance there, those pointy teeth are the *Dubh*, the Black Cuillin. The locals call 'em the Devil's Mountains."

Clouds cast deep charcoal shadows across the widespread crags. A few jutted to ragged points. In the foreground, the Red Cuillin were rounded, with russet and brassy red streaks. As they drew closer, Deirdre admired the mixture of spring grasses, heather, and boggy moss blanketing the shoreline. It was an awe-inspiring sight. Skye appeared windswept and wild, more so than Glen Shiel. She could only imagine how desolate yet beautiful Uist would be. A quiver of excitement joined her already unsettled stomach.

"Ye best keep yer distance from them—that's no' easy land to travel. Stay to the coastline. Sir Stirrat, there's a road from Broadford."

Aleck straightened his back. "I thought we made port in Sligachan."

The ship pitched as a crewman adjusted the rudder. Deirdre gripped the front rail, her inadequate sea legs shaking.

Captain Tuach shook his head, greasy hair dancing about his round face at the change in direction. The sail flapped and then stiffened as it caught a full wind. "Regrets, sir, but the squall is no' holdin' the sails well. We need to make port and wait for better wind. It may no' be til the morrow. Ye can wait, or ye can make it there by land. 'Tis a few hours' ride by horse. I've lads ashore that can assist ye, sir."

Crystoll approached. "It won't be much longer that route, Sir Stirrat. I've journeyed that way before."

Aleck responded with an indistinguishable murmur-moan.

Several men lowered oars and rowed to give the ship more speed as they drew near the shore. Chimney smoke from the thatched cottages comprising Broadford, an even smaller port than Caol Loch Aillse, percolated the midday haze. A few ships were already docked. The village teemed with life, which lifted Deirdre's spirit a bit. Traders worked along the muddy shore, carrying cargo to and from ships. A sailor jumped onto a large wet rock, balancing precariously, and then hopped to the next, a heavy crate upon his shoulders. Others did the same, unloading freight like ants with crumbs. Captain Tuach secured the sail and tossed ropes to the lad awaiting him on the dock.

Their cheerful captain disembarked and shook hands with another man who came to greet him. They chuckled and talked while Tuach gestured to Deirdre and Aleck in reference.

Crystoll went ashore first of their group, followed by Aleck, after he helped Deirdre down the plank. Aleck thrust a hand out in greeting to Tuach's acquaintance.

"G'day, Sir Stirrat. Tuach tells me ye'll be needin' an escort north," he said with a partially toothless grin. He tilted his head toward Deirdre. "G'day, ma'am."

Deirdre regained her footing and ignored her dizziness.

"We need only horses and directions." Aleck paused and looked at Crystoll. "See to it that Deirdre is accommodated at the inn, and I'll meet you there," Aleck ordered, pointing to a building of whitewashed stone. Aleck then turned from them and conversed with the man.

Crystoll said with a halfhearted nod, "Aye, sir."

Deirdre felt the tension rise within Crystoll's docile lifeblood. She knew that he was not pleased with the situation and did not take kindly to being ordered by someone other than her father. She was secretly glad he had arrived though. At least he knew the route to Uist. After the encounter with the vagrant MacDougall men, she felt safer with Crystoll's additional presence as well. As much as she trusted Aleck, she knew that Crystoll would protect her by any means necessary.

The idea of warm food after the cold morning sail enticed her. "Come, Crystoll. Let us see if Jemma's reputation holds true."

"Aye, my lady."

She linked her arm in his and they walked the short distance down the overgrown path to the inn. They wouldn't have pleasant accommodations until they reached Uist, as Captain Tuach had warned, so she was eager to partake in some warm food now.

An hour later, her stomach brimming with food and drink, Aleck arrived. Deirdre didn't need her special ability to know that he was irritated.

"We need arrangements for the night, Crystoll. We can't acquire horses until tomorrow morning, but I've spoken to the stable master, and they will be ready at dawn," Aleck said.

"Aye, Sir Stirrat." Crystoll rose. The meal, and more likely the whisky, had apparently calmed his mood, for his usual amber energy lacked the strain Deirdre had felt earlier.

Aleck fell into a seat next to Deirdre. "Here," she said, pushing a plate of meat, bread, and cheese in front of him. She subtly pushed a goblet of whisky beside it.

He ate quietly.

"I'm sorry for the delay," Deirdre mumbled a short while later, unsure what else to say.

Aleck pushed the half-finished food away. He drained his whisky in two gulps, then tapped a nervous hand on his thigh. "We rode hard the past two days. A rest will help you." He pointed out the window. "Tuach said there's a grove of trees yonder with an agreeable view. Can you endure a short walk? It will help your legs."

"I'm not an able seafarer, am I?"

"You did well."

He summoned a half smile, a small dimple appearing on his right cheek. How had she not seen that before?

"How does your leg fare?" she asked as he rose with a minor hesitation and sharp intake of breath. She wasn't going to ask about his nose. It was still bruised from the MacDougall encounter and her accidental kick of him at the stable back in Dornie. He looked ragged.

"Och, I've had worse."

He stepped with a crooked gait as they proceeded out of the tavern and up a worn path. Men and their pride, she thought.

She blew a breath out, slightly winded and still a little wobbly, as they ascended. Aleck's red warmth glowed something fierce again, and she had devised a notion about it. Whenever his emotions were heightened—or so she presumed—his lifeblood was stronger, masking her from seeing within him and feeling his emotions. His lifeblood was like a protective shield. God knew why she couldn't break through it. Perhaps her aunt would know.

A rocky precipice overlooking Broadford greeted them as they crested the small foothill. As she sat upon a sun-warmed granite slab, she let out a loud sigh. She stretched, allowing the rock's heat to soothe her as her gaze fell upon the water below. The sea was calm as a gentle surf broke upon the shore.

Although her belly was full, her mind and body were not in agreement. The nausea was a constant reminder of her father's order. Her hope still hinged on the idea that maybe Edmund would have another child and her father would change his mind. Pesky questions still lingered so it was time to ask a few more. "How long do you think you'll be on Uist?"

Instead of relaxing and enjoying the view, Aleck paced stiffly, cringing. Their two-day ride apparently had not helped the healing process. "As long as it takes."

"It?"

He paused. Opened and closed his mouth. He then returned his stare to the sea, although he stopped his pacing. As he crossed his arms, the muscles strained in his back.

Aleck's elusiveness was beginning to drive her mad. The same distressing thought surmounted all others: she hardly knew Aleck. She felt only heat from him. What that heat meant was a mystery.

"I want to know." She offered no explanation but added, "You can trust me."

"I prefer it if once we reach Uist and you settle things with your kin, that Crystoll returns you home, Deirdre. It's for the best. You do understand?"

"Of course," she said, although she didn't completely agree or understand the urgency to return home.

She still wanted answers. No more evasion! For her to pull information from him, she decided to do some sharing herself. "You're aware that my father's allegiance is to the Cause...and he has yet to support a Claimant, but he'll likely be swayed if the alliance is mutually beneficial." She bit her lip. Aleck didn't appear to be a man persuaded by bribery, even if it included the entirety of Glen Shiel.

He spun around and approached her, even-tempered. "What do you want to know, Deirdre?"

She was taken aback at his response and her own question that followed. "Who are you?"

"Why do you ask things to which you already know the answer?"

She would not relent. "Why did you lack a vassal and horse? Edmund was correct. You had ventured far and alone."

"My escort ran off, stole the horse. And I prefer to conduct my own trade affairs."

"You said the animal grew lame."

He gave a hard, obvious swallow. "I hired an escort once I reached Argyll to take me through the Highlands. He was a despicable man, and one night while I slept, he stole my horse and many of my belongings. What I wore when I saw you was all that I had left, save for what I had in the satchel that I had rested my head upon to sleep."

His tone lacked guile, but something didn't feel right with her. "Why did you lie about your horse?"

"My father used to say that I was more headstrong than a bull. Pride, I suppose."

Her own pride kept her from arguing. Regardless, she was determined to get a straight answer from him. "Tell me about your family. How are you related to Laird Cunningham?"

His mood darkened with her question. "Tell me about yours."

"What do you mean? You've met my family."

"Your kin in the isles. You could've told me that was why you had wanted to come along. Are they Norse? There's no shame in that."

Well, few people also have a Seer for an aunt and a Healer for a mother, she wanted to answer. "I didn't think you'd understand."

He reached down and took her hands. "What's not to understand? They're your kin."

She pulled her hands from his. She wished he would stop doing that. He clearly was bothered by her presence, and those kisses—oh those kisses—had been a mistake.

He massaged his upper thigh.

"Does it hurt? Should I check the dressing?"

"Och, this? No. It'll be fine."

"What about your family?" she pressed.

He sat beside her and spun a ring on his finger. "My parents are dead."

"Oh." Her limbs felt suddenly heavy. "No lady awaits you at home?"

"Not yet." The tiniest smile stretched across his unshaven face.

Perplexed, she turned away. She allowed his lifeblood to soothe her. It was puzzling how he both vexed and mollified her. She ventured another question. "Crystoll said my father still wishes an alliance. Do you wish the same?"

"You're a woman with deep questions."

"And you're a man who keeps avoiding them."

He reached for her hand, and she wiggled away. "No. You think I am a dim woman who will fall for your charms and-and caresses. But I am no fool. I demand answers." Her galls burned and she turned her face away from him, toward the sea.

"The truth?"

She crossed her arms and turned back around to face him. "Yes!"

"I journey to Uist for trade alone."

She'd be damned if it was trade. His emotions were vague and shadowy beneath that lifeblood! She hushed her troubled spirits. *Tell me the truth!* her mind screamed.

He grabbed her hand and rubbed his thumb over her knuckles. "Do you believe me?"

No. Yes. "Aye," she said. "My father though, he…" She stopped herself. "Will you stop doing that?"

"Doing what?"

"Touching me." Although her words said one thing, her body said another. She didn't pull her hand from his this time. Warmth flowed through his palm into hers.

"Why?"

She found no explanation to support her demands. She turned her eyes downward. Again, she noticed the scope of raised, white scars that covered his hand. With her other hand, she lifted the end of his shirt sleeve to expose a trail of scars leading up to his elbow. She scrutinized the ancient injury, feeling the bumps under her fingertips. The wound had caught her eyes a few times before, but now that she saw the extent of the damage, it took her breath away. "How did this happen?" she said so softly, it could have been lost on the wind.

"I was young."

A man of conflicting actions and words, he cupped her chin and drew her gaze to his. He then leaned down and kissed her in a non-gentlemanly way.

His kiss freed her in a way she didn't expect. She reciprocated, for why not partake in joy, as fleeting as it was?

They kissed, unhurriedly, enjoying the delicious feel and taste of the other's lips. The days of their journey had left his chin covered in stubble that tickled her face. He drew his lips down to her throat and kissed the hollow at the base. She inhaled, and her pulse quickened.

His breath trailed down her cleavage, and she felt her desire heighten. She stroked his head, digging her fingers through the length of his hair and down to his shoulders. She tightened her embrace, chest against chest. His heartbeat reverberated within her. He laid his hand on her knee, but it went no farther. His touch was scalding hot even through the fabric of her skirts.

The vision of him in the wood flashed behind her eyes, and she pulled away for the briefest moment, but he wouldn't allow her to escape—Aleck was a man lost to the oblivion just as she. As he pulled her closer, she released a small yelp. He parted her lips, his tongue exploring.

Finally, she broke free. "We...should..." she panted, her cheeks hot. Should *what*? Stop? Or delver further into the delights of flesh...?

Abruptly, he released her. "Forgive me." His eyes were squeezed shut as if it pained him to pull away from her.

Breathless, she said, "We should return."

With a nod, he rose as if nothing had happened, his face and posture all stoic, but the hot lifeblood pouring from his body said otherwise.

She followed him down to the tavern, too delirious to speak. Her lips hummed from the kiss. And she wanted more. So much more.

Alasdair was grateful for the crisp dawn air and a long ride. It had become painfully obvious that he needed to part ways with Deirdre. Whenever he touched her, it was like being shocked by a bolt of lightning. He was drawn, even compelled, to touch her, kiss her…and yet he knew in the deep fathoms of his soul that he could not cherish her the way he wanted. It was as though an ominous echo from beyond the grave whispered words of warning in his ear.

His mother had been dead many years, but she still haunted him. She had been a loving soul accused of spellcasting by his father, the vile beast. If only he could have saved her. He tightened his hold on his reins and urged his horse ahead with a kick. At least when they rode, it prevented discussion and questions, and Deirdre was full of both. Now with Crystoll as their shadow, both remained mute.

The trail around the Cuillin and along the eastern coast had moderate grades with flat stretches, and they rode the horses at an easy canter.

Despite the sunny start to their day, a few hours into their ride a thick mist had overtaken the trail, concealing the blackened crags around them. They weren't far north of Broadford when they reached a washed-out point.

Alasdair halted his horse.

Crystoll rode up beside him and stopped. "The stable master mentioned this spot where the tide comes into the marsh. We need to cross it. The trees are too thick there to bypass it on horseback." Crystoll pointed to their left. "If we go that way, we need to walk the horses by foot, and it would take longer. What say you, Sir Stirrat?"

"Let us ford the wash. At least the water appears shallow." Small waves lapped the shore, and a calm current drew past them in the inlet.

Crystoll nodded. "He mentioned that at high tide the water would be up to the horses' bellies or shoulders and could be dangerous. We're fortunate to have caught the low tide."

"I'll cross first." Alasdair looked over his shoulder to Deirdre. She agreed with a shrug. He eased his horse through the sandy beach and entered the wash. The water reached the horses' knees, and he rode at a gentle trot. Thick fog settled in the wide inlet, wrapping them in a hazy cloud. He couldn't see the other side. For an unsettling short while, it felt as if he rode in the middle of a loch, surrounded by water and silence, save for the occasional bird call. He cast repeated glances behind him at Deirdre, who managed quite well. He wouldn't have thought otherwise.

A short while later, they emerged from the eerie gloom and slowed the horses to a walk to rest them.

Time drifted and before long, late afternoon was upon them. Alasdair was so consumed with his thoughts that he didn't immediately notice when Deirdre's horse flattened its ears and began to prance. It let out a shrill whinny.

Deirdre's eyes were wide. She halted her horse, but its hooves danced madly. It shook its head and snorted, nostrils flaring.

"Oh my God..." She clutched her head as she almost slid off her unruly horse. Alasdair was quick to her side, steadying her.

"*En sky av hvite død skjult i svart...*" Deirdre mumbled under her breath.

"What?" Alasdair bristled. Deirdre spoke in the same unusual language as she had before when she was by the loch, where they first met. The words sounded familiar to him and not because he had heard her utter them. What was this language?

He shared a look with Crystoll, who lifted his shoulders in equal puzzlement as he settled Deirdre's horse from her other side, while Alasdair kept her upright with a palm on her back.

Alasdair scanned the area. The coastal trail was rocky, weaving through moorland. Waves of large undulating rocks encircled by sea grasses surrounded them. There were no trees, no deer or other animals to aggravate her horse. The prevailing sea wind swept over the rolling hills and clusters of granite. It was even more disconcerting than the tidal wash. He saw nobody. Nothing.

"They're coming!" she said, her voice shaky.

"Who?" Alasdair and Crystoll asked in unison.

"I see nothing," Crystoll said.

Alasdair controlled his breath and listened. "I hear nothing."

Deirdre whimpered, her hand clutching the side of her head. "*Hvítr andlát...*"

"Perhaps she has another headache," Alasdair said, half-believing himself. Had the woman gone mad? Was she chanting?

"Another headache?" Wrinkles furrowed Crystoll's forehead.

Through the thickening fog they couldn't see the ocean, but Alasdair heard the distant crashing of surf. Their only option was to ride to their right, where the hills sloped to the sea. To their left, walls of granite and volcanic rock served as a forbidding nature-made palisade guarding the Black Cuillin. He squinted ahead. The fog obscured the trail. "What is it, Deirdre? We do not understand you."

Deirdre seemed to wake from a trance. "Aleck...we need to get off the path. They're right behind us." Her face blanched.

"I don't hear or see anything, Deirdre," he ground out. At least now she spoke normally. The wind whirled in his ears. Her horse was responding to something, either a smell or sound or to its own rider's agitation. It continued to stamp its feet, dancing in place. He was about to ask "who" again when her next words struck him.

"They'll kill us," she said, tenacity awakening in her voice. "Cold death..." Her outreached hand hung in the air, as if reaching for something within the fog. She returned a clenched fist to her head and moaned. "They're coming!"

Deirdre and her horse were clearly spooked. Alasdair kicked his heels into his horse. "Make haste!" He rode around a bend and spotted a gentle slope to a rocky scarp. Good enough. "This way!" They were barely hidden behind the scarp when he heard the approaching horses.

"Get that beast under control!" Alasdair breathed hotly at Crystoll, who dismounted.

"Please dismount," Crystoll whispered to Deirdre. Her fingers were tight on the reins, knuckles white. "My lady, come down!"

She slid from her horse and collapsed upon the ground. "By the heavens! Lord, white and cold, so cold."

Alasdair unsheathed his broadsword.

Crystoll pulled out his crossbow, loaded an arrow, and aimed it at the road. All three grew quiet as the riders rounded the bend on the path. Alasdair was grateful for the bellowing wind that swept the shoreline. He risked a peek around the scarp, praying that their horses had left minimal hoof prints on the trail.

Men rode by in a distortion of color. It was hard to make them out through the fog. The lead horse was jet black, its rider with matching hair and bright burgundy jacket. Several men rode with him. Alasdair pressed against the cold, unforgiving rock, closing his eyes and suppressing the urge to run from his hiding place to slaughter the baron.

Damn the man. He had found him.

The baron couldn't possibly have discerned Thomas's location on Uist! Moray would have never given up such information under the most brutal of torture. Alasdair clenched the hilt of his sword harder. Moments passed, and quiet returned. The men had rode on, unaware of their presence.

Alasdair finally released his breath. "What in God's name was that about?" He glared at Deirdre.

With her head hung low, she stared toward the sea.

Crystoll still aimed his crossbow at the empty path. "How many men did you see? I saw maybe four?"

Alasdair couldn't afford to raise more suspicion about himself. "Aye, four or five riders. Perhaps they're English? It was too foggy to see." Admittedly, that was a lie.

"English? They've no posts on Skye." Crystoll lowered his crossbow and wiped sweat from his face on his sleeve.

Alasdair feigned ignorance. He directed his question to Deirdre. "Would the MacDougalls come seeking revenge?"

She didn't answer, seemingly frozen with pain or fear.

"MacDougalls? Why would they be here and seeking revenge?" Crystoll raised an eyebrow. "Besides, those men didn't look like any MacDougall I know. Why would the English be here?" he repeated.

"We had a confrontation with two MacDougalls near Ardelve. They tried to steal from us."

"What?" Crystoll began to pace, resting his crossbow on his shoulder in readiness. He kept returning his look to the quiet path.

"It's of no importance."

"No importance?" Crystoll knelt beside Deirdre and set his bow down. "My lady, we ought to return home." He lowered his voice, but Alasdair still heard him. "The MacDougalls...my lady, we should tell your father."

Deirdre snapped alert. "No."

"Deirdre, he's right. You should return home with him," Alasdair said, disheartened by his own words.

She shook her head. "No."

"But—" both men began.

"Crystoll, you may return home, but I am going to Uist." Her words could not disguise the troubled look in her eyes.

Alasdair voiced reason. "It would be wise to keep our distance from them. None of us like the English, and I believe your laird shares the same regard about King Edward."

Sharp and dubious eyes stared at Alasdair, but Crystoll nodded. "Aye."

Alasdair tried once more. "You should return home with Crystoll, Deirdre."

"No! I am coming with you." Fire burned in her eyes.

Alasdair shrugged. A part, albeit a selfish part, was happy she chose to come with him. "We need to ride through the Cuillin then."

Crystoll attached his crossbow to his satchel. "We're unfamiliar with the way."

"We can backtrack and circle round the mountains from the south and take the west coast instead," Alasdair said, strategizing aloud.

Crystoll appeared to ponder it. Deirdre agreed for him. "Aye."

"Were those men after you?" Crystoll spoke in a breath of challenge.

Alasdair tightened his lips and clenched his jaw. "I'm offended you would suggest such a thing."

"Sir Stirrat, if I find that you are not the man of honor you claim to be, then God help me..."

Alasdair ignored him. "Deirdre, what in blazes happened back there?"

"Mmphmm, not now, Aleck," she said, already mounting her horse. "I'm not staying here tonight."

Once they were safely camped for the night, he would ask her again. Her behavior had not just been odd, it had scared him as well.

Crystoll shared a look of misgiving with him.

They both mounted their steeds. The decision had been made.

Deirdre rode in a daze. Returning to Broadford would have aroused suspicion among the merchants and locals. Instead, they veered off onto a secondary path that went west, north of the coastal wash they had crossed earlier in the day.

She couldn't shake the feeling of foreboding that intensified within her. The lifeblood she had felt on the coastal trail from one of the men in the English patrol party was more than disturbing. It was frightening. A lifeblood unlike anything she had ever felt before, it had pierced her with a numbing death. Whereas Aleck's lifeblood breathed heat and life, this other one cast only cold, white death. Through the years, she had felt the unscrupulous thoughts of many other men, especially those of nobles seeking an alliance with her father. The MacDougall sentry in Ardelve had fallen into that dark realm as well. But, by the heavens, *this* had been different. His energy went beyond dark. It radiated from a black soul so depraved and evil that she prayed she would never encounter it again.

The farther away they got from that energy, the better she felt.

A few hours later, they rode into a village on the western edge of the Black Cuillin.

Crystoll plopped several coins into the hand of an older woman who had coaxed her husband, of similarly ripening age, to disclose the directions of a pass through the Cuillin.

"Be wary of the Sith," the older woman advised.

"The Sith?" Aleck asked, dark eyebrows slanted into a frown.

"*Themselves*," the woman said, drawing out the word.

Aleck's face was blank.

The woman *tsked* at him, her look impatient with Aleck's apparent lack of understanding. "The faeries...the Sith," she said, drawing the word out. "Through that pass. That's why nae a person ventures there," she said, shaking her head. She focused her cloudy eyes upon Deirdre. "Ye see, 'tis the souls of the *Lochlanach* that roam the dark crags. Those crags, ye call them the Cuillin, used to shine white as the moon when I was a wee lass, aye, they did."

"Aye." Her husband bobbed his head vehemently.

"Then the *Lochlanach* came and used them as pillars of sacrifice, leavin' their blackened souls behind. They're the Devil's stones."

"Aye," her husband agreed again. "They're drawn to light, so dinna leave a fire glowing at yer camp."

The woman's loose gray hair bounced with a nod of her head. "Aye! Do ye hiv any bells?" she asked, laying a bony hand upon Deirdre's wrist.

Despite the woman's age, Deirdre felt a warm lifeblood flow from her. "I'm afraid not."

"Weel, they hiv blades," the man said.

"Aye, blades," the woman echoed.

"Keep yer dirks close. They're afrait of the iron in 'em." He squinted through gray eyes.

"Och, that's right! The iron. Keep them close," the old woman repeated, tapping Deirdre's hand. She then pulled Deirdre aside. "That dark one, there," she said, pointing to Aleck. "Keep close to 'im. He'll protect ye. Here, take these, to stave *themselves* off as well." She shoved a kerchief full of bannocks into Deirdre's hands. "Dinna eat them!"

Deirdre and her downcast escorts inclined their heads in polite gratitude and set out, all skeptical of the warnings, attributing them to old folklore.

Deirdre grew more guarded, regretting their change in direction. She could understand why the locals were superstitious. A chill filled her core as evening began to cast somber, peculiar shadows among the jagged gravestone-like rocks and heather moorland.

Hours later, they reached another impasse as the sky began to darken. Crystoll and Aleck spoke heatedly in front of her.

"We should make camp here. It's getting late," Crystoll advised.

"We're not far enough inland yet," Aleck countered.

Deirdre made the decision for them. She dismounted and guided her horse to a patch of grass. It nibbled, happy to rest. She pulled the bannocks from her skirt's pocket and contemplated eating one but thought otherwise and rewrapped them.

Aleck dismounted and heaved an exaggerated breath. "No fires?"

Crystoll mumbled under his breath. Ever since the near encounter with the English on the other road, his lifeblood flared with discontent. "I'll locate wood. The trees are sparse. We need to stay out of sight. Perhaps over there," he said, pointing to a small grove of ash and birch trees.

Aleck approached Deirdre from behind. "Are you well?"

"Must you always ask after my wellbeing?"

Spinning her around, he rested his hands firmly on her hips, intimate in gesture, but also preventing her from moving away. "Why should I not? What was that madness all about?"

She lowered her eyes; she couldn't avoid his questions anymore, not now that they were safely away from the English patrol. She had plenty of time to come up with a lie, but she had found nothing suitable. "'Twas my horse. It was startled by something."

He lifted her chin with a hand. A reproachful look glared down at her. She was shocked by his bluntness. "Your horse? Do you believe me to be a fool, Deirdre?"

"I had a headache," she added.

A scowl settled on his features. "You can be honest with me, Deirdre. How did you know those men were behind us?"

His eyes didn't leave hers, and she found herself shuffling her feet, wanting to pull herself from his boiling gaze.

"How did you know those men were on the road?" he asked again, raising his voice.

She crossed her arms and tore her chin from his hand. "Why divert our trip in an opposite direction, and a difficult one at that? The English wouldn't bother with us—with me, or Crystoll. Unless we were hiding something," she accused. She shuddered in remembrance of the riders.

He shrugged. "The English don't like any Scot. It is wise we avoid them."

She grew bold. "Why? We are no threat."

He was unmoved by her persistence. "Do you want to deal with the English, who shouldn't be here on Skye, at the dawn of a revolution? For a woman well acquainted with politics, I would expect you to agree."

She wasn't sure if that was a compliment or not. "I don't understand why they would be here. There are no English garrisons on Skye."

"Aye."

"They should be no concern of ours," she said through gritted teeth.

He was silent.

At least his questions had stopped. She had evaded them for now. What was she supposed to say? She was not a witch. Not many would believe her. A devastating hell would rain down on her father if the rumors of witchcraft spread beyond their village. He would be ruined.

She spoke slowly, trying once more with him. "King John is in prison. The Claimants, I've been told, all reside near Edinburgh. Nobody is here stirring up trouble for this bloody Cause."

"How do you know for certain? Your father himself admitted his position in the Cause. There are supporters everywhere."

She flung her hands out. "Just *tell* me what it is you know, Aleck."

He countered, "Only if you tell me how you knew they were near...that they would kill us."

Her fingertips grew numb and she wrapped herself in a hug. She couldn't tell him about her gift. She was a curse on her family and clan. "No."

"Then we are at a stalemate."

She turned.

He reached for her arm. "Deirdre..."

"Unhand me!" she shouted, despite his soft tone. Tears, like frozen raindrops on her lids, threatened to fall. The gloom settled in her bones as a strong wind whipped through the maze of pointed crags.

Aleck's voice was low, uncompromising, but gentle. "Please, Deirdre." He stepped closer, hovering over her, his hands firm on her shoulders.

She ripped herself from his grip.

Crystoll emerged from behind a tall, slender crag. He chuntered as she bumped into him, causing him to drop a few branches and tinder. "What the de'il?"

Rushing past him, she allowed the hurt to unravel her. She fled down the hill as Aleck and Crystoll argued behind her, their words lost on the howling wind. Her boot caught between two rocks, she stumbled, and settled where her body found the ground, neatly tucked against another large granite slab.

To her surprise, a few moments later, it was Crystoll who came to check on her, not Aleck. He sat beside her.

She had since stopped crying, but her pulse was fitful. She blew a breath out and let Crystoll's amber lifeblood relax her. Despite it, she felt his troubled emotions and knew what he was going to say before the words left his lips.

"My lady, I think we should return home."

"I can't, not yet."

"Are you ill, my lady?"

"Nay. 'Tis the ride, and...everything," she said in a choked whisper.

"My laird doesn't tell me everything, not how he used to confide in—" He stopped himself from saying her dead husband's name. "—in my predecessor. He trusts me, my lady, and he..." He paused and scratched his forehead.

"What is it, Crystoll?"

"I am to protect you, my lady..." He looked over his shoulder. Deirdre followed his gaze. Aleck led their horses to the grove of trees. "...from *all* dangers. Perhaps we should part ways with Sir Stirrat."

She rose. "Thank you, Crystoll. You've always been kind, but I shall see my aunt, and then we may return home."

"Then may I suggest we proceed without him?"

"No, I think we should stay together. With those English about, we're safer with him." English or not, she did not want to see those riders again. She shivered; the icy lifeblood still sickened her.

"As you request it, my lady."

Exhausted, she forced herself to join Aleck at the camp. The darkness of night took over in the setting sky, and a heaviness found residence within her. Aleck preoccupied himself with a fire and preparing the salted fish he had acquired in Broadford. He hardly gave her a glance when she sat across from him.

Perhaps Crystoll was right. They should part ways with Aleck. However, there was something about him, something that stirred her, scared her, but also aroused her. As irrational as it sounded, she felt protected when with him.

Alasdair refused to sleep. The strangeness of Skye, filled with dancing shadows and random sea bird calls, was enough to make the sanest man turn mad. Of course, the mood of their camp was not the only thing keeping him on watch. The baron's proximity had him glancing at every shadow, sitting upright with every sound. He also regretted his quarrel with Deirdre.

However, it was justified! First, she had seen Crystoll from afar before it was humanly possible. He dismissed that as coincidence or hope or perhaps she had known he was going to come all along. The second time though—it was as if she *had known* the baron was behind them. Not to mention those strange words she spoke. They were burned in his memory. He didn't travel with parchment or quill, but he had a good recall of things he heard.

He couldn't explain it. God, she baffled him.

Had he kept on his way and not ventured to Dornie, he would have been to Uist by now, with the vital information placed safely in Thomas Comrie's hands. Instead, here he was.

He touched his thigh, the injury from Edmund's arrow still tender. Curse it all! He sorely wished he had never met Deirdre MacCoinneach.

Muffling a groan, he tossed a rock into the dying fire. Nay, by God's hands, that wasn't his wish at all. Besides, in his condition and lacking coin, he would not have gotten this far without the money and horse from Laird MacCoinneach, by way of Crystoll.

Perhaps the time had come for him to slip away from Deirdre. She had Crystoll now, after all.

Christ, he couldn't do that. Not with the baron so close. The baron executed unbridled atrocities like no other. He would not let her out of his sight.

Crystoll's usual soft-spoken voice intruded upon his thoughts. "I can stay watch, Sir Stirrat. You can sleep."

"You know bloody well you can call me Aleck," Alasdair grumbled, his eyes falling upon Deirdre. She slept, albeit restlessly.

"I'd rather not."

"Do as you wish."

Though Alasdair was not pleased that he had to prove himself to him, he respected Crystoll. Although outwardly reserved, Crystoll was also a man of integrity and loyalty and would honor his laird's wishes, even if it came down to sacrificing his own life. Friction between them or not, Alasdair was grateful to have the soldier by his side.

Alasdair was ready for answers, and Crystoll was the only person left to ask. "Did you hear the horses when we were on the sea path, Crystoll?"

"Not until they were upon us."

Although he couldn't see Crystoll's expression in the darkness, Alasdair heard the detachment in his frosty voice.

"Deirdre heard something, though?"

"No."

"Then how did she know about the English patrol?" Alasdair controlled his disposition. God, and what she said. Those words. And that they would kill them. How could she know that?

Silence.

Very well. He would play another card—disclosure. Well, not complete disclosure. "My efforts take me to Uist. What I haven't told you is *what* that work entails."

Crystoll straightened but kept his gaze on the low burning embers that popped as the last limb succumbed to the flames. "Trade."

Alasdair took a deep breath. Christ, was he really doing this? His argument with Deirdre had convinced him that it was time to share a little more. "You and your laird are well aware of the contenders and the Cause." Not waiting for a response, he continued, "For Scotland to prevail against King Edward, we need a substantial force. What I do will help the Cause." He paused for emphasis, then added, "...regardless of the Claimant."

Crystoll turned to him. "And?"

"I relay information to a person of importance on Uist at Laird MacRuaidhri's keep. Edward's attacks in the south will not end. You and I are not fools. With men fighting for rights to the crown and John weakened and in prison, war and blood will be spilled everywhere, including the Highlands."

Crystoll seemed unimpressed. "Who has sent you on this charge?"

"Does it matter? A man of worth and connection. Scotland will triumph."

"Are the English looking for you?"

"King Edward knows nothing of me," he lied.

"Laird MacRuaidhri is, er, *was*, involved in this arrangement?"

"At some point, we'll all be asked to endorse a Claimant, won't we?" Alasdair said with a shrug. "Either that, or side with England."

Crystoll asked nothing else, although Alasdair suspected he had more questions.

"I advise you not to tell Deirdre. She's far from home, and I don't want to see her worry."

"Aye," Crystoll agreed with hesitation. "However, if she asks me, I'll not lie to her. She is my laird's daughter..." He whispered, "...and she's not like most ladies."

"I know." Alasdair stared at the hypnotic flames, feeling a shred of peace at unburdening himself with some of the truth. By God, there was more. "Now you."

"I've nothing to hide."

"Don't play the fool, Crystoll. That's not what I meant." He picked up a twig, poked at the fire, then loosely gestured to Deirdre with it. "What was she saying back there? It sounded foreign." *And familiar*, he thought.

Crystoll shrugged. "Maybe Norse?"

"She's never been to the isles and the Norse culture has vanished, along with its language. At least that's what I was told. Is she learned of the language?"

Light from the fire flickered in Crystoll's stare, illuminating his brown eyes with unnerving glints of yellow and orange. "How familiar are you with the isles and their..." He paused, scratched his nose, and continued, "...lore?"

"Enough." Alasdair suppressed a groan. Not him, too.

"The isles' people have special powers."

"You sound as daft as that old couple and their talk of the faeries." *Or Moreen*, he thought, though he didn't voice that opinion. He groused, "Highlanders and their superstitions." A chill settled within him. Highlanders weren't the only ones who participated in irrational hunts and feared the unknown.

"Deirdre's mother came from Uist, descended from the Norse."

"So?"

"The people of her mother's family are rumored to have had *gifts*."

"Gifts?" Alasdair saw what he implied. "Are you saying she is a witch?" He could hardly say the word. With it came the flashes of memory: his mother's screams, the burning flames upon his skin. "My friends of Uist have no mystical powers."

"They're not descended from the Norse. Nay, Deirdre is *special*, born of the Ancients."

"What in blazes do you mean?"

A sliver of a smile cracked on Crystoll's tired face.

He closed his eyes and said no more.

CHAPTER SEVEN

They set out again in silence through the gray daybreak, the sun still hidden behind the craggy spires of the Cuillin.

Alasdair regarded Deirdre as she took the rear of their riding party. He had muddled things with her. He was a hypocrite to judge her for her secrets. Perhaps once they reached Port nan Long her wall would come down, he could kiss her more thoroughly than he ever had, and she would open up to him in more ways than one. He shifted in his saddle. That was a thought best left to dreams.

He slowed his horse to a walk beside Deirdre. She gave him a curt look. "Forgive me, Deirdre." It was all he could say.

"I'm sorry you ever found me by that loch."

He hadn't expected that. "Bleeding Christ, Deirdre. I didn't come to Eilean Donan seeking an alliance or marriage, but—but…" He refused to lash out at her, and he was already falling over his apology.

Her silence said more than her words could have conveyed.

Alasdair leaned in, aware that Crystoll was not too far ahead of them and probably heard their discussion. He whispered, "I didn't expect to meet you."

"I'm sorry to have disappointed you."

Alasdair remained steadfast. "I want to help you."

"Or help yourself. Glen Shiel is an enticing seat for any noble."

"Deirdre, not this again—"

"If you want an alliance with my father, might you seek out my sister Caite instead?" She rubbed her temple, uneasy. She gave a slight moan.

"Is it your head?"

"Why do you care?" she snapped. Her horse became restless.

"I don't seek a marriage alliance, Deirdre. Your father may wish it, but it was never my intention. What must I do to convince you of such?"

She stared at him, blue eyes piercing. Sweat beaded on her brow. Her hair whipped into her face, and she shoved it behind her ear with an exaggerated sigh. By the saints, she was striking when she was angry. She seemed more than just angry though. He looked quickly behind him. Nothing was amiss. Was it her horse again?

He drew his horse right beside hers as they came around a blind bend, where the trail narrowed among the trees. He grabbed her hand. "Give me a chance to earn your trust, love."

The word slipped over his tongue before he could take it back. His mother had always said the same endearment to him. He had meant it in highest regard, but it felt different saying it this time. He'd used the phrase on a lass or two in his younger years, but he never used it for more than mild flirtation.

"Aleck, I think we need to—" Deirdre began, shaking, her face turning pallid.

Crystoll hollered. "Bloody hell!" His horse reared up so suddenly he was tossed.

Deirdre's horse began to dance and snort.

What now? Alasdair looked ahead of them. His own curse was cut short.

The baron and his men stood a few horse lengths in front of Crystoll. They drew their swords.

It all happened in a blur of commotion.

Deirdre moaned and clutched her head, sliding to the side.

Alasdair grabbed her by the arm before she fell. God, not now. What was the matter with her? "Stay up, Deirdre!"

He tore her hands from her head, shoved the reins into them, and shouted, "Go back! Ride hard!" He slapped her horse's hide. Her horse reared, front legs coming off the ground. For once, she did as told, getting her horse under control and turning it around.

He unsheathed his sword and rode straight for the baron and his men. God's fury, they had waited for them! They had caught them on a blind bend, unsuspecting. How had they gotten in front of them? Blazes, he had not seen the signs, the dolt. He had been distracted as he begged Deirdre's forgiveness.

Somehow, Crystoll rose, unscathed, and drew his sword as well. His horse ran off down the path ahead of them. Carney, who Alasdair recognized immediately, dismounted and charged Crystoll. Alasdair knew that the baron's fat soldier was no match for Crystoll.

Ronat, a despicable creature whom Alasdair was surprised to see alive after his last encounter with him, galloped past him down the path toward Deirdre. Alasdair prayed Deirdre could outride him—or hide. If the baron was the devil, then Ronat was his right hand, a cut-throat man who would do anything the situation called for.

Two other soldiers, as well as the baron, rushed Alasdair. He lunged and dodged as metal clanged. He was unhorsed, despite his best efforts. Fighting side by side with Crystoll, he countered and thrusted. He knocked one of the men down.

Carney and Crystoll's fight distanced from the group, leaving Alasdair to contend with the baron and another soldier. "Give it up!" the baron barked. Despite his age, he was a virile fighter, and Alasdair's stamina waned as he fought the two men.

The baron moved just in time to the side, deflecting Alasdair's strike. He countered, grazing Alasdair's shoulder. Pain tore down his arm to the hand holding the sword's hilt. He rolled to the side, shoved the soldier, and made a last attempt at the baron. With all his force, he knocked the sword from the baron's hand. He stood above him, the tip of his blade resting on his chest.

"Do it and she dies," Agmus said through gritted teeth.

Alasdair wiped sweat from his brow. He looked up to see Ronat approaching, Deirdre in his grasp. He held a dagger to her throat.

Damn it all to hell. "Release her!"

The baron cackled.

Pure menace danced in Ronat's face. He tightened his hold upon Deirdre and she whimpered.

Alasdair dropped his sword. He was no match for Ronat's ruthlessness. He would slit her throat then and there.

"No!" Deirdre cried as she squirmed in Ronat's arms, but he pulled her closer.

The two fallen, but still breathing, soldiers rose and restrained Alasdair.

A moment later, Carney returned with Crystoll in tow. "What do I do with him?"

Alasdair was dumbfounded. Crystoll should have had the upper hand against the slow-moving brute Carney.

"Bind him, over there," the baron ordered, pointing to a tree across the path. Carney did as told. He tossed Crystoll's crossbow into nearby bushes. Crystoll spat at Carney, who responded with a punch.

"Ye certain I can't kill him?"

"Nay, he can watch his friend die." The baron turned to Alasdair. "I'm disappointed in you, Ali."

"I'm not the disappointment to his country," Alasdair said.

The baron gestured to his two soldiers. They pulled Alasdair over to a tree across from Crystoll. "No, that tree," the baron ordered, pointing toward a slender birch. The bark peeled and the tree was dry and mostly dead, its innards exposed and brittle. They bound his hands behind the trunk, nearly twisting his shoulders out of the sockets. They then collected limbs, twigs, and dried brush and gathered it at the base of the birch. Carney approached, opened a small vial, and dumped a black oily substance on the placed tinder.

Alasdair clenched his teeth so hard his jaw ached. The devil was going to burn him? He nearly laughed at the cowardliness. The baron was never one to do his own dirty deeds after all. Why run him through when he could make him die slower, for all to see? "May you burn in hell, Baron."

"No, that will be you."

At least the soldiers had left Crystoll attached to a tree with no intention of killing him...yet. Cowards. They were all despicable.

Agmus turned to the soldiers. "Search his things." They got Alasdair's restless horse under control and riffled through the satchel on the saddle. They pulled out the wax-sealed rolled parchment.

Alasdair ground out, "You have what you wanted. Unhand her."

"On the contrary, Ali. I have exactly what I want." The baron approached Deirdre and ran a finger down her shoulder. Deirdre outwardly quivered.

"Light it."

Carney did as told, a snide smile spreading across his face as he lit the tinder behind Alasdair.

"No!" Deirdre screeched, but Ronat was rough with her, pulling her even closer, squeezing her against him.

"Hush, lassie. I'll take good care of ye."

She fought against him, but it was futile. Her swats were like a kitten against a boar.

The group then mounted their horses. "Wait!" Agmus said to one of the soldiers. "You."

One of the two soldiers halted in his mounting, drew his leg back down, and stared at the baron with a timid look. "Aye, Baron?" his youthful voice squeaked. "You stay. Make sure that he dies," he said, pointing toward Alasdair. "And when he's dead, run this man through." He moved his finger to Crystoll. Agmus's tone lacked question. "Slowly."

The soldier drew his sword in response. "Aye, Baron."

"And kill the horses."

Agmus kicked his feet into his horse. He called over his shoulder. "Meet us at the set point." With that, he was gone.

Deirdre rode with Ronat. All Alasdair could do was apologize to her with his eyes as they disappeared down the path in the direction of the mainland. His hope fizzled, but at least Agmus didn't wait around to watch him die. For the baron's overconfidence, Alasdair was grateful. Or perhaps he still retained a sliver of decency to not watch him die. No, it wasn't that. Alasdair knew him too well. The baron was a coward who had others do his bidding.

Alasdair began to test his bindings as soon as the riders were out of sight.

He shared a look with Crystoll. They still had the soldier to contend with. Sweat beaded on the man's forehead as he approached Alasdair's horse, his sword drawn. Crystoll released a low guttural sound, one usually used to summon a horse, except it had the opposite effect. The two horses that had remained by them whinnied, stamped their hooves, and began to trot down the path.

"Och!" The soldier chased after them. "Ye wild beasties!" He whistled for them to stop.

Crystoll continued with his sound, drawing the horses farther away. He had quite the skill for horse persuasion, Alasdair thought.

With the man distracted for the moment, Alasdair tried again. Pain lanced his shoulders as he slowly twisted his body upright and to a half standing position. The fire had already lit well enough that the logs and dry tinder were catching, hissing, and crackling. The heat licked at his boot heels.

Crystoll also fought with his bindings. "Can you get free?"

Alasdair puffed a breath as he wriggled. Fire scorched the tree, ever closer to his chafed wrists. "No. You?" He swept a look down the path. The man had caught up with one of the horses but hesitated with his order. Instead, he grabbed its reins and led it back to them.

"Trying. I've a small dagger, hidden," Crystoll said, winded. He knelt, his legs straddling the tree. Twisting his torso, he reached with his fingers for his boot and the knife hidden within it. "Argh!" His face grew red with effort. "Got it!"

"Hurry!" Alasdair groaned, biting his lip. The flames were hot, eating the dried birch. He pushed his tied ankles out in front of him, arched his back against the tree, and stood as far from the flames as possible.

Crystoll cut himself free. He hurried to Alasdair and cut him loose. Alasdair stepped away and leaned over, wheezing.

The soldier ran toward them. "Och, you! Stop!"

He was no match for Crystoll, who dodged the broadsword swings, jumped to the side, and then thrust his small dagger into the man's side. The man yelped, dropped his sword, and fell to the ground, his hand cupping the wound.

Alasdair fought to get his pulse under control and his breathing steady.

Crystoll kicked dirt onto the flames. Dry birch bark crackled and hissed as fire consumed it. He bent over and dampened the fire with large handfuls of dirt.

"Are you going to tell me what in God's name that was about?" Crystoll wiped sweat from his brow and ground his words. "By cravens, you're not being chased just like the sky is not blue! They were *not* English! Those were Scots! We still may be able to catch up with them." He was already making for the horse as he spat curses under his breath. He got the frightened horse under control and whistled for the other one, which immediately returned.

"I told you how sensitive my mission was." Alasdair grabbed his reins.

"That man was a Scottish baron!" Crystoll shook his head as he collected his crossbow from a gorse bush. "What did he take? That parchment?"

"It doesn't matter. We need to help Deirdre."

"God's teeth, Aleck. It does matter. Who is he, and why is he after you?" Crystoll mounted his horse.

"I'll explain on the way." He clicked his tongue and guided the horse down the path. They passed Deirdre's horse, which danced about, quite vocal about its nervousness.

"Wait!" Crystoll seized the flailing reins.

"Leave it. It will slow us down." Alasdair grabbed the sack of Deirdre's clothes and left the heavier satchel, which seemed to be filled with books of some sort, on her horse.

"Do you know where they're going?" Dirt smudged Crystoll's furrowed brow.

Alasdair gritted his teeth. "I've an idea. We're going to need to head them off somewhere. How good are you with that crossbow?"

"Probably better than you."

"Good. We're going to need it."

The path ahead was rocky, narrow, and shrouded with trees. He tried to open to a full gallop, but his horse resisted and he settled for a cantor with Crystoll right behind him. Eventually, the path opened back up, and they allowed their horses to a full gallop.

Alasdair prayed that he wouldn't be too late. Loss of Robert Bruce's letter and plans was a calamity. Without them, he couldn't convince the men on Uist to finish the navy on his word alone. He needed those plans. He needed Bruce's seal and promise. Thank God the baron couldn't decipher the details of the navy's whereabouts. Only Thomas and the foreman had the key to the code, and they were safe on Uist.

Despite the importance of the mission, he found something else drove him on. He needed to save Deirdre from the clutches of the devil himself.

Why didn't I see him? Why didn't I feel him?

Deirdre's mind raced with questions.

There was no doubting the fact that Aleck's blazing lifeblood had drowned out her ability to sense the baron's icy lifeblood until it was too late. Or perhaps it was her own emotions that had prevented it? Either way, she now rode in the saddle in front of this rank man, Ronat. She dared not ask where they were heading.

Oh, God, Aleck. A sob caught in her throat.

And Crystoll. It was all her fault. He was only following orders. Now they were both dead because of her.

Her captors were quiet. They weren't Englishmen. The baron spoke in Scots dialect, as did his men. What the hell was going on? She kept her eyes on their surroundings, praying that Aleck and Crystoll were still alive and would find her. The scent of burning wood was charred in her mind. But how could they be alive? Aleck had been left tied to a burning tree, and Crystoll equally tied and to be run through. She couldn't suppress the tears.

The man she rode with, Ronat, nudged her and spat over his shoulder. He leaned in closer, his breath rotten on her neck. "Dinna fret, lass. Ye've got us to keep ye company." He rested a hand on her upper thigh and squeezed it roughly. He pulled up her skirts enough so that he could slide his hand underneath on her bare thigh skin. Nausea rippled through her. She swatted his hand away, and pushed her dress down firmly.

He chuckled and retreated.

They rode for hours without rest. Sleep must have superseded her wariness, for she drifted off. Before she knew it, she was jolted awake when the men began arguing.

"We can't ride around."

"Then we cross it."

"It's too deep, and my horse carries two."

"It's getting dark, Baron Montgomerie. Shan't we make camp?"

"No! We cross. You take the lead, then Carney and I shall follow. Ronat, bring the rear," he ordered.

The long shadows of twilight stretched across the inlet that washed out the trail. As they entered the water, cold seeped through Deirdre's submerged boots. The water was deeper than it had been when they crossed yesterday. Much deeper. High tide greeted them in its full mightiness. She felt the subtle pull of the current as the water flowed out to sea, and their horse struggled against it.

By mid-cross, water was at the horse's belly. The water was black glass in the dimness. A thick fog curled and moved over it, more eerily than before. She shivered, not from the cold alone.

They rode for what seemed like forever, encircled by dark, slowly moving water. The horses sloshed and trudged. Deirdre calculated how soon they would reach Broadford and the harbor. She spoke, boldly. "Where are we going?"

"To the mainland."

"Why did the baron take me?"

"Ne'r ye mind. Quiet yerself." Ronat huffed.

"I've no riches nor any doings with the uprisings in the south. Please release me."

"Shut your mouth!" He struggled against the current as the water got deeper.

Her heart raced with the reality of what was happening. The baron, whoever he was, wanted something from Aleck. She had known it all along! The image of him tied to the tree, provocative hate shining in his face as he spoke to the baron, was branded in her memory.

Then, they left him there...to burn.

And oh heavens, the baron. He was a vile man. He was aged, with graying black hair and dark blue eyes. His lifeblood was the icy chill she had felt on the coastline north of Broadford. He radiated a white and rancorous death. Her head ached when she thought of it. She pushed it aside with all her might. Thankfully, he was at the lead of their riding party, and she was able to dampen his energy with the coldness of the surrounding water.

She tried to locate Aleck with her senses. Was he alive? God, she was far from him. She doubted she could feel his energy, but she had to try.

With deep breaths, she closed her eyes, slowed her pulse, and focused on Aleck's lifeblood.

Nothing.

She tried again.

A long moment passed, then suddenly heat struck her. Fiery red heat.

He was alive. He was near.

Yet she saw only blackness around her.

Suddenly, one of the horses ahead screamed. Disorder broke out, and the men hollered. Their horses splashed loudly, skittish. Before she could react, Deirdre lost her grip on the horse's neck and slipped off into the water while her captor fought to control the horse.

"In the trees! Carney, get your bow!" the baron yelled.

Cold hit Deirdre with full force. She immediately found her footing on the rocky floor. She stood upright. The water was chest-high and her clothes weighed her down. Her captor and horse disappeared, swallowed by darkness and commotion. Shouts, splashing, and neighs.

"Find her!"

Now was her chance. Which way?

A hand grabbed her ankle. She squelched a scream and instinctively took a deep, soul-drenching breath as she was pulled under. She clamped her eyes shut to prevent the sting of the saltwater. She fought the grip upon her, but it was strong. Twisting in the water, she punched out at anything. A hand found her cheek, fumbled, and then came back to it. Heat seared into her skin. Another hand found her hand and clasped it. It squeezed. Red hot fire.

It was Aleck. His soul breathed life into her with a blazing heat she had become familiar with. Her feet hit the rocky bottom and she tried to stand, but he held her below the surface. He kicked and pulled her farther out of the inlet to deeper water. She understood.

They stopped again, and he held her close. They sat under the water for what seemed an eternity. Her lungs burned, and her ears rang with the muffled sounds above. She regretted not inhaling deeper. Stars danced in her shut eyelids. After holding on as long as she could, she pushed up, and his hand pulled away. She broke the surface and drank in the cold evening air with a hefty swallow.

Aleck surfaced next to her. He spoke simultaneously as he breathed in. "We...must...swim out farther."

She swam with him into deeper water, every stroke heavier than the next. They reached a point where she couldn't feel the bottom anymore. "Aleck, I-I'm cold. What are we doing?"

Her layers of gown and kirtle and boots weighed her down as if she were carrying stones.

"Come."

They swam farther. She no longer heard sounds. Only her heart, fighting to pump warm blood through her body, drummed in her ears. "Almost there," Aleck said. Her muscles quickly grew fatigued.

The water became shallow again, and through the dissipating fog, she saw the coastline. She suspected that they had swum north. They dragged themselves out and shivers consumed her. "W-Where is C-Crystoll?"

"Safe."

Aleck took her hand, and they trudged along, her boots leaden.

"H-How are you alive?" she said, clinging to him with a hug once they reached a makeshift camp, both of them sopping and shivering.

He kissed her briefly and pushed her wet hair back over an ear. "I'm too hard to kill," he said, smiling. His lips were cold. "We need to get warm. The sun has set."

They reached a cluster of large pinnacles and wide boulders, shielding them from the evening wind. A collection of firewood sat next to Aleck's plaid and satchel. The remnants of a fire burned, almost snuffed. The few embers were enough for Aleck to relight it though. He got to work on the fire with his flint, some kindling, and fresh logs. His fingers fumbled. "You need to undress, Deirdre. Put the plaid on. I don't have your cloak. We need to warm you."

"They'll find us. They'll see the fire."

"No, there's a thick copse of trees, and these rocks will hide it. And Crystoll will continue to lead them south. If we don't undress and get under the plaid, we'll freeze."

Finally the tinder lit. He leaned down and blew on it to feed the fire. She pulled off her heavy, soaked boots. Then she undressed, her fingertips numb and shaking. She struggled with the laces up the front. Yanking on her sleeves, she pushed her gown down, followed by the kirtle beneath. In the end, she was left standing in her thin chemise pasted to her body. Aleck looked up. "All of it. The pl-plaid is there." He turned his gaze away to provide her some modesty.

She peeled off the chemise and wrapped the plaid around herself.

"Sit there." He pointed to a makeshift pile of grasses and leaves. "You don't want to lose heat to the ground."

Aleck rubbed his hands before the growing fire. He then knelt and stripped down to nothing. She sat as close as she could to the fire, her eyes locked on the flames and not on the naked man before her.

"We need to lie together. Share warmth," Aleck said.

Deirdre hesitated for a moment. His lifeblood had dimmed to a warm orange. He was losing strength. She opened the plaid and lay on the thick leafy bed he had made. "Come."

He curled behind her. In front, the fire began to thaw her skin, and from behind, Aleck's lifeblood grew warmer and radiated into her as they lay skin to skin. He breathed erratically upon her neck, and his shivers were like shockwaves. She had to keep him awake.

"How did you know you'd be able to find me here?"

"I didn't, but I suspected that the baron would take you to the mainland with haste. He wouldn't have gone around that inlet. Fording at this spot is the quickest route. Crystoll suggested it. We were fortunate it was high tide."

"How did you get here before us?"

She wiggled, pressing her body as close to his as she could. She yanked her thoughts from those less virtuous. He was still shivering.

"We rode our horses hard. With your horse carrying two, we knew your party would be slower than us. We doubled back through that copse on foot. Crystoll stayed there. He released a few arrows to distract them. I grabbed you in the water. Simple plan."

His smugness assured her that he was lucid. "Simple plan, och? And a fire and camp, too? How did you know I could swim or hold my breath under water?"

"Remember the loch, when we met? You told me you were an able swimmer and could hold your breath for a long time. I gambled on that."

She chuckled lightly. "Although my father didn't approve of it, I spent many summer days testing my limits under water as a girl. Of course he said a lady shouldn't do such a thing, so now I do it in secret."

He stroked her arm, sending gooseflesh rippling down it. "You were naked then, too." He kissed the back of her neck.

Her pulse quickened. She had hoped to avoid this discussion again. "I thought we were done with this, Aleck."

He was quiet as his hand fell upon her hip.

She distracted him with talk. It also kept her alert. "You're an impressive rider—and swimmer—for a trader. You've soldier's skills."

"My father saw me trained by some of the best." She remembered his gentleness with her wild mare Delilah. There was more to Aleck than he disclosed, although now was not the time to question him about the baron. That would have to wait until morning.

"There is a way to warm us." He laid his hand flat and caressed the round curvature of her hip down to her bottom. He then cupped her breast, and she let out a breath. "But only if you want it."

Her blood was pounding all right. Her nipple grew stiff as the gentle tip of his finger caressed it.

His hand left her breast and glided lower, tracing her belly in a slow circle. She trembled beneath him, unsure if it was from her body fighting to return to a normal temperature or from his touch. She nearly moaned aloud.

His entire body stiffened. She shifted and allowed him more access to her. His lips found their way to her shoulder, then her earlobe, and she didn't fight him. A tentative and light hand reached between her legs. She gasped and squeezed her eyes shut, the sensation overpowering everything else. He rubbed her so softly that it made her pant with an unheard of desire. Oh by heavens, she lacked the words to protest and lacked the will to stop him. It felt too good, and she gloried in his touch.

A flooding ache radiated from within her. She yielded to the burning sweetness that took over her body, and she quivered uncontrollably.

"Warmer?" he whispered in her ear.

"I-I, yes, we—you..." she stammered, her head spinning. His lifeblood glowed bright red again, and she was sure he was well warmed. She wanted to roll over and do so much more. Instead, he held her tight in his arms.

"Hush, love. Sleep." He kissed her neck, and she only took a few moments to drift off.

Alasdair awoke to a dead fire but a blazing woman in his arms. Every part of his body was stiff and tired. He slipped from beneath the plaid, escaping the cocoon their interlocked naked bodies had made. He pulled his dry clothes from his satchel and put them on as he watched Deirdre sleep.

Their clothes from last night were damp. He folded them and put them in a satchel. Their drying would have to wait. Thankfully, Deirdre had another kirtle and chemise in the satchel he had grabbed from her horse. She only had the one gown though. It would take some time to dry. He laid dry garments beside her. He regretted not having grabbed her horse, but there hadn't been a way to bring the animal along on their hasty ride to save her.

He debated whether to wake her. They had to meet Crystoll soon. He blew out a deep, pent-up breath. He was caught in a nightmare. The baron had his plans, signed by Bruce himself. What if he found a way to decipher them? Deirdre could have been hurt or worse. He was hopelessly delayed. Would there even be any workers left on Uist by the time he arrived?

He laid his head in his hands. They needed to hurry and leave no traces for the devil to find them. He knew all too well that Baron Montgomerie never left any loose ends. Certainly, he was dead set on killing them all now.

Alasdair knew why the baron had taken Deirdre—to hurt him. He had disclosed as much as he could to Crystoll on their ride to the tidal wash but skirted around the dangers imposed upon Deirdre's family. The baron didn't know who Deirdre was—yet—or who her father was. So long as Alasdair continued to run, the baron would follow *him*. Laird MacCoinneach was safe for now. Or so he hoped.

There was another thought that he couldn't dislodge. Crystoll's revelation echoed in Alasdair's memory. *Special.* Deirdre. Blazes, what did that mean? Between Moreen's explanation of the ridiculous curse, the local folks' superstitions, and Deirdre's reaction to the riders, Alasdair was going daft.

He continued to watch her sleep. She lay like an angel. How could she be linked to the unnatural? But what about his mother? She had been a woman of faith and still died, caught up in the lies of his father.

He felt wretched. Was he surrounded by a world of unexplained powers, or was it only the fear of the unknown that drove people to persecution of the innocent? Deirdre had a pure heart. She loved her family and valued simplicity. However, she hadn't been the most forthcoming when he questioned her.

This type of thinking was madness, and he wouldn't waste any more of his time on it. All that mattered now was getting her safely to Uist and getting himself to Thomas. With the baron this far north, the navy had to be readied soon.

Deirdre stirred. Her cheeks were rosy from sleep. Sleeping intimately with her last night had nearly uprooted his resolve. It had taken all his strength to not make love to her last night on the rocky shore.

She opened her eyes from beneath a mound of tangled dark hair.

"Good morning," he croaked, taken aback by the astounding blue-green beauty of her eyes.

She smiled.

Well, that was a good start, he thought.

He pointed. "Your clothes are there. The others need to dry."

He walked around the rocks to allow her privacy, but after last night, modesty was behind them. His fingers still vibrated from the feel of her soft skin beneath them. He cleared his throat and scanned the area while she dressed. They were on a small coastal outcrop with large black pinnacles, curved hills, and slabs of granite. He was amazed that he had not only been able to locate such a secluded spot, shielded a distance from the coastal trail, but that he'd also been able to find it whilst they had swum in the dark away from the flooded inlet. It had been a miracle.

Now it was time for another miracle. They were to meet Crystoll at the set meeting point and get as far away from the baron as possible. Crystoll had been adamant about returning to Glen Shiel with Deirdre, now more than ever.

Alasdair trudged back to their campsite. Deirdre was dressed and running her fingers through her knotty hair. "I'm afraid I've no cloak for you. It appears it was lost last night."

She spoke in a broken whisper. "Who was that man?"

He took her hand, grabbed the satchels, and led her through the hills and rocks toward the tree line. "Baron Montgomerie, a lowland noble with more power than he should have."

"He was after you?" For once she didn't confront him in a huff.

His guise was falling apart, and he was on the verge of telling her everything. Not yet. He needed to see her safe first. "Yes."

"Why?"

Deirdre wasn't ignorant, as he had already learned. "Trade is only part of my business in the isles." *Liar, it has nothing to do with trade.*

She lifted an eyebrow for him to continue.

"I have, or rather I *had*, important information to relay to Lady MacRuaidhri and her vassal. I'm but a messenger."

Another lie.

"Why does the baron want it?"

"It's important to the Cause. I'm afraid I can't say more, Deirdre. It's safer if I don't." He turned to her, his spirit weighed down.

"Why did he call you Ali?"

"I was acquainted with him a long time ago. He knew my father." *More lies.*

"He's a Scot."

"Even Scots can be turned for the right amount of power or money." That was enough explaining for today. He had said the same things to Crystoll, who was as unconvinced as Deirdre. "Crystoll wishes you to return to Dornie. I beseech you, please go with him." He couldn't find the words to tell her everything.

Her brows drew together. "Do you want me to go home?"

He took her hands in his. "It doesn't matter what I want."

"What about my father? Should he be wary of this baron?"

"No. Did the baron question you?"

She shook her head. "No. He never spoke to me."

Alasdair blew out a breath. "Then your family is safe." *For now*, he thought. *Lies, lies, lies.*

She swallowed, her face composed. "I'm going to Uist."

He looked at her sideways. "All right, but you'll need to convince Crystoll of that decision."

They continued in silence for a while, until Deirdre spoke again and looked around. "My horse? My other sack?"

"I'm sorry. The horse and other sack are gone. We couldn't burden the horses. All I could manage were your clothes. Was there something you needed in it?"

"No." Disappointment showed on her face.

Alasdair approached her and skimmed a hand down her shoulder. "What was it?"

Her eyes grew wet. "A book of my mother's."

"Perhaps it will turn up? We'll find the horse on the trail?" His false optimism did nothing to ease her.

"Perhaps," she repeated, face cast down.

Two days passed in a wearisome blur. They had secured a new horse for Deirdre, and by God's graces, they remained unnoticed as they rode along the wet and weathered coastline dotted with small villages and even smaller crofts. Along the way, Alasdair had formulated a plan with Crystoll. Although he argued a good case to return home, Crystoll had ultimately acquiesced to his lady's wishes and came along with them to Uist.

They drew upon a substantial coastal village, south of the MacLeod holdings on the western coast.

Alasdair gave Crystoll a sanctioning look. Crystoll assumed his rank and guided his horse behind him. It was time to implement the plan.

Alasdair pulled his assorted rings from his satchel and slipped them onto his fingers. The thick gold ring from his father always chafed his skin and seemed to weigh down more than his hand. Now dressed in the formal clothes that he had packed, with his hair slicked behind his ears, he appeared as his birthright.

He nodded once more to Crystoll, who agreed by blinking. Crystoll hung back beside Deirdre.

The sound of their horses drew a few curious people out from their cottages, while others remained hidden, cautiously observant from behind shuttered windows. They stopped at the first cottage, where an older woman sat on a stool out front, churning butter. She didn't look up from her work until Alasdair spoke. "I seek a village merchant."

She stared blankly.

He deepened his voice with authority. "A trader with the isles?"

Gray eyes and a flat-lipped face glared at him. She continued with her churning.

Alasdair splayed his hand out on his thigh, flaunting his rings. The woman still churned. He waved Crystoll forward. Crystoll brought forth the bag of coin. The slightly heavy, but rapidly shrinking, bag made an enticing jingling sound as he opened it, finally drawing the woman's attention. She rose and stepped forward and stuck out a calloused hand.

"Gorrie MacAuley lives yonder," she said, pointing toward a gathering of cottages, sheds, and a tavern north of them on the path. "He's the person ye seek."

Crystoll paid her a coin. A quiet dock alongside a lopsided woodshed welcomed them. The empty float rammed against a rock wall. A young lad ran across their path, chasing a stray sheep down a hill. Smoke saturated the dreary sky from the chimney which meant somebody was home in this equally dreary shack.

After two knocks with no answer, Alasdair opened the door. "Stay out here," he ordered Deirdre. She nodded.

An older, grubby man snored on a cot by the hearth. No one else was about. The room reeked of fish and body odor and Alasdair shared a look with Crystoll, who lifted a thin eyebrow and shrugged. With his hand hovering on the hilt of his sheathed sword, Alasdair poked the man in the ribs with a finger. "Gorrie?"

The man stirred, snorted, and rolled to his side. Alasdair poked him again. Nothing.

Crystoll took out the bag of coin and rattled it.

The man bolted upright and yawned, his breath pungent. Alasdair coughed and cleared his throat. "Gorrie?"

The man scratched his privates, closed his eyes, and cracked his neck. He then eyed the pouch. "Aye. Who asks?"

"Sir Stirrat of Lennox. I need passage to Uist on the morrow."

Gorrie licked his lips, rose, and hobbled over to a rickety table. There, an empty goblet sat beside an equally empty plate. He frowned when naught but a drop came out of his flask. "I don't leave for another week."

"My wife is ill. I must take her to the stones at once. There's a woman there who can help us," Alasdair said, hoping the superstitions of the folk in the region would work to his benefit. It had been Crystoll's idea, and after the strange behavior of the old couple who had explained the passage through the Cuillin, Alasdair was willing to use this guise.

Their explanation drew minimal interest from Gorrie, who proceeded in rifling through the jugs he had on a shelf. Not finding what he wanted, he frowned. "I've no shipment to take to Uist until next week." He glanced at Crystoll's pouch.

"We'll pay you handsomely if you can rouse your crew for departure on the morrow."

Crystoll stepped forward. He deposited two coins in Gorrie's hand. "An advance. You get the rest tomorrow when we leave." Alasdair removed his flask from his belt loop and handed the remainder of Moreen's ale to the merchant. He had been saving those last few drops.

Gorrie snatched it, drank, and then let out a belch.

Alasdair's hand danced on the sheath holding his sword, flaunting his jeweled rings. Gorrie's glazed over eyes were entranced.

Alasdair displayed his hand. "Ruby and gold. One of these would fetch a good price."

Gorrie groused, "I've no need for rings."

Alasdair stepped closer, lowering his voice to a firm, imposing tone. "Pluck out the ruby and sell it. Melt down the gold. It'll feed you for a year."

Gorrie didn't disagree. "Ye've got horses?"

"Aye, three. Just my vassal, wife, and I."

If Gorrie was suspicious, he didn't let on. "On the morrow," he agreed, scavenging another area of his cottage for a drink once he drained Alasdair's flask.

"On the morrow," Alasdair said with a nod as they left the cottage.

Deirdre paced outside. Alasdair smiled at her, and she returned it with her own. "On the morrow," he repeated to her.

CHAPTER EIGHT

The open sea.

Aboard a ship with drunk, reeking men.

Aboard a *rocking* ship with, drunk, reeking men.

And longer if the wind didn't cooperate and the ship was becalmed. Deirdre stood at the bow, attempting to alleviate her seasickness mingled with early pregnancy nausea.

A forceful gale hit the large cog ship, and it teetered in the undulating sea. Stowed below in a stall designed for smaller livestock, their horses neighed in protest. "We should've sold them," she said to Aleck. "That compartment is meant for sheep, not horses. They can barely stand."

He tottered over to her. "Probably, but they may be harder to come by on Uist."

"I suppose."

A booming laugh emerged from the men. Crystoll remained unaffected by the ship's motion and had already found himself in kinship with several of the crew. For a moment, Deirdre felt a pang of remorse, remembering how close Crystoll and Cortland had been. The sadness lingered as she thought of Cortland. Unlike with Gordon, her first arranged marriage, she had truly cared for Cortland. He had been a good man. She struggled with her conscience, coming to terms with the fact that her gift was somehow responsible for taking his life. And now she carried his bairn. She suppressed a groan. She prayed her aunt would have answers. Now her mother's book—the only thing she had of hers—was gone, too.

"Come with me. You're shivering." Aleck began to pull her from the deck rail.

"I am well."

"Deirdre, the men can hear your teeth chattering from the stern. It sways below, too, but it's warmer." Aleck flashed a white toothy grin. The bruising on his face from their altercation with the baron was now a nasty bluish-green.

"Besides, you need to rest," he urged, taking her by the elbow.

"All right, although you should, too." She'd lost count of how many injuries he had acquired since their first meeting. His arm, his leg, his nose, his other arm and God-knows what else from the baron's attack...

She allowed him to lead her to their quarters. They had left at midday, and it now drew upon sunset. The moderate warmth from the cloudy day had been overtaken by the chill of open water, western wind, and dimming light. Sleep sounded wonderful, although she doubted her queasy stomach would be more forgiving down below. At least it would be warmer.

They proceeded through the narrow passageway to a room at the stern. Her legs wobbled as she felt along the wall for support. The horses whinnied. Deirdre couldn't imagine their discomfort. The captain, Gorrie MacAuley, had a private cabin on the vessel. She wondered how much coin it had taken to not only barter passage on the ship but also to obtain such privileged accommodations as the captain's chamber.

"Sit," Aleck said.

She hesitated, crinkling her nose at the sight and smell of the scratchy blanket on the wide cot. She tried not to think about what creatures hid within it. She had journeyed aplenty with her father and Edmund, but never at sea. She tried to think of pleasantries. Mmphmm. It didn't help.

"It's not that bad, is it?" Aleck lit a candle on a table.

"To what do you refer? The tossing ship or the questionable odors that arise from it?" She gathered a smile.

He laughed. "Both, I guess."

"I'm sorry, Aleck."

He stopped in his lighting. "For what?"

"For disrupting your mission." She found herself frowning.

"Don't be. I should be the one apologizing." He softened his voice and sat beside her on the cot. It creaked with his weight. His shoulder touched hers, and she felt the spark of heat. He was like a hearth that never went out.

He took her hand. With a gentle fingertip, he traced each finger. It sent gooseflesh along her arm, and she retracted it.

"You're afraid of me."

"No."

"Did I hurt you?"

She swallowed, remembering their intimate night on the beach. "No. Your touch is..." She paused. He stared at her, his eyes dark in the shadows of the wooden room.

The air was stale and warm, and she leaned forward. She rested a hand on his unshaven chin, the stubble rough on her palm. She felt her muscles untangle instantly.

He placed a hand on the small of her back but didn't pull her forward. She felt empowered, yet vulnerable in his arms. Her growling stomach intruded upon their moment. Again.

"Always hungry, och?" He laughed. "I've meat and bread here." He rose, ducking as to not knock his head on the ceiling. Footsteps scraped above them as he handed her a plate.

The salted deer appeased her famished appetite. "Please eat, too."

He grinned. "I enjoy watching your lips move."

His arousing look sent a shudder through her. Their closeness in the dark room, the salty meat, and the swaying ship was a comfort beyond words. Her nausea slowly began to dissipate.

She finished eating, wanting to say more, but felt her eyelids grow heavy.

"You should try to rest." Aleck lifted the questionable blanket, took the plaid from his shoulders and laid it on the mattress. "I'm tired myself. I can sleep on deck." He motioned to leave.

She grabbed his elbow. "No, come rest with me."

It was an invitation. She pulled off her gown, so she wore just kirtle and chemise. Her heart hammered as she tucked herself within his arms, fitting against his contours, her back against his chest. At least they weren't naked, she thought, heat flushing her cheeks.

The sound of her heart quieted as she listened to his deep breathing. He stroked her arm and shoulder as he had before. This was the Aleck she enjoyed. Not the arrogant, overly confident noble who evaded her questions. Not the tense stranger from afar. Not the warrior who killed her MacDougall attacker and rescued her from the baron. No, it was the gentle man who radiated a soothing vibrant hue of rich lifeblood...the man who showed compassion in their intimate encounters, tapping into her soul with each touch. She felt his heartbeat fall into rhythm with hers, their breaths and beats intertwined.

Drunk with tranquility, she closed her eyes, hoping to dream of nothing.

Deirdre awoke in the middle of the night to a black void. She blinked several times to rouse her senses. The rocking jarred her back to her reality. Water lapped against the ship's hull in a recurrent song.

Slosh, rock, slosh.

Cold penetrated her bones, and despite the presence behind her and heavy arm over her midsection, she didn't feel Aleck's hue. She bolted upright. A blinding pain snared her as her head hit the low wooden ceiling which curved at a sharp angle beside the cot. She mumbled under her breath and felt the wound. Dizzy, she lay down.

He moaned beside her. "You all right?" he asked groggily.

"Mmmm. Aye." Color flashed before her eyes, but as she lay still, it faded and blackness returned.

He pulled her close to him, snugly positioning her bottom against his groin.

She twisted under him. "Aleck, I need to tell you something." Her movement had the opposite effect she had hoped for.

"Hmmm?" His lips fell upon her neck. He nuzzled against her, and his hand slipped down to her hip. Fingers trailed up her waist to her bodice and unlaced the top strings of her kirtle. Her breasts fell forth in the loose chemise. A mixture of relief from their tight enclosure, the discomfort of early pregnancy, and the tingling sensitivity of desire caused her to sigh at the freedom from the lacing. With a sleepy, hungry hand he cupped one breast and she didn't push him away.

God, whenever she wanted to tell him about everything—the bairn, her ability—he did this, and she felt powerless to stop him. She rolled to face him in the dark. With her eyes closed, she could sense her way to his lips. She was drawn to the scars on his arm, and she traced a finger down the rough, rippled skin. Once again, she found herself wondering about it. The lack of light in her room triggered a realization—fire. They were from fire. They had to be. She had seen burn scars before on some of her father's soldiers. He had been burned.

They kissed and touched in the hazy hours of dawn for what seemed like an eternity, and she felt herself fall asleep at times, but then again awake and resume the stroking and kisses as they drank in each other. Her lips burned with the fire that he released in every touch, and she succumbed to the potency of it all and lost herself.

The dreaminess of their kissing began to fade as her mind wandered. They weren't married, and she had allowed their intimacy to delve too far already. This was exactly what her father had wanted. God's graces, she just couldn't do it.

"Oh, Deirdre. I..." Aleck croaked with sleepy desire. His muscles tightened against her, and she felt him wrestling with his own restraint.

She wanted to be with him, more than she wanted to admit to herself, but she also feared for him. What if...?

He stroked her hair and kissed her with a whisper of a touch.

Slosh, rock, slosh.

The sounds of the water against the boat drowned the racing of her heart, the stab of worry in her chest.

A riot of emotions poured through her throbbing head.

He lifted her chin in the dark so she faced him, though she saw no more than the outline of his face. "I desire to be a good man to you, Deirdre. I know about your husbands before, and I'm sorry that happened. I want to show you that you can love again."

She couldn't believe her words as she spoke them. "I never loved them."

There was nothing else to say. He held her close and continued to stroke her. She let his touch and the rocking of the ship lull her back to sleep.

After a long night aboard a large cog ship with a woman he was burning to make love to, an unruly crew of sailors, horses that desperately needed to be let run, and rocky waves, Alasdair was more than happy to set foot on dry land. He had a mission to accomplish, and nothing would stop him. Once they reached the safety of Lady Annella MacRuaidhri's keep, he made up his mind that he would thoroughly bed Deirdre—and tell her the truth. Marriage or not, he needed her. Damn him to hell for it. Perhaps there was still a chance for a union if her father wished it.

Deirdre shared a broad smile with him as she stepped on solid ground, unaware of her allure. "Uumph!" Still pale from seasickness, she was unsteady on her feet and accepted his offered hand. She dabbed at her face with a neck kerchief. Despite the chill in the air, sweat beaded on her brow, and her dark hair was matted against her high forehead.

He tightened his hold on her hand. "Your body will set right by tomorrow. Are you certain you are able?"

"Yes."

It had rained the entire sail, resulting in a tumultuous sea and strong tailwind. However, as they reached the shoreline, Uist was warm and pleasant. "You've really never been here before?" he asked.

"Sadly, no."

He guided her over the rocky shore. From the corner of his eye, he saw Crystoll handling matters with Gorrie and collecting their goods, including the three skittish horses.

"My father wouldn't allow it," she added.

He could sense her forced look of detachment. "I pray that you find what you are looking for, love. I'm sorry about the book."

"Me, too."

Even he had not been able to believe his lie that they would find her horse, satchel, and book after the encounter with the baron. He thoroughly regretted that he hadn't taken the entire satchel for her. Now her mother's book, whatever it was, was lost. He really did pray she reconnected with her kin. He knew all too well what it was like to grow up with no mother, and in his case, a distant angry father.

His gaze fell upon their surroundings. Aside from the cottages, stables, and docks that comprised the seaside village of Loch nam Madadh, he saw endless bogs and low hills plastered with peat in all directions. Thomas had been correct about it being a desolate place. They could ride across Uist in less than a day, encountering naught but lochs and a few peasants' homes.

Crystoll joined them a short while later. "Did you pay him well?" Alasdair asked.

"Aye. I paid extra for him to keep watch," Crystoll said, handing the reins of a horse to Deirdre.

"Good."

"Watch?" Deirdre asked.

"For the baron. If anyone of his likeness gains passage across to Uist, then Gorrie is to send a messenger immediately to us," Crystoll said.

"Are we in further danger, Crystoll?" she asked him, and then she turned to Alasdair. "The baron stole whatever it was that he needed. He wouldn't need to bother with us anymore, right? He doesn't know who I am or who my father is."

Crystoll directed a subtle glare at Alasdair. Thick suspicion hung in the air.

"He's not one to worry about anymore," Alasdair lied.

Deirdre nodded, but her face reflected otherwise, as did Crystoll's. Even Alasdair couldn't believe his lies anymore.

Soon after, they were headed north. "We'll be there by nightfall," Alasdair encouraged Deirdre, who still appeared off-balance after the voyage.

Crystoll's voice was colored in neutrality. "How well did you know Laird MacRuaidhri?"

"I seek Thomas Comrie, and the laird's widow, Lady Annella. I didn't know Laird MacRuaidhri."

"Och, I see. It's been a few years since my last journey here. We visited before the laird died. Who is Thomas Comrie? Laird MacRuaidhri had no male heirs yet," Crystoll said, scratching his head.

"He's acquainted with Lady Annella through mutual friends and serves as marshal to oversee the laird's soldiers and estate. Are you aware that Lady Annella is also a cousin of one of the Claimants?"

"No. Who?"

Alasdair licked his lips and kept his eyes forward. *Choose wisely between friend and foe. Full disclosure earns trust with friends and deceit with foe.* This time it was words of his mother, not his father, which echoed in his mind. "Robert Bruce."

Crystoll and Deirdre were both shocked into silence.

When they reached the undersized keep of Lady Annella MacRuaidhri, Deirdre was more than ready to welcome a warm, soft bed that didn't require making it out of moss, leaves, or sticks and that didn't roll throughout the night, threatening to toss her.

Thomas Comrie received them cordially, even if he looked surprised to see more than Aleck. "Ah, my friend," he said, hugging Aleck.

Aleck extended an open hand to Deirdre. "Thomas, may I introduce Lady Deirdre MacCoinneach, and honorable soldier to her clan, Crystoll Murchison."

Crystoll bowed, and Deirdre stepped forward.

A largely pregnant Lady Annella greeted them. "Welcome, Lady MacCoinneach. It's a pleasure to meet you. Your father has told me great things about you," the fair-skinned, blonde lady of the manor said as she approached them. She took Deirdre's hands in hers and smiled. Her cheeks glowed with healthy rosiness, and her eyes were full of clarity.

Lady Annella's virtuous lifeblood had a relaxing effect, and Deirdre's chattering teeth ceased. She liked her already.

A young girl popped a curious head out from behind Annella's billowing skirt. Deirdre smiled wide, and the girl squealed and resumed her hiding place. Annella laughed with maternal affection. "Christina." She pulled her daughter out with a firm tug and clasped her hand. "Say hello, sweetie."

"Goo' day, me ladeee." The russet-haired girl stood beside her mother, large, curious eyes staring, and legs dancing in usual toddler fashion.

"My condolences about your laird and husband, Lady Annella," Crystoll said with a bow. "I send my laird's regards and his regrets for not visiting."

"Thank you, Mr. Murchison. 'Tis a pleasure and surprise to see you again. 'Tis been a long time."

"You must be hungry and tired. Come inside, please," Thomas said in an equally gentle voice as Annella. "We'll see to the horses." He waved to two stable hands.

Deirdre observed that his lifeblood was an ideal counterpart to Annella's; his was akin to an earthy, golden ale on a cold day. Intuition told her that they'd be safe here. Thomas embraced Aleck, and they spoke in a whisper, heads close, as they strode on the path ahead of the group.

The keep was small but robust, more house than castle, and heated by two large hearths on each end. A settlement of thatch-roofed cottages and outbuildings surrounded the two-floored stone house, which lacked a curtain wall. It was open and exposed to the sea, wind, and enemy. Its advantage was that it sat on a tall cliff, standing watch over the northern sea. Deirdre wondered what it must have been like living here during the wars of the Norse.

Oh my God, she was here. She was *here*. All the troubles getting to Uist suddenly vanished with that realization.

She was surprised to be treated to a hearty supper an hour later with foods not native to the isles. The room was not a grand hall; instead, it was intimate and comfortable. Christina ran in circles chasing a cat while the adults ate. A dutiful maid hovered around the toddler. Deirdre watched the lass with fondness. Children brought life to homes. Their lifebloods were always pure and lively.

"I'm afraid I was not aware of your husband's death, Lady Annella. Please accept my condolences," Deirdre said. It still irked her that her father never told her about her aunt or how involved he had been with the clans of the isles.

Annella smiled with grace. "Thank you, kindly. My husband, Alan, prospered here. He was always a laird who took care of others first before himself." She shared a look with Thomas. Respect reflected in his deep chestnut eyes. Deirdre felt the emotion that beamed between them in that tender moment, and it coursed through her blood with serenity. Thomas was handsome, with brown hair, a soft round chin, and narrow, but strong shoulders. He had a soldier's stature. Although not laird, he possessed a regal air to him.

Deirdre nodded for Annella to elaborate.

"He had a trusted trade of fish with the mainland, allowing us the comforts to which we are accustomed. Our village folk, near and far, are skilled for the life on Uist. Our seas burst with life, unlike our boggy land," Annella said, chuckling to herself. "We also share with our servants and the tenants. There are no ruthless kings or nobles here. Uist was abandoned by the Norse after the Battle of Largs, but we hope to see its rebirth as more Scots return."

The meal passed pleasantly. There was no mention of the impending war with England or Aleck's real reason for coming to the isles. Instead, Annella led the conversation, regaling more delightful tales of the isles' prosperity. At the end, Thomas rose. "Aleck and I must tend to a few matters. Annella, perhaps Deirdre would be interested in joining you in the solar?"

"Of course."

Thomas stood behind Annella and planted a light kiss on her cheek. He then turned to Crystoll but not without a fleeting glance at Aleck, who gave the smallest of nods. "Crystoll, please come join us."

"Let's leave the men to their business," Annella said, looping her arm with Deirdre's.

"Mama!" Christina yelped, following at her heels.

"Come, sweetie," Annella said, taking her daughter by the hand. Christina bubbled incoherently.

The solar was on the second floor, a chamber complete with a large window facing out over the cliff to the blustering sea. Though Deirdre was put off by their exclusion from the discussion, she had secretly longed for a woman's company since their departure from Dornie, and Annella was proving to be amiable already.

"Come by the hearth and rest. I've made the journey several times. It's not easy." Annella urged her to sit beside her on a plush bench in front of a roaring fire. The seat was embroidered with an intricate floral design, and Deirdre ran her fingers along the threads. "This is beautiful."

"Thank you. I sewed it while I carried Christina." She motioned to Christina's maid. "Leslie, please see Christina to my chamber."

"Aye, milady."

Annella kissed her young daughter's forehead and handed her to the maid.

"Nigh-nigh, Mama!" Christina cooed with a wave as she left the room.

Deirdre rose and walked to the tall slender window. The wind whistled through the half-open shutters. The setting sun's rich hues of lavender danced on the whirling busy sea below. For a brief moment, she felt the hum of life within the household. All the lifebloods felt pleasant, content, and safe. She sighed aloud.

"I find solace here. Sometimes it's the only thing that calms me in the winter," Annella said. She pulled fabric, needle, and thread from her basket and laid it in her lap.

"I've a similar room at Eilean Donan. A smaller window. I can see off across the loch. I favor retreating to my garden to escape the bustle of the village though."

"The life of lady can be taxing. We all need a place to rest. Anything to keep my hands busy keeps my mind quieted."

A wave of nausea rippled through her, reminding Deirdre of her responsibilities as laird's daughter. "Aye, indeed."

They talked on lighter topics while they drank a honey water infused with fragrant herbs and Annella sewed a small girl's kirtle in her lap. Deirdre enjoyed the hearth's warmth on her back as the fire crackled.

"This is for Christina. She's keen for a lass and wears through clothes quicker than the stable lads. She'd rather be chasing the lads and animals, than sitting with her mother." Annella rubbed her bulging belly and sighed with a glance over her shoulder to the window.

Deirdre wondered how far along Annella was in her pregnancy. She appeared at least halfway, or more. Since Alan was dead for two winters now, she presumed the unborn child was Thomas's. Deirdre had seen the glance that passed between her and Thomas at dinner and his delayed release of her arm when he assisted her with sitting. She also felt the love between them—a honey hue, warm and tender. They were lovers. Deirdre knew it wasn't unusual for people to have relations prior to marriage, especially if they were betrothed. Or widowed. She thought of her intimate moments with Aleck.

Annella caught her gaze.

"Forgive me."

"What brings you here, Deirdre, if I may ask?"

"My mother hailed from Uist. I was told that I may have kin here." She wanted to ask her more about Aleck and his doings here, but it was not proper and too soon to ask such a thing. She suspected that Annella knew something about it, especially if her lover Thomas was involved with him. And Bruce was her cousin!

"Kin? Whom do you seek?"

"An aunt, Venora, but I've never met her, and I don't even know if she's still alive."

Annella tapped a finger to her lips. "I shall ask around. I believe there is an older woman by that name." She rose, dropping her needlework on the bench. "Come, you look worn. Here I am chatting, while you must be exhausted from your trip! Thomas will keep Aleck engaged into the wee hours. Let me show you to your chamber. You will have our nicest room."

"Oh, I can't ask that of you."

"Nonsense. You're a guest." She added with an artful look, "Aleck will have the chamber beside yours."

"Och, we are not, er, together..." she stammered. Deirdre felt a full blush come on.

"Of course you're not."

Doing anything other than sleep was the last thing on Deirdre's mind. However, as she settled into the plush thick mattress, a blazing fire glowing in the hearth, she pondered what tomorrow would hold for her.

For once, the images of the man in the wood, or rather, the images of *Aleck* in the wood, did not haunt Deirdre's sleep. She awoke feeling rested. Shortly after, a servant appeared and prepared her a bath. With a long soak, she was able to wash away a week of grime. She took her time dressing, enjoying the feel of a fresh dress, borrowed from Annella, upon her clean skin. She thought of Aleck and gooseflesh prickled down her back.

Pulling back the drapery on her lone thin window, she stole a look outside. The sun was high in the sky. She sensed that today would be a good day. She was here. She was here!

Annella greeted her in the small dining hall. Through an arched doorway, scents from the kitchen wafted into the room.

"I'll have my cook prepare you something," Annella said with a wave to a nearby servant, who at the order, darted into the kitchen.

"I'm sorry that I missed the morning meal. That bed was a welcome to my tired body."

Annella chuckled. "It's already past midday. You were exhausted."

"Oh goodness. Forgive me for sleeping so long."

"Don't fret, Deirdre. Your body needed the rest."

After her meal, which was oh-so-warm and agreeable, Annella led her out to their gardens. "Perhaps you can help me?"

"Of course." She drummed her fingers at her side. "Lady Annella—"

"Just Annella, Deirdre, please."

"Annella, have you had a chance to locate Venora?"

"Och! I forgot. I shall do that before supper."

"Thank you, kindly. Perhaps I can come with you?"

"No need. I can do it. You need your rest."

Deirdre fought the urge to press her host further. Disappointed, she set to work. Another half day of waiting would not be unbearable.

After an hour, Deirdre plopped down and stretched. The mundane task of planting, weeding, and digging helped pull her mind from all her troubles. She rubbed her fingertips together, the feel of the dirt between them comforting. She appreciated the moment away from the chaos of life energies that inundated her body. Her powers had grown stronger each day since...

She picked dirt from her beneath her fingernails. Since when? She had thought it was since she had become pregnant, but that wasn't true. It was perhaps two weeks ago when the pulses had begun to glow stronger. And it was two weeks ago that she had met Aleck.

An amber glow hovered nearby. Annella's lifeblood was strong, pure.

"I'm ashamed to have just met you and am already troubling you with drudgery," Annella said, her melodic voice interrupting her thoughts.

"It's no trouble."

Annella dropped her basket, now filled with fragrant herbs. She arched and pressed her fist into her lower spine. "Och, my back cannot take much more." Her cheeks were tinged pink, and her eyes glistened to match the clear sky. The sun illuminated streaks of gold in her flaxen hair.

"How are you feeling?"

"Good, most days, but getting more tired as the wee bairn grows."

A look dimpled Annella's cheeks as her gaze was drawn over Deirdre's shoulder. "Ah, Aleck."

Deirdre had been so distracted by her work and with the thought of locating her aunt that she had not felt his lifeblood until he was upon her. A large, and as always, earnest, hand squeezed her shoulder. Heat warmed her skin. She offered him a delighted look. "Good day, Aleck."

His eyes blazed with a brilliant sheen, and a grin ruffled his mouth. Having grown quite the beard while on their trip, he now was freshly shaven. Even the cuts on his face were healing. His hair was washed, still damp, and pulled in a low leather thong. "Care for a walk?"

"How's your leg? If anything, now is a great time to rest it?" Deirdre said, although his gait had seemed unbothered since arriving and she knew he would not heed her suggestion anyway.

Annella's forehead creased with a frown. "What happened to your leg?"

Aleck waved the question away. "Nothing. 'Tis fine."

"Go. We're done, and I need a rest. I'll see you for supper," Annella said with a gentle shooing of her hands.

Before Deirdre could respond, Annella turned and strode from the garden, a basket of vegetables precariously balanced upon her hip.

"Where are we headed?" Deirdre asked.

"Hmm. We've a few hours of good light. How about we stroll down below the cliffs?"

She nodded, grabbed her plaid to keep out the sea chill, and looped her arm through his. After maneuvering down the rocky path, they reached an isolated pebble beach below the large outcrop upon which the MacRuaidhri keep rested. Aleck pointed out a larger boulder, flat and worn by the sea. Deirdre sat, blowing out a breath and taking in the crashing surf.

"I must leave to tend to a few matters of importance tomorrow. It's not far. You should be safe here with Annella."

A sudden wind gusted, and her hair danced about. She tucked a few unruly strands behind her ear and pulled her plaid closer. Aleck noticed and leaned in next to her. She mused over what to say. "The Cause is important to many, my father included. Change is indeed coming to Scotland." She inhaled the salty air on her tongue.

Bruce was a strong contender. Aleck was wise to support him. She still wasn't sure what his mission here entailed, but she had her suspicions and she understood why he had been so secretive.

Aleck clasped her hand in his, flesh burning into hers. "You've been understanding, Deirdre. I thank you for it."

Ever since their intimate beach encounter, the wave of tension that pounded between them seemed to lessen. She had been ready to part ways with him at one point, too frustrated with his lack of candidness, but now she felt otherwise. With tenderness and coaxing, she had loosened the strings that he tied around his heart. She wished she could return the honesty. Whenever she found herself wanting to tell him about it all, she couldn't.

"Are you certain he won't come after you here?" Deirdre couldn't bear to say the name of the man whose lifeblood tore through her like an icy blade.

"Aye. He doesn't know where we are. You will be safe with me, Deirdre. I promised you that."

"And Dornie? My family?"

"The baron has no discord with him. Your home is safe. Have you located your kin here yet?"

"Not yet. Annella is seeking out my aunt."

Without a thought, she lifted her chin and kissed him. She lost herself in the softness of his touch as he stroked her wind-blown hair and cheek. The calm coolness of late afternoon washed over her.

After a long, luxurious kiss, she pulled from the embrace. The usual sun-kissed glow of Aleck's face seemed diluted by fatigue. She brushed his arm and let her fingers fall on his hand. "Will you tell me what happened?"

"It was a fire."

She squeezed his lower forearm. "Does it bother you?"

He drew her hand from his arm and laid it on his thigh. "'Tis from when I was a lad..." He drifted off, the memory setting his jaw. A tightness appeared in his eyes. "My mother died in the fire."

He didn't elaborate, and Deirdre's heart ached for him. She had lost her mother to an illness—ironic since her mother had been a Healer. To see his mother die in a fire must have been wrenching for him. "I'm sorry, Aleck."

Wishing she could transfer her own energy to mollify him, she shifted her weight so that her hip rested beside his thigh. Cold seeped into the crevices between their bodies, slithering beneath her skirt. She lifted her plaid and shared her body warmth with him, for it was all she could do.

They sat for a while, both drinking in the quietness. She shoved all negative thoughts aside. Eventually Aleck would tell her more about the incident with the baron and more about his mission here, or so she hoped. She supposed that there were things he couldn't discuss with her—not yet at least.

Mostly, her thoughts fell upon her purpose for being here. She longed to locate her aunt. Tomorrow she would press Annella again.

The sun dipped down lower in the sky, a dull orange orb slowly blanketed by the charcoal clouds of impending night. She rested her head in the crook of his shoulder and closed her eyes. The steady rhythm of his heart calmed her. By God's graces, she finally believed. He was the one. She didn't understand why, but he was her lifeblood's partner in a way that was indescribable and unattainable by their intimate embraces alone, passionate and physical though they were. When Aleck touched her, a fire within her roared to be quenched.

The last bit of ginger glow disappeared, and with it, her heart settled into its own new place of peace.

CHAPTER NINE

Alasdair's impatience to meet with the naval workers grew, and now that he had made it to Uist, the thought of waiting any longer pushed him to his brink.

"They are morose, Alasdair. I'm not sure what more we can do. Thank God you have the letter!" Thomas said as they turned toward the stables in the early morning mist.

"About that," Alasdair said, with a brief look over his shoulder. Crystoll was still in the kitchen readying their meal satchels. "I need to tell you something."

Worry drew Thomas's eyebrows together. "What is it?"

"The baron...he found us." Alasdair tried to release the tightness from his chest by blowing out a deep breath. It didn't work.

"Where? Not here?" Thomas stopped with saddling the horse. His look fell on their house. All was quiet.

"No, on Skye."

"God's fury, Alasdair. Why didn't you tell me as soon as you arrived? I'll send my fastest riders to Loch nam Madadh to watch the docks."

Alasdair raised a hand to settle his friend. "Dinna fash. I think he lost our trail on Skye. We're safe here— for now. We paid good coin to a man to watch."

"Did you see *him*?"

Alasdair rubbed his arm where the cut was still healing. "He ambushed us. Tried to kill me and took Deirdre, but we retrieved her." *And I certainly awakened the devil with that move.*

"Dear God, Alasdair. What if he knows you came here? Does he have the letter?" Naked alarm fell upon Thomas's face.

"Aye, he does."

"We're not safe!" Thomas ran both hands through his hair, sending the short brown strands standing on edge. He began to pace like a ruffled rooster.

"The plans and letter don't mention which isle or port. You and the foreman are the only ones that possess the key to decipher the code. I'm confident they lost our trail when we sailed across the sea. I have a man there keeping watch, like I said. He will send word," he repeated.

"That's not enough. I'll feel better with my men watching the docks, too."

"As you wish, friend. Do *you* think he is aware of the navy?"

Thomas shook his head. "Moray's sources say no. I've my suspicions though. As long as Moray holds out, then our navy is secure. Yet now that the baron knows you were on Skye, he may deduce that you've fled this way to gather forces or allies."

"Or I am just fleeing."

"He knows you don't run from anything." Thomas shook his head and rubbed his chin.

"Then perhaps I am gathering men, and not a naval force?"

"Mayhap."

"No harm will come to her," Alasdair said. He knew how much Thomas cared for the MacRuaidhri widow.

"She's Bruce's cousin, for Christ's sake."

"He may think she's still on the mainland."

Thomas just muffled a guttural sound of discontent.

Soured by the discussion, Alasdair pressed on with what he needed to say. Over the past two nights, with Crystoll's presence after dinner, he still hadn't felt comfortable with disclosing everything about the fleet or the baron. However, he knew that telling Crystoll the rest of it was inevitable. "The fleet must reach the secured location. I have the oath of the rightful Claimant. It should be enough to sway our men to continue building. The coin will come."

"It'd better be enough."

Alasdair reached into his pocket. He had hoped it wouldn't come to this, but seeing as Bruce's seal and letter were now gone, it was all he had left. Thank God he had kept Bruce's golden ring in his pocket this entire time.

Thomas eyed it. "He gave you this?"

"Not exactly. Moray stole it for me."

"What? You stole Robert's ring? Why in heavens?"

"In case I lost the letter," Alasdair said. "Bruce owns many. In fact, it's too small for his finger now. He won't even miss it. The important thing is it has his insignia on it, see?" Alasdair rolled the simple gold ring between his thumb and forefinger.

Thomas chuckled. "You never cease to amaze me, Ali."

"Time is short, Thom. Edward marches north. You've heard about Dunbar and Berwick?"

"Aye."

"You understand how pressing this is."

Again, Thomas looked toward the house. "Do you trust Crystoll?"

Alasdair nodded. "Aye.

"We need to tell him, then."

"Not yet." Alasdair rolled Robert's ring between his fingers.

"What about Laird MacCoinneach? Do you think we can persuade him to declare Bruce as the rightful Claimant? Simon has come to the isle several times for trade. Fostered a strong relationship with Alan MacRuaidhri. I inherited that kinship..., but he and I are still figuring the other out. I am not the laird here, just a vassal following MacRuaidhri's dying wishes, so, Simon has yet to return."

"I do think we can guide him toward siding with Bruce, but..."

Thomas put his hands on his hips, frowning. "You muddled things up, didn't you?"

Alasdair shrugged. "I had to get out of there. The baron was close, and..."

"What did you do, Ali?"

"I left in the night. Deirdre came with me. She had kin here she wished to meet. An aunt?"

"Dear heavens, man. You stole his daughter!"

"Christ, Thom. It's not like that. She came willingly."

"Why the devil are you limping?"

Alasdair smirked. "Och, that's another tale." Alasdair looked back at the house. He had a few more questions before Crystoll arrived with their satchels. "What do you know about the MacDougalls?"

"The MacDougalls?" Thomas scratched his chin. "Their seat rests south in Argyll, Castle Dunstaffnage, I believe. The laird's son came north two years ago, not far from Loch Carrann, seeking an alliance with clans there and with the Earl of Ross. They're not a clan you want to be associated with. Why do you ask?"

"We were attacked by two of their sentries near Ardelve. There's animosity between them and the MacCoinneachs. A man attacked Deirdre." He swallowed hard, trying not to remember.

"Curses, you've had a rough time of it."

Alasdair thinned his look. He needn't more guilt lancing through him.

Thomas said, "Aye, well, I've heard that the laird, Steafan MacDougall, is loyal to the Comyn claim to the throne and against Bruce."

"What about the Earl of Ross?"

Thomas's mouth tightened. "I'm not certain. I think he sides with Comyn. The earl's power is wide and his pockets deep. The MacDougalls may be north seeking the same thing we do and with the earl in their bed..."

"I'm afraid it may be too late for discretion." He rubbed his still sore nose.

"I agree. You need to make yourself a ghost. Annella and I will be staying here. I can't bring her to the mainland in the midst of war, not with the bairn coming. I've seen enough bloodshed."

"We both have."

"Aye. Let's hope that God's grace is in Robert Bruce's favor then."

"Thom, are you familiar with any Norse?"

Thomas lifted his eyebrows. "Devil, Ali. You bemuse me today."

Crystoll emerged from the house and came toward the stable but stopped to greet one of the stable lads.

Alasdair cleared his throat. "Thom?"

"Aye, aye. I've learned some Norse since moving here. Some folk still use their old tongue in their daily talk and tasks. Some cling to their past with pride, or perhaps as a reminder. Why?"

Alasdair swallowed hard. The words Deirdre had spoken were seared in his memory. "What does *En sky av hvite død skjult i svart* mean?"

Thomas tapped his creased forehead. "A sky, no...a *cloud* of white...white death," he said, pausing, reflecting. "Dressed, no, *veiled* in black. Hmm, that makes no sense. 'A cloud of white death veiled in black'? Where did you hear it?"

Alasdair pursed his lips. "It doesn't matter." White death? Veiled in black? He raked his memory for what else Deirdre had said. She had said something about an icy death.

They were silent for a moment as they returned to readying the horses.

Crystoll reached them, his arms filled with satchels for their long day's ride to the hidden harbor. "Morn."

Alasdair shifted to a cheery mood. "Good morning, Crystoll."

Thomas's translation clung to Alasdair. As much as he felt the pull to complete his task and run from the lies that surrounded him, at this moment he found he wanted nothing more than to return to the comfort of Deirdre's arms. There at least, he could let his ghosts remain buried if only for a few hours. Later, he told himself. Later. He would tell her. Aye, that he would.

By midmorning, they drew near the harbor. They had ridden their horses to a small collection of crofts on the coast's edge, where they then took a boat across the choppy sound. After the boatman fought against rough waves and moored their vessel in the hidden harbor, and rowed a smaller boat to shore, they disembarked.

"Och, let me assist ye," Crystoll said, grabbing a side of the small boat as a rope got loose. "You go ahead," he said to Alasdair and Thomas with a nod.

They made for the small sailor's croft.

"Are you going to tell me the other reason you're acting like a lad who lost his sweetbreads?" Thomas asked once out of Crystoll's hearing range.

"No."

Thomas buckled over with laughter.

"I amuse you?"

"I don't make light of our matter, Ali. It's imperative we get the fleet situated and relay the information to Moray. Och, but there's no harm in enjoying the finer pleasures of life while we still have our own heads," Thomas said. "And you amuse me sometimes."

Alasdair eyed his companion and long-time friend. "You've enjoyed yourself, I can see."

Pink tinged Thomas's ears. "I never planned for it to happen. Alan trusted me, and his last wishes were for me to care for her. I didn't expect to feel this way. Alan was my friend."

"Is the child yours?"

Lively twinkle shone in his friend's eyes. "Your pluck never changes. Aye, the bairn's mine, but Christina is Alan's child. I suppose I need to marry Annella?"

Alasdair shrugged. "I'm not the best person to ask about the proper ways of marriage and courtship."

"That is indeed what it is, isn't, it? You are besotted with the laird's daughter. That explains the odd faces you keep making. She'll understand when you tell her the truth—and women always learn the truth. Better to tell her now. Besides, what's not to love about you?" Thomas knocked his shoulder with his.

Alasdair looked behind them. Crystoll surely had a skill for making friends with boat crews. The boat was now secured, and he chuckled lightly with the captain, sharing some lively story using grand hand gestures. Alasdair turned back ahead and slowed his steps so they didn't reach the croft yet. "I'm not sure she will understand my deceit. She has the strongest perseverance I've seen, but she has a delicate heart. I don't know how I'll tell her."

"Alasdair, are you admitting you've a soft spot for her? You, the man who never lets a woman close to his heart?"

He cracked his knuckles and avoided Thomas's gaze.

"Och. You love her! And if she loves you, she will understand why you lied."

Alasdair grimaced. "I never said I love her."

"Of course you didn't." Thomas pointed to his face. "Your eyebrows did. Hmm, yes, and that dimple, and that crease there."

They were almost to the croft. He tried to outpace his friend, but Thomas was quick to keep up.

"Don't avoid this conversation, Alasdair."

"Are you going to marry Annella?" he snapped. "And quit using my name!" he whispered hotly with yet another look back. Crystoll was far behind them on the trail.

Brown, frank eyes looked at him over his shoulder. "Yes, *Sir Stirrat*."

Alasdair groaned and hurled a fist out at his friend, who dodged and laughed instead.

"Yes. I love Annella, but this conversation is not about me," Thomas said matter-of-factly. The high wind of the coast caught in his short and wild hair, but a smile spread his face like a man who held a deep affection for a woman. "We've been preoccupied lately, as you are well aware."

"And Christina?"

"I devote myself to her, as if she were my own."

The words struck Alasdair with a familiar chill.

Alasdair's father was nothing like Thomas, who took in a child not his own. Instead, Alasdair's own father had tried to burn him beside his mother. After the fire, his father never regarded him the same way, refusing to believe that Alasdair was his own son. He had sent him away to schools, mentors, court. Not until Alasdair returned home, trained and ready to rule, had his father spoken to him…and revealed his true motives. All his father cared about was land and power, and if that meant allying with the English, then that's what he would do. The man didn't realize he was working for naught—what good was land if you had no children or family to pass it on to?

As if reading his mind, Thomas said, "I'm sorry, Ali. I didn't mean anything—"

"I know, Thom."

"You can't blame yourself for it."

Alasdair gritted his teeth. "He tarnished her name and killed her. She was innocent. He tried to kill me, too. What kind of soul does that?" His breath came in ragged gasps as anger yielded to grief. His arm might have healed, but the fire had left a gaping hole in his heart.

Thomas steadied his look on Alasdair. "It's not your fault. We're all flawed, friend. Your mother's heart went astray, and who's to blame her? Your father exploited that. You can't let it kill you. She wasn't a—" He stopped himself. "Forgiveness frees your heart and soul, Ali."

"I do forgive her. I will never forgive him."

Crystoll reached them.

"Come," Alasdair said, grateful for the intrusion. They stepped past the croft and around a bend. A knoll obscured the inlet and the ships sheltered within it. Unlike Uist, this small isle was hilly, rounded, and the perfect place to hide tall ships. Alasdair held in his breath, preparing for the worst. By the few men he had seen near the croft, he assumed the number by the ships would be fewer.

It was Crystoll who gasped first when they reached the summit of the knoll. Before them sat, bobbing in the water, two dozen large cog ships, sails down, but halfway built. At least fifty men busied themselves along the beach, carrying wood and planks, oars, and fabrics of sails yet to be hung. They looked tired, thinned, but determined. And they were working.

"We may not need that ring at all, friend," Alasdair said. "Your message sounded dire. This is anything but that."

"I don't understand. My last visit here was a month ago; we had ten ships, and the men were deserting the project and bickering with each other. Now look. I don't understand how this could happen," Thomas said, ruffling his hair again. The foreman below spotted them, waved at Thomas, and plodded up the hill.

"Perhaps word of Edward's attacks arrived sooner than we did," Crystoll said, as was his astute manner.

"Mayhap," Thomas said, scrunching his brow. "I tried to persuade them, but my words did not hit their mark. I'm sorry, Al-Aleck," he stammered, sending Alasdair's heart to skip a beat a moment. Crystoll didn't catch Thomas's near slip with his name. "There was naught I could do. I kept coming, talking with them, but they…"

He shook his head. "So I went to the mainland to gather more workers but to no avail. I had just returned home this week with nothing but more supplies."

Alasdair couldn't help but smile. "Perhaps miracles do happen."

"Sir Comrie!" The foreman stopped, breathless from the ascent. He wiped sweat from his brow. "I was beginning to think you had forgotten about us."

"Well done, Mack." Thomas clapped a hand on the foreman's back and walked with him toward the supply crofts. "I've brought more food and drink for the men, some cloth from the mainland for the sails, and…"

They continued on their way as Thomas recounted his list of supplies.

Alasdair stood in awe. His father may have been a beast, but he was always right about one thing: Highlanders were not to be reckoned with. War was in their blood. Something had stirred these men on to continue. Now he had Bruce's ring and would promise them the coin they required for their loyalty and hard work. A great burden felt lifted from his chest. The navy still had a long way until it reached completion—the ships had to be sea-ready and the men trained—but Bruce would be pleased with the progress.

Aye, the fleet would be ready. Aye, Scotland would prevail.

Deirdre fell into a rhythm with Annella over the next few days. They worked in the gardens in the morning, broke for a midday meal in the solar, followed by whatever overseeing the keep needed, and then joined Thomas, Aleck, and Crystoll for the meal come evening. She had to keep herself busy while she waited to see her aunt. Annella had located Venora in the village but learned that she was away. It had been a few days since then, and Deirdre was getting beyond impatient.

"Does she leave often?" Deirdre asked, as she pulled up a tough weed.

"Apparently. I asked Mary, a widow who lives near her. She told me that Venora can be found about the countryside in the spring, collecting herbs and visiting friends in the towns on the south isle. Hopefully she'll return soon."

"Have you met her before?" Deirdre felt Annella's hesitation.

Annella chewed her bottom lip as a pensive quietness took over their conversation. "I'm afraid not."

Port nan Long was a small village, and Annella seemed to know everyone. Passersby were always eager to chat with her, and she with them. Deirdre found it odd that Annella offered no explanation as to why she knew little of Venora. She decided to let the subject be. There was nothing more she could do about it now.

Although late spring was upon them, the warm weather struggled to reach the isles. Spring's nip joined them daily, and by late afternoon, Deirdre was grateful for a rest by the warm hearth as she and Annella came in from the garden. She was surprised to see Crystoll pacing near it this evening.

"My lady, a moment, please?" he said, his expression like stone, although Deirdre felt the unrest within him.

Annella excused herself. "I'll fetch us refreshments."

When Annella was out of hearing range, she spoke to him. "What vexes you, Crystoll?"

His face was grave. "My orders were to bring you home, my lady. Is it not time? Your father has surely received my message by now. I know he worries about you."

His angst radiated through Deirdre, and had to steady her heartbeat with a few deep breaths. "He'll understand when I tell him why I left. No punishment will be imposed upon you, Crystoll."

His worry didn't dissipate, and she rubbed her aching head.

"There's something else?"

"Have you found what you needed here, my lady? Will we be able to leave soon?" He straightened his back and balled his hands.

She lowered her eyes. "Not yet. It appears my aunt has left Port nan Long for a while, but we are hopeful of her returning soon."

Crystoll crossed his arms. "My lady, if I may be plainspoken?"

"Of course."

"That incident with the baron. I don't...I feel it's better if we get you home soon. Aleck, he...what if the baron comes here? The message I sent to your father is coded, but even so...and I sent it before our *incident*."

"It will be all right, Crystoll. We're safe here," she said, although she didn't completely believe herself on that matter despite Aleck's reassurance.

"If you say so, my lady."

"Crystoll, please speak it."

He paused and looked over his shoulder toward the kitchen. He lowered his voice and placed a hand on her shoulder, drawing her away from the entranceway. "You are well aware of what's going on?"

"Aye, Aleck has told me."

Crystoll raised an eyebrow. "Do you know all of it?"

"Tell me."

"You know that Aleck relays important information to Thomas from Robert Bruce, aye?"

"Aye."

"A few days ago, my suspicions were confirmed. They are readying a naval fleet. They have two dozen ships already."

"A fleet?" Deirdre muffled a gasp. She had been correct. She felt slightly stung that Crystoll knew and she didn't. Aleck didn't fully trust her yet. God, these men!

"Men can be turned by greed, and this baron is one of them. I support our laird in his decision to back a Claimant, and if it be Bruce, so be it. This war has come to our home, my lady. Eilean Donan is gateway to the isles. This war is bigger than we had thought."

A part of her tried to deny it, but she had known all along. "It's beyond our control. Our fate is determined by how we choose to fight it, Crystoll."

"Aye, my lady." His amber glow intensified, as did the pain in her head. She wanted to tell him to quiet his emotions. Obviously, her words didn't placate him.

She took his hand in hers. "Please give me more time, Crystoll, and then we can take our leave?"

Annella returned, carrying a tray of goblets with a steaming drink, cheese, and honey cakes.

He bowed. "Aye, my lady." He left the room. Annella and Deirdre made their way to the solar and sat by the hearth.

"Is something amiss, Deirdre?"

Deirdre stared into her goblet, whiffing cloves and spices, as she sat. "It's Crystoll. He's wishes to return home. It's the Cause. I'm afraid we've become entrenched in it unwittingly, and my father worries for my safety."

"Aleck's told you of it?"

Deirdre nodded.

Annella pursed her lips. "This bloody war. You would think we could escape it here, but in fact, the war will be coming here soon enough. Our country has been ravaged by an evil king and selfish contenders. Uist is the ideal location to prepare the navy."

Deirdre wanted to say more, to share with her the qualms she had about the baron, but she couldn't gauge how much Annella knew about him or about Aleck's doings.

"Aleck and Thomas appreciate Crystoll's help," Annella said.

Deirdre could almost feel the death that would come with the war. An odd feeling gripped her. She needed to talk of other things. "Thomas is kind."

"Aye."

Deirdre spoke hesitantly. "You are not married yet?"

"No," she said with subtle click of her tongue. "Alan was a good husband. I bore him a daughter. Christina is a beautiful, spirited lass. Our marriage had been arranged, but I grew to love him. I favored him through his last days. I made a vow to see that his lands were cared for properly. That's why he didn't pass it on to his nephews—his brother Dubhgall was a keen man, as well, but died a few years before my husband. Alan knew they would fight over it. Alan was a quiet supporter of the Claimants, as am I." She tittered. "Well, out of obligation, aye? My cousin being Robbie after all. And Thomas, he, well…" Her pearly eyes glazed over, wet with tears. She paused and shifted her weight. "…He's an honorable man."

"I'm sorry, I didn't mean—"

Annella waved her words away. "It was a dark month after Alan died. His nephews pressured me into relinquishing all rights. I'm young but not dim. Alan shared his secrets with me. I was familiar with running his estates. Then Thomas came. Alan had sent for him before his death. It was too late." Grief clouded her eyes. "Alan had already died by that time."

"You don't need to tell me more," Deirdre said softly, placing a hand on Annella's arm, feeling her host's pain.

A delicate musing look returned to Annella's face. "Thomas helped me. I think on his deathbed, Alan trusted that Thomas would take care of me in more ways than one," she said, rubbing her round belly. "We're married in spirit. We don't need vows before an altar to be in a marriage of the heart."

Annella's bluntness vibrated within Deirdre. "He is a braw man, Annella. How did Aleck and Thomas meet?"

Annella flicked an imaginary speck of dirt from her skirt. "Through a mutual friend years ago."

"Aye." So there were still a few things Lady Annella was not willing to share. Deirdre ventured another question. "Are you familiar with Baron Montgomerie?"

Annella coughed and tapped her chest. "Forgive me! Too much ginger!" she said, fluttering a hand at her flushed cheeks.

Deirdre doubted it.

She cleared her throat. "Aye, I do. He's a dreadful person. He's against the Cause and not a man you want to meddle with. Why do you ask?"

Deirdre pursed her lips and lied, not knowing if Thomas, who seemed kindred with Aleck, was informed of their encounter. "His name arose in conversation with my father, that's all." She waved a hand in feigned ignorance.

She was not dim either.

The next morning, Annella came to Deirdre's bedchamber. Joy bubbled in her voice. "Venora has returned!"

Deirdre hurried with getting ready. She ate her morning porridge with shaky hands and was out of the house before Annella could even say goodbye and good luck.

Despite her exhilaration at locating her aunt, Deirdre trembled when she came upon the rustic croft a short distance from the center of the village. A brutal sea wind pummeled her and the equally unsheltered home. Her boot snagged on a hidden rock, and she nearly fell. Shaking, but summoning courage, she approached the door. To her surprise, a woman—her aunt?—answered immediately after her knuckles rapped upon the old oak door.

"Ah! You're here! Come, lass, I was expecting ye." Deirdre held in a breath as she took in her aunt. Eyes, deep blue and flecked with green, stared back at her. Long dark hair streaked with gray tumbled around her shoulders, and her face reflected a curious scrutiny.

She was aged but not unattractive and could almost be mistaken for Deirdre's mother—whose painting hung in Eilean Donan. An upturned smile welcomed Deirdre inside.

Venora motioned to the two seats by the hearth. Unsure how to start, Deirdre sat and crossed her arms.

She was here. Here. With her aunt...her kin! "I'm Deirdre."

"Ye've the look of yer mother." Venora's cool fingers tilted Deirdre's chin left and then right as she inspected her.

Deirdre swiped at her wind-blown hair and tucked it behind her ears. "She is dead."

"Aye, she is."

"Did you know I was coming?"

Venora smiled, fine wrinkles creasing around her thin lips.

Deirdre rocked, her vision going soft. This was more awkward than she had expected. She raked her mind for the questions she had rehearsed. "Have you met my father?"

"Once, long ago."

"You didn't see him during his visits here in the past few years?"

"No."

"Did you know about me, Edmund, and Caite?" She balled her hands and stared at the low flames in the hearth.

"Aye, I did. One day perhaps I can meet them, too." With an emphasized sigh, Venora sat.

"Moreen told me about you."

Venora's expression went from serious, almost pained, to one shining with the light of joy at the mention of Moreen's name. "Oh, Moreen! How fares she?"

"She's well. She's been a blessing to me since my mother died when I was a child."

"Your mother is greatly missed." She tapped Deirdre's hand and shook her own head as if chastising herself. "Excuse my manners. I may hiv the Sight, but sometimes I forget formalities. Would ye care for some drink?"

Deirdre nodded.

"I'm sorry that I was away when ye arrived, dearie."

"This was an unplanned visit. You wouldn't have known." Or would she have? Fragrant herbs burned in a bowl near the hearth, sending a wisp of smoke dancing through the room. Her muscles felt tight as a clammy sweat chilled her and her head became heavy, foggy. She clenched and unclenched her fists, encouraging the blood to flow.

There was a lot she wanted to ask. Oh heavens, what were those questions?

"We've time to talk more, dearie. Ye will be back. Ye must hiv a lot of questions." Venora had a low voice, but it was crisp and clear. "I suppose ye want to hear about yer ma. Let's start with that." She busied herself with collecting a few cups, a plate of biscuits, and putting a kettle on the fire.

"Aye."

"Our father, Blasius, was Norse, but some would call them *Lochlanach*. Ye ken who they were?"

She nodded again, her tension beginning to unwind.

"He was a powerful ruler here, in the day when the *Lochlanach* roamed these isles. He stole one of the young women native to these isles—my mother—and forced her to his bed. He saw her healing gifts and wanted them in his own kin. The *Lochlanach* were a bloodthirsty lot, and yer grandfather was a man hungry for dominance, for much more than can be offered by Mother Earth. He believed in the glory of afterlife, and became maddened with the Silver Veil. The Norse decimated the people here and took the land. Not that there's a great deal to take, mind ye. They had eyes on the mainland, but the king, and nobles like yer father and grandfather, stopped them. It was a perilous season in our country." She paused to ensure that Deirdre was paying attention, and then continued.

"All that remain are the descendants of the Norse King Haakon and the few native folk, the *Silver Folk*."

"The Silver Folk?"

"The stone believers, and the gifted, of course. Some call them—call *us*—Ancients," she said, eyeing Deirdre carefully.

Gifted. Deirdre cringed.

"Don't fear it, lass! Never allow them to cast ye out. The Ancients are yer kin! Ye're a special woman, and I can feel the energy in ye. Ye've grown more powerful lately, aye?"

Deirdre swallowed and shifted her weight in her seat. Nobody had ever read her so clearly.

Sensing her discomfort, her aunt continued, "Don't be afraid, Deirdre. Embrace yer power. Use it for good. That's why it was bestowed upon ye. 'Tis a blessing. Yer mother had the power, too. She was a Healer like yer grandmother, but ye already ken that. She suppressed it around our father, but she held great power. Och, I hiv seen her use it. She saved many lives, including yer father's. She wanted to leave this dreadful place and she fell in love with 'im, though he was the seed of our father's enemy."

"How? Why? My mother had healed Da?" How had she never heard this tale before?

"Yer da came to Uist on trade with yer grandfather and uncle, Desmond. They met with our father." Her words held heat as she continued, "Our father wouldn't negotiate, wouldn't trade, and wouldn't relent. Yer mother wanted to intervene, to prevent our father from unleashing his men upon yer da's clan—but it was too late. Blood had been shed. Swords drawn in battle." She paused, as if choosing her words carefully. "Soon after, Simon was besotted by yer ma. I saw and felt their immediate connection. She ran away with 'im, much to our father's ire."

Deirdre suspected her aunt told mixed truths. What was lie and what was truth? Had her mother really run away with her father...or was there more to this tale? A deep, cold sadness hardened Venora's voice when she spoke of Deirdre's mother. There was something else her aunt held close to her heart, something she was not telling Deirdre.

Deirdre had never seen her parents in such a romantic light. Her father had come to Uist, a stranger to their land, and her mother had fallen in love with him. Her father was a firm but compassionate laird, who used words and strategy over blade. She had never seen him use his sword. A battle on Uist with these Norse? Bloodshed? She only knew about the Battle of Largs, when all the clans came together to fight the Norse. This was something else. Who was this father of the past? And her mother had run away with him?

The secrets, the tales...sounded all too familiar. She shoved that madness aside. She had not fled her home to be with Aleck. She had come to see her aunt.

Venora's eyes dazzled with her Sight. "Och, dearie. Ye're besotted, too."

Deirdre bit into a biscuit. "I came here to see you."

Venora grinned. "Of course ye did."

"You mentioned my Uncle Desmond. I know him not. Do you mean Uncle Kendrick?"

"No, dearie. Kendrick is not your Da's brother. Desmond was his brother, but...he died. Kendrick is...my brother and yer mother's brother. He was born here, on Uist. He was a Feeler, like you."

Was? He was no longer a Feeler? This gift could be lost or taken?

Kendrick was her mother's brother, not Father's? Why would they lie to her about that? "Why did Father never tell me—?" She grimaced. Just like he never acknowledged her ability. To protect her? "How did our family get such power?" Deirdre just now realized that she couldn't feel Venora. She radiated no lifeblood, no emotions. She was unreadable, not masked like Aleck, but completely unreadable, and Deirdre relied on watching her aunt's face for any hint of emotion.

Venora shrugged. "Some say it was a power born by the merging of the *Lochlanach* and the Ancients, the Silver Folk, long before my father arrived. Don't believe that though. These special people—*my* people—have existed far longer than any of us, and our powers lie in the stones."

Deirdre pinched her nose. Her head whirred with a muted sound but not from a lifeblood. *The stones again. Oh heavens. What was with these people and these magical stones?*

Venora beamed. "Ye're a beautiful union of both *Lochlanach* and the Ancients, both with long pure bloodlines. That is why your ability is so strong."

Deirdre's face must have revealed her confusion.

"It makes sense if ye allow yerself to believe." Venora cleared her throat. She leaned back, closed her eyes. The fire's colors moved over the delicate curves of her face. She had high, round cheekbones, deep-set eyes, and a small chin. If Deirdre's mother were still alive, would she have the same streaks of gray, the subtle wrinkles around her eyes?

Venora then opened her eyes and spoke in a low, flat tone. "There's an ancient story of a people, many thousand years ago, the ones who built the stones...an old man had lost his wife, and he grew dark and mourned her. In his bitterness, he forced his slaves to build the stones so that he could attract a selkie. He heard of the mystical ability of the selkies being able to shed their seal skin and walk on land and he wanted his wife back. One selkie came, enticed by the beauty of the stones. Overtaken with the loveliness of the selkie, he caught her and forced her to his bed. The selkie died birthing a son...a son who had the abilities to walk as a human but possessed the magic of a selkie. It's from that son whom the people of Uist—the Silver Folk or Ancients—are descended. Then the *Lochlanach* came and wanted the same power. And our bloodlines...mixed."

Deirdre shook her head. "It can't be true."

Venora poured two cups of a hot herbal-infused water and handed one to Deirdre. The cup warmed her hands, but she did not drink it.

Her aunt's voice rose to an almost shrill sound, filled with passion. "It goes against yer Christian ways, but search inside yerself, for ye ken it to be true. The bairn will have the gift, too."

Deirdre's head began to spin, and her hand fell upon her middle. Of course Venora could see the life growing within her.

"It's not his." Venora smirked.

"His?" Deirdre choked on her words.

"The dark one that came with ye. Aleck, ye call 'im. Ye've not yet shared yer bed with him." Venora chuckled as she sipped her tea.

"No." Deirdre was shaken to the core at Venora's clairvoyance. Heavens, how had the conversation turned to this?

Venora clucked her tongue. "Lie with him soon, lass, or else he'll ken."

"He's not my husband." She fought to remain composed. "Besides, I'm afraid I may, I may…I wanted to ask you about…"

"Marriage! That's not stopped women from sharing their bed with a man they love."

"I don't love him."

Venora grinned knowingly while taking a long sip from her cup.

Deirdre felt the sting of tears in her eyes. "How do you know all this?" she began but stopped herself.

Bony, frail fingers squeezed around Deirdre's. "I'm a Seer, lass. It's my gift. It's my curse." She clenched her jaw. "Dinna get het up, lass. It's not yer undoing. It's good ye came. Never regret it! Use yer gift for good. Our ancestors were a rich people, not in coin, but in their wisdom and understanding of nature. They recognized there is a fine veil between the realm of the human world and the other world, and they were able to exploit it. Yer purpose is grander than ye or I will ever comprehend. Go to the stones. There, ye will feel the hum of the earth. There, ye can embrace who ye truly are. The earth will tell ye."

"I don't understand. Why?" Upheaval flooded her head with questions. "Why?" she repeated, in a weak whisper.

"Soon enough ye'll learn why. And trust yer visions."

"I am no Seer."

"Oh, dearie. Ye've the power to feel people's souls, but ye've seen that man—this Aleck—" She drew his name out. "—in the woods in yer dreams. Trust yer instinct when these visions come to ye. This black-haired one, he is good. Alas, I sense another dark one—oh, his soul is sick."

Deirdre swallowed, unable to control her shaking. "It's just a dream. I don't see things like you."

Venora shook her head side to side, a grimness sinking her mouth into a grimace. She suddenly rose. "Forgive me, I've strained ye. Please, go visit the stones. Then ye will see."

Deirdre stood, spellbound. Her mind raced with more questions. "May I visit you again?"

"Of course, dearie. Of course. I ken ye will."

Alasdair searched the gardens, expecting to find Deirdre after another exhausting day with the workers, but she was nowhere to be found. Oh, how he longed for her company not out of a need for comfort, but to revel in the successes of the day.

With success came challenge though. By some miracle, the men had been working all this time, but now that he arrived, they expected payment. Although he had memorized the plans and orders in Bruce's letter, the men were not as convinced as he was to keep working, even with the ring as proof. A few more had left, but the rest stayed on. Promises would only garner him so much time. Moray vowed to return to Uist in a month with the full payment, but in the meantime, Alasdair's responsibility was to persuade these men to keep working. The navy had to be operational soon. They had two dozen ships but needed at least a few more. The men were tired and had families to feed. By God's miracle, they had come this far. He had a feeling there was something else, though, that had spurred them on.

Crystoll's coming had proven almost providential. He was an able body and, by fortune's luck, was acquainted with a few of the men. Alasdair wondered if Crystoll had been a sailor before becoming a soldier. Crystoll was able to assimilate among the workers, form friendships and trust, and keep them working.

"Will that be all?" Crystoll's voice intruded. He emerged from the stables after settling the horses from their day trip to the harbor.

"Er, yes, Crystoll."

Crystoll turned to head to the keep.

"Thank you, Crystoll. Will you come with us again tomorrow?"

"Aye, Sir Stirrat."

Alasdair followed him and when he reached the hall, Deirdre came hurrying in, a basket of herbs hanging from her arm. Alasdair grabbed her elbow and pulled her aside. "I couldn't find you in the gardens."

She batted a hand, but not before he saw a glint of apprehension in her eyes. "I went for a stroll along the coastal trail," she said, pausing. "And I found my aunt."

His spirits lifted. "That's wonderful news. Was she agreeable?"

"Very."

"Good. I'm pleased you were able to find her. Does she live nearby?"

"Not too far from here. She lives by the loch, outside the village."

"Could you please inform me when you do leave the keep? It's not my place to prevent you from seeing your kin, but..." He paused and scratched his forehead. He didn't want to worry her and forced a casual smile. "It is safer if you stay near. At least take one of Thomas's soldiers with you next time?"

Her face grew wary. "Safer?"

"You're in an unfamiliar area."

She tilted her head, paused and pursed her lips, but then nodded with a smile.

A claw gripped his thoughts. What if the baron *did* pick up their trail? What if he found the women here while he, Thomas, and Crystoll were off tending to the navy? All this time he had been worried about the baron discovering the navy, but seeing Deirdre walk in through the hall, her basket in hand and a glow on her face...by heavens, it sent his heart spiraling down a path he had fought ever since he met her.

After supper, Alasdair escorted Deirdre to her room.

A servant was already preparing the hearth. She stood, curtsied, and departed.

Alasdair paced to the slender window. He blew a deep breath out. *Tell her.* "Are you content here, Deirdre?"

"It's quiet, but I like that."

"I'm certain your father worries about you."

"Crystoll sent a messenger home," she assured.

"Och, aye." He rubbed the growing stubble on his chin.

Deirdre sat on the hearth bench. She leaned her head to the side, untied the ribbon in her hair, and wove her fingers through it, loosening the plait. Her hair fell in a ripple of dark, slightly damp waves. The firelight flickered on her rounded cheekbones.

He swallowed as he approached her, for she was a glorious sight to behold, even more so with that pink pout as she fought with her hair. "How would you feel about staying here longer?"

She paused and stared at him, unblinking.

"With me," he added. *For several years*, he wanted to say. He felt compelled to sit beside her. She turned from him, either absorbed in her task or purposely avoiding his gaze.

After a long moment, she stopped in her work, cradled the brush in her lap, and closed her eyes. "Much has happened since we met. I should return home soon, Aleck."

Every time she used his false name, a knot formed in his stomach. With all his planning, he had never anticipated...well, *her*. God's teeth, why couldn't he bring himself to tell her? He wondered if she would forgive him for his transgressions. He stroked her hair, it smooth like silk. His hand fell to her shoulder, and he felt her stiffen.

She opened her eyes, and they shared a look.

Alasdair's hand lingered on her.

He leaned down and kissed her. He was finished with words and would rather use his lips for other things. Thinking upon all the *other* transgressions the two of them shared, he moaned. God, he needed her touch. It lifted the heavy weight from his soul and brought him to a place of no burdens.

She sighed with a sweet purr and allowed his aggressive advance, arousing him further. He could wait no longer. His body ached and throbbed everywhere. He shifted on the bench. Placing his hands on her waist, he drew her closer and kissed her harder.

She laid a hand on his cheek and pulled back.

Through gasps, she said, "Aleck, I'm confused."

His fingers found the ties of her gown's bodice and began to undo them. She didn't resist. "About what?"

"About this. About us. We shouldn't..."

"I want to be with you, Deirdre." He drowned her words with another kiss, one so thorough that all she could do was to partake in it. He held her with a grip that refused to let go, heart against racing heart. His hands slid down her back.

"We're not married..."

"We could be," he said. He wanted to tell her that many couples consummated their relationship long before marriage, and Deirdre wasn't a chaste maiden. She had been married twice. Regardless, he had to respect and accede to her decision.

However, there was no harm in persuasion...

He finished unlacing the front of her kirtle next, and her perfect breasts fell loose beneath her thin white chemise. Reminded of their naked encounter on the beach and the luscious kisses they shared on the ship across the sea, he moved with urgency.

In between raspy breaths, she continued her futile fight. "Aleck..." she moaned, surrender stealing her voice.

He countered with another titillating kiss. She melted in his arms and drew her hands around his neck, encouraging his tongue to explore. It sent shivers of fiery desire through his entire body. With that, he swept her into his arms and carried her to the bed. Three weeks of torture had been enough. "I've wanted you, Deirdre, since the day I first saw you by that loch," he whispered in her ear. "Be with me, love? Just this once?"

There was a long pause before she said, "Yes," in a strong exhalation. As they fell onto the plush bedclothes, their movement extinguished the two candles on the bedside table, leaving the room in the dim glow of the hearth. He brushed his lips against each round nipple, the taste of her salty skin more delicious than any meal. Pushing her skirt up, he was unable to go slow, as much as he enjoyed the feel of the soft skin on her thighs. They can do slow later. He inhaled the scent of her hair at the nape of her neck, perfumed with rose water.

He ravished her lips in a way he had not before as her fingers danced down his neck and back. She pressed him to her body, arched, and parted her legs, open and receptive. He undid his trews and drew against her, skin to skin. Hungry desire coursed through him as they joined.

Her flesh was inviting, and together they found an intuitive rhythm that felt both raw and refined. Passion pounded the blood through every part of his body down to his fingertips and toes. He made love to her in anything but a delicate way, contrary to what he had envisioned, but he couldn't control himself. He lost himself as pleasure rose within him like an insurrection. She moaned and writhed beneath him, arching farther, and hips dancing against him. "Oh, love..." he said, hoarse and drunk by the feel of her around him.

As their eyes locked and he saw the passion in her face, he knew there was no turning back. If that damn curse were true, at least he would die happy tonight.

Deirdre awoke with a start as a coldness enveloped her. The hearth had gone out, and the room was filled with dark shadows, a meager shaft of light coming through a crack in the shuttered window. The chill sent gooseflesh down her bare arms. She pulled the bedclothes to her chin, realizing her nakedness. She rested a hand on her still flat belly, remembering it all.

Gentle snoring emerged from Aleck. His lifeblood blazed bright, and she found herself wanting to cry! She pressed her body against his back. *He is not dead*, silent words told her. Something had happened to change her fate...or what happened to Cortland and Gordon were just coincidences. Was it really not her fault? Was she truly not responsible? A profound thought illuminated within her. She hadn't killed Aleck! Relief washed over her. She wanted more of him...to know he was real, that this was real.

Her fingers fell upon herself; she could still feel his wetness within her. Her nerves seemed heightened more than ever before, and her own brief touch roused her desire. She drew her hand to his body and traced it down his ribs to his bare bottom. Her nipples hardened against the hot, damp skin of his back. A tingle mixed with early pregnancy strangeness led to a perplexing sense of arousal. Aleck's snoring stopped as her hand slid along his narrow hip and fell on something more intimate.

A soft moan escaped his lips as she treated him to the same sensation that he had given her when he had touched her on the beach. He rolled flat, and she took advantage of the moment and his hard longing. She fondled him in a way that caused his breath to become erratic.

Then, she floated over on top of him, her breasts against his chest. She could smell the muskiness of him and before a word could be said, she kissed him. Her hair fell in a waterfall about his face, shrouding them in a tent of clean fragrance and complete darkness. He cupped her cheeks and allowed their tongues to dance together. She then did the unthinkable, something she had never done before. The desire was too great not to do it...she slid onto him, reaching a new level of awareness and being.

By God, it felt better the second time. Deirdre could not remember it being this intense before. Both Cortland and Gordon had done their husbandly duty, and it had left her feeling incomplete. She gripped Aleck's shoulders, her nails digging into his skin as they swayed together.

He guided her, his hands upon her skin as scalding as the lifeblood he radiated. He helped her find a motion that swept them both to a point of breathlessness. Aleck didn't stop as she crumpled upon him. He held onto her, whirled her around and pressed her into the bed, continuing the cadence. She bit her lip until it was painful, holding the scream of pleasure that begged to be released. He silenced her with his mouth, heavy and demanding. The stubble on his chin scraped her face, but he wouldn't yield and she didn't want him to.

Her hands roved over his body, down his back, eager and willing. She wanted to touch every part of him. She wanted to fuse his body with hers. As he brought her to the edge again, her heart nearly burst.

Aleck was heaving, his hot breath in her ear. "Oh, love." He collapsed onto her, heaving.

Her eyes grew wet, and she began to shudder beneath him. What in God's name had just happened? As they lay unmoving except for their pounding hearts, she had to wonder. Was Venora right? Did she love Aleck?

CHAPTER TEN

After a week of searching the extent of Skye, the trail had disappeared. Even coin would not buy Agmus results. It wasn't as if he was bloody English, but these Highlanders were stubborn heathens. As he skirted the shores of Loch Alsh back to Dornie, his anger grew to an intolerable level, and he led his soldiers at a swift pace, forcing them beyond their limit. The jolt of the horse jarred his bones, but it fed his resolve and he rode on.

Not only had he lost his advantage—that woman with the eyes that bore right through him, much like a witch—but he had spent a week riding all over damnation trying to find her. Somebody would suffer. He eyed his three soldiers. They were fools.

God's teeth...the letter from Bruce, although it would likely cripple Alasdair's plans by not having it, held no information. The cursed parchment was encoded. His soldiers could only wield swords, not decipher codes. He was left with no bartering piece, nothing to substantiate his cause, and he was unsure where the impetuous man had gone. He presumed one of the isles, but which? Bruce was not in hiding. Or perhaps Alasdair had turned back and gone north, fleeing into the depths of the Highlands?

No, Alasdair would never run. Agmus had taught him too well.

Alasdair's ambush at the tidal crossing had been unexpected. Next time, Agmus would just run the bastard through and eliminate all his troubles. Now all he had was a piece of parchment only fit to wipe his arse.

"Hold!" Agmus brought his tired horse to a halt and lifted a flat hand. He tapped his fingers on his thigh, working each swollen knuckle and cold fingertip. The movement hurt, but it would help. He wished he had packed more of his willow bark for his joints; he was down to the last drops in his flask. He had disposed of his herbalist when she said that there was nothing else she could do. Rest in his countryside and no more riding, she had recommended. He was no lout!

He lifted his leg over the saddle, feeling the ache settle in his back. Carney came to his aid, but he shoved a foot in the man's jaw. "Leave me!"

"Get wood," Ronat ordered. Carney hobbled away, holding his bloody chin.

Agmus landed with a thud, sending a shockwave up his left side to his hip. He had reworked the plan over in his head meticulously. Everything needed to fall into place; there was no room for error. He directed a glare to Ronat. "Make camp. We rest for a few hours."

"Aye, Baron."

With his decision made, Agmus settled down for the night. "Carney and Ronat, you two stand watch," he ordered when they returned with wood. "Fall asleep and it will be your head, Ronat."

He then took a hefty swallow of the last of his willow-bark ale and pondered his plans again as he closed his eyes to attempt sleep.

In the bleak predawn, a body landing atop Agmus awoke him with a painful start. "What in damnation?" He gasped for breath, pinned.

Carney appeared above him, blood splattered on his round, unshaven face. He scowled and rubbed his split upper lip. "Up, you!" He lifted the body off Agmus and tossed the dazed man against a tree. "Baron, we caught these men trying to steal our horses."

Ronat held a dirk against the throat of a second captive.

Agmus stood and brushed himself off. He glanced about, squinting in the minimal light. "Where is..." He forgot the fool's name. "...our other soldier?"

"Retrieving the horses," Carney said, spitting blood.

"How did you let this happen?" He glared at Ronat. The arse was lucky he was behind the man in question, or Agmus would have pounded him to the ground.

Ronat responded with an insolent look beneath dark eyebrows. The scar on his cheek throbbed with the clench of jaw.

"Who are you?" he asked the man under Ronat's blade. Filthy from head to boot, with long loose hair, the stranger narrowed his eyes. He remained silent with an almost impish grin. He didn't look to be suffering for food but he wore no armor, which was typical of the Highlanders. Not a vassal. An emissary? A lookout? Or a foolish thief?

"Is that one dead?" Agmus cocked his head to the other captive leaning against a tree.

Carney nudged him with his boot and the man moaned, gripping his belly. "Nay, not yet."

Agmus lifted his sword, approached the injured heathen, and shoved his blade through his gut. The sharp jolt of the strike rippled up Agmus's arm to his shoulder, but he refused to succumb to it.

The man cried in shock and bled out slowly, ending with a gurgle and his eyes agape. Agmus was slow and meticulous as he wiped the blade on the dead man's shoulder. "Well, now he is." Lifting his cleaned sword, he pointed it at the first captive. He tightened his grip to white knuckles to prevent his arm from shaking. The sword felt heavier with each passing day.

Although outwardly not frightened, the man was quick to relent with upraised hands. His eyes didn't leave Agmus's face though. "Our laird is MacDougall, and this is *his* land."

Agmus blew out a breath and laughed. "Your laird approves of attacks on nobles riding along a well-known road? You're aware that thieving, against a *baron*, is punishable by death. I represent King Edward. An assault on me is an assault on our sovereign. Why should I let you live?"

He grimaced as Ronat pressed the dirk harder against his throat, drawing blood. "I was ordered to take precautions."

"Precautions against whom?"

A corner of his mouth turned into a malicious smirk. "Anyone who might be our enemy."

Agmus gritted his teeth but didn't allow him to see his weakness. "You Highland clans are like bickering lads.

When will you learn to stop fighting amongst yourselves and instead yield to our king?"

The man puffed out a huff.

"Do you have a particular enemy in the area?"

His opponent stared him down. *Bold*, Agmus thought. This MacDougall could be an asset...or an obstacle. Agmus wielded his sword with lightning speed and stuck it at the base of the man's throat. Ronat removed his own blade but kept his grip tight on the prisoner from behind. Agmus pressed, drawing more blood. His upper arm quivered, but he allowed hatred to keep the blade straight, focused.

The man yielded. "MacCoinneach. L-Laird MacCoinneach...but he never comes through here, not until when we saw his men a few weeks ago. I've been ordered to watch the area for their return."

"And steal nobles' horses while ye wait?" Carney stepped forward.

"Aye, well...that..."

Agmus couldn't believe his luck. He sheathed his sword. "Who were these men you saw pass through here?"

"The laird's daughter. A noble and his wife and one of the MacCoinneach soldiers, not far behind 'em." Agmus forced a stoic look, masking his delight. "Well, then. You'll take me to your laird unless you'd prefer the worms dine on you tonight."

The thrill of discovery awoke a new sensation within Agmus. He had let his physical ailments rain on his spirit too much lately. Newfound information was rejuvenating. It had to be Alasdair. God damn it, he would track down that bastard son of his if it was the last thing he did on this bloody earth.

Alasdair slipped out of bed at daybreak, allowing Deirdre her needed rest. After dressing, he reached the hall and found Annella awake and at the table. Christina sat in her lap, sipping a cup of steaming milk. "Does something trouble the lass?"

Annella yawned. "Nay, she sometimes likes to rise when the cows do."

"Aye." He sat and wiped the sleep from his eyes.

"Watch her a moment, and I'll fetch eggs and milk for you." Annella already pushed the girl into his crossed arms and proceeded to the kitchen before he could protest.

Christina squirmed as he held her. Giving up on restraining her, he let her down and followed her as she toddled from thing to thing. She reached for the fire stoker. "No, no..." He swiped it from her. She reached her pile of wooden blocks by the hearth and tossed them about. "No, no..." he said again, grabbing the blocks and plopping them into a nearby basket.

Fatigue paled her normally rosy cheeks, and her curly locks were in a tangled mound atop her head. She looked up at him, her brown almond-shaped eyes searching his. He inhaled sharply as it struck him for the first time. That gaze was too familiar. She inherited Annella's fairness in skin, but the rest of her was unlike mother or Alan. He wondered...

She reached the corner of the hearth and leaned too close to the fire; he scooped her up. She let out a huge wail. "Hush, hush. 'Tis all right." He patted her springy hair and wiped fresh tears away. Well, she did have Thomas's temperament, too, always fretting. Hmm. If Annella had been with Thomas all this time and was able to convince him of Christina's legitimacy, what about...? The woman did have a sparkle about her and was quite persuasive. He brushed a hand through his hair, wondering.

Annella hurried into the room, empty-handed. She laughed out loud when she saw Alasdair holding Christina. "Taking a liking to her, have you?"

He mustered a shrug. "She's a busy thing and not well."

Christina squealed as Annella took her.

"Mama," she said with a pout.

"She'll be well. Her new teeth hurt. Sometimes she gets a fever when that happens. I slip a few drops of whisky in her warm milk, and she feels better." She sat and coddled Christina, whispering sweet words to her. She looked up a moment later. "Thom shall be awake shortly if it is he you seek? Och, the food is in the kitchen. Sorry, Ali. I heard her fussing and came right out..."

"Och, aye, thanks. Don't bother him. It can wait until he rises." With that, he stood to leave.

"Alasdair?" she said quietly.

No one was near enough to hear her address him by his true name. Even so, he wished both she and Thomas would cease using it. He cringed. "Aye?"

"Deirdre is most agreeable."

"Aye, she is."

"I think she'll understand if you tell her. You can't let this go on much longer."

"I know." He paused and sat again. Instead of talking about Deirdre, for he already knew the purgatory that wrapped around his conscience like entwined ropes, a question nagged at him. "You'd do anything for Robert Bruce?"

"Aye," she said with a nod, distracted by wiping Christina's nose. "Why do you ask?"

"The men...the workers. When Thom wrote to me a month ago, they were stalled, stubborn, refusing to work. Then I arrive and now the men have nearly two dozen ships finished. I do wonder why. What persuaded them to carry on."

"Men are like that."

"Not the men I know."

Her clear blue eyes were alight with confidence. She looked over Alasdair's shoulder. Nobody was coming.

"Ann..."

She swatted her hand at an invisible fly. Annella was never one to fall for intimidation. She purposely fussed over Christina, who wiggled to get down again. "Sometimes men just need a wee coaxing."

"Hmm." He was right. He watched her stew as she bristled with defiance.

Huffing a breath, she said, "After Thom wrote to you, he went to the mainland, north, seeking more men to replace those we'd lost, while also gathering supplies. So, I went to the workers."

His look must have conveyed his thoughts.

"Och, don't fret. I am not blind to bloodshed and lies. Robbie is my cousin, after all," she said, crossing her arms.

"I brought them more food and spoke with them." She paused, exhaling loudly. She swiped her hand along her skirt and held his gaze. "I promised them each ten more coin."

"You what?"

"Have you grown deaf on your travels? Ten coin." She stuck out her chin.

Christina mimicked, "Ten, ten, ten, ten..."

"Ten more *each*? Blazes, Annella, if Thomas knew..."

"He doesn't need to know. My cousin, The Bruce, as some would like to call him," she said with stern emphasis but with a wrinkled nose in distaste at his apparent nickname, "has plenty to give."

She shocked him into silence.

"I'm no fool, Ali. I understand the importance of all of this."

"Aye, you do." No wonder Deirdre had taken a liking to her. With a nod, he rose, and left through the kitchen. After a bite of hard-boiled eggs and a swallow of milk, he stepped outside. A brisk and dark morning received him. He had slept restlessly, despite the release of energy. Rubbing his arms to stir up some heat, he sat on a patch of grass and watched the sun slowly rise over the eastern horizon. Then he did something he had not done that much in years.

He prayed.

God seemed to be ever-present in his life, hanging over him like a rain cloud that wouldn't leave him alone. Or perhaps it was his conscience that beleaguered him and not Himself. If God was in heaven, looking down, even laughing at him, then the devil himself was here on earth—in the form of Baron Agmus Montgomerie, his wretched father.

Annella was right. He needed to tell Deirdre the truth. He couldn't keep it from her any longer, and damn himself to hell for making love to her under the name of Aleck Stirrat. She had nestled her way not only into his bed, but into his heart.

As the sun eased above the horizon, lost in a milky haze of morning mist, and not feeling any liberation from his ruminations, he returned to the house. Realization hit him as he took the path in long, purposeful strides.

He was alive.

Oh, that bloody curse.

He had forgotten about it. He had been correct all along. The curse never existed. He had not shared a hundred kisses with Deirdre before he bedded her, and here he was walking, breathing...alive.

A tremor dashed down his back. His arm itched, and through the fabric, he rubbed the scar that branded him from hand to shoulder. He may have been a God-fearing man, but he was a believer in humanity and creeds. He clenched his fist and rubbed his arm more vigorously. Between his father's second attempt at trying to kill him, the naval workers' behavior, and his bloody guise possibly ruining his relationship with the first woman he'd ever cared about, he was about ready to burst apart.

He cooled himself down by the time he reached the hall, at least for appearance's sake. Thomas sat at the oak table alone.

"Not happy to see me?" Thomas asked.

The chair scratched the stone floor as Alasdair pulled it out and slumped onto it. He shrugged and looked at his friend with a loud sigh. Brown almond-shaped eyes stared back, conveying what words could not.

A hand glided over the subtle rounded swell of Deirdre's belly. "Hmmm..." she murmured. Aleck's touch sent prickles of excitement all over her body. Her eyes popped open, and she awoke from the dream.

"Love..." His voice was muffled under the bedclothes, and she wasn't able to discern what he said. He was naked, body hard and pressed against her.

"I'm not dreaming?" she asked, becoming aware.

He stroked her shoulder and traced a single finger along her collarbone, down to the hollow of her neck. "Nay...I need you, Deirdre." A vulnerable passion filled his voice.

In response, her lips sought his, and hotness welcomed her. After another day without him, she desired his touch more than she thought she would. When they saw each other during the past few days, they had fallen into a rhythm that lacked awkwardness. It felt natural to be around him after their night together, much to her surprise. He now slept in her bedchamber. There had been no words. They both just knew.

The smell of sweat and salty sea on his skin made her hungry, but not for food. The room was black, but she felt along his body as he lay beside her. She matched each curve and muscle with what she had seen in daylight, learning the intimate parts of him—his muscled arms, the valley in between his shoulder blades, the indentation at the top of his buttocks, and the raised ripples on his scarred arm. Beneath her fingertips, she could almost feel the burned memory of the scars.

She paused, rose, and lit two candles on the table.

She returned to Aleck and sat in his lap.

He let out a happy moan. "Och, I do like you in my lap." He traced a finger down her naked shoulder.

She couldn't help but smile.

She drew her inspection to the two cuts on his arm. "How are they healing?" The one from their very first encounter by the loch which Gilford had mended looked satisfactory, but the other injury from their confrontation with the baron fared not so well. It was swollen and pink. It would need a new poultice.

"Och, well."

"And this?" She drew her hand to his thigh, which also looked good, considering. Gilford was a good surgeon.

He slid his hand over hers. "Och, well."

"And these?" she said, running her fingertip down the bridge of his nose, which was still slightly bruised from numerous assaults, hers included.

"Och, well," he said yet again, his voice growing deeper, the words slurred with sleepy desire.

She sighed. "Any more aches?"

He smirked. "Och, *well*..."

She lightly tittered but then said, "Is this customary for you to be so...so..." She lacked the words. "Injury-prone?" She scrunched her brow. The wounds weren't exactly his own doing.

He drew her hand to his chest. His heart thumped steady and slowly beneath her hand. The lightness of the mood dissipated as he cupped her neck and brought her mouth to his.

He breathed his fiery lifeblood into her as she felt his need grow stronger, matching hers. He switched spots with her, rolled on top, and slid between her legs. She gasped, clutching his back, urging him not to retreat. Images of their first night together flashed behind her eyes. She rocked her hips and muffled her own moan as pleasure found her once again.

He slowed and continued the dance of bringing her to the brink and then pulling back, teasing them both. His arms moved gently down her shoulders. She caressed his body in return, allowing her fingers to roam and reach all parts.

Dark, black-blue eyes stared back at her, heavy with thought. Oh, how she wished she could read his emotions.

He muttered a mixture of curses and sweetness under his breath, hot and moist in her ear. Physically connected, they swayed. Their connection delved deeper than that of the flesh. A shared contentment and peace flowed from his lifeblood, and she clung to it. Deirdre felt the change. The red heat of his ever-present spirit turned to a white hot glow. It wasn't like the white of death and evil, but rather the glow of a poker removed from the flame. It melted her soul.

She succumbed to it all, unable to guard her heart any longer. "I love you, Aleck," she said through wet eyes as he brought her to a swirling, turbulent storm of emotions.

He collapsed upon her, silent, the only sounds in the room the pounding pulse in her temple and his uneven exhalation. He spoke so quietly that she wouldn't have heard him if his mouth wasn't beside her ear. "And...I love you."

The following morning, as Crystoll and Aleck went off with Thomas, Deirdre decided to visit Venora again. Still unraveled from all that her aunt had told her, she made her way to the cottage.

Venora greeted her with a warm expectant look. She picked up a basket by her door. "Come, dearie. I need to collect willow bark."

They strode along a narrow path away from the cottage and village, picked their way down to the shoreline, and emerged at a basin where a low-lying loch sat. A few tall willow trees guarded the loch, out of place compared to the rest of the landscape.

"My father planted them here. He brought the seedlings from the mainland. He may hiv been a sick soul, but he understood the importance of simple remedies to help with aches and ailments. My mother and sister also used plants for easier curatives," Venora said in answer to Deirdre's unspoken question.

Deirdre pulled out her knife and set to work. She cut several thin branches off the tree. As she sliced the bark off the small, slender branches, she felt Venora's studying gaze.

"Ye've skills with gardening and herbs, hiv ye?"

Deirdre recognized by now that nothing Venora said was a question, for she already knew the answers, but she obliged her anyway. "At home, my duties are to tend to the household and gardens. My mother had left behind some of her books. I don't understand most of them, but a few of her remedies were easy to follow. Willow bark is good for pains. It's nothing our local herbalist and midwife don't already know." Her mother's books reminded her of the one she lost, somewhere in the Cuillin of Skye.

"Ye still don't believe."

Deirdre looked up from her work, knowing she could be direct with her aunt. There was no point in fruitless talk. "I would like to know more about my dream."

Venora sat beside her, lifted a branch, and began to scrape it with her knife. "Do ye hiv just the one?"

"Yes, it's the same." Deirdre explained it to her.

"That's a vision, dearie. Not a dream."

"Are you certain?" Deirdre pulled her attention from her work for a moment to watch her aunt's face. Being unable to read Venora's emotions was more disturbing than her inability to read Aleck's.

Venora didn't answer. She just smiled.

"What does it mean?"

"Dreams and visions can be interpreted various ways. The black-haired man from the wood is the one ye love, aye?"

She twisted her hands in her lap. Then she ran her finger along the knobby willow twig. Once again, Venora had been correct. Deirdre had confessed her love to Aleck in the wee morning hours, and he had done the same. Not only had she given him her body—out of wedlock, God forgive her—but she had given him her heart. Her lip trembled. Inadvertently, she had seduced him, exactly as her father had ordered. Each day was another day farther into her pregnancy and toward a deadline of deceiving Aleck.

"Oh, dearie, something troubles ye more than this dream. Dinna fret o'er it." Venora tapped her hand. A blue calm stillness sank into Deirdre's skin.

There was no undoing what had already been done. "Was I *fated* to find him?"

Venora blew a breath out and laughed. "I dinna believe in fate."

"What does it mean then?"

"Ye alone can interpret them, dearie. I am a Seer, but I can't feel the way ye do. I can't understand another's visions, only my own."

Deirdre wrinkled her brow. This wasn't enlightening at all. "The other day, you spoke of another man, with a black *soul*. Who was that?"

"Ah, dearie..." Her face was uninterpretable, but she shook her head vehemently. "Stay away from him. Only death surrounds him."

Deirdre frowned. "It's too late for that." She rubbed her forehead. She couldn't take much more. "Aleck—I can't feel his emotions like all the others. His lifeblood is too strong. Do you know why?"

"There's a purpose to everything, dearie."

Deirdre sighed. That was no help.

"Be mindful of Sir Stirrat's past."

She lifted her face and stared at her aunt's emotionless eyes. "Of his past?"

"This man ye love, his mother died in a fire."

Deirdre swiped at invisible tears. Venora may have been a Seer, but she didn't understand how to communicate well with others. She lacked prudence, and Deirdre struggled to make all the connections. A part of her grew disheartened. Venora was nothing like she had envisioned. She swallowed, shoving those thoughts aside in a hope that Venora couldn't sense her disappointment. "He already told me that."

"Not in the way you think, dearie."

A heavy, stifling fog engulfed Deirdre, despite the clear day. "What...do...you mean?"

"She was a witch." Venora's face studied Deirdre for a reaction. Seeing none, she continued. "Well, she was not a *witch*," she said with emphasis, "...or a *natural variance* like us, lass, but she had wronged some people and suffered greatly for it."

"It can't be." Deirdre wanted to stand, to run to the keep but was unable to bring herself to do so.

"She was burned at the stake. This dark man of yers, he almost died with her. His father pushed him into the flames along with his mother."

She thought she may retch. Oh, poor Aleck. "His father tried to kill him?"

"Ye hiv doubts?"

Deirdre contemplated.

"A Seer cannot lie."

When Deirdre tried to speak, a garbled sound came out.

Venora rose, basket in hand, ready to leave. "Ask him. He'll tell ye."

She nodded feebly, like a fool.

"Dinna fash, dearie. All will fare well," Venora assured.

Her mood lifted slightly. "All will fare well?"

Venora's mouth spread into a large warm grin replacing her usual dour expression. Truth was a seedling growing in her aunt's seaweed blue eyes. "Aye."

Deirdre wanted to ask her more, but she couldn't. She didn't know what Venora meant. What would be well? The war with England, her relationship with Aleck, the pregnancy, her Feeling gift, her clan's future...

"Which reminds me," Venora continued, releasing a melodious hum as she dug into her pocket. She pulled out something wrapped in a small piece of green fabric. She pushed the item into Deirdre's hand. "This was yer mother's."

Deirdre's fingers fumbled with the wrapping, and she hesitated. She traced the embroidery of delicate blue flowers. A pure, almost ochre color emanated from the item within it.

"Close yer eyes. Open it up. Feel its lifeblood."

Deirdre did as told even though non-human objects held no lifeblood. Although the stone her fingers fell upon was smooth, hard, and should have felt cold, it was warm, like a hot rock taken from a fire. The radiance she felt blazed through her palms down to her elbows. It rushed up to her shoulders and flew through her lungs. She breathed out, feeling the hot breath of life, of healing.

She opened her eyes. The rock was simple, shiny and black, and silky like a river stone. "What is it?"

Venora spoke in a soft, fond voice from a far off place. "A Healer's stone. Yer mother left it here. She had a few of these. It wasn't the source of her ability, but it did help her harness powers from beyond the Silver Veil."

Deirdre carefully rewrapped it, and held the stone to her chest. "What do I do with it?"

Her aunt shrugged. "I may hiv the Sight, but I only see what is shown to me. Take it home with ye."

Deirdre tucked it into her skirt pocket.

"Go to the stones of Fhinn first," Venora added.

The days began to pass in a blur. Deirdre assisted Annella around the house and garden, but she felt restive. Another week passed.

"I think it's my time to return to Dornie, Annella," Deirdre said with sadness one morning. Although she had enjoyed the company of her new friend, her time here had been too long. She envisioned her father's enraged face, nearly matching the russet-auburn of his beard. Heavens, and she tried to avoid Crystoll, whose lifeblood grew increasingly agitated as the days passed.

"I'll miss you," Annella said, surprise absent in her voice. "I know you must go home."

Deirdre pulled out a stubborn weed, grunting with the exertion. "And I will miss you." She frowned. "My place is in Dornie, with my family."

"I'm sorry there's not more here for you, Deirdre, other than your aunt. I sense that meeting her wasn't as fruitful as you hoped?"

"I am afraid so. It left me feeling uncertain." She shrugged. "I suppose I expected more." She spoke with a hesitant whisper. "Did you know that she's a Seer?"

Annella's face said it all. "Come walk with me, Deirdre." Her friend rose and stretched.

They lifted their baskets and proceeded to the kitchen's pantry to drop off their vegetables. Winded, Annella turned to her. "Somewhere private."

Deirdre followed as Annella led her on the outside path from the keep.

Crystoll emerged from the stable. "Good day, ladies." His always-pleasant smile didn't hide the unease Deirdre sensed. He was a whirlpool of anxious emotion. "A word, my lady?"

Annella took his hint. "I'll check on the mare that was delivered yesterday."

Crystoll thanked her, and waited a moment before speaking. "My lady, I don't mean to harry you, but I had hoped we would soon return to Dornie."

"Have you spoken to Aleck? Perhaps he—"

He grimaced. "No. His place is here, my lady. I've been able to help him, but I am afraid he may be here for a while. It's imperative that I bring you home." Crystoll lowered his voice, with a quick look over his shoulder. "You've visited with your aunt, aye?"

She nodded.

"Then your purpose has been met. I beseech you, my lady, I must bring you home."

"I understand. We will return home soon," she said with a heavy heart. She couldn't delay Crystoll much longer. Her father's orders took priority over hers, and both knew it. Crystoll's compliance was out of friendship, but Deirdre had pressed even that for too long. He would take her home by force if he had to.

Aleck needed to stay here. She needed to return home. By the heavens, she hadn't expected to...to...fall in love with Aleck.

"Forgive my disrespect, but I can't...I don't..." He stopped himself, the side of his mouth pinched into a lopsided frown. "After what happened with the baron, I fear for you, and I'm afraid for Glen Shiel. In my first message to our laird, sent from Skye, I relayed our destination." He paused, releasing a pent-up sigh. "I sent another message upon our arrival here as well. I informed our laird of the baron and the circumstances we encountered."

"You did?"

He ran a hand through tousled hair. Brown eyes watched her. "I had to, my lady."

"What about Aleck?"

Crystoll licked his lips. His face said it all.

"He's been honest with us, Crystoll. We need to trust him."

"Forgive me, my lady." He bowed his head with regret.

She clasped his hand. "I appreciate your honesty, Crystoll. We will leave within the week." Her statement left her with an empty feeling.

He inclined his head, apologized again, and strode to the house, his steps heavy but fast. Annella returned. "Fare he well?"

"He's restless to return home."

A HUNDRED KISSES

"Ahh. I see. That's what I wanted to speak with you about."

Deirdre's fingertips tingled. "Oh?"

Annella guided her down the path away from the keep. They sat upon two large boulders that seemed out of place on a sandy beach. The wind was calm.

"Have you told him yet?" Annella asked, her hand caressing her round protruding belly.

Deirdre's pulse quickened. "Told who what?"

Annella sheltered her emotions well. She cast her look out to the sea. "Aleck. About the bairn."

Deirdre swallowed. "Not yet." If Annella had noticed her pregnancy, she wondered who else had. God, first it was Moreen and her father, then her aunt, and now Annella. "Can you see?" she asked, looking down at her belly.

"No. It's not his?"

Deirdre fell apart. "N-Noooo." Suddenly cold, she shivered.

Annella's warm lifeblood eased Deirdre's unrest a hair. She took Deirdre's hands in hers. "All shall be well, Deirdre. I won't tell him."

"H-How did you know?"

"A woman knows. I saw the signs when you came here. How far are you?"

Tears found their way down Deirdre's cheeks in thick, angry droplets. "Two moons, I think? My mind is a puddle. The bairn is Cortland's. We were married, but he died."

"I remember him when he visited with your father and Crystoll. I'm sorry, Deirdre. I didn't know."

Deirdre whimpered, sobs choking her.

Annella stroked Deirdre's hands. "It's all right, hush, hush. It's all right." She cooed. "What does your father say? It is your husband who shall rule?"

"Aye." Deirdre wondered if Annella knew about Edmund's misfortunes. "My father is forgiving, but keeping Eilean Donan and our clan's future secure...is all he sees nowadays."

"He wishes another marriage?" She nodded woodenly, answering her own question. "I see."

Deirdre was amazed by Annella's perception.

"He wanted to arrange a marriage to Aleck, but no alliance was struck. Aleck was adamant about getting here, and he slipped away during the night, and I—well, my father didn't give me permission to come. I snuck away and came along to see my aunt. My father sent Crystoll after us, and I convinced him to continue to Uist. I'm sorry that I've not been completely honest with you. Och, I've made a mess of it all."

Annella pursed her lips. "What about your brother? Has he no children?"

"He and his wife have not been blessed with living children."

"Ahh, I see."

"There is more." The deception of it all consumed her. "My father asked me to seduce Aleck, make him think the child is his, then force him to marry me for an alliance."

"Ahh. Did you?"

Annella was anything but self-righteous, but Deirdre felt her stare burn into her, despite her gracious lifeblood. "Yes—well, not on purpose. But we did lie together..." She stopped and hung her head in her hands. "Oh, God, what have I done?"

Annella laid a hand on Deirdre's knee. "Tell him. Tell him that it's his."

"What? I can't." The idea she had ignored for weeks hit her like a full force gale. She was prepared to return home, leaving Aleck and her heart behind, knowing full well that she could no longer lie to him. Now she questioned that judgment.

"Secrets can be found everywhere, even within the strongest marriage. I'm sure there are things Aleck hasn't been able to share with you."

Deirdre's eyes blurred with tears. "We're not married though."

"Yet," she said.

"I don't understand... Do you know something I don't?"

Annella sighed, slightly losing her usual patience. "Deirdre, what I say does not leave us."

Deirdre sniffled. "Aye."

"He's a good man. I see that he loves you. Forgive him, Deirdre, for any wrongs he has done. He's passionate about the Cause, and his heart is in it deeper than I can disclose. Trust me, aye?" She waited for a response.

"By the heavens, if I hear another word about the bloody Cause!"

"Deirdre, we can't hide from it all. My cousin, Robert Bruce, is powerful, dedicated, and loves our country. We pray that he prevails. This Cause means life or death for all of us, Glen Shiel and your family included."

"Annella, speak true to me. I can't bear much more of this circumvention."

Her new friend's eyes glistened with tears. "I tell you all that I can, Deirdre." She grabbed her hands again and squeezed. "He loves you, Deirdre. I've never seen him in such a way. When I lived on the mainland, my family knew Aleck well." She paused and rubbed her belly as if reflecting on what to say next. Her gown rippled in the breeze, but it was tighter and bunched at the large belly. She looked down at her soon-to-be-born child with maternal affection. "Oh, don't deplore me, Deirdre. I've grown fond of you during our time together."

"What is it, Annella?"

"Thomas and I, well, I told you that I met him with Alan a few years ago. He and Alan shared a similar opinion on many causes, and they dealt with trade and other political affairs together. I didn't mean for it to happen..." She drifted off, tears trickling down her cheeks now.

"You and Thomas? I mean, before this bairn?"

"It was one night. Three years ago, a year before Alan died. Alan had asked Thomas to maintain the estate and watch over me while he was away. By that time, Alan had grown old, began to develop the sickness in body and mind. He and I rarely shared a bed."

Deirdre couldn't bring herself to ask it, but it didn't matter, Annella already answered.

"Christina is not Alan's daughter." Annella spoke as if at a confessional. "But Thomas thinks Christina is Alan's daughter."

Deirdre shifted, adjusting her own billowy gown. Sweat collected under her armpits and between her thighs. It had not grown too warm, but she noticed that lately her body held more heat and she was easily winded.

"Deirdre, you cannot tell Aleck the truth about the bairn, not yet."

"What?"

"Do you love him?"

"Yes."

"I see how Aleck cares for you. I've seen that look in my Thomas's eyes."

Deirdre shook her head. "Why do you tell me all of this?"

She blew out a breath, staring across the grasses and flat beach. "Aleck's mother was betrayed and murdered."

The vision of it still troubled her. Sickness had taken her own mother. Death by fire was unimaginable. Och, poor Aleck. "Venora told me."

"Do you know why?" Her eyes grew wide.

"His father, her own husband, had accused her of enchantment and had her killed." Deirdre's gaze fell upon the crashing surf. Even its soothing regularity couldn't pacify her.

"He also accused her of unfaithfulness. She had been with child, not of her husband's seed, when she died."

Deirdre gasped at the awfulness. "Oh dear…I didn't know that."

Annella continued, "Aleck isn't his son either, and when his mother was aflame, his father tried to set him ablaze as well."

Deirdre inhaled, reeling from the revelations from both Annella and Venora. So what Venora had said was true. A part of Deirdre had hoped that Venora's version of the story was exaggerated. "What kind of a person would do that?"

"An evil one."

Silence overtook their conversation as they both sat, staring out at the sea, their minds elsewhere.

"One more thing."

Deirdre wasn't sure she could take anymore.

"Don't see Venora again. I understand that she's your aunt, but she is more than a fortune-teller. She is a true Seer."

Deirdre inhaled sharply.

"I'm sorry, but it's why I wasn't the most forthcoming with you meeting her. People call her a witch. I've not allowed, and will not allow, anything to happen to her. I don't believe she's a witch. People use that word out of fear. She's a broken woman though. She has the special powers of her ancestors, and they run strong in her family. But she has a hurting, dark soul and an even darker past. And I do not want to see you harmed because of it."

Deirdre's pulse began to race. She stood to leave, hurt by Annella's request. This was all too much.

Annella rose beside her and took her by the shoulders. "Deirdre, whatever your gift may be, please be careful with it. Aleck's a hurt man, too. His past haunts him. If he knew…if he…" She stopped herself, shaking her head. "He has a temper and passion. I see that with him, and with you. I don't want anything to come between you. In time, peel the truth away, and let him see it all for the beauty that it is. Your gift, the bairn… He will understand. In time. Be slow about sharing the truth. Men needs small bites. Their egos are tender."

"Why don't you tell Thomas about Christina?"

"Thomas and I are happy together. He has always loved Christina as his own, thinking she is Alan's. I love that about him—he loves a child he thinks is Alan's. It would crush him to learn that she is his." She rubbed her brow, heaving a sigh. "It makes no sense, but you see, he was stricken with guilt after we spent that evening together. He never returned to the keep if I was there, until Alan had called for him on his deathbed. By then, it was too late. He saw Christina, and I saw the question in his eyes. He refused to allow himself to have betrayed his good friend even in death. I lied. I had to. But, oh, Deirdre! He loves me and her, but because he thinks that it was one night—an indiscretion—nothing more. His honor would not allow it, thus I won't tell him."

Twisted as it was, Deirdre understood. Men and their pride.

She shrugged. "I tell you this because I am certain that eventually, Aleck will understand." She softened her voice. "Thomas will, too, when I tell him." She rubbed her belly and blew a deep breath out. "As it is now, Aleck can't know the truth yet. If you want to be with him, marry him, then he must think the bairn is his."

"I cannot lie to him."

"Then you need to choose. Lie and live with him, or return home without him."

Deirdre lacked a response. Her heart told her that Aleck would understand. She had to tell him the truth.

The sun dipped in the sky, and shadows danced across the rocks. "Come," Annella said, rising.

They walked in silence until nearly to the stable. "Please heed what I say. He loves you, I see it. You have an unusual connection. You belong together."

Deirdre's thoughts churned.

Aleck's mother had been accused of sorcery, when all she had been guilty of was adultery. Aleck had been burned in more than one way by a father who hated him. If he learned of Deirdre's gift, what would he think? And the bairn, oh that sweet innocence left over from one night with Cortland. Could she convince Aleck that it was his and live with that lie? It all seemed logical when her father had first mentioned it, but in truth, the lie was faulted with cracks.

Secrets between a husband and wife. Annella's words echoed. Deirdre wept inside.

CHAPTER ELEVEN

"Good afternoon, love."

Aleck's warm voice sent a wave of delight down Deirdre's back, and she turned from her kitchen work to find him behind her, a basketful of herbs in his hand. She playfully slapped him. "You creep in here like a cat!"

A striking grin parted his mouth. His beard had grown in more. Deirdre approached him, took the basket, plopped it on the table, and kissed him. She stroked his chin, a pleasant prickle under her fingers.

"I need a shave, don't I?"

"Hmm, perhaps," she said, wrapping her arms around him, not bothered by the dirt that covered his working trews and shirt. She let her hands play in his thick, wavy hair.

He pulled back slightly and squeezed a spray of flowers in between them. "For you."

"Och! Where did you find these? I've looked everywhere, but beyond the herbs in the gardens, all that bed the ground are grasses and peat bogs." She eyed the petite, fan-like blue flowers with orange stamens that caught the light and shone like small flames. She inhaled their delicate fragrance.

"My secret."

Secret. That word sparked a sense of guilt within her.

He gave her the smile that sent her heart quivering. She glanced out the window. "What time is it?" She had gotten lost in baking bread and grinding herbs for Annella's cook.

He sniffed the air. "Time for supper."

"Productive day, I hope?"

"Aye. We finished early today." He reached around her, an arm firmly on her hip, and grabbed a few dried plums off the counter. He remained affectionately close to her. After a swallow, he leaned in and kissed her again, the fruit sweet on his tongue. "What troubles you, love?"

Curse her face for showing her emotions. "It's time for me to return home." She had procrastinated enough. It was now well over a fortnight since arriving. The past two days she had spent going over and over the options Annella laid out for her. She couldn't bring herself to lie to him. Or worse—have him hate her for her gifts or the child. She had to go home. Reality was a sickle to her heart.

He lifted her chin, drawing her gaze to meet his. "We'll return home soon, I promise. I have a final trip to the north, for three days, and then we can take our leave."

"We?"

He took her hand in his. "If you will have me, that is?"

She hesitated, searching for a response. "You'll return home with me?"

"Aye, that is, if...will you marry me, Deirdre? I'd take good care of you, love. I would pledge myself to you. My work is almost finished here. I don't marry you for an alliance with your father. I will make amends with him though. Alas, love, I want you. Just you. This is the last time I ask it of you, and if you don't want to, then I will understand if you wish to leave—"

Audacity gripped her. "Yes."

Tell him about the bairn—his bairn, she bade herself. *Tonight.*

His lifeblood grew stronger, hotter. He leaned down and kissed her at length, tenderly. Energy flowed from his lips to her own, down her throat, and settled within her core.

"After supper, come with me to the stones," she blurted when he came up for a breath.

His hand traced down her back, and he cupped her bottom. "What stones?" He leaned in, his breath heavier on her neck than the light kiss he brushed her skin with.

"You've not heard of them? The stones of Fhinn."

"I don't believe in such things."

She drew out her words. "I've heard they're spectacular to see at sunset. If we go after supper, the sun's rays pass through a cleft stone at the pinnacle, and it spreads glorious light all over the hill. Annella said it's a peaceful place to reflect, and take in the beauty..."

"Annella, oh?"

She felt abashed. "Aye." Did he know about Venora's gift? She had heeded Annella's warning and avoided her aunt, despite the incredible pull she felt to visit her once more.

He squeezed her hand, pulled her close, and planted a thorough kiss on her lips. "I've enough beauty right here, but certainly, let's go there tonight."

After supper, wrapped in the warmth of their plaids, they escaped for their twilight walk. Deirdre needed it. Her soul needed it. With bated breath, she hushed her mind.

The hum of the earth vibrated in her bones as they approached the circle, and the fine hairs on her arms rose.

They drew upon the hill, a slight rising slope that opened up into a wide plateau above the bog and loch that bordered Port nan Long. "It's not too far from here," Deirdre said, huffing with the slight exertion.

They were an hour's distance from the village, and she had regrettably insisted upon going by foot.

They summited the small plateau and reached the wide circle of stones, and Deirdre gasped. Her jaw dropped. "I've never seen such a thing. It's...it's...

"Remarkable," Aleck said for her.

They were awe inspiring. The plateau was covered with brown and flaxen sea grass, and scattered throughout, in the shape of a large oval, were gray and white speckled granite slabs. Some were toppled over to their sides, but others remained erect, standing Aleck's height or taller. There were about twenty of them, and the oval spread wide, a hundred feet at least. A smaller circlet of stones, equally pointy and intriguing, gathered in the center.

Deirdre approached the center ring where the plateau rose slightly, allowing her to take in the vast sea, the loch, and hillocks. The humming grew louder. It wasn't from Aleck, and there wasn't another soul in sight. Perplexed, but captivated, she stood still and listened. Meanwhile, Aleck wandered around the outskirts of the stones, observing and exploring.

Deirdre closed her eyes and let the cool breeze wash over her. She reached into the pocket of her skirt and rubbed her thumb on the Healer's stone. Suddenly, a wave roared within her, and she was nearly knocked off her feet. She inhaled, allowing the fragrance of the earth to work through her body, settle her nerves, and calm her soul. The whirring strengthened, but it didn't hurt. It was a melody, like wind chimes. Although not a balmy day by any means, the sun's rays encircled her, warming her to the core. A tingle began in her fingertips, raced through her arms, down into her chest, and bolted all the way to her toes.

She felt an array of emotions. Love, red hot and deep, throbbed within her body. Happiness, a deep tawny hue, made her soul smile. Humor, an emotion she had not felt in so very long, was a verdant meadow on a spring day, tickling her toes. Sadness, a cold blue, crept into her bones. She grew dizzy with the mixture of feelings and found herself kneeling, overpowered by it all.

A dominant sensation dwarfed all the others. It was the feeling of tranquility as humanity and nature danced in harmony. It rushed through her like a roaring river.

Aleck came to her side. "Deirdre, what troubles you?"

He helped her upright. She opened her eyes. "Nothing."

He eyed her doubtfully. "You fell to the ground."

"I'm well."

"Was it your head again?"

"Aye," she lied.

"Are you certain? Perhaps there is something Annella has to help you?"

"No, no. I am well, Aleck. So very *well*."

Truly, she was. Venora had been correct. She couldn't explain it, but she finally felt at peace with her gift.

Aleck's gaze was drawn to a large upright stone, with two long slabs on either side. It looked akin to an altar. "Come, let's go over there."

They stood near the large stone, which had a deep cleft in the top. Aleck sat on one of the side slabs and laid his plaid down. Deirdre sat, and he pulled her close with a quick motion.

"Mmphmm!" she said with a startle at his rough gesture, but liking it nonetheless. She liked everything about him. Her mouth hurt from smiling.

The wind stilled, and they sat in silence, his arm around her as they watched the sun set. It wasn't an impressive sunset, seeing as the sky had been clouded all day, but it did cast a few hues of color.

Deirdre drew upon her strength. *He would understand*, she told herself. She was about to tell him but before she could utter a breath, his lips fell upon her neck. He drew her closer, and she spun to face him.

She escaped his kiss for a breath. *Tell him!*

Choices crept into her mind. *Lie and live with him, or tell him the truth and return home.*

His touch grew heavy, persuasive. He fumbled with the laces on her gown, followed by more laces on her kirtle.

"Aleck..." she said. It wasn't his fault she was faint-hearted. She couldn't do it. Invisible tears fought to be shed. This had to be goodbye. She couldn't keep with the lie and marry him no less. Aleck would be fine. He'd find another woman, a better match. At least that's what she told herself. Och, then why had she said yes to his proposal?

Curse her muddled mind!

He lifted her onto his lap, and he leaned back against the center tall slab of stone. He undid the strings to his trews and pulled her closer to his chest, pushing the layers of kirtle and gown up and around her hips. His hands were eager, searching, and quick as he slipped up her chemise.

She surrendered, her heart whimpering, and she moved on top of him. She closed her eyes, savoring his touch. His chest pounded against hers as the power of the stones echoed in her bones and brought her to heightened sense of awareness as they made love. His searing lifeblood joined with hers in a fiery passion. God save her, she yielded to it one final time.

In the early morning hours, Aleck took his leave with Thomas. He promised that, upon his return from a final three-day trip to the workers, they would make arrangements for the trip to Dornie. Deirdre was relieved but also scolded herself for her behavior at the stones. The pregnancy was still well hidden, even in her nakedness, but her breasts were beginning to swell and her midsection was slightly stretched.

When he returned from the ships, she would part ways with him and go home. The thought left her feeling hollow.

A heavy heart brought her to her aunt one last time around midday. It was time for her first goodbye. She arrived at Venora's cottage to find her aunt outside, sitting on a rock, drinking from a cup, and staring at the sea. Venora spoke, despite Deirdre's distance of twenty paces.

"Fire," Venora said in a whisper that carried over to Deirdre on the wind.

"Fire?" Deirdre repeated, approaching. Had she heard her correctly?

"It's from where yer power springs."

"What do you mean?"

Venora turned to her, her eyes distant. "This vision, the man from the wood is burned in it, aye? He dies?"

Deirdre nodded. Venora's bluntness never became comfortable.

"And the lifeblood ye feel from Sir Stirrat, 'tis of fire?"

Deirdre gulped. There was no need to respond.

"He suffered his own misfortune from fire, as ye ken already. Fire is the Feeler's gift. Ye're bound to him by it." Venora rose.

"Bound to him?"

Venora blinked and answered with only a smile, awoken from whatever trance she had been in. "The Ancients harness their power from nature...from the land, the sea, and the sky. Healers like yer mother and grandmother used water."

"Oh," Deirdre said, understanding. "I had a book of hers. It had a fish on it. I couldn't read the Norse, but one page showed Eir, the goddess of healing and mercy. Moreen told me about it, but she couldn't read the rest. I had brought it along on the journey to show you, but it got lost," she said, her voice cracking with disappointment.

"'Tis a shame." Venora shrugged. "Och, well. Come with me. I've something to show ye before ye go."

"But we don't leave for a few more days. I can come back."

Venora stopped and cast her a glance, one mixed with both perception and sadness. "Nay, dearie. This is yer last visit to see me."

Ever? she wanted to ask, but a lump in her throat stole her words.

They went inside her cottage, and Venora pulled several books out of a chest. Deirdre's pulse quickened. They all had the same darkened goatskin binding. Each had a simple metal emblem on the cover. The book that caught her eye first had a tree, with limbs rising as if to an invisible sun.

"That's Earth, the goddess Jörd. Her power lies within us all. We are all drawn to it."

Deirdre nodded. "Is that why I like my gardening? The soil feels so...so...I'm not sure how to explain it. When the soil runs through my fingers, it calms my spirit. I find solace among trees and flowers."

A smile stretched Venora's face. "Aye." She pushed another book in front of Deirdre. A single flame adorned the cover. "Fire is where ye'll find yer power."

"Isn't fire used for evil?" Deirdre asked, thinking of all the ways man had used fire: destroying castles, forging weapons, burning people.

"Man can exploit any power. Yet, we're given our gifts to use for good."

"But your father—?"

She waved that thought away. "He was a madman."

Deirdre sat and stared at the book. "May I?"

"Of course, dearie."

She laid her hand upon the cover and nearly scalded her fingers. "It's hot."

Venora touched it. "Not to me."

Deirdre touched it again. The heat lessened to a simmer as she flipped it open. Just like the heat of Aleck's touch settled the more she touched him, but was still a humming undercurrent, so was the heat in the book. Each page was warm but not as hot as the first touch. Although her mother's book of water and healing had been filled with symbols and drawings, the book of fire lacked drawings. It was filled with page after page of writing. Writing she couldn't read. "I read no Norse. Do you?" She looked up, hopeful.

"Aye. We've not the time to go through it all today though."

"Why is it in Norse if these are books of the Ancients? Wasn't their language—?" she said, stopping, unsure if their language had been Gaelic or something else. "Hmm, Gaelic?"

"My father was an evil spirit, but he embraced the power of the Silver Folk, my people. He had their secrets translated into these books. My mother did many of the translations into the Norse tongue for him." She stifled an unhappy moan. "Mayhap he did it to also prevent the Scots from reading it, too. Kept the secret of the powers to 'imself. Dinna fash. We've more time to go through the books. I can explain them to ye. And now that ye ken, talk to your uncle Kendrick." Tears pricked her eyes. "And tell him I think of him often."

"I will. And, I must return home soon."

"I ken, dearie. Dinna fash. Although this book holds the understanding of yer powers, mixed with a few spells," she said in a surprisingly casual way, "yer powers lie *within* ye, dearie." She tapped Deirdre on her chest.

Deirdre pulled her attention from the book. "What about the stones?"

"Ye went."

"I did. I—I felt..." she said, pausing, unsure how to describe the sensations she had felt.

"We all feel the earth. It's the easiest to connect to. The stones hold Jörd's power. It roused ye, did it?"

Deirdre nodded. Aye, in more than one way, she thought, remembering Aleck's touches.

"Mother earth, Jörd, takes care of all of us. My gift lies in the wind. Whispers of souls, breaths of the living, and voices of the past...they all play to me on the wind." She lifted her hand and flicked it ever so slightly, resulting in the candles near Deirdre blowing out and the flames of the fire dancing.

Deirdre stood and embraced her aunt. It no longer felt uncomfortable to do so. "Thank you, Venora!"

"May ye feel peace with it, dearie."

"I must go soon."

"Ye ken where to find me when the time is right, dearie. I've many days left, as do ye."

For once, Deirdre didn't doubt her. Certainly she could see her own future, her own death.

Another question caused her to pause. It had been why she had come after all. "Did I kill my husbands?"

"No, dearie. Yer power did no such thing." Although her voice was crisp and firm, a cloud shadowed Venora's eyes. There was something else she wasn't telling her, Deirdre could feel it.

"I did not?"

"No."

Despite her misgivings, she believed her aunt. "How do I use my gift?"

"Ye already ken how. Listen to the earth. Feel the fire. Allow the power to flow through ye. You and I will see each other again, many years after yer bairn is born."

"You look tired, Deirdre. Can I presume that last night was pleasant?" Annella asked with a smirk as Deirdre joined her in the kitchen later in the afternoon. "Or it was bad?" she second-guessed herself. She stopped in her kneading of bread.

"I suppose both. We went to the stones."

Annella froze in her work. "You took him to the stones after what I told you about Venora and his mother?"

"He didn't mind," she said, feeling herself blush.

"Oh, he did enjoy himself there, did he?" Annella shook her head, laughing. "Did you tell him yet about the bairn?"

Deirdre's smile disappeared. "No."

Annella was silent, but Deirdre felt the frustration breaking through her golden core.

"He asked me to marry him."

"Oh, Deirdre! That's wonderful."

A sudden throbbing gripped Deirdre, and she dropped the dough she was working on. "Oh..." She groaned and hunched over, hand against her middle.

Annella rushed to her side. "What is it?"

Deirdre breathed herself through the pain. She felt a warm trickle down her leg. "Oh my God, I think I'm bleeding. What's happening to me?"

Annella nibbled on her lip. "Let me get you to your bed and call for the midwife."

"No! You can't do that. Nobody knows yet..."

"You are beyond secrets now. You need her! She visits me weekly already. She's not far. I'll send for her. Come with me." The other servants had left the kitchen, but Christina's maid returned, hearing the commotion. "Leslie, please send for Ina immediately and bring a few linens to my bedchamber."

"Aye, milady." Leslie hurried from the room as Annella assisted Deirdre upstairs.

Once Annella and Deidre reached the bedchamber, Leslie returned with the linens. She curtsied and then left without a word. Annella was quick to lay two cloths on the bed, and she slowly eased Deirdre down into a comfortable position. "Here is another cloth to put between your legs," Annella said.

Deirdre took it. "I—I think it's over."

Annella fussed about, adjusting the bedclothes and feather-filled pillow, replenishing the water basin, and opening the window shutter to allow cool spring air in.

"Annella, did I cause this? Aleck and I have been..." she stumbled over her words. Another headache began to overtake her.

"No, you didn't cause it. You may have relations while you carry a child unless there is risk as the midwife would determine. You were carrying well, aye?"

Deirdre nodded. "I felt ill a lot in the earlier weeks, but Moreen had given me ideas on how to help that. The sickness has decreased. I've not yet seen a midwife."

"No, you did nothing wrong."

"But, we..." She paused, biting her lip. "We were together last night." Heat warmed her cheeks, and she patted at the perspiration on her forehead.

"Let's only speak of good things. Tell me about the stones. Did you feel anything?"

The conversation was a welcome distraction, as there was naught they could do. Annella pulled a stool beside Deirdre's bed. Her head was humming with possibilities. "It was divine. My gift..." She still had trouble saying the words. "I'm a Feeler. I can feel the lifeblood—the energy—of people, sense their emotions, and hear the song of life."

Annella's eyes grew wide. "What a remarkable gift!"

"My mother was a Healer. Venora is a Seer. The gift runs in our blood." She pulled the smooth stone from her pocket and showed it to Annella. "It's a Healer's stone that was my mother's. I don't know what it does. My power comes from fire. Although I'm not sure how to harness it," she said, wanting to add "for good," but refrained from doing so.

Annella rolled it in her palm and traced a few striations along the edge. "Beautiful. Don't ever be ashamed of your gift, Deirdre. I hear it in your voice when you speak of it. We are all God's children, unique in our gifts."

"I'm not ashamed. Well, not as much anymore. Yet..." She hesitated. "I can't tell Aleck. I am afraid of what he may think or do."

"He loves you, Deirdre. He will understand."

"I don't think he will. Not after what happened with his mother. Even you said that." Deirdre felt faint. She told Annella about Gordon and Cortland. Tears burned her eyes. "I worry that I may have killed them."

"Nonsense. You didn't!"

Deirdre still didn't fully believe she had no hand in their deaths. "What if for some reason my power had the opposite effect on them? Instead of sensing their lifeblood, I drained it from them."

Always voicing the obvious, Annella looked at her with sincerity. "Aleck's alive, and he shared your bed."

Deirdre's lip quivered. "I cannot explain that. However, we weren't married." Deirdre pulled the bedclothes to her chest in an attempt to lock warmth into her shivering body. What about Auld Kenneth? He died before they could be wed—there was no consummation with him.

"Deirdre, did you love them? Cortland and Gordon?"

The midwife entered, her gaze first falling on Annella. "Does something trouble ye, milady?"

"Not me. It's Deirdre, Ina." She turned to her friend. "Do you wish for me to stay?"

"Please." Deirdre squeezed Annella's hand.

Ina pulled up a stool. "How far along are ye?" She was a younger woman, much to Deirdre's surprise. Curly brown hair fell about her shoulders, but her forehead appeared wrinkled beyond her years. A luminosity of hope filled her face, likely from birthing many babies. Crisp and clear life exuded from her lifeblood. Deirdre felt trust and compassion from the woman.

"About two months." Calculating hurt her head. The days had begun to blur together, and it felt like an eternity since she'd shared her wedding night with Cortland.

Ina bobbed her head, deep in thought as she rolled up her sleeves. "It's early. There's not much I can do."

She lifted the bedclothes and hiked up Deirdre's skirt. With a cloth, she wiped the inside of her legs.

"Ye've bled a little. The color is normal. Hmmm, that's a good sign."

Deirdre bit her lip at the thought of losing the life that grew within her. She felt its subtle essence. It was still there. She hadn't truly given herself the time to enjoy the sweet life. Now that she could lose it, she suddenly wanted nothing more than for the bairn to live.

Ina rested a hand on Deirdre's womb and examined her.

"It's too soon to feel the bairn," Ina said. After cleaning, she sat on her chair. "Two things could happen. The bairn will fight and live. Or it will pass. It's best to let it pass naturally if it does. I can then bring ye something for the pain. Until then, please stay in bed, drink ginger and hot water, and eat." She rubbed her chin in contemplation. "I have some herbals for ye as well."

If she was trying to sound hopeful, she wasn't.

Ina rose. "Sometimes when the seed plants itself in your womb, it can create, this, *hmm*, scar or irritation where it attaches to you. The bleeding comes in a rush and the woman thinks she may lose the bairn, but the life holds on and fights." She unrolled her sleeves and collected her things. "Time will tell if that's the case." She patted Deirdre's hand and reassured, "Rest, dear. It's all ye can do."

With that, she motioned for Annella to follow her. The two spoke quietly outside the door, Ina with excessive use of hand gestures.

Annella came back to her. She tucked Deirdre in, swiped a sweaty strand from Deirdre's forehead, and smiled. "So did you?"

"Did I what?" Deirdre felt light-headed.

"Love them?"

"Och." Deirdre didn't need to think about it. "No."

"Well, you have your answer then."

Deirdre knew there was more behind her friend's smile, but neither spoke further.

Deirdre was physically exhausted, but her mind wouldn't settle itself. The afternoon waned, and Annella returned to visit her several times with herbal drinks and food. Finally in the evening, as the day's light slipped away behind the window shutters, Deirdre fell into a fitful sleep.

She awoke in the night, unsettled and drenched with sweat. She placed a hand on her belly, uneasy. Vibrant strength radiated through her hand.

It wasn't the dream of Aleck that had awoken her.

She exhaled and stared at the hearth. The flames flickered in response to her concentration. After quiet meditation, it all came back to her in a torrent of images and feelings. Dark blue and white, colors of the most sinister lifeblood, flashed before her eyes. Her head pounded as an evil-like buzzing assailed her, and she thought she would retch. She had felt this energy twice before—both times when she sensed the baron. His lifeblood was the epitome of death. Her body shook.

The image of her sister Caite appeared in her mind's eye. It was fuzzy, but she could *feel* the lifebloods in her dream. Caite's warm tawny glow drained to nothingness, to death. The same white, icy energy of the baron was there. She saw him. His black malevolent face stared at her.

Blood, she smelled blood.

Fire, she felt fire.

She felt the death of her sister, and her entire body trembled. It was not a dream. Venora had been right. These dreams—of Aleck and now her sister—were not just dreams. They were visions of what would happen if she didn't stop them.

"What's wrong with Caite?" Crystoll said, appearing behind Deirdre.

She jumped at his appearance in the stable. She had forgotten that he hadn't gone with Aleck on this trip to the harbor.

"Annella said that you needed me," he explained. "Aren't we leaving in a few days, my lady?"

She paused to look down the path in the direction of Venora's cottage through the open door. There was no time to say a proper goodbye. She fought the tears. One day she would return and see her. "We can't wait for Aleck. We must leave." She lifted the hood of a borrowed cloak over her head.

"Did something happen to Caite? I received no message from Laird MacCoinneach. Annella said to speak to you about it." He took the saddle from her and readied the horse.

She chewed her lip. In the early morning, she had told Annella about her vision. Of course Annella was supportive but also concerned and told Deirdre not to do anything foolish. Deirdre lied and agreed, and as soon as Annella was out of sight, she snuck away to the stable in an ironic familiarity. "Caite is in trouble."

He scrunched his brow but didn't ask her how she knew.

"You plan to ride in your condition?"

Anger flooded her cheeks. "Annella told you?"

Deirdre continued with her horse, attaching her satchel, tightening the straps. Another wave of pain gripped her, but she refused to succumb to it. As long as she felt the bairn's light yellow glow of life, she was fine. She could bear it.

"Cortland was my friend, my lady. You and your child are mine to protect."

"Thank you, Crystoll."

"What about Aleck? He doesn't return from the north until tomorrow. I can ride ahead of you and..." He stopped and took the straps from her. "You don't look well, my lady. I'll go. Stay. Please. Aleck can then bring you home."

Losing all sense of formality, she broke into sobs. "Crystoll, she's in trouble. She's going to die." She finished tying her satchel to her horse with fumbling fingers.

"Why must you go? Why can't I?"

She ignored him and tried to mount the horse, gritting through another spasm. Crystoll supported her. She wiped the sweat from her brow, feeling both feverish and chilled. "I need you to come, Crystoll. I need your help."

"Is she ill?" he repeated.

"I can't explain it all. I just *know*. Please trust me, Crystoll," she pleaded.

There was no more hesitation in his voice. "Give me a moment to collect supplies."

Her lip trembled. "Thank you, Crystoll."

Alasdair felt ready to burst. Three days away from the comfort of Deirdre's arms was three days too many. He rode with Thomas to the house, eager to see her again. He was still awestruck, days later, that she agreed to marry him. The time had come. The awful truth was there, hovering over him the entire length of his trip. He would tell her today.

Thomas clapped a hand on his friend's back. "It's done, Ali. We did it! They're working harder than they have ever before. By God, I don't know why, but they are! Two dozen ships completed and another six being readied. By the time Bruce comes, they will be finished. Will you be coming with me to the mainland, to rouse more soldiers?"

"I can't, Thomas. I've asked Deirdre to marry me. I must return home with her and make amends with her father."

Thomas shook his head. "Eilean Donan is a pivotal spot and will help the Cause. Will you be able to secure an alliance even after all that has happened?"

"I hope so." Alasdair knew he did it more than for just the alliance though. God save him, he loved the lass.

Thomas chuckled. "I suppose I'm next, aye? Perhaps before the bairn comes?"

Alasdair hadn't the heart to tell him about Annella's involvement with inspiring the workers, nor about his suspicions of Christina's parentage. With time, that stubborn hen would tell Thomas. He released a pent-up laugh. They had done it. The navy was secure. The men were working. Bruce could handle the rest from here.

"Do you mind taking the horses to the stable?" Thomas asked. Apparently, he was also eager to see his lover.

Alasdair slid off his horse and led the tired animals to the stable. His legs quaked with the steps as he began to think about what he might do with Deirdre tonight. He would tell her after.

As he left the stable, a hooded woman approached him.

"Sir Stirrat?" she asked.

"Yes?" He raised an eyebrow. She was older and although shrouded in her cloak, a radiant and familiar-looking face stared back at him.

"I'm Venora, Deirdre's aunt. Could I request a moment with ye?"

He felt an invisible tug of curiosity and followed her along the path away from the keep. "Is Deirdre with you?" He looked around.

"No."

"Is something amiss?" He itched to return to the keep and find Deirdre.

She dismissed that thought with a head shake.

"I'm delighted to hear that Deirdre was able to find her kin. You are her mother's sister?" A part of him felt ashamed for not taking the time to meet her aunt.

She nodded and drew him farther from the keep as they walked.

A thought dawned on him. "It would be a pleasure to have you join us for supper tonight." He wondered why Thomas and Annella had never invited her to come after learning she was Deirdre's aunt. It triggered a primitive warning within.

A low cackle escaped her lips. "I'm not welcome there"

"Why not?"

Glassy blue eyes glared at him. "My people aren't."

He frowned. "Nonsense. Lady Annella is an agreeable host and lady."

Venora waved a derisive hand.

He tried again. "The Norse and Scots have been at peace for thirty years."

"The Norse are not my people."

He grew frustrated. Was she daft? "Who are your people then?" He regretted the words as they came out, for his mind went instantly to the answer.

"The Ancients, of course."

"Ancients?" he had to ask. Maybe he had heard her wrong.

A sudden coastal wind blew past them, and it rippled his arms with gooseflesh.

"I'm no witch, sir. Ye had better get that thought out of yer mind. My mother was an Ancient, as was her mother."

He could feel her frosty glare down to this toes. An overwhelming desire to leave her presence formed in his gut, but something stopped him. "Then what *are* you?"

"A Seer, dearie, and the powers are strong within my family's blood." Her lips were rosy and tipped, like Deirdre's mouth, but Venora's smile was dark and conniving.

He wasn't going to partake in a mind game. He turned to leave.

"Ye've broken the curse."

Her declaration stopped him short. He turned around and stepped close enough to her that he whiffed the spicy scent of incense upon her clothes. He clenched his fists at his side to suppress his mounting ire. "For Christ's sake, there are no such things as curses, magic, or powers!"

She shrugged. "Seeing as ye're *alive*, it appears that the curse has been broken by a hundred kisses."

He backed up a step. She had his full attention now. "There were no hundred kisses, I assure you." He controlled his racing heart. "Your curse is wrong."

He stood there, silent, ignoring the mocking voice inside his head asking why he allowed himself to listen to such ramblings. Something held him. He studied her face as the wind continued to bellow around them.

She ignored him. "Deirdre's lost two husbands and a man she was betrothed to?"

He stiffened at the question.

"My own daughter lost her husband, as well. She didn't have a strong spirit, and—" A storm of unrest clouded in her eyes. She sniffled and again, waved a hand toward the crashing surf below them. "She couldn't handle her grief, and the sea swallowed her soul."

Silence hung over their conversation. Alasdair's head ached, and he wished to return to the keep, but his legs wouldn't move.

Venora eyed him sharply when she spoke. "Our father didn't approve of my sister Gwyn marrying a *heathen* Scottish laird from across the sea. So he cursed us."

He finished her statement. "He put a curse on his own daughters?" Oh my God, was he falling for her ploy? What was wrong with him?

"Aye. Well, he had no special ability, but our mother did possess such a gift. He forced her to create the curse. Gwyn had gone to the mainland. Neither of us was yet with child though. You can't cast a curse on the living, ye see. It's in the rules."

"Of course," he said, his tone acerbic.

"He didn't curse *us*. He cursed our own bairns, so that they would never be able to experience the truest of love and our bloodline would end with them. He hated the Scots. He didn't want his Norse-Ancient bloodline tainted, and he'd rather see it end than mingle with the impure."

He was speechless.

"Her brother Edmund is also childless?"

He made the connection instantly. Poor Edmund hadn't lost his wife on their wedding night. Instead, he suffered from repeated bairns lost in the womb, as Deirdre had told him. Deirdre's fate was to be left permanently widowed. Yet, not this time. He was alive. "Why did he curse you as well?"

"I had some hand in Gwyn's courtship and her departure from Uist."

Alasdair wondered what kind of father would do such a thing, and the thought stung him.

"Ye understand my pain."

He was more than bothered by her astuteness. "I've not married Deirdre, and we certainly haven't shared a hundred kisses. There is no curse."

She laughed under her breath. In answer to his unspoken doubts, she said, "I'm no witch. I've a gift, as do others in my family," she said, sharing a hard look with him.

Deirdre's kin or not, he had to get away from this woman. Now.

"Some use it for good, some not," she continued.

"Why are you telling me all of this? Did you tell Deirdre?" His heart hurt. He'd seen it in Deirdre's eyes. She had felt the weight of her husbands' deaths.

"She has no knowledge of the curse."

"You wish for me to tell her?"

"I don't wish for anything, sir."

He forced himself to turn. He'd been more than enough enlightened—and unsettled—by this conversation.

"One more thing, Alasdair…"

He halted, as though his feet had grown roots. He blinked. Had he heard her right?

"Aye, *Sir Alasdair Montgomerie*. I ken who ye really are."

His pulse beat in his ears, his own personal war drums, echoing with each thump. He refused to turn around and began to walk away. Her voice drifted to him on the wind.

"'Twas never the kisses, Alasdair," she said snidely. "'Tis *love* that broke the curse."

He strode to the keep unable to hear a word more.

As he passed the stable, Annella hurried to him. Dried tears painted her cheeks. "Thank God you've returned! She's gone."

Alasdair stopped. "Who?"

"Deirdre. She's in trouble, Alasdair. You need to help her!"

"God's fury. Where the hell did she go?" It was a futile question. They had already explored most of the area of northern Uist and besides those stones, there wasn't much here worthwhile to see. He shot a look behind him. Venora had disappeared. "Was this the witch's doing?"

"Who?"

He thinned his lips. "Venora."

"I don't think so. Deirdre left without me knowing. I went to check on her, and she was gone. She came to me yesterday, talking nonsense about her sister, but I thought it was the b—" She pursed her lips.

"Where, Annella?" he repeated, growing agitated. "Home. Dornie. She left yesterday with Crystoll."

"Why in God's name did she do that? We were leaving soon." He ground the words between his teeth.

She tugged on her bottom lip. "She saw something. She saw Caite die by the hands of your father."

"She *saw* something?" *Special.* Crystoll's words entered his mind. A Seer for an aunt. It wasn't possible. Deirdre was not a witch. Witches did *not* exist. It couldn't be. "My father?"

"She knows him only as the baron."

"Tell Thomas where I've gone. I'm not sure when I will return." He paused for a moment, regretful. "I'm sorry we must part, but the route is treacherous and with my father's men about, God knows who she will run into, even with Crystoll's help."

She stopped him, laying a gentle hand on his arm. "Please wait. I'll get your provisions."

He hurried to the stable and prepared a different horse.

Annella returned a few moments later. She braced her look with fortitude. "Alasdair, there is another thing."

He inhaled deeply, attempting to hold in the raw emotion. He could still taste the bitterness of the incense upon Venora. "I've no time, Annella."

Her eyes clouded over with more tears. "She's not well. Yesterday, she was bleeding. I'm afraid for her."

"Bleeding? She's hurt?"

There was a long, fragile silence as Annella swayed on her feet, clearly deliberating if she should speak.

He steeled his voice. "Annella?"

Her hand trembled upon his arm. "It's your bairn, Alasdair. She is with child. She may lose it. She rested, and then her behavior was odd and she was spouting about Caite being hurt. Then she disappeared while I was tending to Christina. Alasdair, she needs this." She pulled a vial out from her apron pocket and shoved it in his hand. "It'll stop the bleeding."

He stared at the liquid-filled vial. "She is with child?" he said, quieter. "What is this?" He clenched his hand, and his nails dug into his palm, nearly crushing the glass. "Venora gave this to you?"

"It's from the midwife."

He didn't believe her.

"Alasdair, not all who have special powers are witches. You must trust me. And trust Deirdre."

He tempered his anger with forced exhalations, and he mounted the horse. "I can't wait, Annella."

She nodded. "God be with you, friend."

Thomas ran down to the stable. "I'm sorry, Alasdair. Be safe."

He rode off, fury powering him on. She was a day ahead of him. With luck, there would be a delay at the docks to Skye, although she might have already embarked. Alasdair knew his father better than anyone. Crystoll and Deirdre were being snared into a trap that would leave no soul of Eilean Donan—or Glen Shiel—alive.

It took Alasdair three days before he caught up with Deirdre and Crystoll on the western coast of Skye. Following his hunch, he had taken the detoured coastal route. It would be the logical path to take, and Crystoll was a logical man.

He found their camp at twilight. It was set back from the coastline and hidden in a patch of small spires and trees. Intuition drew him inland to scan the grove. He was grateful for the internal guidance as Crystoll had done well hiding the camp.

Even with Alasdair's soft-footed approach, he still found himself with a crossbow in his face. "Aleck!" Relief relaxed Crystoll's scowl, and he lowered his weapon. Crystoll followed Alasdair's gaze to Deirdre. "She's not well, Aleck. We couldn't ride anymore."

Alasdair wanted to choke him for leaving without telling him, but instead, he clapped a hand on his shoulder. Crystoll followed the orders of his laird and his laird's daughter. "Thank you for taking care of her."

She sat curled against a boulder; beads of sweat lined her pale face. He scooped her into his arms and cradled her in his lap as was becoming custom. "Deirdre," he said. "Here." He opened the vial. A putridly sweet, earthy scent emanated from it. "Drink."

She licked her parched lips, and her face convulsed. When it appeared to have subsided, she spoke, just realizing he was there. "Oh Aleck...I'm sorry! I had to leave."

"Hush, love, hush. Drink."

"What is it?" she said in a whispered breath.

He moved it to his other hand and stroked her damp hair away from her forehead. She shivered in his arms. "Drink. It'll help both of you."

She obeyed, and he tipped it to her lips. Not until she had finished and made gurgling sounds as though about to vomit, did he suddenly worry that he'd been deceived. Had Venora intended to kill the bairn, to kill Deirdre? His only encounter with her had left him with a bad feeling. Even so, Venora couldn't possibly wish her niece dead. "Deirdre, why didn't you wait for me and especially in your condition?"

A dullness shrouded her normally vibrant gaze. She looked as if she would sob. "What was that liquid I drank?"

"An tincture from Venora to help you and the bairn."

"You met her?"

"Aye." He couldn't say more.

Her face broke. "I'm sorry, Aleck. My sister...the baron took her!"

"Hush, hush, love. It's all right. We'll find her. Perhaps Venora lied when she told you about Caite." He used all his strength to remain steadfast in his caressing, not allowing the heat of his wrath to consume him.

Deirdre put a hand to her mouth.

"Try to keep it down."

She quivered and kept the liquid down. "Venora didn't tell me about Caite."

She is special. Curse those words. He wished Crystoll had never uttered them to him. Alasdair didn't want to know the answer, but asked anyway. "Tell me, Deirdre."

Her tears returned. "Oh Aleck, I'm sorry. Don't cast me out. I meant to tell you. I can feel things. I can see things."

He was spellbound as he listened. Or perhaps he was actually *spell* bound. *No, Alasdair. She is not a witch. Trust her. Trust her*, a voice told him.

She continued in a rush of words. "Please believe me. I never asked for this gift."

"That day we rode along the eastern coast, you sensed that the baron was near us? You felt him?" He wrestled to control his breathing. He tried to remain open to the explanation.

She nodded. "And Crystoll?"

She nodded again, her face paler.

"The day we met. In the loch. Was this all a ploy?" he asked, unable to hold onto his resolve. Had she lied and manipulated him this entire trip? Was the curse her doing? Her father was a sly ruler; perhaps he had used his own daughter to seduce him into an alliance. *She can't be a witch*, his inner voice said again.

"No!"

"It was all a lie." He rose, feeling as if he may be sick, too. The heat that twisted within him, fighting to remain quenched, released. He had to ask the final question that arose with her confession.

"Is the child even mine?" Dear God, he didn't want to know.

She hugged her arms around her middle.

Crystoll approached. "She's hurting, Aleck. I don't understand what this is all about, but can't it wait? She needs to rest."

She stammered, "It-It's not like that! I meant to tell you. It was just the wedding night."

Red singed the corners of his eyes. "Cortland? You carry his seed, and you intended to deceive me? You could have just told me! I would have understood." He recoiled. Annella had lied, too. Were they all lying to him? Dizzy, he stumbled. Crystoll was there to catch him. He pushed him away and punched him without thinking. Crystoll fell and landed on the ground in a heap.

"You used me. Your father used me," he said miserably.

"No, please, it wasn't like that!" she said, reaching out to him, too weak to stand. "I meant to tell you."

"When?"

She cowered.

He strode to and mounted his horse.

"Wait! Where are you going?" It was Crystoll who spoke. He rose, holding his midsection where Alasdair had walloped him.

Alasdair needed to leave, to process this all. But even so, he said, "Take care of her, Crystoll, and whatever you do, don't take her to Eilean Donan."

"What? Och, aye. Why? Wait, Aleck!" Crystoll said.

Seeing as they were sharing secrets, he left them with his final words, more angry with himself than with her for getting caught up in her family's lies. "It's not Aleck, so bloody well quit calling me that."

"What?" Crystoll was clearly bemused by everything that was going on, but he recovered his valor. "What?" he repeated as he pulled his hunched frame upright. "You bastard! *You* lied and used us!"

"Consider us even. No more lies." Alasdair waved a hand in the air, more disgusted in himself than in their lies. "It's Alasdair Montgomerie, and I have my father to kill."

CHAPTER TWELVE

Deirdre slept hard. Whatever Venora had put in that concoction had crushed her senses, and after the confrontation with Aleck, she could hardly keep her eyes open. *Aleck.* That wasn't his name. She refused to allow herself to think about it all. During the night, her body had settled itself; the light bleeding and cramping stopped. The lifeblood of the bairn glowed stronger within her.

Now they blazed across Skye. "Ride harder, Crystoll! We may be able to make the same ship home."

He shook his head. "He has a night ahead of us, and Aleck—err, Alasdair, or whatever his damn name is—is an able rider. All we can do is continue to Eilean Donan and speak with your father. Besides, we must keep at a slower pace for your sake, my lady."

She grimaced, shifting in her saddle as the terrain switched from the smooth flat paths of the western coast to the rugged Cuillin foothills. "He said not to go home."

"We need to return. I beseech you, my lady. Let us ride home. And please, I will listen." He pulled on the reins to slow his horse so that he flanked her.

"How can I explain it to you?" she asked, not surprised by his audacity. She had grown fond of Crystoll's genuine nature. She liked to think it had been instilled in him by Cortland.

"I'll believe you."

She told him all—starting with her pregnancy, her father's idea, Venora and her mother's past, her gift, and the curse or whatever it was that caused her husbands to die.

"Yet Alasdair is not dead." He stated the obvious, echoing Annella's reasoning.

She shrugged. She still didn't understand it herself, and said so.

"I always knew you were special, Deirdre."

"How?"

"Caite. She confided in me, which confirmed my suspicions, but I've known you since our wee days. Remember how I always followed Cortland, tended to the stables, and helped the laird even as a lad?"

"Aye, that was because you're fond of my sister."

He blushed. "Aye, aye. That was part of it. I was drawn to *you*, too. I see how you respond differently to other people. You always try to remain inexpressive, but, I see it sometimes—a glimmer in your eyes or how you back away from the less virtuous men your father invites to the hall. You know something that others do not."

"I'm just observant," she said.

He forced a smile. "You know that is not it."

"This gift has been my undoing." Her lip didn't quiver for once when she said it.

"No, it hasn't. It saved us from the baron that day. That was when I was certain. Aye, Caite likes to weave tall tales, and maybe I was imagining things, but I saw it in your face."

Deirdre struggled to take it all in. "Baron Montgomerie is Alasdair's father. I can't believe it."

"He tried to kill his own son."

"Twice," she added, her heart aching for Alasdair.

"What?"

"When he was a child," she explained. "What would cause a man to turn on his own people and try to kill his son?"

"Fear, my lady." Crystoll added in a mournful voice, "And power."

There was no more need for discussion. She needed to get home.

Alasdair pressed on as though he rode into the black fire of perdition itself. He blocked everything from his mind and prepared himself for the battle. Though he pushed the horse beyond its capable endurance, it held its head high, neck tense with the fury.

A few days after leaving Deirdre on Skye, he reached Dornie. He dismounted and led his tired horse through the village, allowing himself to fall into the shadows of the bustling afternoon market. Other than the occasional glance of recognition, most people ignored him, and he remained inconspicuous.

None of the usual guards were on the bridge leading to the keep. Alasdair's fears were piqued, and he proceeded with caution. He led the horse to the stable in the bailey. Three horses paced about, not the usual ten. The laird must be away. The young stable lad who he had saved from Deirdre's wild mare greeted him. "Sir Stirrat! Ye've returned!" Youthful eyes searched behind him. "Where are Lady Deirdre and Mr. Murchison?"

Alasdair forced a welcoming smile. "They'll be here shortly. Ewan, is it?"

The boy, of maybe age seven or eight, beamed and nodded.

"Is your laird present?"

The boy lowered his gaze and kicked at a pile of hay, searching for something. "Nay. He's gone."

"Do you know where?"

Ewan crouched down to pick up a cat that was hiding in the hay. "Nay. Sir Edmund is here."

"Any other visitors?"

Ewan shrugged, too distracted with teasing the cat. He waved a piece of hay, and the cat swatted at it, tail curled and swaying. Ewan looked up with wide eyes.

"Sir Stirrat, ye're bleeding," Ewan pointed to Alasdair's leg.

His trews were wet with brown-red blood. His hunting wound had reopened.

"Shall I fetch Gilford?"

"No, it'll be fine." Alasdair patted him on the head. "Thank you, Ewan. Be mindful of skittish mares, aye?"

The boy nodded and scurried out of the stable, the cat in his arms.

Alasdair inspected his wound. Another bandage would have to wait. It had been doing well until he pushed himself the past few days.

Ignoring his dislike for Deirdre's brother, he hurried to the keep anyway. He found the servants preparing food for the evening meal in the kitchen, which was a good sign, but he didn't lower his guard. Some bowed or inclined their heads in greeting. "Welcome, Sir Stirrat," one said with a placid smile. Moreen wasn't present, though he wasn't surprised. In the few days he had been there, she appeared to be a phantom—here one minute, gone the next, bustling about barking orders. His hand hovered over his sword's hilt at his waist, and he glanced around the corner into the hall. The hearth, already lit for the evening, crackled in greeting. He stepped lightfooted into the empty room.

Half expecting it, he ducked when a person leapt at him from the dark shadows beside the hearth. The adversary's fist landed in his right arm instead of his face. Alasdair stumbled, his arm still sore from his previous injuries.

Edmund was an agile fighter and lunged at him again. Alasdair's sword slipped from the sheath and fell to the floor in a clatter. He retaliated with his own more accurate aim. His fist met Edmund's gut, and Deirdre's brother faltered. They scuffled on the rush-covered floor, kicking, punching. An on-target thrust caught Edmund squarely in the chin. "You filth!" Edmund said, cursing profanities under his tongue as he spat blood.

Alasdair pulled himself upright and darted for his sword. He grabbed it and held it out. "I've not come to harm you, friend."

Edmund's look pierced him. "I'm not your friend, Alasdair Montgomerie."

Alasdair paused.

"Och, your secret is no longer that, Alasdair. My father's sentinel returned from Lennox with interesting information."

"Where is the laird?"

"My laird has gone to Clan Donald to seek help from our neighbors. Apparently, an evil baron, whom you are well acquainted with, has taken my sister and is causing unrest in the glen. You brought this evil to us." Edmund stepped forward into the blade, its tip resting on his chest. "Either kill me or be gone. I've done no wrong. You're the lying traitor."

"Lying is one thing, but treason is another. If I'm a traitor, so is your father and anyone else who supports the Cause," Alasdair said calmly.

"My father is no traitor!" Glaring, Edmund stepped back.

Alasdair sheathed the sword. "Are you ignorant to your father's doings? He supports the Cause, as do I."

"That's another blatant lie. He's yet to declare allegiance. They have special places for liars in the pits of hell." Edmund crept toward him, fists balled at his sides. He winced and let out a wheeze, then hugged his middle where he'd been punched.

Alasdair countered with a step closer, hand outstretched in pity. "I want what you want, Edmund."

Confused wrath drew Edmund's dark brows together. His blue eyes glowed with the same passion as Deirdre's, and a small muscle flicked in Edmund's angled cheek, and it shocked Alasdair to see the likeness. "I daresay you don't."

"What did the baron tell you?"

Edmund's jaw tightened. Abruptly, his demeanor changed, and he fell into a nearby chair and let his head sink into his hands.

Alasdair lowered his voice. "Dammit, he got to you, too. What did he promise you?"

Edmund lifted his head. His mouth took on an unpleasant twist. "There'll be no reclaiming the Scottish throne. My father hasn't formally declared support for a Claimant, but if he does, then he's as foolish as you. King John is finished. Power lies with the English, and they'll crush us if we revolt. Loyalty to the English crown is the only way. Don't you see?"

Alasdair shook his head, and distaste formed in his throat. "Land. You want land. Of course he would offer you that. Deirdre inherits Eilean Donan. You've nothing, Edmund. No heir, no land. You're willing to betray your family and the clan for land?"

Edmund chuckled. It was not the cackle of a happy or devious man, but that of a defeated soul.

"I know the baron, my father, better than anyone else. He's played you, Edmund, as he does everyone, to get what he wants. He speaks of only lies and empty promises. I can help you. Where is Caite?"

"You can't get her. She's hidden. I-I..." He stopped himself. His features hardened. "The baron will kill her if my father declares support for a Claimant."

Alasdair approached and sat beside him. "There's always time to repent, Edmund. The Lord forgives us all."

Edmund scowled. "Have you repented yet, Alasdair? You lied to my sister."

"I've made my peace."

"If you've made your peace, where is she?"

"Safe and far away from here."

Alasdair searched Edmund's face. The spirit in his eyes died. Alasdair ground his teeth to prevent himself from losing control. "Where is the baron?"

"Waiting to collect you," Edmund said in a bare whisper, as he tried to cover a small sob.

As if on cue, the front hall doors burst open, and several English soldiers entered, swords drawn, escorting the devil himself into the gloomy hall of Eilean Donan.

Deirdre stumbled and fell as the horrible buzzing assailed her. She cried out and covered her ears, hoping to quiet the sound that resounded in her skull.

"What is it?" Crystoll was quick to her side. "Do you feel the baron?"

She moaned with a newfound pain. Deep breaths were not helping. For once she didn't lie and call it just a headache. "Aye. And Caite. Make haste."

"Is she hurt?"

"No."

"Can you stand and ride?"

"I think so." She was grateful that the vision had hit her when they stopped to rest.

Her eyes burned. She could see the baron clearly with his dark black mane of hair streaked with ashy gray, wicked smirk, and painfully piercing eyes. Though she sensed the sickness in him, and saw his wince of pain as he lifted his blood-covered sword, he still stood above her sister in the hall of Laird MacDougall's keep, powerful and deadly. She recognized the familiar insignia on the tapestries in the castle. Caite was in the MacDougall keep, and that's where Deirdre had to go.

"Please give me a moment to rest."

"Aye. The path gets lost in the copse here. We'll need to circle around. I'll collect the horses and scout the best way." He hurried away with a brief look over his shoulder. She nodded her permission.

She closed her eyes. Crystoll's energy grew fainter as he distanced himself. Other energies competed within her. In addition to Caite's lifeblood, she felt the warring push and tug between two others: the red hot fire of Alasdair's lifeblood and the icy white death of the baron's. Both came from the same place. She grabbed her satchel. Once Crystoll was out of sight, she ran in the direction of the MacDougalls' land, northwest of home. *I'm sorry, Crystoll.* She presumed that he would give up searching for her after a while and return home, hoping to find her there. She hated lying to him, but there was no other way. She had to go alone. He was an asset and a skilled fighter, but she couldn't bring him to his death. This was her own battle and she refused to have his blood on her hands, too. He was a good tracker. She would need to hurry.

She prayed that her hunch was true, and her father's men were also on their way.

The closer she got to MacDougall land, the more uncomfortable Deirdre became. She got better at suppressing the excruciating sounds in her head, but she couldn't stop the heat and cold that blanketed her skin. Alasdair's lifeblood fought with the baron's and it nearly tore her in two.

Not the best at navigating, she partially regretted not bringing Crystoll, though it was a mission she had to do alone. She justified it with the fact that he could return to Dornie and assemble more men. She would garner them more time or offer herself in trade. After stumbling on undergrowth, she took a moment's rest to lean against a tree.

She told herself that she was doing this for Caite. Alasdair didn't want her anymore. She had lied to him, deceived him, unforgivably. Her lip trembled, and the tears fell over her cheeks. He had also lied, all for his damn Cause.

Determination pushed her, and she hobbled through the thick hedges and trees. The energies calmed themselves once she concentrated on the task of getting through the woods.

A few more hours passed, and dusk was upon her when she found a road. A sudden perceptive wave hit her. She dropped to the ground.

On instinct, she returned to the cover of the woods and waited. A slow and repetitious sound of chain mail echoed down the dirt road. She crept closer, hidden beneath shrubbery, to get a look. She moved on hands and knees, hoping the dusk shadows would hide her. Dressed in full English military regalia down to the mail, swords, helmets, and shields, at least a dozen men marched by.

It didn't take more than a moment to feel the bitter cold clutch her heart. The baron was here. She watched them pass. The baron's men rode in the rear, three of them. She didn't allow his evil to overtake her heart, and she pushed his lifeblood from her. Instead, she opened her heart to *him*—to the man who had brought a new meaning to life energy. She searched through the soldiers. In the middle, Alasdair walked as if he were marching to his death, shoulders slumped and head down. His hands were bound, and he was linked by a rope to a horse.

She wanted to jump from the trees and help him, but that would mean certain death. *Alasdair! What are you doing?* her mind cried.

His head raised, and he jerked it in her direction. He stared at her spot in the trees for longer than a breath, and then snapped his gaze forward. None of the soldiers noticed, but she did and she ducked behind a thicker gorse bush. She waited until the group passed before she continued on her way, following at a distance. She hoped she would reach the soldiers by nightfall, and she prayed she had the courage to do what needed to be done.

After a day of being dragged by a horse, Alasdair's feet and wrists throbbed. He leaned against the tree trunk, knees up, gaze lingering on the fire. He didn't allow his pain on the outside or inside to show as the soldiers busied themselves in the makeshift camp and settled in for the night. Pondering all day still left him without a plan.

His father paced with a straight back. Only Alasdair knew the extent of the discomfort Agmus felt. He was surprised his father could ride in his condition. It had been years since he last visited his family home, and even then the herbalist was telling his father not to ride for long distances anymore.

Two soldiers sat nearby on guard. "How far is the keep from here?" one man behind Alasdair asked the other, shifting in his mail. As usual, the English were decked in all their pride and glory.

The other man yawned. "We'll be there tomorrow by midday. MacDougall is supposed to be a ruthless *laird*," he said, slurring the "r" to mock the Scots vernacular. "He was swayed easily enough by the coin. That heathen was bragging about it," he said, pointing a chubby thumb at Ronat. They both mumbled respective obscenities and took hefty swallows from their flasks.

Putrid, stale ale fell off their breath. "Even the heathens can be turned for the right amount," the other agreed.

"There's bad blood betw'n the two clans."

"It has to do wi' the witch daughter, I think."

"Well, we know how the baron feels about witches."

They both laughed.

"What of 'im?" the larger soldier said. He poked the tip of his spear into Alasdair's stomach. A pockmarked grin spread the soldier's unhandsome, heavy features.

"This traitor's comin' wi' us to the White Tower, unless they hang the bugger first."

Alasdair needn't hear more of their drunken conversation, so he turned away. His father paced and barked orders. Fatigue won out, so Alasdair soon found himself dozing but he was jolted awake when a sudden commotion filled the camp. Several men grabbed their swords and followed Ronat into the woods across the clearing.

"You two, stay with him!" Agmus ordered, flicking his hand to two additional English soldiers. They clanked over to Alasdair and stood guard. Agmus paused, deliberating. Apparently, four men were enough to guard his prize. He went with his men to investigate the disruption. Instinctively, Alasdair rubbed his bloody chafed wrists together, the ropes too tight for his liking. His fingers had grown numb. It was no use.

He heard no shouting, no fighting.

Soon after, the men returned, cursing jovially.

"I found this bonnie flower by the loch," Carney said, his voice laced with scorn as he shoved his female prisoner. "Might want to pluck her petals."

Deirdre.

Her hair was unkempt and clothing torn from travel.

Bloody hell. A pain squeezed Alasdair's heart as the soldiers pushed, poked at, and fondled her. One groped her bottom, and she kicked his shin with her heel. He slapped her and laughed. Alasdair clenched his fists, his nails cutting into his palms. What was she doing here? Where was Crystoll?

Agmus grinned at Alasdair. "Well, look who we happened to find roaming the woods all alone? It appears that our wee fish has returned."

Alasdair suppressed his anger under a look of indifference, or at least he hoped it appeared that way. Inside, he wanted to throttle someone, Deirdre included. "Sit her there," Agmus ordered, pointing to a large boulder across the clearing from Alasdair. "Bind her well. We don't need her to run off on us again." He approached Deirdre. "Well, there is no water to lose you in this time, my bonnie selkie." He chuckled to himself.

They sat her down, and her shoulder hit the boulder. She muffled a cry and hung her head.

Agmus paced the clearing, clearly pleased with himself. He rubbed the gray and black curls of his beard in feigned reflection. "What a pleasure it is to have Lady MacCoinneach with us this evening. It appears that you would also like to join your sister for our *ceilidh* tomorrow? I doubt there will be much singing or dancing though."

Her look took on the stabbing hate which resembled her brother's blue scowl. Alasdair hid a smirk. That woman was all fire.

Agmus snickered and strode to Ronat. They spoke in whispers.

As the camp settled for the night, Alasdair's exhaustion overtook him again, but he refused to fall asleep, not while Deirdre sat no more than twenty paces away. The fire popped, the men discharged their bodily functions in usual crudeness, and most fell asleep. The four guards that were posted near him alternated shifts. Only two men flanked Deirdre. His father rested against another tree, Ronat at his side. In spite of his black, hardened façade, Agmus lacked the resilience he once possessed. His body had become frail in the past few years as the disease in his joints begun to win the battle. Not until that devil closed his eyes, did Alasdair look again at Deirdre.

She, too, remained awake. He could hardly see her features in the dim firelight, but she spoke to him with her eyes, which were as dark as the night instead of their captivating blue-green.

He wanted to scream to her, *What were you thinking?*
Please don't be mad at me, her face pleaded.

He mustered a grin, as much as it hurt his split lip. *I'm not.* He tapped his hip with his tied hands, as hard as it was. *Do you have a dagger?*

She shook her head. *No.* She tilted her head ever so slowly, raising her chin in the direction of Carney, who sat slouched by the fire. Then she shrugged.

They each sat quietly, staring across the clearing into the wee hours. Deirdre's gaze fell upon the fire. In a sleepy daze, she blinked and the flames licked up high as a fresh log succumbed to the fire, popping. She blinked again and looked at him.

He mouthed the word "sleep" to her. Most of the soldiers were passed out, his lunatic father included. A few guards remained awake, and occasionally they changed shifts, stretched, or relieved themselves. Deirdre pulled her cloak around her, lay to her side, and closed her eyes.

Alasdair watched her sleep, his own eyelids growing heavy. Tomorrow would be a long day. Only God knew how it would play out. Deirdre's arrival put a knot in it all. He had been willing to lay down his life to save her family. Damn, she was stubborn! Even with the lies and hurt she had unleashed upon him, his sins were just as bad, or worse. It was he who needed forgiveness. There was no denying that inside that sleeping beautiful mess of a woman lay a powerful embodiment of unwavering strength. As he relented to exhaustion and closed his eyes, once again he turned to prayer. 'Twas all he had left.

Alasdair found himself again roped to a horse come morning for another day of walking. Deirdre rode with Ronat, their horse taking the lead.

After an hour, the road narrowed, and the horses slowed, so Alasdair was able to catch his breath. Even though Carney rode the horse at a slower gait, two days of being dragged along had paid its toll on Alasdair's body. Draining energy slowed his steps and blisters hurt the bottoms of his feet.

The soldier behind Alasdair shoved him. Carney pulled the rope tighter, forcing Alasdair to be right beside him. He spat on his captive. Alasdair glared at his bloodshot eyes. "You're a fool, Carney." The fat soldier kicked him in the face.

Carney tugged on the rope, bringing Alasdair level with his leg. "Keep moving."

"He will kill you when he's done with you," Alasdair said with a bloody smirk, pleased that he had riled Carney. It was time to stir up trouble.

Deirdre stole a glance behind her. Carney and Alasdair were moving toward the center of the group. Carney dragged Alasdair by a rope attached to his saddle. Alasdair's face was bruised badly, his complexion more yellowed and pink than his usual healthy glow. He glanced up at her, his one eye partly closed and swollen. Blood seeped from his lip and new nose wound. Dried blood caked the back of his head as well as the rope binding his wrists. Black hair, soaked with sweat, fell in his face. In the darkness of night, she had not seen the extent of his damage. God, he looked like death... Yet his lifeblood burned strong.

She rode in the front of the saddle with Ronat. His hazy brown lifeblood was extremely weak, blending in with the surroundings. He would die soon, if not by a blade, then by the black sickness that spread through his veins. His emotions made her ill. She worked hard to tune his lifeblood out.

As if he knew she had been thinking about him, Ronat laid a hand on her thigh. In repeat of his earlier behavior, he hiked up her dress on one side, which was easy to do with her legs straddling the horse. She was in no mood for his pawing.

She fought against it, pushed at his strong hand, but to no avail. "Don't ye get any ideas, lassie. The baron doesn't ken the true way to keep a woman obedient." His hand slithered inward between her legs, and she searched for distracting thoughts.

"I daresay this is not the way either, you pig."

He removed his hand, shoved it down the front of her bodice, nearly tearing the wool gown. He fondled her breast and pressed her back to his chest in a tight hold. "Och, that's better." He shifted his weight in the saddle. "Best ye get used to me, ye bonnie thing. I doubt yer lover will live to see sunset. And I'm hungry. Hmm, nice," he said with a laugh as he played with her nipple.

She felt him stiffen behind her, and her stomach churned unpleasantly.

"Carney, watch our prisoner. I need a break," he called over his shoulder.

Carney rode up to them, Alasdair stumbling as he tried to keep pace. "We just left. Can't it wait? He won't be pleased," he said with a head nod to the front of their riding party.

Ronat shifted again in the saddle, and Deirdre used this moment to dislodge his hand. "I don't care. He's ridden us o'er damnation for months with little coin. I want a moment, and the lass'll be joining me. We'll catch up to him in plenty of time."

Deirdre followed his gaze. She counted Ronat, Carney, and six foot soldiers. The baron had ridden ahead an hour before but not without a death threat to the men guarding them. Deirdre had been surprised by the move, but seeing as they were outnumbered, unarmed, she was a woman, and Alasdair a bloody mess, she assumed the baron had thought himself secure. That was the one emotion she had felt over all of the others when she was near him—his blind overconfidence. Try as he did to mask it, she had felt his despair and darkness as well.

"Down," Ronat said, pushing her off to the ground.

He dismounted and grabbed her hand, leading her to a grove beside the road. Graces, she could have used a dagger now. Carney had taken the one she brought from Uist.

"Ronat. He'll hiv yer head if she's harmed," Carney warned.

Deirdre shot Carney a pleading look, but his eyes were glazed over. His lifeblood was also weak, though she felt the hesitation within him.

"Don't ye worry. Ye can hiv her next. Keep watch."

Deirdre looked over her shoulder at Alasdair. Pink heat formed at the base of his neck and throat, and his jaw clenched. His fiery lifeblood blazed. She could almost feel his pulse beating faster. Anguish gripped her heart, but she knew he could do nothing.

As soon as Ronat was out of earshot, Alasdair acted fast. He assessed his situation with little optimism. Six English foot soldiers, all carrying swords or spears, flanked him. Thankfully, none had a bow. Carney took a moment to urinate on a tree beside him and followed it with retching from his overindulging the night before. Alasdair prayed the rope was long enough.

He had no time. Now was it. Deirdre had only moments to fight off Ronat.

He jumped on Carney from behind and, using the small length of rope that hung between his tied hands, flung the rope over Carney's head to choke him. Caught off guard as he tied his trews, Carney struggled to squeeze his fingers between the rope and his neck. He coughed and gagged.

Tighter, Alasdair thought. He mustered all his strength and wrapped more of the rope in circle around Carney's throat.

He yanked Carney close against his chest, backed up, and pressed his own back to the horse's belly, and squeezed. He stretched the minimal length of rope between his knotted wrists whilst also pushing Carney forward with a knee in his back. The pain bit him nearly down to the bone, but he pulled with all his strength, choking the bastard.

A soldier rushed in from the side and tried to grab his shoulder. Carney heaved and sputtered, stamping with his feet and clawing at Alasdair's hands. It was enough commotion to block Alasdair from attacks. He wedged against the horse harder. The animal danced its hooves, preventing other soldiers from getting closer.

The choking was not enough to kill Carney, for Alasdair's arms burned and his strength dimmed, but it gave him the time he needed. Alasdair dropped the rope from around Carney's neck, and shifted his hands down around Carney's belly, wrapping him in a tight hold. He managed to slip the dagger from Carney's belt. He angled his wrists in and shoved the dagger inward with full force.

Alasdair released his hold, and Carney fell to the ground. "Ye bloody bastard!" he moaned, writhing as he bled out, now grabbing his belly.

Alasdair kicked him aside and stepped forward to face his opponents, wielding only bloody hands and wrists. A soldier came at him with a sword but instead fell into him. Startled, Alasdair staggered to the ground, near the horse's rear hooves, the soldier atop him.

The horse danced about, hooves coming close to his skull. Alasdair rolled to his side and wrestled with the injured soldier. An arrow protruded through the man's shoulder.

Alasdair reached for the dagger stuck in Carney's belly. The other soldier on the ground punched him in the chin. He fumbled, found the dagger, and swiped blindly. The man cried out and fell as the dagger sliced the back of his calf.

A few more arrows whizzed past, and two other soldiers fell to the ground.

A familiar voice hollered. "Stay down!"

Edmund and Crystoll rode into view. Edmund reached him first, dismounted, and helped Alasdair upright. He took the dagger from Alasdair and freed him of the ropes. "Deirdre?" was all Edmund could muster.

Alasdair took the dagger back from Edmund's hands and made for the forest. The sounds of metal left him with the assurance that Crystoll and Edmund could handle the other soldiers.

Alasdair broke through the thick hedges and found Deirdre and Ronat.

"Get off me, you beast!" Deirdre screamed. She scratched Ronat's face.

He slapped her, turned her around, and shoved her face against a tree. He pushed her skirts up.

Alasdair's wrists burned from the rope, but he came upon Ronat with the dagger and stabbed him between the shoulders. Ronat screeched and fell. He tripped over a large knotty tree root. He gasped and gurgled on blood.

Alasdair fell to the ground and punched Ronat in the face, knuckles growing bloodier by the moment as he pounded him. He kept punching, feeling bones break in Ronat's nose and jaw. He grunted, cursed, spat. The sweat poured down his temple, mixed with blood from his reopened head wound.

A hand landed on his shoulder. He spun around and punched. Deirdre had the wits to duck. "Stop, Alasdair! He's dead!"

He froze and then sank to his knees. Gasps of anger clashed with sobs of misery, and he stared at Ronat's pummeled body. The man's face was unrecognizable.

Deirdre was there, clasping her clean, porcelain hands around his trembling bloody ones. "It's all right," she whispered. She brought his hands to her lips and kissed them.

Through blurry eyes he found her face and clung to the serenity her blue-green gaze offered. She brushed a swath of his hair from his eyes, and traced his cheekbone down to his jaw. He wanted to kiss her, but he banished that thought.

She led him to the road.

Edmund and Crystoll were dragging the bodies into the woods. Blood painted the ground. "Don't bother," Alasdair said. "He'll already recognize that something's amiss when the group doesn't arrive."

"Edmund!" Deirdre ran and hugged him. She looked around. "Are you with father?"

Edmund shrugged out of the embrace. "Deirdre, I—"

Alasdair interrupted. "Thank you for coming, Edmund." He surveyed the situation. The only two horses, besides Edmund's and Crystoll's, were both injured from the battle. They were unusable.

"Father? Is he coming?" Deirdre asked.

Crystoll and Edmund shared a silent look. Crystoll wiped blood off his sword and sheathed it. "We don't know. He wasn't home when I reached Dornie. I—We couldn't wait. We came directly here. I told Moreen where we're heading. If your father returns, she'll relay the message."

"We can't possibly go alone," Deirdre said.

"Weren't *you* heading there alone?" Edmund accused.

Her eyes dropped.

Alasdair intervened. "How much farther is the keep?"

"On horse, by nightfall. On foot, tomorrow morning," Crystoll said.

Alasdair contemplated. "You two go ahead. We'll follow on foot. We can't burden the horses, and we'll slow you down. Scout the area; find a weakness in their guard. Don't proceed in until I am there. It'll give your father another day and if he's not there, then we'll have to do it ourselves."

"What about Caite?" Deirdre said. "He may kill her after this," she said, waving her hands at the dead bodies.

Alasdair sighed. "We will try our best."

"We should go with them!"

"We'll slow them down. Deirdre, we need them to scout the area first. We need your father's men." If they get there in time, he thought.

She pursed her lips but nodded. He knew she understood.

He turned to Crystoll. "Are you familiar with the MacDougall laird and keep?"

Crystoll said, "Enough. He has able men, but they're scattered."

"He also has at least six English foot soldiers, and possibly more if the baron has arranged it," Alasdair added, seeking agreement from Edmund. He nodded subtly. He didn't want to mention the fact that none of them even knew *if* Laird MacCoinneach was on his way.

After leaving Deirdre and Alasdair with supplies, both men mounted the horses and left at a full gallop.

It was a time for a reckoning.

CHAPTER THIRTEEN

Deirdre's soul was weary. She rubbed the shoulder where Carney had shoved her into the boulder last night. Then she moved down to massaging her achy wrists from fighting Ronat's aggressive hands. Even the physical pain couldn't surmount the hurt that welled within her though.

"I'm sorry about your father, Alasdair," she said, the feel of his name rolling off her tongue still foreign.

"Me, too." He poked at his swelling face, wincing with each touch.

He looked poorly, but that wasn't the reason she kept her sights ahead and not on him. "Why does he hate you?"

"He sentenced my mother to death for being a witch—I watched her burn." He paused and tightened his scarred hand. He stopped and turned toward her, searching her face for her reaction. "You don't look surprised."

Her lower lip trembled. "Annella told me." *And Venora*, but she dared not breathe that to him. "I'm sorry, Alasdair. It wasn't your fault." She touched him lightly on his scarred arm. For once, he didn't push her away. The ripples vibrated with his memory—which she felt like sharp pricks of a needle—beneath her fingertips.

A muscle quivered in his jaw. "But it was. I am not his son. He sent me away for education and training, unable to stand the sight of me. I'd hoped upon my return that his heart could be swayed, but alas…one cannot change their soul. How could he love a bastard son?"

She knew otherwise. Both men shared similar features, and even though they had opposite life energies—cold and hot—she had *felt* their blood connection. She knew that expressing that sad truth to him would not ease his heartache.

His shoulders stiffened, but he said nothing.

Deirdre reached out to his face. "You should let me clean that."

He assessed her quickly. "What about you? Did Ronat hurt you?"

She threaded her fingers through her hair, self-conscious. She pulled two small leaves from it. "No."

"How did they find you?"

"I let them capture me."

"What?" With all the bruising that had appeared, his face flared with death.

"A distraction?" she said feebly, then recovered her resolve. "To delay and distract them, while Crystoll returned home to get father's men."

"That was bold and unwise." He shook his head.

She actually agreed with him. "How did *you* get captured?"

He groaned, rubbing his ribs. "That doesn't matter."

She grew annoyed. "What do *you* plan to do?"

"Kill him."

His callousness pierced her. "What about Caite?"

"We're doing our best to get her."

"What if he kills her?"

"I won't allow it."

She couldn't hold back the wetness at the back of her eyes any longer. She may not have been able to sense his emotions, but she knew soreness when she saw it. "Please forgive me, Alasdair," she said, her voice breaking.

He didn't speak. Instead, he held her. The comfort of his arms was better than words. She cried into his blood-stained shirt. He stroked her hair and whispered to her. "Hush, love, hush."

"Can we ever go back to before?"

"I'm afraid not."

She pulled from him, and stared at her feet. Her heart squeezed as she realized that he would never again want her. She sniffled, unable to bring herself to look at him. "I understand."

He lifted her chin, forcing her to face him. "Oh, love. I meant that we can never return to before—to our former lives. I can't imagine my life without you," he said, a half smile cracking through his split lip. "If you'll still have me."

"Oh, Alasdair. I-I wish I'd never married Cortland, or—or…"

"Don't ever wish to undo anything. It's all meant to happen. God has plans for us. I was the fool to think I was more righteous than He. I'll not be resentful and run from struggles like my father. I shouldn't have left you like I did. I should have listened."

"You have strong faith in a power greater than us," she said, thinking about her own ability.

"Can you forgive me?" His words were tender, like the kiss of the wind.

"How can you forgive me, though? I lied the most dreadful of lies and this ability of mine—"

He put a finger to her lips and shook his head. "No more, Deirdre. No more. We cannot undo the past. We're here together, and that's all that matters. God gave you a gift that I don't understand, but I should not cast judgment because then I am just like *him*."

They continued, their hands linked. They walked bruised but not broken.

"Did you see me?" she asked much later as dusk drew near.

"See you?" he repeated.

"When you were along the road yesterday, I was in the woods, watching, and your head turned in my direction."

"You were watching?"

She exhaled and blinked, exasperated. He hadn't seen her. It was all her imagining. "Aye."

"It sounds daft, and I was delirious, but I swear I *felt* your presence."

"You had?"

He swiped sweat from his brow and shook his head. "Aye. Like the yellow glow of the sun. Daft, huh?"

Deirdre looked ahead as the road narrowed and traversed rockier terrain. Trees flanked them. Two smaller mountains lay ahead and beyond that was the MacDougall holding. There was no way they would reach it by nightfall.

"We need to make camp," Alasdair said.

"Aye." Her entire body agreed, and as much as she wanted to get to Caite tonight, it was not possible.

Alasdair voiced her fears. "Don't worry, they'll wait for us."

"But Caite—she may already be dead."

Alasdair shook his head. "Nay. He'll want to see me suffer first and use you in his plan. Why else would he have taken you earlier? Hurt you and he hurts me. He won't touch a hair on her head until I'm found."

Deirdre closed her eyes, searching within. When she was near Alasdair, his red hot lifeblood transcended all others, and she had to block it. It took a moment to locate her sister. No, Caite wasn't dead. She felt her sister's strong lifeblood even though it was dim and far. She had a strange feeling about it. "What about my father?"

"A father's weakness is his daughter."

"What if—" she began.

"Don't fret, love. That option isn't available anymore." His attempt at a smile made him look deranged.

He pointed to a group of oaks and a thick patch of gorse. "Here. We'll rest and leave before daybreak."

Once they made a fire, Alasdair sat, groaning with each slow, stiff movement. "I'm afraid I'm in no shape to hunt or fish."

"I'm not hungry," she said, partly true.

"Good." He lay on a bed of forest litter. "Come rest with me, Deirdre. My strength will return come morn."

"I hope so because I can't wield that," she said, sticking her thumb out at the sword he had taken from a dead soldier.

"Hmm." His eyes were already closing.

"You need to be tended." She rose.

"We've no supplies," he said sleepily.

All they had was a satchel from Crystoll. She searched the contents; it held a flask each of ale and water, a few bannocks, hard cheese, some coins, and a spare dagger.

It was enough. She cut small pieces from the hem of her skirt, soaked them in an ale and water mixture and blotted Alasdair's wrists.

He winced but kept his eyes closed, resting as she worked. She meticulously dabbed at his damaged wrists and knuckles. She leaned down and kissed his hand, where the scars rippled, wishing she had willow-bark tincture, or better yet, her mother's Healer abilities. Alasdair snored lightly. She watched him, ignoring her own fatigue.

Resting a hand on his chest, his strong heartbeat thumped beneath her palm. She closed her eyes and thought of good things. Like she had at the stones, she allowed earth's beauty and life's essence to stifle all negative thoughts. She spoke to her mother's spirit. *Heal him. Heal him.*

Nothing.

She tried again, her gaze drawn to the small fire beside them. The flames lured her with their heat, almost in a hypnotic way. *Heal him.* She watched in astonishment as the flames flickered in response. *Heal him*, she said louder in her mind. One large flame licked up higher than was possible, then lowered. She turned back to Alasdair and concentrated on his lifeblood. Nothing had changed. It was still warm, but not the fiery hot it once had been.

Quiet tears fell down her cheeks, and she turned her attention to the wounds again. In the low light of dusk, deathly black shadows formed in places where blood had pooled in his face. She cleaned his lip and blotted a cut on his jawline. She stroked his messy hair. He moaned and took her hand, pressing it against his cheek. His eyes cracked open. He whispered, groggy, "I was ready to say goodbye to you, but I was walking there on the road, and I thought of you. Damn, I could almost feel you. I had to find you. Then you appeared in the camp. God had forgiven me. Now you have. I am blessed."

His jaw quaked under her hand.

He pulled her down to meet him and kissed her. She had missed his touch more than she could say. Despite his injuries, he moved quickly, sweeping himself up and over, switching positions with her. He ran a hand down her cheek. "I can't be without you, Deirdre."

"Alasdair, you're injured," she said, gasping for breath in between kisses.

"Say it again."

"What?"

"My name." His voice was gruff but filled with desire.

"Alasdair," she said, his name rolling off her tongue with ease.

"Are you...well?" he asked belatedly, lifting off her body, leaning on one elbow. He cupped a palm over her belly.

"Yes, we both are," she responded. In all the commotion, she had forgotten to tell him that the bairn was fine, that she was better.

"We shouldn't. I don't want to hurt you."

She felt the delicate glow of life. "All will be fine. I can feel it."

There was no time for formalities or gentleness. He shoved up her skirts, exposing her to the cool night air. She welcomed his presence. He moaned as they took each other tenderly. Pressed into the hard ground, she relished the pleasure he unleashed. Her mind and body fragmented as she grew close to the edge. The surreal insurgence of sensations attacked her as the cadence took over.

He cried out and stopped, resting his head on her chest.

They both fell asleep, deep into the realm of darkness, completion, and peace.

Alasdair awoke to find Deirdre spread out beneath him, her delicate white legs still wrapped around him and covered in the morning drizzle. The thought of their interlocked bodies aroused him, and he kissed her sleeping face, brushing aside her matted hair. She stirred.

He began to slide off her, but she stopped him. "No, stay," she said. He kissed her in the wet dawn, drawing out the joining of their mouths. He had little energy left in him.

"Are you really well?" he asked, rolling to his side and smoothing her skirt down. His finger lingered on her thigh.

Branches sheltered them, but a few droplets made their way through. Their litter bed had begun to grow soppy. He pulled the cloak over her.

"Aye, mmm." She rubbed her belly in subtle emphasis.

"Did that potion really work?"

She smiled thin-lipped. "Aye." Her smile then disappeared, replaced by a sad frown. "I wish this child was yours."

"It will be," he assured her, rubbing her covered belly. "And we'll have more," he added. "I didn't hurt you? I shouldn't have...last night...I..."

"I *am* well, Alasdair. We know what's coming for us. We could d—" She stopped herself. Neither could seem to find the words to speak the most plausible certainty.

That thought stirred him further. He couldn't be with her enough, touch her enough, and make love to her enough to fill the void within. He wanted to lie with her here the rest of his days. He kissed her. Long, slowly, and thoroughly. His cut lip and sore jaw throbbed, but the gratification of their joined lips surpassed it.

He unlaced the front of her gown, then kirtle, and pushed down the loose chemise beneath. He drew a fingertip around her nipple. Gooseflesh rose up over the mound of her breast, and he brushed his lips over it. He nestled into her chest, enjoying the woodsy, yet feminine scent of her and feeling her breaths rise and fall. She weaved her fingers through his hair and massaged his scalp.

He propped up on his elbow, and interlaced his fingers with hers. "I love you, Deirdre."

"I love you, too, Alasdair." Dreamy eyes stared back. "Would you think me foolish to say that I've always known...that you'd be the one? That I'd find you?"

"Find me?" he asked, in all seriousness. "Och, but I found *you*." He stroked her chin. "Well, Aleck Stirrat, that ignorant dolt, found you by that loch. I'm sorry I lied to you, Deirdre. I had to do it for the Cause." Her stare wreaked havoc upon him. She had dried blood smudges on her opal cheeks and rounded chin, obviously a marking from their love-making for her face was uncut. He brushed her chaotic hair from her forehead and tucked it behind her ears. He licked his thumb and cleaned his blood off her face.

Her lower lip trembled. Over the past few days, he had fought the reality of it. He was a God-fearing person, but he had also been a foolish man filled with a fear of the mysterious. His mother had died due to her indiscretions. She had not been a witch. Perhaps a part of him had believed the accusations. A shudder of shame vibrated through him. "My father is a dark soul."

Veiled in black, Deirdre's Norse words echoed in his mind. *Icy death.* By God, she had felt his father's presence. It all made sense— well, some sort of sense, now. A *cloud of white death veiled in black*. She had seen his father's coming. She had felt him.

She was silent but attentive, probably watching his face doing tumbles as he put it all together.

"I often wonder about my mother," he hesitated, clearly perplexed as to what his mind was thinking. Could she have been descended from these magical peoples? "I never told you that she was from the isles, too. South, not Uist, but I don't know which. My father said she was a witch, but perhaps she was like you? I never saw her do anything though. I was young."

"Perhaps," Deirdre said, her voice soft. She stroked his shoulder. "But she was not a witch."

"No, she wasn't." Aye, he believed it. There was a long pause as he contemplated it all. "If she did have powers, like you, does that mean...I, that I..." He couldn't say the words. When Deirdre had hid in the trees, his intuition told him to look that way. He had seen nothing but leaves and branches. However, a feeling deep in his stomach told him that she had been there.

"Have a power?" Deirdre finished for him.

He gulped, perspiring with the thought.

"Maybe. Do you feel or see things?"

He shook his head. "Nay, not really. Only that one time when you were by the road. I've never dreamed of you, yet when we met, there was something familiar about you. I fought it for so long. I—" He stopped and rubbed his knuckles across his forehead.

Deirdre was special, and when she was ready, she'd tell him more. An exceptional ability blessed her. The way she looked at or responded to people was intense. "How did you know I would come?" he asked, purposely gentle with his tone.

She blinked, then refocused her gaze. "You'll think it daft, or worse."

"No, I won't."

She pursed her lips and heaved a sigh. "I used to have these dreams of a man from the wood." She closed her eyes. "He had waves of black hair, eyes like a deep dark loch, long nose—albeit, not as bruised as yours is," she said with a chuckle. "A man with an *energy*," she said, drawing out that word, as if pondering upon it. "...hot to the touch. Like a scalding hearth. When I saw you that first day at the loch, I knew it was you." She began to shake beneath him.

He stroked her cheek. "You've dreamt of me?"

"Aye."

"Does it hurt when I touch you?"

She shook her head. She opened her eyes and touched his face for effect. "Like the sweetest fire."

The sun peeked through the trees, reminding them of their mission.

"It's time," she said for him.

"Aye. One last kiss," he said, leaning down.

They reached the MacDougall keep by midmorning. Crystoll and Edmund were hidden in the forested hills that encircled the stronghold and its neighboring loch. Alasdair was grateful they had not risked going in alone. Just as they ducked under the protective cover of the trees, the clouds unleashed their fury.

"What do you know about the keep?" he asked, pulling his plaid over his head and kneeling to join their companions.

Edmund spoke first. "It was abandoned for a long time, but the MacDougalls came north from Argyll about ten years ago and reclaimed it. You're familiar with their contention with the Donalds?"

"Yes."

He continued. "My father is loyal to the Donalds. By being allied with them, we have strained any hope to partner with the MacDougalls."

Deirdre added, "Then there was Auld Kenneth."

"That wasn't your fault, Deirdre," Crystoll interrupted.

"He died before we could wed. They blame me."

Alasdair felt the agony in her voice. He squeezed her hand. "Nonsense. Regardless, the baron has used that situation."

Tenting his hand over his eyes to shield himself from rain, he assessed the wooden tower house. It was a lonely keep, resting on a higher knoll, and lacking village or town. A loch bordered the rear of the simple stronghold, and open meadows abutted both sides. A moderate-sized palisade guarded the courtyard. From his view, Alasdair observed six men standing guard. But how many were within? Overall, it appeared abandoned. Ghostlike gray clouds shrouded the landscape. Alasdair knew full well that looks could deceive. A forceful gale blustered, and boats tethered to the docks bounced in the upturned loch.

"My father's men aren't here yet." Edmund tapped agitated fingers on his knee.

"Perhaps we were wrong?" Deirdre asked.

Edmund shook his head. "No. He's coming. He went to the Donalds for reinforcements. He's not willing to turn from the Cause and not with Caite taken."

Crystoll added, "No more of the baron's men have arrived either."

"That's reassuring," said Alasdair. "But we do not know how many wait within."

"He'll be here," Crystoll said in confidence.

Alasdair agreed. "I suggest that two of us go in."

"I've searched the grounds and found a way." Crystoll motioned toward the rear of the keep.

"What about a distraction?" Edmund offered.

Alasdair considered their assets. Between all of them, they had a handful of daggers, swords, and one crossbow.

Their opponent held a stronghold potentially filled with English foot soldiers, MacDougalls, and perhaps Comyn's supporters. Circumstance did not favor them. "Word surely has reached the baron that we've escaped. How many MacDougalls do you think he has?"

"An unknown number. Laird MacDougall's men live scattered across the area," Crystoll said. "After we arrived last night, there was stirring within the bailey."

"I should go in," Deirdre spoke up.

"No," all three men said in adamant unity.

"I could—"

"Absolutely not." Alasdair grabbed her hand.

She glared at him.

Alasdair softened his tone. "I don't want you to get hurt again, love. Or worse."

"But Caite... This is my fault. I should be the one."

Alasdair was firm. "No fault lies with you. You *know* he wants me and will use both you and Caite to get to me," Alasdair said, placing as much sincerity he could into his words.

Deirdre's mouth was tight and grim. Rain dripped down her forehead, and she swiped at it.

He took her other hand in his. Her fingers were icy. "I beg you, Deirdre. Please. I don't want you in harm's reach as well. He'll not hesitate killing you after what happened to the soldiers on the road."

"Then what's stopping him from killing Caite?" she countered.

"Do you feel her?" he rebutted, even though he knew she was right.

She closed her eyes for the briefest of moments. "Aye. She's alive. I don't want you to get hurt either," she said, placing a hand on his cheek.

They both knew that this was his battle. A realization dawned on him, and he didn't know why he didn't put it all together earlier. Deirdre's dead husbands. Edmund's misfortune with babies. Caite...was her fate to die before love could ever be found? Was this when it would happen? No. He would not let Deirdre's sister die.

"The baron doesn't know *who* attacked his men, and all of them are dead," Edmund said prudently. "So I've an idea." He paused before saying, "I go in."

Crystoll agreed. "It may work."

"I owe it to her," Edmund pleaded.

"I don't understand," Deirdre interrupted. "It's not your fault Caite's there. The baron—he's a dark man. He took her to lure out Alasdair and to persuade Father against the Cause."

Edmund curled a hand and rubbed it on his thigh. "It is. I'm sorry, Deirdre. The fault rests with me alone."

"What?"

"He promised me...he promised me..." He stumbled on the words as he averted her gaze. "Oh damn it, it doesn't matter!"

"What did you do?" she said tremulously.

Edmund swallowed hard, clearly disgusted with himself. "I was a fool."

Silence engulfed the group. Deirdre took her brother's hand, squeezed, and tilted her head in forgiveness.

Alasdair patted Edmund's back. "The past is behind us. All that matters is that you're here now. If the baron doesn't know you were involved with the attack on the road, then he can still trust you. Remember though, when he's done using you, he *will* kill you." He turned to Crystoll and stabbed his dagger into the dirt. "Lay it out."

Crystoll drew out a map and motioned with his fingers. "Six guards flank the palisade, here and here. Two boats are tied to a berth on the loch. The main entrance is through the palisade and the courtyard. Most of Laird MacDougall's men reside or have been posted in other areas in the region. I doubt he's gathered many men for the baron's purpose. The MacDougalls look out for themselves. So we are looking at maybe a few dozen men."

"What do you know about the Earl of Ross?" Alasdair asked.

Crystoll's eyebrows raised. "He's for the Cause, but we aren't certain which Claimant he supports. Why?"

"Thomas suspects that the earl sides with Comyn. The MacDougalls may support him as well."

"Hmmm. So he may have more men than expected."

"It doesn't matter. I'm going in." Edmund sheathed his sword and rose.

"Wait, you need to understand who we're fighting," Alasdair began.

"I think I already do," Edmund snapped.

Alasdair sighed and looked at Deirdre when he spoke. "I'm sorry that I've not told you all more. The baron, my father, is one of the twelve Guardians. He was placed among those men not to assist Scotland with the Claimants, but as a spy many years ago. King Edward wishes to see all the contenders dead, and my father's job is to implement that order."

Both Crystoll and Edmund appeared unaffected by his statement.

He added, "I also have it under good authority that my father killed the child Lady Margaret six years ago."

"What?" Deirdre said. "The queen? She was sick. She died on passage to Scotland. He couldn't…"

"Trust me, he did and under Edward's authority. If you kill the baron…you will be hanged by Edward. I can't have your blood on my soul." Alasdair blew a deep breath out. "I must be the person to kill him."

All three nodded, although Deirdre wrung part of her skirt in her hands, clearly bothered.

"Edmund, tell him you arrived after Crystoll and a few others had already attacked the soldiers. Convince him you've not been swayed."

"After Edmund goes in, I'll distract the guards so you can get in there, too," Crystoll said.

"Aye. Can you manage to get to the west side of the palisade and release those docked boats to draw their attention there? They may just think the boats got loose."

"Aye."

"Deirdre, I need you to cover me." Alasdair clasped her hand. "Can you handle the crossbow?"

Crystoll already removed the bow from his back and handed it to her.

"Yes," she said firmly.

With that said, Edmund disappeared through the trees.

Deirdre's eyes didn't move from the entrance in the palisade. The moments felt like hours. Edmund had been received warmly by the guards at the front and was led inside. She still couldn't believe what he had done. Well, she could. The glowing life within her was a constant reminder of her brother's pain. Her child would inherit Eilean Donan and be future laird of the clan.

Alasdair looked over his shoulder again. "They'll be here," Crystoll encouraged.

Deirdre wasn't so sure she shared his confidence.

Alasdair pushed his shoulders back. "Do it," he ordered Crystoll.

Deirdre looked at the bow in her hand. "Be safe, Alasdair. I—"

He stopped her with a brief kiss. "No goodbyes." Then he was gone, moving between hills. Crystoll took what he needed and crept to the opposite end of the palisade. The wooden fence enclosing the square tower and courtyard hovered no more than a hundred paces way, yet seemed to be mountains away in Deirdre's mind.

Alasdair crouched among the hills, inconspicuous. He came dangerously close to the entrance without being seen, moving like a cat closing in on a mouse. The guards remained huddled under an overhang, distracted by the rain. Meanwhile, Crystoll navigated along the tree line, down to the loch shore, and over to the boats. Deirdre tapped a nervous finger on the crossbow's stock as she watched the plan unfold before her. Two of the boats began to drift in the billowing loch, and as Crystoll reached a hiding spot, three of the guards ran to the loch's edge. They argued and gestured, jumping into the water to retrieve the tossing boats.

Three men remained at their posts near the entrance. Alasdair would never be able to get through unless she fired and hit all three. Cortland had taught her the crossbow, but she wasn't a soldier and hardly adept at it. It was heavy, and her aim horrific. She loosed one bolt, and it flew off into the trees. What a futile plan! She cursed under her breath, vowing that she would encourage her own daughter—if God blessed her with one—to learn how to use a bow and arrow and mayhap even a sword. She set the crossbow down and rose.

While the other three guards were preoccupied with the boats, she stepped out from the grove and took the narrow dirt road to the entrance, her heart pounding and hands trembling. Her legs felt like sacks of grain after sitting for so long, but she trudged on, becoming soaked in the process as the rain fell in torrents. She shivered on her approach but forced a look of indifference and strength. "Good day, gentlemen."

One of the guards recognized her. "Grab her!"

This was her moment. She felt Alasdair's lifeblood nearby. She pulled her dagger from her pocket and lunged. She missed the soft flesh of one soldier's midsection and cut his arm. She struggled and fought in vain as another soldier restrained her. Slamming her foot down on his boot, pain raced up her shin instead of injuring her attacker.

"Let go of me!" She wriggled in his grip and spat at the soldier in front of her.

He came forward and slapped her.

Her arms hurt as the man behind her dug deeper into them to control her. She began to lose strength. Her head lolled, chin against her chest, but she forced it upright.

A shadow behind the men moved in the hills. Alasdair stood a few paces behind the men. His lifeblood throbbed red. She pleaded to him with her eyes. *Go in!* He paused. Indecision contorted his face. *I'll be well*, she said with her mind.

The injured man drew his dagger.

"Wait! We can't kill her. Baron's orders."

"I don't care! The witch cut me." He stepped forward.

A raw buzzing erupted in Deirdre's ears, and her knees buckled. She cried out and cradled her head. The baron's lifeblood overtook her. Damn it! Not now!

It was enough to puzzle them.

Alasdair was behind one, sword drawn, if the man so much as made a move forward to hurt her.

"Pick her up," the guard said, sheathing his dagger.

She sagged more in relief. As the one propped her back up, she looked beyond them and saw the muted image of Alasdair ducking inside, unnoticed.

They dragged her through the gatehouse. The courtyard was empty, with a handful of guards—all English—within. Blackness lured her, but she found her footing. Her eyes fell upon everything as she searched for Alasdair. He was gone. She breathed a sigh. At least he had gotten in.

The men pulled her through a side entrance, down a maze of dark hallways, and then into the large hall. She wrestled with the cold that numbed her to the core as she raised her head in preparation to be presented to the baron.

Even though she had expected it, she gasped when she entered the hall. Caite sat beside the hearth, tied to a chair, battered but alive. Edmund was beside her, equally restrained and emanating rage in pulsating waves that struck Deirdre. There were too many men to count. Scot and English filled the hall. Lifebloods and emotions of all sorts...most brown and earthy, stale and bitter, angry, eager, worried...hit her at once. She stumbled as if struck by lightning.

"Baron," her captor said as he brought her in. She wobbled on her feet but forced herself to remain upright.

The baron turned. Light illuminated his face and for the briefest, albeit sickening, moment he looked like Alasdair with the glint of delight in his blue eyes, and the lopsided grin. "My darling Lady MacCoinneach! Once again, you've blessed us with your company. You seem to be unable to part ways with us. I'm afraid the ambush on the road didn't serve you well." He waved toward the throng of men filling the hall.

Her throat dry, she managed to speak. "I've come in my sister's stead. Release her."

"Why in heavens would I do that? I now have all of Laird MacCoinneach's children."

She passed a brief look at her brother. Edmund made the subtlest of motions, shaking his head left to right. His eyes narrowed to slits. His usual robust ginger glow turned red with heat and anger.

"Oh, don't look to him, lass. He'll betray you too easily. Like a rat with a crumb." The baron snickered. "Sit. You must be chilled." He motioned to the guards, and they brought and bound her to a chair near the hearth, though she was separated from her siblings. "Laird MacDougall, is this the witch who killed your father?"

Steafan MacDougall stepped forward. Deirdre cringed; he had the same air about him as his father, Kenneth, the old beast. Steafan approached her and lifted her chin with a fat hand, as if inspecting a piece of meat. "Aye, this is the wench." Steafan turned toward Agmus. "She's not to be killed. She is mine."

"Of course," Agmus said.

A foul, ashen lifeblood radiated from the tall, heavy-set laird. Gray stone-like eyes smirked as he hovered over her. He scratched his thick auburn beard, then drew his hand lower and fondled himself in gesture. "Aye, she'd do just fine." Several of his men laughed, and a rumble of jeers ran through them. Laren, Stefan's younger brother, a man who exuded a kinder lifeblood, was nowhere to be seen. He was not one to be so easily swayed by coin. She had no voice of reason among all these men.

She tried anyway. "I didn't have a hand in your father's death. He was old and enjoyed his libations too much." She stuck her chin out.

Steafan leaned in to her, his hands on the chair arms. His breath reeked of rancid food. "What about your husbands? Did they die from being fat and old, too?"

She had no response.

"That wasn't her fault!" Caite spoke up. Deirdre shot her a pleading glare to be quiet.

"Och, her husbands, young able soldiers, both died after bedding their wife, and that is not evil-casting?" Steafan countered.

The MacDougall soldiers laughed and shouted obnoxiously.

"Och, we'll make sure we cast the devil out of her first, just to be safe."

"Our father will kill you." Edmund struggled against his restraints. "All of you," he said, turning his wrath upon the baron.

"Your father is a fool," Steafan said.

"We've done nothing to any of you. Set us free," Deirdre said. Unpleasant lifebloods and depraved emotions roared through her body. Agmus stepped closer, his energy rending through her.

Edmund drew the attention back to him. "So you plan to kill every person who supports the Cause? There are many contenders and a greater number of supporters."

"If it's necessary, but empty promises work fine," Agmus said. With a quick flick of his wrist, he signaled to the English soldiers in the hall. They all pulled out their swords and began killing Laird MacDougall's men. Cries and slicing steel echoed off the rafters as commotion broke out. Steafan's men were outnumbered by at least twofold.

Caite screamed as two scuffling men bumped into her, their blades drawn and coming close to her face. She curled into herself and sobbed. Deirdre watched, horrified, as men dropped to the floor one after the other. She bore their pain as each cried out and died. She felt shock, anger, fear. Her body quaked as if she was experiencing it all herself. Waves hit her like she was drowning on the open sea.

Steafan wasn't as slow as his semblance would indicate. He cut through several of the English soldiers. "Baron, what is this?" he cried, winded as he dodged strikes. One soldier grazed his arm, and Steafan's sword dropped. Steafan fell to his knees.

Revolted eyes looked upon him as Agmus approached.

"You promised us." Steafan spat the words.

"The only vow I make is to King Edward. You have served your purpose, Laird MacDougall, and are released from your debt." Agmus plunged his broadsword through Steafan's gullet. Steafan crumpled to the ground, stone-eyes wide with shock, mouth agape and voiceless. "All Cause supporters must be eliminated."

Agmus pulled his sword from Steafan's throat and turned to Deirdre. "It's sad how the promise of land could turn any man, even a brother on his own sisters. Tsk, tsk, tsk." He angled his sword at Edmund. The closer he stepped toward them, the icier Deirdre felt. His look was enough to chill her to the bone, but his lifeblood was debilitating. Icy death lanced her lungs. She gasped for air.

"Don't you hurt him, you bastard!" Caite cried out. Dried tears smeared her cheeks, and her hair was disheveled about her shoulders. Blood was splattered on her face from the two men who had fought near her. Although Caite tried to put on a brave face, Deirdre felt her sister's fragile spirit. She had never been exposed to such brutality before.

"What will you do with us?" Deirdre felt her own rage dwarf the defeat that stabbed her heart. She wanted to hit him, but her mind—and ropes—held her in place. Agmus turned back to Deirdre. *Yes*, she thought. *Keep his anger directed to her, as much as it hurt her.*

His dark eyes leered. "All witches burn."

"I'm no witch."

"On the contrary, lass. I can spot an abomination better than any man."

"Let Edmund and Caite go," she ordered. She swallowed hard. She knew he was not a man that could be convinced of anything, except maybe his own fears. "Or I will strike you down!" she bluffed.

He shook his head, feigning pity. "Tsk, tsk. Sometimes the innocent perish with the guilty." He lifted his sword and approached Edmund again.

"Your fight is with me." Alasdair burst into the room, sword drawn.

"Ah, my son, speaking of the *innocent*. Great of you to join us."

There would be no talking this time. Alasdair lunged toward his father, sword raised. Several guards hurried to the assistance of the baron. Alasdair cut through them without a moment's hesitation.

The baron's remaining men came forward. "No!" Agmus ordered. Deirdre saw the subtle limp in his gait, but the fire in his eyes compensated for any weakness. "He's mine." He took a swipe at Alasdair. "It's a shame you'll have to see another woman you love die in flames." Agmus ordered his men forward toward Deirdre and her siblings with a flick of his chin as he fought with his son. "Light it all!" The soldiers took the torches down from their brackets and hurried around the room. They lit the tapestries, walls, and anything that could burn. Deirdre thanked God that they didn't attempt to light the wooden chairs they sat upon.

Agmus wasn't done. "Go!" he ordered his men. "Ready the horses."

"But Baron..." one soldier said. At least twenty men remained.

"Go!" he seethed.

The soldiers fled the hall, and Alasdair struck out at his father again. Despite his age and obvious sickness, Agmus was skilled with the blade and repeatedly countered, dodged, and deflected as they maneuvered around dead bodies. Deirdre squirmed, struggling to free herself. Edmund and Caite did the same.

"I can't, Edmund!" she said.

He grumbled, too, muscles flexing as he rubbed wrist against wrist. "It's too tight."

Alasdair and Agmus continued their dance of swords, one that surely would end with death. Though the baron grew winded, he kept pace with his spryer son.

Alasdair hollered curses at his father and fought with stealth. Deirdre recoiled as his lifeblood burned white-hot.

"I've taught you too well, son."

"Don't you dare call me that." He charged and caught Agmus on his left arm.

Agmus stumbled and laughed. "Och, the lies a child believes. You *are* my son, Alasdair. Like it or not. Your mother may have been a lying whore, but I planted my seed within her, and she birthed you. The bastard child that lay in her womb on the fiery stake, however, wasn't mine. Here you are again, defending a witch. It's no good. When will you learn, Ali? She'll die, too."

"You're wrong. Only you will die today." Alasdair exhaled and leapt. He caught Agmus in the thigh, and Agmus fell, blood spurting from the wound at an alarming rate. The baron clamped a hand on his leg and dropped his sword. Alasdair hovered over him, chest heaving, sword held up to run him through. Deirdre's ears buzzed with the overwhelming sounds of both his and Agmus's lifebloods.

Heat consumed her and not just from Alasdair's lifeblood. Fire had begun to overtake the edges of the room. A beam near her lit as the flames moved from tapestries to wood. The hall almost growled as the blaze ate it hungrily.

Agmus coughed, gagged. "Alasdair, *son*. Please..."

Alasdair knelt beside him and dropped his sword in a clatter. "Why should I help you?" He wheezed the words out, and hurt filled his eyes.

For the first time, Deirdre felt his emotions. They had broken through his shielded lifeblood. Like when she was at the stones, an array of emotions slapped her—sadness, disappointment, loneliness, anger, emptiness...

She whimpered in pain for him. Dear God, she felt it all at once.

"I—I..." Agmus began. He closed his eyes and lay back.

"Why did you do it?" Alasdair asked, his voice cracking.

"She lied. She betrayed me. She betrayed us both. I wanted no memory of her," Agmus said through gritted teeth.

Alasdair leaned in closer. Deirdre felt his hollow grief.

"As long as you live, you will be a reminder." In a sudden movement, Agmus grabbed the dagger at his waist and thrust it into Alasdair's stomach. Alasdair fell, shock widening his eyes. Agmus then slowly rose, cackling.

He dragged himself from the room, leaving a bloody trail behind him.

The flames ate the timber that lined the walls, sprinting to the roof. Heat devoured the room. Deirdre felt helpless, tied to the chair, watching Alasdair's lifeblood leave his body. Her vision flashed before her eyes. *The man from the wood.* Not a forest but rather a wooden house—the timber keep—went up in a blaze around them. Alasdair lay, still, blood draining from the gaping wound. *Oh my God*, it was her vision. His lifeblood weakened.

Damn it, no, he won't! Deirdre fought her bindings but coughed and grew tired as the room thickened with smoke. She closed her eyes, dizzy, succumbing. In an ironic twist, something she had feared most, being burned for her abilities, was going to happen. She cursed Fate. There was no way to stop it.

Suddenly, a burst of warm amber penetrated her thoughts. Fingers fumbled on her tied hands. "My lady! Go!" It was Crystoll. He untied Edmund and Caite. "Go, go!"

"Not without Alasdair!" Deirdre ran toward him.

"Go with Caite, Deirdre. I'll assist Crystoll," Edmund ordered, shoving her.

Caite grabbed Deirdre's hand. "Come," she said, dragging her from the room. They fled through the main entrance. Deirdre stumbled over a dead MacDougall's body as spots of color danced before her eyes.

"*Come with me*," a woman's voice said. Deirdre reached the middle of the courtyard, looked around, and saw nobody except for Caite. The palisade and small buildings within the courtyard had yet to catch fire. Flames consumed the timber keep and licked angrily from the roof. Crashes filled the air as the roof and walls collapsed.

A moment later, Crystoll and Edmund emerged, Alasdair leaning against them, haggard but upright.

Another crash sent shudders through her core. "Lay him down." The three of them eased him down. Blood still oozed from his wound. She refused to cry.

The sounds of horses and men broke into the courtyard's chaos. "Go!" she said to them. They hesitated.

Deirdre discerned her father's warm yellow lifeblood. "It's Father! Go!"

Edmund knelt beside her. "Deirdre, this is my fault."

"No it's not! Go with Caite and Crystoll. It's Father. Get help. We need linens and water and... Just go!"

Caite hesitated, but Crystoll grabbed her by the arm and Edmund followed. They ran through the gatehouse.

Deirdre knelt before Alasdair and prayed. She didn't cast a spell or evoke spirits. She prayed. *Mother, help me. Heal him.*

Nothing. She cursed under her breath.

She then realized she had the Healer's stone. She pulled it from her pocket and turned it around in her palms. She squeezed it and felt the earth's heat. She stared at the flames devouring the keep despite the rain. Hues of crimson and ginger dance before her. She tuned out the painful sounds of wood giving and the beams collapsing, and just watched the flames as water hit them and they hissed, persistent. "Heal him!"

She focused on one spot, and in response to her command, the fire licked up in a wild flame. She slowed her breath, centered on her steady heartbeat, and closed her eyes, the firelight still burned to her memory. "Heal him," she said again, her voice shaky as she harnessed the fire's power. Didn't her mother's healing power use water? Rain soaked her and pelted Alasdair's body. She cupped the hand with the Healer's stone upward.

She instantly felt a gale of glowing life. It was her mother, not present beside her, but present in her mind, in her soul. She was as beautiful as Deirdre remembered her, with black hair, pale blue eyes, and round features. A unique luminosity emanated from her, one that Deirdre couldn't describe. It wasn't a lifeblood, for she was dead. Now only a spirit burned into her memory. A foggy white haze encircled her mother.

Her mother's eyes smiled back at her.

Put your hands on him.

Deirdre did as told, her eyes still shut. Alasdair's lifeblood was weak.

Her mother laid her hands atop hers. An indefinable heat poured through her palms, into Deirdre's hands, and out her fingertips in a rush, like molten rock. Alasdair winced and gasped but then settled down, his eyes closed.

Her mother hummed foreign words under her breath. She rocked side to side, her hands over Deirdre's. The same sensation she had felt at the stones overtook Deirdre. Her heart pounded so fast that she thought it may burst from her chest. Thunder rolled in here ears.

Deirdre lost herself to it. She cried without tears. She prayed without words. She embraced every sense around her: the sound of the fire eating the keep, the rushing wind, the cold dark night as rain hit the ground, the crashing waves of the loch, the stringent scent of blood...and Alasdair's weak, but pumping heartbeat.

The thunderclaps turned into a roaring. Her hair danced madly about her face. It was as if the wind would pick her up, but she knelt, firming herself to the ground.

Heat almost as hot as a fire itself hastened down her arms and into her palms. *Heal, heal, heal*, she thought.

Then all was quiet and static.

Deirdre rose and stepped back, immobilized by fear, no more prayers to be spoken.

The image of her mother left her as she opened her eyes. She was gone.

She knelt down, hung her head in her hands, and sobbed uncontrollably.

"Deirdre, love."

Her eyes shot open. She felt the dim fiery glow. "Alasdair."

Crystoll and Edmund returned by her side a moment later. "Can we move him?" Crystoll cast a wary look to the burning keep.

Several of her father's soldiers appeared and were already lifting Alasdair.

Deirdre forced herself to walk through the gatehouse, numb from the experience. *Let him live*, she prayed.

Outside stood at least forty riders on horseback. They surrounded the remaining English.

Under the archway, she stepped past the body of Baron Agmus Montgomerie. He lay dead in a pool of blood, dark eyes open and staring blankly. No lifeblood came from his corpse, and a great burden lifted from her soul.

Alasdair awoke to the sound of lowered voices. A sharp, unfamiliar pain rushed through him as he tried to move. He closed his eyes and took deep breaths.

"We need to move him again. We're too close to the MacDougall keep, or what's left of it."

"We can't! He's lost much blood," Deirdre's voice implored.

"Look how well he's healed so far. It's a miracle," Crystoll said.

Silence. More heated whispers. Then footsteps and a door closing.

Alasdair stirred and groaned. He cracked an eye open.

He tried to sit up, but Deirdre pushed him down. "Rest."

His head throbbed, but the worst pain was his middle. He felt as though he'd been run through with a hot poker. The memory of it all came flooding back. "Is he dead?"

Tears pooled on the edges of her eyes. She held a cup of something cold and bitter to his mouth. "Aye. I'm sorry, Alasdair."

He swallowed. "Don't be sorry, love. There was no saving him." Despite knowing his father was dead, and by his hand no less, Alasdair didn't feel comforted.

"What will we do?" Deirdre rested a hand on his chest.

"Live at Eilean Donan as long as we can."

"What about the Cause? The uprisings. The English..." she started.

He lifted a hand and touched her cheek. "Then we stay and fight with Bruce or return to the isles. I'll go anywhere with you, Deirdre. If we must leave, then so be it."

"This Cause means much to you. The navy..."

"The navy is almost ready. Robert Bruce will be here soon. I've done my part for the Cause. Now I do my part for you."

He reached to kiss her, but stinging gripped him.

"Rest, Alasdair."

A week passed, and to Deirdre's surprise, Alasdair recovered with unheard of vigor. He insisted upon walking outside today. A warm spring day greeted them. They had relocated to a cottage near the Donald holding. "There's more you need to know, Alasdair," Deirdre began.

He leaned in and kissed her, his lips eager but soft. "You're special, love." He interlaced his fingers with hers. "We spoke of this, remember?"

She ignored his look. "When I healed you..."

"You healed me?" he asked, lifting his shirt to reveal his bandaged abdomen.

She traced a finger around the dressings that encircled his wound. "Well, I had help. My mother—"

He hushed her with a kiss.

"Will you stop that?"

He grinned. "Sorry. Your mother?"

Her words came in a rush of mixed excitement and liberation. "Her spirit was with me. I don't know how to explain it. She wasn't *there*, but she was here," she said, pointing toward her heart. "She was a Healer. She helped me heal you. My aunt had given me a Healer's stone that was my mother's, and I used it. I felt my mother with me. Fire is my gift, and water was hers, and she used it for healing."

"Fire? Are you a Healer, then? Is that your gift?"

"No. I am a Feeler. I can feel the life energies, lifebloods, good and evil exuding from everyone. I can see into their souls, sense their emotions. Your father's lifeblood was pure death, a white coldness." The words slid off her tongue, smooth and redeeming.

"I know."

"What do you mean?"

"On the path from Broadford, you spoke in old Norse. And earlier, at the loch, when we first met. You said, *En sky av hvite død skjult i svart*."

"I don't remember that. I don't know what that means." She rubbed her head, having no memory of saying such a thing. "Norse? How?"

"It means 'A cloud of white death veiled in black.'"

She inhaled and understood, whispering. "Your father. It describes him. I felt him before I even knew about him? I wonder why?"

"Because you are gifted, love." He stroked her hand.

She closed her eyes and enjoyed his touch. She continued, "And, and I...see things. Like that dream I had of you. I also had one about Caite. That's why I had to save her. You haunted my dreams long before I met you, Alasdair."

"My love, you're gifted beyond my comprehension. You've told me and shown me. You don't need to explain yourself more. I believe you. Whatever happened to do this," he said, lightly tapping his bandage, "was a blessing, a gift. You're blessed with a beautiful ability. You use it for good," he said, dark blue eyes gleaming.

"But your mother..." Uncertainty still disquieted her. "Perhaps she had been gifted, too, as you thought? And your father knew about it—and feared it."

He shook his head and put a finger to her lips. "No more talk of that. I know not what abilities she had, or if she had any at all. My father's heart was so broken that he believed what suited him."

"You believe me then, Alasdair?"

"Och, I do. Fate brought us together. Regardless of fate, magic, or God, my soul and heart are yours. You are my fire."

She melted into his arms, heedful of his injury. The great affliction on her heart had finally been lifted. "I always thought I was cursed."

"Well, I rectified that."

"What do you mean?"

"A hundred kisses, or true love, call it what you want, but your curse is broken, my love." With emphasis, he leaned down and kissed her, the warm rush of love pouring into her like fresh water.

Breathless, she pulled back and looked at him. "What do you mean by a hundred kisses?"

He smirked, scratching his head. "I suppose Moreen and Venora never told you?"

She shook her head. Norse words. A *real* curse? She had thought the curse was her powers. How had she not seen all of this? "I really was cursed?"

"Supposedly, you and your family and Venora's kin were cursed by her father so that your bloodline dies with you." He paused. "Edmund's lost bairns. Venora's daughter was also cursed to live without love, and she tossed herself into the sea. Your curse was that you needed to be properly wooed. One hundred kisses before sharing your bed, or else, well…" He drifted off.

She filled in the rest. Her heart ached. Gordon. Cortland. Oh, and poor Edmund. "I don't think we kissed *that* many times, not one hundred before we, uh…" She felt herself blushing, despite all they'd been through.

"Nay, I don't think we did. Love made up for it. We broke the curse with love."

"Love?" It was true. She had never loved Gordon or Cortland, not the way she loved Alasdair. "It was that simple?"

"Simple, och?"

She smiled back.

He lowered his hand to her belly. "I will love our entire family."

She lifted her chin and seized his lips.

His red hot lifeblood tickled her tongue, quickened her heartbeat, and settled in a warm spot in her womb. The life growing within her danced in response to the sudden heat.

The glow that passed between them paused at Deirdre's core, and a shockwave hit her as she felt her own life energy for the first time. A brief vision of their future blinked behind her eyes—an image of her and Alasdair by the stones, watching the sun set, as their children played.

"Alasdair Montgomerie…that is your name, aye?" she said playfully.

He nodded. "Aye, love."

"Good. I want to be certain that I know your *real* name before we wed."

"So you will have me?"

"Aye. And perhaps we can start counting those kisses once more. I think you owe me a few."

"Gladly," he said, leaning in for another. "I plan on sharing thousands more with you."

JOURNEY THROUGH THE HIGHLANDS...

P **eople, clans, and places...oh my!**
Want to learn more about The Hundred Trilogy? Visit my website (www.jeanmgrant.com) for some book extras. Learn about the MacCoinneach & Montgomerie family lineage, the clans, culture & lore, places, and so much more with a glossary, Scotland map, and family/lineage chart. Be warned! There may be spoilers. Read with caution...and sweet abandon.

Purchase the rest of the series at various retailers online:
https://www.jeanmgrant.com/bookshelf

Want to know when the next book is coming out? Sign up for my newsletter on my website at:
https://www.jeanmgrant.com/contact

Read on to continue the journey through medieval Scotland.

The Hundred Trilogy

Norse invasions, Scottish wars for independence, and the plights of the mystical isles' people come together in The Hundred Trilogy. In each standalone book, delve deeper into the mystical powers of the MacCoinneach clan...a powerful family descended from the Ancients of the Isles. Each person is gifted with an ancient power—healing with water, intuition with fire, and prophecy with wind. But with each gift comes a curse. Can they overcome their afflictions to bridge peace...to find love?

A Hundred Breaths

1263

Gwyn of Uist is a merciful Healer but loses breaths of her life with every healing charm. She barters an alliance with a Scot bent on revenge against her Norse kin, in the hopes to save her brother from their abusive father. But can she and Simon MacCoinneach outwit her betrothed and bring an end to the Norse-Scottish bloodshed when it will take all her breaths to save Simon on the battlefield?

A Hundred Kisses

1296

Deirdre MacCoinneach feels the lifebloods of everyone around her...but vows to discover if her gift killed her husbands—twice. Under the façade of a trader, Alasdair Montgomerie travels to Uist with pivotal information for a claimant seeking the Scottish throne. A cruel baron hunts him, leaving little room for alliances with the lass he meets along the way. Amidst ghosts of the past, Alasdair and Deirdre find themselves falling together in a web of secrets and the curse of a hundred kisses...

A Hundred Lies
1322

Rosalie Threston's fortune-telling lies have caught up with her and she's on the run from a ruthless English noblewoman. Rosalie finds refuge in the halls of Eilean Donan castle deep in the Highlands, and in the arms of the laird's mysterious son, Domhnall Montgomerie. Terrible visions plague Domhnall and he avoids all physical contact to temper them. When an accidental touch reveals only delight, he wonders if Rosalie is the key to silencing the Sight. Mystical awakening unravels with each kiss. But can Domhnall embrace his gift in time to save her life, even if it means exposing her lies?

Seeker
A novella, part of the Mortar & Pestle series
1322

Aileana Montgomerie lacks the mystical ability of the Scottish Ancients like her kin. She seeks a purpose but what good is her bow and arrow if she is denied the right to fight for her clan? Brodie MacDougall is ordained to be the next war chieftain of his clan. Chronic pain and nervous vapors force him to spend his days alone, not lift a sword and charge into battle. Can his strategic skills alone keep him one step ahead of his conspiring brother? After magic cast by mystical Mortar & Pestle, the seat on his brother's council is no longer dependent upon his health...but on Aileana's strength. With rumblings of unrest among their clans, will their love foster an alliance or be a step toward war?

Also by Jean M. Grant

A Hundred Breaths
A Hundred Lies
Seeker
Soul of the Storm
Will Rise from Ashes

ABOUT THE AUTHOR

Jean has a penchant for the misunderstood, be it sharks, microbes, or wounded characters. A scientist by training, she now spends her days as an author and champion for her children. She draws from her interest in history, science, the outdoors, and her family for inspiration. She serves on the local library board of trustees and is an advocate for community, inclusion, and diversity.

A nature enthusiast who adores the national parks, Jean also writes for family-oriented travel magazines and websites. When not writing, she enjoys gardening, tackling the biggest mountains in New England, and going on adventures with her husband and children, while taking snapshots of the world around her and daydreaming about the next story. If she were stuck on a deserted island, her three essentials (besides family, food, water, shelter) would be: coffee, lip balm, and endless pink sticky notes.

Find out more about her books by visiting her website: www.jeanmgrant.com

SCOTLAND
1263-1322

Made in the USA
Middletown, DE
18 February 2025